Emerge

TOBIE EASTON

Month9Books

Published by Month9Books, Raleigh, NC 27609
Cover Designed by Beetiful Book Covers
Cover Copyright © 2016 Month9Books

Month9Books

PRAISE for EMERGE

"Romance, fantastical lore, and adventure—the most fun I've had reading in a long time!"—Wendy Higgins, *USA Today* and *New York Times* bestselling author of the *Sweet Evil* series

"Clever, well-written and insanely unique, *Emerge* brings us deep into the lives of mermaids, where coming of age has never been so magical."—Award-winning author Jennifer Gooch Hummer

"An unforgettable siren song of characters who will hook your heart"—Skylar Dorset, author of the *Otherworld* series

"This clever twist on an old tale will hook readers with its humor and lure them in with its heart. A charming story filled with rich world building, authentic characters, and an irresistible and surprising romance"—Lori Goldstein, author of *Becoming Jinn*

This tale is dedicated to anyone who has ever sat in a bathtub and pretended to be a mermaid.

Chapter One

I can't swim. No matter how sparkly and tempting that water is. No matter how it glistens in the sunlight, ripples in the California breeze, or reflects the swaying palm trees. One quick dip and my legs will go poof.

Besides, I'm late for P.E. Again.

I run past the swimming pool and heave open the glass doors to the auditorium. I can't keep relying on the twins to get me to school on time. I've got to learn to drive, but I need better control of my legs first. What dope thought giving a car foot controls was a good idea?

All my classmates turn to stare, already in gym clothes. We finished volleyball last week—thank the tides!—so today we're starting a new unit. About half the class wears P.E. shorts and t-shirts and stands near the entrance to the yoga studio. The other half mill around in bathing suits. So lucky.

I scan the room for the coach. If she's not here yet, I can pop into the locker room and be in yoga before she knows I'm tardy. I rush toward the changing rooms, salvation in sight, when out marches a woman whose long blond hair is at odds with her bulging muscles. Coach Crane. She was a professional wrestler on one of those gladiator shows in the eighties, and her biceps are bigger than my head. She stops in front of me, her massive frame towering over mine.

"So nice of you to show up." A drop of her spittle lands on my cheek, and I scrunch my nose, unable to wipe it off without her noticing.

"I'm super sorry. My sisters—"

"Hurry up and change," she says, stalking past me. Phew! Maybe this day won't be a total shipwreck after all. Then she adds, "Put on your bathing suit. You'll be in swim class today."

I spin around.

"What? I'm signed up for y-yoga, not swimming," I say. *Stay calm.*

"Yoga's full up. You have a swimsuit, don't you? It's on your list of required materials."

I have a swimsuit in my locker, but it's for show. No matter what happens, I can't get into that pool. Sure, I can maintain my legs all day on land, but as soon as I hit the water, my natural instincts will take over. My tail will emerge, scales and all, and I'll expose my whole family. I'll put the entire Community of land-dwelling Mer refugees at risk. My breath comes in quick, shallow pants.

"My mom filed a note in the office," I say, clinging to the story my parents concocted for such an emergency. "I'm taking private swimming lessons with this coach my parents hired and I'm not supposed to have any outside instruction."

Rather than help me, this story makes Coach Crane's nostrils flare. "I haven't seen any note, so today you're swimming. Now go change. I'm not going to tell you again."

"No." Did I just say that? Hands cup over mouths as the room erupts in whispers. No one gets why I'm making a fuss. I wish Caspian were here. What I wouldn't give for one other Mer who'd understand. "I'm not swimming."

I've never disobeyed a teacher before. But as much as Coach Crane scares me, that water scares me more. If I swim in the pool, the next place I'll be swimming is a government laboratory tank, being poked and prodded and then chopped into sushi-sized pieces. "Please. My parents'll kill me. And I just got over the flu," I lie, floundering for a good excuse.

"Listen up ... " the coach sticks one meaty finger in my face. Panic seizes me, and my legs tremble. My control over them is slipping. At this rate, I won't even need to get in the water to reveal myself. If I lose my focus, I'll be flat on my fins.

"Coach Crane?" One of the guys steps forward from the group of yoga students. Clay. His dark hair shines under the fluorescent lights as he shoots me a reassuring smile. "She can take my spot in yoga. I have swim trunks."

"Clay, that's not necessary. She needs to—"

"I'd rather go swimming." He cuts the coach off, determination in his hazel eyes.

Twenty pairs of restless feet tap against the rubber floor. I'm holding everyone up. Then a sweet, chirpy voice pipes up from the throng by the doors. "At this rate, none of us will get to do anything. Can't Lia and Clay just switch already?" It's Kelsey, my closest human friend. She twists one of her corkscrew curls around her finger and stares blatantly at the clock.

Coach Crane looks from the clock ticking away on the wall to me to Clay and back to me. "Fine. Ericson," she motions to Clay, "go get into your trunks. And you," she pins me with a fierce glare, "go change into your gym uniform. You'd better be in that studio doing downward dog in less than five minutes."

I nod. The coach storms off, and Kelsey winks at me before she goes out to the pool with the others. I draw in a shaky breath. Am I really off the fishhook? I look around for Clay to say thank you, but he's already disappeared into the boys' locker room. That's better, anyway. I promised myself I'd stop talking to him unless it was one hundred percent necessary.

I change and step out of the girls' side of the locker room, adjusting my shorts for the gazillionth time. Exposing my legs still makes me self-conscious. I should head straight to the yoga studio, but instead I find myself walking to the door of the boys' locker room. It would be rude not to thank Clay, wouldn't it? Of course it would! I wasn't raised by wolf eels. He stood up for me today when everyone else just whispered. So, I really don't have a choice. I have to stay right here and thank him. Yep. But maybe that'll give him the wrong idea. If he comes out in the next thirty seconds, I'll—

The door swings open, and Clay appears. In his swim trunks … and nothing else.

It's like my brain is full of flotsam. I can't focus on anything except the expanse of smooth skin over defined muscles. But it's a momentary weakness. I wrench my eyes away from his chest and up to his face.

He gives me a casual, self-satisfied smirk, but excitement sparks in his eyes. "What? No shirtless guys at your old school?"

I've been here almost a year, but everyone still treats me like the new kid. At least last year I transferred after swim season.

"Tons," I answer. "Shirtless, nearly naked, all the time." It isn't a lie. Mermen never cover their torsos unless they're venturing into the human world, and my old school—the one I attended before I hit puberty and got my legs—was all Mer. "I'm just checking to make sure Malibu Hills Prep is up to par." Did that sound witty? I hope so, but I'm never sure. Something about seeing Clay shirtless is different. And not just because his lean body bears the type of taut muscles I'd want to sculpt if I were even remotely artistic. No! Bad thoughts. *He's human,* I scold myself. *Off-limits.*

"Feel free to check me out all you want," he says, "but you're going to be late for yoga."

The wall clock tells me he's right. The last thing I need is more trouble from Coach Crane.

"Don't worry about Coach Crane," he says, as if reading my mind. His tone changes from cocky to kind. "She just doesn't like anyone questioning her *authority*." He infuses the word with sarcasm and rolls his eyes. Like it's our own private joke.

"Thanks. For stepping in back there, I mean. You didn't have to do that." I have no clue what I would have done if he hadn't.

He gives me one more genuine smile. I tug on my shorts again.

"The shorts look good on you," he says.

I'm not so sure. No matter how many humans I see walking around in micro-minis or bathing suits, bare legs still strike me as daring. "They're not too short?" I ask.

"That's why they look good on you." With that, he flips his towel over his shoulder and walks off toward the pool.

Was he teasing me? Flirting with me? Both? It doesn't matter. I never should have talked myself into thanking him. I have to keep my distance. He doesn't have a tail. End of discussion.

That's why I've made sure we're not friends. Not anymore.

And I have to keep reminding myself of that for the rest of the day. Three hours later, I'm chatting with Kelsey by my locker—and I'm *not* thinking about Clay. I'm not thinking about how brave he was to stand up for me or how he smiled that little half-smile at me from across the gym or how flattered he looked when he caught me staring. Nope. I'm not thinking about Clay at all. But can I help it if he happens to be smack-dab in my line of sight?

The fact that he's talking to another girl at the other end of the hall shouldn't bother me. Clay can talk to other girls. He should talk to other girls. But why does he have to talk to a girl who looks like that? Who *is* that?

"Who is that?" I ask Kelsey, nodding toward the girl. Whoever she is, she's gorgeous. High cheekbones, sapphire eyes, and sleek black hair. Not to mention a lithe body that boasts more merchandise in the chest department than I'll ever have.

"Don't know. Never seen her before," Kelsey says. "I guess you're not the new kid anymore. Good deal, right?"

New Girl giggles at something Clay just said. The feminine

sound tinkles down the hallway, and Clay laughs in response. She rests a perfectly manicured hand on his arm.

I hate her.

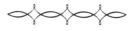

I bet she can walk in heels, I think to myself as I try to balance with four-inch spikes strapped to the bottoms of my feet. I've got to stop comparing myself to her. Any issue of *Seventeen* would tell me what I'm doing is unhealthy, but it's been three weeks since she started at Malibu Hills Prep and I hate her more than ever. Every time I see her, she's clinging to Clay like a slimy, black mussel clinging to the pier. Not that he seems to mind …

I take a few wobbly, unnatural steps and clutch a nearby shoe rack for support. "Maybe I should stick with flats."

"No way!" Kelsey whines as she struts forward in a pair of impossibly high blue stilettos. She grabs my hand and pulls me in front of the full-length mirror. "Legs look so much better in heels."

She's right. The shoes lift my calves, making my legs look longer, making me look taller. I've been dying for a pair of heels for as long as I can remember.

"I don't get why this is so hard for you, Lia."

Of course Kelsey doesn't get it. But let me ask you this: Would you let a toddler wear heels? Of course not! They've only been walking around for three years. How could they be expected to balance? Well, I'm in the same boat. I only got my legs three years ago, and it took me a good six months to learn to control them—and another year and a half before I could hold them in place all day without breaks. That's why my parents waited until last year to decide I was finally ready to start a human school. So while all my human friends probably got platforms by age thirteen and have been wearing heels for years, I've always settled for a comfy ballet flat. Judging by the way I'm stumbling around the store, maybe I had the right idea.

"Try balancing more of your weight on your toes," Kelsey instructs.

A low voice interrupts her. "You know, I almost bought that same pair last week, but I couldn't walk in them either."

With slow, tiny steps, I turn away from a display of sling backs to face Clay. "What are you doing here?" I toss a few stray strands of my long hair over my shoulder and try to look cool as I scramble for something non-embarrassing to say. "This doesn't seem like your type of place."

Like many of the upscale boutiques in Malibu, this one has that studied elegance carefully contrived to help shoppers justify spending way too much. Kelsey dragged me in here when she saw the blue stilettos in the window. I have to admit, their stuff is gorgeous, but they only have a few pairs of shoes for men, and all of them are super trendy. They don't look anything like Clay's well-worn Doc Martens. A lot of the guys at school look like they're trying to mimic Abercrombie ads and falling painfully short. Not Clay. He tends to do his own thing.

"Baby, I found a pair." The sing-song voice from across the store makes my stomach plummet. It's her. Mel Havelock. I don't know if it's short for Melissa or Melanie or something equally generic, and I don't care. She stands by the designer athletic shoes, holding up a pair and humming some inane tune as she beckons Clay over.

"I'm not exactly here of my own free will," he confides with a conspiratorial smile. He starts to head over to her, as if drawn like a magnet. Then, as he passes a rack of discount boots, he turns and looks at the heels still gleaming on my feet. "Gold suits you," he says, before walking the rest of the way.

"See you Monday!" I call out lamely. Mel gives me a curious look before wrapping her arms around Clay's neck and kissing him right there in the middle of the store, her hands tangling in his hair.

I want to leave. Now.

But Kelsey's trying on some baby pink t-straps. "They should at least get a dressing room if they're going to do that," she says. She knows it bothers me to see the two of them like they are now, with their heads close together, smiling and laughing.

"No, it's fine. I'm … happy for them."

"Liar."

"So, which pair are you getting?" I ask, hoping to hurry things along. I should be home already, helping prepare for the gala.

Kelsey accepts the change of topic. "I'm thinking both." She shoots me an impish grin that brings to mind a small child who takes two cookies before dinner when she's only allowed one.

"How about you?" she asks. "Don't tell me you're going to part with those. You look so beautiful in them … as long as you stay upright."

I shouldn't buy them. It's probably a waste considering I can only make it a few steps. Still, the deep golden color is the exact same shade as my tail when the sun shines on it. Wearing these would be like getting to show off the part of myself I always have to keep hidden.

"I'll take them."

Her smile broadens.

On the way home, I try to focus on Kelsey's excitement over the self-defense class we're about to start in P.E. now that yoga and swimming are over. "I'm going to be like, *pow, pow*! Take that! *Pow!*" She throws practice punches against the steering wheel. But all I can think about is how Mel has managed to completely enthrall Clay over the past three weeks. I know I have no claim on him, but it was much easier ignoring my feelings when I didn't have to watch him so fixated on someone else. I've barely spoken two words to her. But every time she touches him or whispers something flirty into his ear, I want to kick her in that toned butt of hers.

I sigh and stare out the window as we get closer to my house. At least I'll have the gala tonight to keep me occupied. Nobody parties quite like the Mer.

Chapter Two

Kelsey and I pull up to the front gate of my house, and I thank her for the ride.

"No prob, Bob," Kelsey says. "Want me to drive you to the door?"

I tell her it's fine and jump out of the car. I don't want her to see the catering trucks in the driveway and realize there's a party she hasn't been invited to. Waving goodbye, I type in the entrance code and wait for the large iron gate to open just enough so I can slip through. I make my way down the winding, gravel driveway, swinging the bag that contains my shiny new shoes. When I turn the final bend, two catering trucks do indeed wait there. They're parked on either side of the circular stone fountain centered in front of the door.

Okay, so my house is kind of massive. With its clean white lines and imposing entrance, most people find it impressive. To me, it's home. I'm so lucky to live in a place this beautiful. At least centuries' worth of sunken pirate treasure hasn't gone to waste; my parents and the other board members have used it to ensure our entire Community can flourish here in Malibu.

As soon as I walk in, my eyes are drawn to my favorite feature of our house. Across the entrance hall and the step-down living room beyond it, floor to ceiling windows look out onto a breathtaking view of the Pacific Ocean. As soon as I lay eyes on the sparkling sea, the waves whisper to me. Call to me.

"Aurelia, there you are!"

Emeraldine, my oldest sister, stands at the top of the stairs, her hands on her slim hips. "I thought you'd be home an hour ago. If you want me to do your hair, you'll have to hurry. The caterers are already here to drop off the food, and I promised Dad I'd help him bring it all downstairs and finish setting up after they leave." Emeraldine's voice is measured and even as usual, but a few tendrils of stress uncoil beneath it.

"Hi to you, too," I say as I make my way up the stairs. "Where's Mom?"

"At the Foundation. She should be home in half an hour at the latest."

I have to hurry. My mom made it clear she's counting on my sisters and me to make a good impression tonight. She and my dad have enough to worry about and I don't want to disappoint them. My father is the public face of the Foundation for the Preservation and Protection of Marine Life; he's the one in charge of securing government support, presenting scientific research to universities, and working with marine animals at zoos across the country. My mother, on the other hand, is responsible for the Foundation's less conspicuous workings—basically keeping the entire Community of land-dwelling Mer afloat. Tonight, every member of that community will be here, in our house, so I have to be perfect.

Once we're settled in my bathroom, Em brushes my hair. In the mirror, I examine the intricacies of her hairstyle. Half of her rich, chestnut-colored hair is pulled up into three tiers of buns in progressively diminishing sizes that top her head like a wedding cake. The rest hangs in flowing, perfectly shaped curls down her back, and the whole coif is studded with pearls.

"How was your day at school?" Em asks, her voice adopting a familiar mothering quality.

"Good. How was yours?" I shoot back, trying to sound like an equal instead of a child she has to take care of when our parents are busy. Em commutes from our house to Pepperdine University, about ten minutes away. She's studying business, which couldn't sound more yawn-worthy to me, but she's into it. "Classes are fine," she replies as she picks up a small section of hair above my temple and begins a series of the tiniest braids, which she intersperses among my natural waves. She sounds distracted, and we lapse into silence. Worry lines crease Em's forehead, and her hands fumble the braiding, causing her to drop a handful of bobby pins.

They shatter the silence as they scatter across the floor, and I bend to help her. "Okay, what's up with you?" I ask, handing the pins back.

She's quiet as she pins the braids so they frame my face. Just when I think she's not going to answer, she admits, "Leo and I had a fight."

"You two never fight."

"Well, we did today." Unshed tears lace her words, and I want to say the perfect thing to comfort her. How many times has she held me, consoled me while I cried? She deserves it back, but I'm drawing a blank, so I decide to be the best listener I can be. "What happened?"

"We've been talking about marriage lately—"

"But you're only twenty-one!" The moment I say it, it's obvious I've put my fin in my mouth. I know better than to mention age around Em.

"Which means we only have seventy, maybe seventy-five years together, tops!" she snaps in response. "That's nothing!"

It's an old disagreement between us. Em is the only one of us who was born Below. She spent her first few years under the sea, hearing stories from a grandmother I've never met. Stories insisting that one day, the curse on the Mer would break and we'd have our immortality back. To someone who believes she should get to spend eternity with her future mate, seventy-five years really does sound fleeting.

Now that Em's older and has realized all she'll ever have is a lifespan as short as a human's, she feels robbed. Many Mer—practically all the older ones and any younger ones raised at sea—feel that way. Like they're entitled to more. Like they're cursed.

I've never felt cursed and neither have my other sisters. I'm pretty sure it's because we were raised on land, reading human books and watching human movies. I've never expected to live longer than a human. For Em, though, the idea of the clock ticking ever closer to her eventual death is a deep source of pain.

"We just want to maximize our time together as much as we can," she says.

"I understand." And a part of me does. "So you and Leo were talking about marriage … " I push on.

"And I mentioned that he didn't have to worry because I was fine with a traditional Mer marriage." Her voice trembles and her eyes shine with those same tears I heard stuck in her throat a moment ago. "And … and he blew up at me. He said he couldn't believe I didn't want to be monogamous." Like everything else in our culture, Mer ideas about marriage go back thousands of years, before the curse stripped us of our immortality. Since for most of our history, married couples stayed together forever—and stayed young forever—fidelity was never a requirement. Just thinking about it squigs me (all the married couples that come to mind are my parents' friends), but it kind of makes sense. If you lived for countless centuries, it would be understandable that you'd … roam periodically … then return to your mate. Still, it doesn't strike me as something Em or Leo would want.

"So you want his permission to slut it up, huh?" The voice from the doorway is matter-of-fact.

I turn my head, disrupting the latest pinned braid, to see that Lapis has entered the room, Lazuli close behind.

"I absolutely do not!" Em answers, dropping my hair and folding her arms across her chest.

"Relax, I didn't say there was anything wrong with it," Lapis continues, trying to sound reassuring. "If I'd been with the same guy since I was fourteen—"

"Gag me," Lazuli interjects.

"I'd want the chance to swim with some other fish, too," Lapis finishes. Lazuli nods, her blond hair bouncing in its already completed curls. The two of them flash Em identical smiles.

"I don't want any other fish!" Em gets out through gritted teeth.

I put my hand on her arm and shoot the twins a reproachful look. At eighteen, they're a year older than I am, but sometimes it doesn't feel like it. "Then why did you tell Leo you wanted a traditional marriage?" I ask, careful to keep any judgyness out of my voice.

"I thought that's what he wanted, too. He's a guy! And like Lapis said, we've been together since we were fourteen. I didn't want him to think I had unrealistic expectations."

"But I thought you wanted to … " How did she phrase it? " … maximize your time together, since you'll only have seventy-something years?"

"Yes," Em answers, nodding. "I want to maximize our time, but I also want to maximize our happiness, or what's the point? And isn't it arrogant to assume we know more about what makes a happy marriage than the generations of Mer who came before us? Or that we know how we'll feel decades from now? I just think Mer who have actually been married must understand more about this than we do." She sighs. "But as soon as I said I was open to keeping our marriage traditional instead of monogamous, Leo started yelling at me. It was so unlike him."

A tear finally spills over onto her cheek, solidifying into a perfect drop-shaped pearl on its way down. She plucks up the pearl, looks at it without really seeing it, and drops it into my box of hair accessories.

"He said he could never do that to me, but that if I wanted to be with someone else, I was free to." She breaks down into sobs, and pearls clatter against the tile floor. "That's not what I meant at all. I just thought, well, he's always been traditional, and so have I … and even just seventy-five more years is a lot to demand of a person … "

"Humans manage it," I say.

"Yeah and end up in divorce court after cheating on each other," Lazuli points out.

"Forget what you think he expects or doesn't expect. Do *you* want a traditional marriage?" Lapis asks Em, serious now.

"I want the option," she says, sniffing back more tears. "I don't like that Leo's just shutting it down—it's a decision we should talk about together. It's not that I want anyone besides him, but it's how Mer marriages have always been. Accepting the monogamous, human version of marriage feels like … we're abandoning our culture." She shakes her head. "I just always thought I'd have a certain type of marriage, and I don't think I can throw all that away."

"Then you two need to talk," I say as I collect the pearls from my bathroom floor. Em cried a lot—I might have enough for a bracelet. "He'll be here tonight, right?"

"I think he's still coming."

"Then you can take him somewhere private and straighten this out. It'll be fine." I really hope I'm telling the truth. Em loves Leo more than anything.

"Come on," Lazuli says, "finish up Lia's hair so we can help you decide on an outfit."

"Wear something hot enough and you and Leo won't even need to do any talking," Lapis concludes.

Em splashes her face with water from the sink. "Fashion advice from the two of you? No thank you."

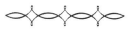

After Em escapes downstairs, I get talked into letting the twins help me pick out what to wear.

"Why are all your clothes so boring?" Lapis complains.

"Where's that *siluess* I gave you for your birthday?" Lazuli asks.

A *siluess* is a piece of clothing worn on the torso when the bottom half of the body is in tail form. It comes from the Mermese word for chest covering. Mostly, I wear bikini tops, but that would be far too casual—and too human—for tonight.

"What's wrong with the white one I wore last time?" I reach past them to where my *siluesses* hide behind a few years' worth of Halloween costumes and pull out a delicate white one covered in tiny puka shells.

"It's so babyish." Lazuli snatches it from me and hangs it back up. "You should give it to Amy—she'll fill it out soon enough. Besides, isn't Caspian coming tonight?"

"So?" I pretend not to see what she's getting at.

"So that boy is a total foxfish. It's just too bad his family is—"

"Nothing's wrong with his family. And we're just friends."

"Whatever you say."

I'm about to continue arguing when Lazuli pulls a hanger out of my closet and holds it up in triumph. "Here's the one I got you!" It's a tiny scrap of lace that looks more like something that belongs on a Victoria's Secret model than on me. The fabric is so thin that, as soon as it's wet, it'll leave nothing to the imagination.

"That's too frilly," Lapis says. "You can borrow something of mine."

Somehow, that scares me more. Lapis and Lazuli may as well be named Leather and Lace. While both have the jealousy-inducing ability to exude sexuality without even trying, Lapis is more rocker chick about it, while Lazuli sticks to pastels and candy-colored nail polish. I don't want to end up in some strappy, studded getup of Lapis's any more than I want to wear the lacey piece of fluff Lazuli still clutches.

"You know, I think I've got this covered," I say, trying to shoo them out of my closet. "Why don't you two go get ready?"

"And just what are you going to wear?" Lapis asks, folding her arms across her ample chest.

"Um … this!" In an effort to end the conversation, I pull out the most risqué *siluess* I've ever purchased. Like today's golden heels, I bought this because it was too beautiful to part with, but I haven't had the courage to wear it. It's a shining midnight blue fabric dotted with small mother of pearl pieces. When I saw it, it reminded me of stars glittering in the night sky above the ocean. It's low cut and reveals the entire expanse of my abdomen, so it should be enough to satisfy the twins.

"That'll work," they say in unison.

What have I gotten myself into?

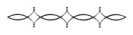

Once the twins leave, I change into the dark blue *siluess*, a simple wrap-around skirt, and flip-flops. I put on a bit of Mer-made waterproof makeup and head downstairs. Now it's my turn to play big sister.

When I reach the entrance hall, I take one last longing look out at the ocean before I walk to a door behind the main staircase that's disguised as a coat closet and open it. The row of coats that usually stands a foot or two back from the door has been removed in preparation for tonight, leaving a long corridor in plain view. I walk along it until I reach another staircase at the end. It winds down, down, down and opens onto an antechamber.

Shelves and hooks line the walls, and a deep canal filled to the brim with satiny salt water cuts across the floor, starting in the middle of the room and flowing out around a bend. The rest of the floor slopes downward, toward the canal. I step around the water, slip out of my flip-flops, and push them to the very back corner of one of the higher shelves. Tonight, this room will serve as the shoe-check it was designed as, and I want to be able to find mine easily. I untie my wrap-around skirt and hang it on a hook, then sit at the smooth edge of the canal. Normally, Mer wait to use this room one at a time so we're not all hanging out together naked from the waist down. If any other Mer did happen to be in the room with me, custom dictates they'd turn politely away during my transformation, offering me privacy while I temporarily reveal my human body. But since I'm alone, I take the time to relish what comes next. With a deep breath of damp air, I close my eyes and let my tightly-held control slip away.

Transforming creates the familiar sensation of ocean tides pushing and pulling against my legs. I'm connected to the sea, connected to its magic, connected to the generations of Mer who have come before me. The bones and muscles shift and fuse and it feels *so* good. Like I can finally stretch out. When the mystical tide recedes with a final tingle, I open my eyes, look down, and see my golden tail shimmering in the light of the wall torches.

One push of my arms and I'm sliding down the slope and into the canal. Water reaches up to my waist and runs over the gilded scales of my tail like liquid silk. I shiver in delight. Now that I'm in the water and in my true form, the call of the ocean thrums through my body like a heartbeat. It makes me want to swim.

With a flick of my fins, I'm down the canal and swimming around the corner, past the walls that hide the antechamber from view, and into the main ballroom. Like all the rooms that comprise the hidden grottos underneath our house, the ballroom is a cave formation with seating and tables carved from the rock. The walls shine opalescent, like the inside of an abalone shell.

My chest remains above water while my tail wades beneath. Toward the center of the room, the water is deep and I'm just dying to do a backflip into the cool, welcoming ripples. I want to dive down as deep as I can, feel the skin below my ears open into gills, and let the water flow through me—become a part of me. But Em would fillet me if I ruined my hair before any of the guests got here, so I'm careful to keep my upper half above water.

I make my way through the ballroom, the dining hall, and the other public grottos before turning a corner into the private quarters. I swim past my own downstairs bedroom and toward my cousin Amethyst's room.

"Come in!" she calls in response to my knock on the archway wall. I part the curtain of hanging seaweed and head inside.

Amethyst, who goes mostly by Amy, lies on her sea sponge bed listening to music on the waterproof MP3 player my father bought her. The bed is elevated, so the water comes to only about half a foot above it. This way, the long, light purple tail that matches her name can stay wet while her torso remains exposed to the cool evening air wafting through the grottos from outside. When I enter, she takes out her earbuds and places the device on the rock formation that serves as her nightstand.

"Lia, you look so pretty! Did Em do your hair?"

"Yep. And the twins helped with the outfit."

"It's bold. I really like it." Her smile is huge and her enthusiasm infectious. Before I know it, I'm mirroring her grin. "I couldn't wait for you to come down. Something so insanely huge happened today! Staskia got her legs!"

Oh no. It's started. Staskia is the first of Amy's close friends to get legs, and now that she has, I won't hear about anything else until Amy gets hers. As if in a hurry to prove my prediction right, she immediately launches into the story.

"It happened in the middle of history class. Stas was embarrassed but you could tell she was like super excited, too. The first time, her legs only held for a second, so thank goodness Mrs. Cordula had time to cover her up with an extra skirt before they came back."

This story isn't ending any time soon, so I grab her hairbrush and a few pins and settle on the bed. I'm not as skilled a stylist as Em, but I'm decent. My fingers work quickly, but they don't compare to the speed of Amy's voice as she tells me every detail. "She's got all ten toes and pretty nicely shaped calves. Her legs aren't too long, but her tail never was either, so I bet I'll be taller.

At least she has nice ankle bones. Do you think I will? Lia, I'm so afraid I'll have cankles."

"You won't have cankles. No one in our family has cankles except Aunt Dolores, and she eats like a porpoise."

"When do you think I'll get mine? Staskia is only three months older than I am, so I'll probably get them soon, right?"

I know the answer she wants, but it's impossible to predict. I didn't get mine until I was fourteen, but that's on the late side. Lapis and Lazuli were early bloomers at eleven. Em got hers at thirteen, the age Amy is now. "When did your mom get hers?"

"She was fifteen, but you know it takes longer Below. I just can't wait to be able to go to the movies and go shopping and go out to dinner … " She trails off, but I understand how frustrating it can be. Until Amy gets her legs, she's pretty much restricted to the underground canal system the Foundation has put in place. She can swim through the tunnels to her school, like all the children in the Community who have yet to get their legs, and to the underwater entrances of friends' houses, but she can't get upstairs to the rest of our house unless my dad carries her. Right now, the whole human world is a mystery to her.

A conus shell lies on her desk. "Did you get a shell call from your parents?" I ask. Amy's parents still live Below, but they sent her to live with us when she was a baby to keep her safe.

"Yep. I'll record an answer after the gala, so I'll have plenty to tell them." She hesitates, then asks, "Staskia's legs are so cool. What if when I get mine, they're short or pasty or misshapen?"

I put down the brush and move so we're facing each other. "Hey, legs always suit the Mer, so whenever you get yours, I know they'll be beautiful."

She blushes. "You really think so?"

"Absolutely."

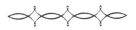

An hour and a half later, guests fill the ballroom. Mermaids and Mermen float around the buffet tables, dining on caviar and tuna tartar. A few are already dancing, swimming in intricate circles and figure eights around each other. In one corner, a band plays classical music on turritella shell flutes. And with every passing minute, another guest swims out from the privacy of the antechamber, resplendent in a jeweled tail and their grandest seashell or gemstone accoutrement.

My face aches from smiling so much at my parents' friends and colleagues.

"So, Aurelia, I keep telling your mother she simply must invite me over for dinner so we can discuss instituting *konklili* restrictions."

I nod but inwardly hope my mother can put off MerMatron Drusy for as long as possible. The only reason she wants to spend an evening in our home is so she has plenty of fodder for the rumor tides. Since my parents run the Foundation, my sisters and I are like mini-celebrities. Not in the fun, free designer swag sense, but in the everyone-scrutinizes-our-every-move sense.

Even Lapis and Lazuli, who usually push the barrier reef as far as they possibly can, are on their best behavior. In the center of the ballroom, they move together flawlessly in a classical Mer dance called an *allytrill*. As the deep blue tails that inspired their names twirl underneath them in the water, onlookers applaud. I wish I could impress everyone that much. Tonight, it's up to all of us to be shining examples of land-dwellers who effortlessly blend human assimilation with the preservation of our Mer traditions.

Just as I'm attempting to construct a diplomatic response to MerMatron Drusy's remark, something over her shoulder tugs the corners of my mouth into my first real smile of the night. Caspian.

"Please excuse me, ma'am. I see a friend who I really must go welcome," I say, keeping my tone as formal as possible. She follows my line of sight and voices her unsought opinion.

"You don't mean Caspian Zayle? I have to admit, I'd heard

the two of you were friendly, but I never believed it. Dear, take my advice: be careful. A sweet girl like you shouldn't be mixing with—"

"I'll keep that in mind," I say, cutting her off. She looks affronted, but Caspian is swimming toward us.

His arrival has the added bonus of making MerMatron Drusy murmur a few excuses and swim off toward a group of Foundation officials.

"It's about time," I say to Caspian as he pulls me into a hug. "I'm dying here. Save me from the small talk."

"That I can do." His deep voice smoothes the rough edges of my frayed nerves, like freshwater over river rocks. "Your parents have done it again," he says, glancing around the lavishly decorated room. "When do the guests of honor arrive?"

"I think in a half an hour or so. There'll be an announcement."

He's listening to my words, but his eyes dart down to take in my *siluess*. Sure, he's seen me in bikini tops before, but the *siluess* is somehow more overt, more suggestive. I fight a blush. *This is Caspian,* I scold myself. *He doesn't care.*

As expected, Caspian doesn't say anything lewd. He settles for a straightforward, "You're looking more traditional than usual tonight, Lia."

He's right. By Mer standards, I am. "Well, we are opening our doors to a whole new group tonight. Might as well welcome them in style. Besides," I joke, "it's not like I'm showing any more skin than you are."

Like all the male guests', Caspian's torso is almost entirely bare except for a thin strand of limpet shells strapped diagonally across his chest that complements his strong, silver tail. My sisters like to tease me, saying that since his tail is silver and mine is gold, it's some sign we'll end up together. I prefer to think of it as a symbol of the friendship we've shared since we were guppies.

And that friendship hasn't changed now that we're older. Sure, it was kind of strange when his voice dropped and he packed on the musculature of a pro-athlete (he does more laps a day than an

Olympic swimmer), but he's still the same Caspian who helped me bury my tail in the sand and molded me a pair of legs when we were six. The same sandy blond hair that falls into the same knowing, ocean blue eyes.

Those eyes grow haunted as we swim past a couple old biddies who are so caught up in their own blather they don't see us. I tune into their conversation the instant they mention Caspian's father.

"It's no wonder Sir Zayle isn't here. He and his wife never dare show their faces at events like these."

"But, Gretchen, I've heard they dine with the Nautilus family in private."

"I hope not. It's bad enough their son is here. Sure, he seems like a fine lad now, but I'm telling you, you have one bad clam in a family, and sooner or later, there's bound to be another."

The protective best friend part of me wants to spin around and tell those Merwitches exactly what they can do with their cruel gossip. I want to shake them by the shoulders and scream that it's not Caspian's fault there was a siren in his family. But causing a scene would make him more uncomfortable. So instead, I use all my self-control to keep my mouth shut as I lead him far away from them and toward the extravagant buffet.

"Casp, they have no idea—"

"It's fine, Lia. I'm fine."

It's so unfair. Sure, next to murder, sireny is the highest crime known to Mer—and for good reason. A siren song is a spell that steals away the free will of a human and forces him to do anything the siren commands. I get shivers just thinking about it. But Caspian shouldn't be blamed for something his great-great-aunt did.

Carrying plates brimming with halibut skewers topped in a spicy dulse seaweed sauce, we make our way to one of the quartz-encrusted tables that line the ballroom's perimeter.

"So, tell me about school," I say in an attempt to make him forget the callous words.

"School's good." He pauses, wiping his mouth on his napkin.

Caspian's parents aren't as progressive as mine and don't want him to lose touch with his culture, so they've enrolled him in the all-Mer high school set up by the Foundation. "There's a dance next Friday."

"Ooo! Who are you taking?" I poke him in the chest when he doesn't answer right away. "Who? You can tell me."

"I don't know yet." With his broad build and strong jaw, Caspian looks like the catch of the day, every day, and—even despite his family name—he could probably have any girl he wanted if he put himself out there. But he's always been the quiet type.

"You have to take someone. Do it for my sake! I'm surrounded by humans at school, so everyone's off-limits."

"But there's someone you'd want to date if there were no restrictions?" His eyes turn intensely quizzical.

I laugh it off. "No, no. That's not what I meant. It just must be nice for you to be yourself at school and date whoever you want."

"Not whoever I want," he mumbles.

"Sure. Pick a Mermaid you like, go up to her, and be your honest, straightforward self. Girls like that."

"I thought girls like the cocky, bad boy types."

My mind flashes to Clay in his butter-soft leather jacket and trademark smirk. "Girls just like to feel wanted," I insist. "So, you go up to a Mermaid and tell her that she's, I don't know, made an impression on you and you'd like to take her to the dance." Yep, I'm great at giving dating advice as long as I don't have to follow it.

"You've made an impression on me and I'd like to take you to the dance," Caspian says.

"Yeah, just like that."

He opens his mouth to continue, but the conch horn blares and everyone turns their attention to where my mother has taken her place at the front of the room. "Maids and Men, I'd like to welcome you to our home." My mother's voice is pleasant but authoritative. "This is a special occasion for all of us. We are adding to our Community—adding to our strength."

Palpable excitement suffuses the room. Everyone waits in anticipation of my mother's next words.

"Of course, we're overjoyed at the opportunity to embrace more of our kind, but we mustn't forget what caused this exodus. We must all be sensitive to the trials the new members of our Community have so recently endured."

With the two hundredth anniversary of the Little Mermaid's grievous mistake occurring in a few months, conditions Below are worse than ever before.

Her real story's not as happy as the one most humans know today. When Hans Christian Andersen first wrote it down in the 1800s, he bungled a few things, but he got the gist of it right. The Little Mermaid rescued the drowning prince and sang to him on the shore in front of a temple. When she saw a maiden from the temple approaching, the Little Mermaid dove into the sea to hide. Since the prince woke up with the maiden by his side, he believed she was the one who'd sung so beautifully to him. I bet you can already see what's coming. Tragedy with a capital "T." The Little Mermaid traded her voice to the Sea Sorceress in exchange for permanent legs that would allow her to live a human life on land with her prince and would keep him from ever knowing what she truly was. To cement the deal, the Little Mermaid agreed to die if she couldn't get the prince to marry her.

Despite the fact that she couldn't speak, at first, her beauty and grace seemed to win him over (what kind of man wants a woman without a voice? It's gross if you ask me, but whatevs). Anyway, everything would have been rainbows and wedding cake except the prince's father announced he'd arranged a marriage for the prince with a princess from the neighboring kingdom. The prince declared he wouldn't marry a woman he didn't love, and I'm sure the Little Mermaid breathed a huge, silent sigh of relief. But when little miss princess arrived, she was ... wait for it ... none other than the maiden from the temple who the prince believed had sung to him. He declared his love for the human princess and asked her to marry him. Of course, his choice devastated the Little Mermaid.

Desperate to get her back, the Little Mermaid's family made a bargain with the Sea Sorceress. If the Little Mermaid killed the prince with the sorceress's enchanted obsidian dagger, his blood on her legs would transform her back into a Mermaid. But she refused and threw the dagger into the sea. She valued the prince's human life above her own immortality, so the magic in the dagger cursed us all with human lifespans as soon as its blade touched the water.

Merkind blamed her father the king for her mistake and executed him, throwing our entire society into a state of anarchy and war that's lasted ever since.

That's why my parents and a group of other brave Mer who feared for their lives and yearned for a better future for their children finally did the unthinkable—they ventured onto land. Now, nearly twenty years later, they've built a life here.

"There's no reason for our people to live under the terror of constant warfare any longer," my mom continues. "No reason for them to fight and die in defense of one false ruler over another, hoping against hope that this will be the one who finally keeps his promises and finds a way to break the curse."

"It can't be broken!" someone shouts from the crowd. I recognize him; he sits on the Community's advisory board alongside my parents. Others agree, echoing his words.

My mother nods. "There's always a new ruler. Always someone claiming to have a better plan, when all they really have is an angrier army. How many of these warlords have overthrown the previous leader—raged battles that bloodied the ocean floor in their quest for power—only to fail once that power was theirs?"

Mer all around me hiss or shake their heads. "Senseless violence," a woman next to me mutters.

My mother holds up a hand, and the room falls silent. "We cannot break the curse. But we can choose to leave the violence behind. Each one of us has chosen a life on land—a life of peace. And tonight, we welcome our brave brethren who are making that same choice."

I glance around me. Now people's faces beam with pride.

"Some of our newest Community members have been here for several weeks," my mother continues, her regal, opalescent tail swishing through the water underneath her, "so you may have already met them at the Foundation. A few others have just arrived. We waited to celebrate so we could welcome everyone at once. I have every confidence you will do your utmost to make our kin feel at home here."

My mother nods to my father, who swims beyond the doorway and returns with ten new Mer swimming behind him. The group consists mostly of young parents with small children, but a few outliers wade in back. The whole room erupts in welcoming applause.

But I'm not clapping. I'm frozen in shock. Among the refugees is the last face I ever expected to see.

Chapter Three

Mel Havelock is front and center in the group of Mer refugees. A slender, coral-colored tail tapers down from her tiny waist, and a *siluess* decorated with actual coral barely covers her chest. She looks more like a spoiled princess than a refugee. How is this possible? How can Mel be a Mermaid?

While my mouth practically hangs open, my parents usher the group to the front and offer a few more words of welcome before allowing our new Community members to disperse into the crowd. Mel and an imposing older man who must be her father stay and talk to them.

"Lia, what's wrong? What are you staring at? You look a little freaky." Caspian shakes my shoulder when I don't respond. I work to regain the power of speech.

"That girl," is all I manage.

"The really pretty one?"

"Yes," I hiss. "She goes to my school. I had no idea she was Mer."

"Oh, well that'll be nice. You'll finally have another Mer

friend at school with you besides the twins."

"No. Not nice. Very not nice. She's horrible."

"What has she done to you?"

"Well," I picture her possessive hands all over Clay, "it's hard to describe."

Caspian looks confused. "But she's horrible?"

"She's dating a human!" There, I got it out. I wait for Caspian to get appropriately outraged, but he just looks thoughtful.

"Well, that's not smart."

"Not smart? Not smart! They're constantly together. She spends hours with him every day after school. All it takes is one moment when she's not a hundred percent focused—one tiny slip of tail—and she'd put all of us in danger." By the end of my rant, I'm practically panting. How is Caspian still so calm? "How are you still so calm?"

"Maybe she doesn't realize the risk."

"Then she's an idiot as well as a—"

"Aurelia, can you swim over here please?" my mother calls.

"Stay next to me," I murmur to Caspian as we make our way toward my parents and the Havelocks. Mr. Havelock has rigid posture and holds his head an inch too high, which makes him look pretentious.

"Aurelia, Mr. Havelock has been telling us that you know his daughter Melusine already," my mother says in her quintessential hostess voice.

"How fun that you girls are already friends," my father says, clapping Mr. Havelock on the shoulder.

"We're not friends," I blurt out. My mother's eyes narrow, and I search for something else to say.

Melusine beats me to it. "We haven't really gotten to know each other yet, Mrs. Nautilus."

"Well, now that you know you have so much in common," her father says, "I am certain the two of you will have plenty to speak about." Mr. Havelock's voice has the slanting, sibilant quality of a Mermese speaker who's not used to speaking English. "Who is your young man?" he asks with perfect, studied grammar, his eyes shifting to Caspian.

"This is my *friend*," I emphasize the word, "Caspian Zayle."

"Pleased to meet you, sir," Caspian says as he shakes Mr. Havelock's hand. "I hope you're finding everything to your liking here on the surface."

"Zayle? As in Adrianna Zayle? Yes, I had heard your family was living here now."

"Filius, you must understand … " my father begins, his tone full of censure. Then, Mel's father surprises me.

"No need, Edmar. I fully support what you are doing here. A fresh start for everyone. I respect that. Without it, I would not have come, not with my family's reputation. I almost didn't, but after my wife died … " He's quiet for a moment, then continues, "I wanted better for my Melusine."

"I won't lie to you," my father says, shaking his nearly bald head, "there were people who petitioned against your request for refuge. Up here in the human world, we all view humans as equals, and we bring up our children to do the same. Not surprisingly, some members of our Community thought you must share your family's *udell* predilections." My eyes widen. *Udell* is an ancient word for human hater. Melusine's an *udell*? Then why is she with Clay?

"Never. I have never understood their hatred of mortals, and I have raised Melusine according to my own moral standards, not my family's."

"Well, now that you're here, you can show everyone through your actions that your family's *udell* history does not extend to the two of you," my mother says. "Of course, we'll help in any way we can."

Mr. Havelock looks gratified and lifts his head even higher. "Just knowing that we have your illustrious family on our side will help fortify us," he says grandiosely. "And knowing my Melusine has new friends makes me feel that I made the right decision in coming here." He looks at Caspian and me, and I get the feeling

I'm being manipulated.

"Melusine, why don't you go get to know Aurelia and Caspian better while my husband and I show your father around? I'm sure that will be more enjoyable for you than endless introductions to Merfolk twice your age." My mother's eyes twinkle with sincerity, and I surge with the familiar sense of pride I get watching her handle social situations with so much grace. Did it skip a generation?

After some brief, "Pleasure to meet yous" all around, Caspian and I lead Melusine to a side room that's less crowded and up to an empty table. Most of the Mer our age have found their way here, and the atmosphere is more relaxed.

"I'll go get us all some seaberry punch," Caspian says. I want to think of an excuse to go with him, but that would be crazy rude. So, here I am. Alone with Melusine.

"I can't believe I didn't know you were a Mermaid," I say, voicing the thought that's been racing in repeated laps around my mind.

"I know. You looked floored," she replies in a syrupy sweet voice. She doesn't have a trace of her father's Mermese accent. She must have worked hard to get rid of it before coming on land.

"Did you know? About me, I mean? Because it's been like, weeks since you started school, and you never said anything." I keep my tone light, non-accusatory, but I can't help thinking how strange it is. Had she been purposely trying to trick me? And, if she had, why?

"I wanted time to explore on my own. I've heard so many conflicting ideas about humans and their world. I knew the moment I revealed myself to you, you'd go out of your way to be my welcoming committee—show me things and explain things. I wanted to draw my own conclusions first, without anyone else's influence."

If I had been in Melusine's place, I'd have wanted any help I could get. In fact, when I started at Malibu Hills Prep, I bombarded the twins with an endless list of questions. I hate to admit it, but Melusine's determination to try things out on her own is kind of … brave.

"Wasn't that difficult? How have you even been able to maintain your legs for so long so quickly?"

"Nothing's quite as … inspiring as a challenge. I practiced for months before we surfaced."

"You mean you can keep your legs in water?" Awe creeps into my voice.

"Here you go, ladies," Caspian says, returning with our drinks.

"We were just talking about why Melusine didn't tell me she was Mer before tonight," I fill him in.

"Isn't it such a fun surprise?" she asks.

I'm not really the type who likes surprises. Okay, surprise presents or baked goods are welcome, but I'm a make-a-plan-and-stick-to-it type of girl, so I don't like to be caught off guard. Still, it's not like Melusine could have known that. Maybe it's time I stop hating her on principle and try to get to know her. After all, she's left everything she knows and moved to a foreign place. It's gotta be really hard for her.

"So, Melusine, Lia tells me you have a boyfriend at your school," Caspian says, concern evident in his rich baritone. Leave it to Caspian to face the seriousness of a situation head on.

"His name's Clay. We instantly connected."

And just like that, I hate her again. I haven't spent a year keeping Clay at tail's length just so he could date another Mer. I've put my duty to the Community first, and she needs to, too.

"You know how dangerous that is, right? For all of us?" This time, I don't care if I sound accusatory.

"Relax," Melusine says, sounding far too calm for my taste. "I'm not putting anyone in danger."

"Lia's worry is understandable," Caspian says. "There are reasons the parents up here don't let their kids date humans. I've only just met you, and I'm sorry if I'm overswimming here, but if this guy … What's his name? Ray?"

"Clay," Melusine and I both correct at the same moment.

"Clay. If Clay ever finds out what you are—"

"Not a chance. Maybe some people have trouble maintaining their legs," she shoots me an appraising look and I don't like how self-conscious it makes me, "but I have excellent self-control."

"And your father hasn't found out?" Caspian hedges.

"Daddy knows!"

"He knows you're with a human?" I sputter.

"Are you kidding? He's thrilled. I guess he thinks it'll help people realize we're not *udell* like the rest of our family. Daddy trusts me."

Her dad approves? My life is so totally unfair. My parents are all for assimilation, but they'd never let me be in a relationship with a human. Even if you forget the risk of exposure, the emotional risk is astronomical.

I mean, talk about heartbreak. It's not like we could ever be married—try hiding a tail from someone you live with. No matter how much self-control I had, that would be impossible. It's not like any of us can maintain legs while we sleep. See, that's the real reason the Little Mermaid went to the Sea Sorceress. Humans have this part of the story so wrong. She didn't go to the sorceress to get legs; she went to permanently banish her tail so she could ensure her precious prince never found out what she really was.

"You can't possibly have a future with him. What's the point?" I ask Mel.

"Please don't tell me you're one of those neo-romantic Mermaids who believes I should get married before I even go to college? I thought one of the reasons we moved up here was to learn how humans make the best of these pathetically short lives. A lot of humans don't even think about marriage until their thirties."

"I'm not talking about marriage. I just mean, if there's not even the possibility you could stay with someone, be yourself with them, what kind of a relationship is that?"

"Gosh, Lia, how old are you? You do know we're in high school, right? I'm just having a good time. The whole point of being young and living in the human world is so I can experience life before I wither and die." She smiles and lets innuendo seep into her voice, "Clay is a fun guy to have those experiences with."

I sit in stunned silence. I'm not a sheltered idiot; I know that dating around is normal. I don't think the first boy I start a relationship with will be my one and only. I'm not Em. But isn't it a waste of time to put in so much energy—to risk heartbreak—for something that could never last? That's what I've always told myself, and that's why I've followed my parents' rules against dating humans.

I'm still thinking about it long after Melusine, her father, and all the other guests leave. I'm lying on the sea sponge bed in my downstairs bedroom, unable to turn off my thoughts. Maybe I'm wrong to take my parents' rules so seriously. The twins don't. Oh, they agree about not dating humans—all the guys they've ever been serious about have had tails. But they've each had human hookups at parties, and our parents have never known the difference. It was just never something I could picture myself trying. My parents have sacrificed so much to save us from the undersea wars and forge this life for us here. I don't think they deserve to be lied to.

Have I made a mistake? Sure, Melusine can't have a future with Clay, but she's spent the last three weeks hanging out with him, laughing with him, kissing him. I could have done that. I could have gotten in a few glorious weeks of kissing Clay. What would it be like to be able to hold onto those strong arms, stare into those deep hazel eyes, kiss that full, smirky mouth? I could have had that. But even as I let myself enjoy the oh so sweet idea, I know it wouldn't have been worth it. A few weeks with Clay and I'd have fallen—hard.

I should be happy his relationship with Melusine can't last, but instead I'm worried that she doesn't seem to care about his feelings. I don't want to see him get hurt. I snuggle deeper into my sea sponge, letting the layer of salt water cover me like a blanket. Clay's a person, not a piece of eye candy. Or lip candy … yum. I lose myself in the fantasy, and my sleepy mind floats away. I might not be able to be with Clay in real life, but at least I can dream about him.

Chapter Four

You know how sometimes when you go to sleep with your head full of worries, you wake up with a fresh perspective and realize in the light of day that your overly tired brain was overreacting? This is not one of those mornings. The moment my eyes pop open, thoughts of Melusine and Clay consume me—and now, I'm officially angry.

By the time I walk up to the kitchen for breakfast, my temper boils right under the surface. Amy has already swum off to school using the tunnels, like she does every morning. It's just Em, the twins, and my parents at the breakfast table as I slump into a chair.

"What's swum up your butt?" Lapis asks.

"Language," my mother scolds from across the table.

"Nothing," I grumble as I grab a sprouted bagel. Like most Mer, I don't do well with processed foods, but whole grains are safe. Usually, one of these bagels topped with as much salmon as I can pile on is my favorite breakfast; today I don't have much of an appetite.

Lapis turns her attention to Em. "So, you talk to Leo last night?"

"Yes ... we talked," Em says, barely forcing out the words.

"What did you—"

"Just drop it. Please." Em looks down and pokes at her salmon with her fork.

Concern paints my mother's face.

My father claps his hands once, breaking the somber mood. "I thought the party last night went just swimmingly. Pun intended!"

"We certainly had fun," Lazuli comments. The sly look she shares with Lapis proves the two of them definitely got up to something.

"You girls must all be excited to go to school today, what with another Mer in your midst," my dad says.

"Oh, yeah. Lia, did you know that Melusine chick was a Mermaid?" Lapis questions.

"Nope," I say, my annoyance obvious.

"I want you girls to be welcoming," my mother says as she sips her sugar kelp tea. Especially you, Aurelia, since the two of you are in the same grade. Do you have classes together?"

"Unfortunately."

"What's that supposed to mean?"

"I don't like her."

"Why ever not?"

"Her boyfriend's a human!" I shout. There. I wait for my mother's reaction. Maybe she'll be so freaked she'll get the Foundation to put a stop to it.

"Yes, her father told us." My mother's voice is way too calm, and my father just nods solemnly.

"Well? Can't you do something? Order an injunction or—"

"Aurelia! We're not dictators. You know very well that the Foundation's job is to keep the peace, not limit anyone's freedom. Now, I wholeheartedly agree that it's not proper parenting ... "

"But we all came up here to raise our children the way we see fit, Lia," my dad says, covering my mom's hand with his. "Filius assured us that Melusine has a particularly strong hold on her legs and that he supervises her with the boy regularly. We may not agree with it, but she's his daughter, and it's his choice."

"At least it will prove to the community they're not *udell*. That'll be a help. We can't have anyone thinking prejudice against mortals is acceptable," my mother finishes. They both look at me like they expect me to understand.

"So, that's it? You've lectured us for years on the dangers of getting 'romantically entangled,'" I purposely use their own words, "with humans, and you're just going to let Melusine do whatever she wants?"

"Melusine is not our responsibility the way you and your sisters are." My mother's tone grows firm. "No matter what Mr. Havelock lets his daughter do, we expect you to continue living by the rules we've set down. They exist to protect you."

"And we're very proud of the choices all you girls have made." My father's smile is genuine.

"This is way too much lecture for me to handle before 7:15," Lazuli says as she and Lapis rise from the table. "Lia, we'll meet you at the car."

Once my parents and I are alone, my mother comes and sits next to me. "I can tell you're angry at this girl, but her father promises he won't let her put any of us at risk." I plaster on a comforted expression. If my mom knew I'm more angry about *who* Melusine's dating than the consequences it could have on the Community, she'd flip a fin. "I want you to think about what a hard time she must be having. You know, her mother was killed in an uprising earlier this year."

The news sinks into my bones. I knew her mother was dead, but I hadn't realized it was so recent or that it had been violent. I'm lucky that, living on land, none of my immediate family has fallen victim to the wars. My anger fizzles.

"Imagine how hard it must be to come up here to a whole new place and know no one. Try to reach out to her, okay, kiddo?

I bet she needs a friend." My father's eyes are beseeching. With a sigh, I nod. "That's my girl," he says, and my mother squeezes my hand.

Great. Now I'll have to be nice to her. My parents don't ask very much of me, like ever. They saved me from a life in a warzone, they created an entire Foundation to secure my future, they spend a small fortune sending me to a school I really like, and they don't limit my shopping budget. "Don't date humans" is one of their only strict rules. Now that they've asked me to be friends with Melusine, I don't have much of a choice. They deserve that much from me. Plus, maybe if I'm nice to her, I can convince her seeing Clay's a bad idea.

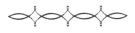

The twins and I get to school early, and when I enter the main hallway, Melusine stands alone by her locker. I take a deep breath. I'd better try this before I lose my nerve.

Yes, a part of me wants to unleash my girl-claws and rip her to shreds, but another part of me knows it's totally irrational to hate her just because she gets to have hot make out sessions with the guy I like. I've chosen not to risk being with Clay, and now I have to act like someone way more mature and live with that choice. We all need to stick together up here, and that means it's my job to be the bigger Mermaid and reach out to her.

I walk up to her locker. "Hey." I hope I sound natural. "I'm glad you came last night."

"Are you?" Her gaze is calculating, like she's appraising me again. I don't like it.

"Sure. Um, my sisters and I sometimes grab sushi together after school. We're going today and I thought maybe you'd like to come." I rush through the invitation before I can talk myself out of it. She's new. She has no friends. She needs this.

"No, thanks," Melusine replies coolly, shutting her locker.

"Oh, well, maybe another day this week?" I should be glad she's said no and drop it, but I can't forget my promise to my parents.

"Look, Lia, I know you're only trying to be besties because your parents told you to be nice to me."

"That's not true," I insist. We both know it's a fat lie.

"I've been at this school for three weeks, and you didn't say so much as hello to me until last night at the party."

"I'm sorry. I—"

"Save it. I can survive without your friendship. I'm used to being on my own." She turns and stalks past me down the hallway. Does that mean I'm off the hook?

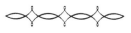

As soon as the bell rings, I have more to worry about than Melusine's determination to be a loner. I hate having P.E. first period.

It would be an overstatement to say I'm as excited as Kelsey to start self-defense, but no matter how brainless a teacher Coach Crane is, I figure since the subject is new for everyone, we'll start with some light punches and blocks. That, I can handle.

When I walk out of the locker room in my P.E. uniform and enter the gym, one look at the coach tells me I'm wrong. Her thick muscles are covered by even thicker padding strapped to her arms, legs, and torso. This is a woman who didn't even bother to wear a helmet when she taught us lacrosse. The fact that she feels the need for so much protective gear does not bode well for the safety level of today's activities.

"Gather up!" she calls as we make our way over to where she's set up a whole patchwork of mats. "To start our study of self-defense, we're going to test your instincts. You'll come up one at a time and fight me. That way, I'll get to see what your individual strengths and weaknesses are."

"We're not working on techniques first?" asks Hannah, a wide-eyed girl who looks as scared as I feel.

"I want you to see how you'd do if someone attacked you today. Hopefully that will motivate you to take this seriously."

I know how I'd do if some psycho attacked me—I'd die. I don't need to be beaten up by my P.E. coach to figure that out. What I do need to figure out is how I'll get through this class with my still-shaky leg control. What if I get all twisted up in my own limbs and make a fool of myself? Epic flail. And the coach won't make it easy. She still has it in for me because I refused to go swimming, and now she'll have the opportunity to knock me unconscious.

She paces back and forth, the soles of her Skechers sinking into the mats with each step. "Now, for the men in the room, I want you to focus on punches. We'll steer clear of the face for today, but feel free to hit me anywhere else—I'm wearing protection." The few guys who snicker at the double meaning fall silent when she pins them with a death glare.

Punches. Okay, I can handle punches. I'll plant my feet and try a few solid punches to her padded stomach. Maybe this won't be so terrible.

"As for the women, the occasional punch is fine, but I want you to focus on kicks. A woman's strength is in her lower body, and I want you to get used to taking advantage of it."

Kicks? As in balancing on one leg while the other is up in the air trying to hit a moving target? I'm shark bait.

The shark in question forms us into a curving line so we can watch each other's fights while we wait. I catch Clay's eye from where he stands at the end of the line, and I must look nervous because he shoots me a "Don't sweat it" smile before turning his attention back to the coach. At least Melusine's not in this class; seeing her land what I imagine would be a series of perfect roundhouse kicks would make me crazy jealous.

Kelsey goes first. She punches the coach twice in the torso then stands back to try a kick. It's not very high, but it hits the coach against her upper leg pad with a solid *thwack*!

"Nice job," I say as she comes to stand next to me.

"Thanks. It's not so bad. You'll do fine."

I doubt it. My lower half tends to work as a unit, since naturally it's one tail and not two legs. That's why walking and running were hard to learn at first. One leg kicking by itself sounds like a face-plant waiting to happen.

One by one, the other students go. While I wait, I practice by discreetly raising one foot a few inches in the air and making a baby kick. The next few girls are the class glamazons, and they make it look easy. One girl, Genevieve, lands a kick so high it strikes the coach's upper arm. Why can't I move like that?

My turn. I move forward, trying not to look anxious. My first step onto the squishy mat almost throws me off balance, but I manage to hold my ground. Coach Crane stares at me with hard eyes and beckons me forward without a word. She plants her feet one at a time, reminding me of a sumo wrestler. I throw a punch aimed at her torso, imitating Kelsey, but Coach Crane blocks it before I get close. I try again, aiming for her left side, but she snaps her arm out, blocking me again. "Come on, Nautilus, you need to make contact. Use your legs."

I grit my teeth and lift my right leg. At the last moment, I chicken out, and kick so low I only manage to tap the side of my foot against her shin.

"You have to do better than that."

I take a step forward, lift my leg, and swing it forcefully back. In that glorious instant, I can visualize it hitting her in an impressive kick to the waist that bows her entire body and finally shuts her up. Instead, my leg misses her, and the momentum behind my kick swings me around so hard I fall onto my butt.

Clay sees the whole thing.

Coach Crane doesn't offer me a hand up. She just calls, "Next!" while I'm left to struggle to my feet on the too-soft mat before the next student can step on me. Why does physical education have to be a graduation requirement?

Face hot, I move to the sidelines while the glamazons giggle. Genevieve, the crowned princess of high kicks, walks over, her BFF Jaclyn in tow.

"Friendly advice? Work on those moves or you'll never get a boyfriend," Genevieve says.

"Maybe you can take one of those stripper pole classes. Loosen up a little," Jaclyn suggests.

My face gets even hotter. "Thanks … I'll keep that in mind."

Oh, no. Clay's heading straight toward us. As if this could get any more humiliating.

Jaclyn gives a flirty wave. "Hey, Clay."

He doesn't say anything. Just stands next to me and stares at them.

They exchange a look, half-confused, half-nervous. The moment drags, and Clay stares.

"Later, Lia," Genevieve says as they hurry away.

Now that Clay's close to me, the muffled notes of a guitar riff fill the air between us. He must have earbuds hidden under the hoodie he's wearing with his gym uniform. I want to thank him for stepping in. But all that comes out is, "How can you listen to that so loud?"

"It drowns out the morons." He nods his head to where Genevieve and Jaclyn whisper to each other on the other side of the mats.

"They meant well," I say, not really believing it.

"No. They didn't."

With Clay radiating silent support, I'm reminded of another moment like this one. It's a moment I try hard not to think about, but right now, I can't help it. In that long-ago moment, having him next to me made a much bigger difference than he realized.

It was last year, right after I'd first started Malibu Hills Prep. Once I could maintain my new legs for a whole day at a time without trouble, my parents had proclaimed me ready. I was used to the feel of shoes by then (well, flat shoes, anyway), and my older sisters had taken me on a few excursions to shopping malls, so even the feel of so many humans close by was familiar. But the idea of actually having conversations with humans? Of trying to make friends? That was totally different territory.

The first few days passed in a blur of new faces and adrenaline. Everyone seemed interested in me simply because I was new, so I spent every day evading question after question: Where did I grow up? Why hadn't I gone to middle school with all of them? How come I didn't want to come to so-and-so's pool party? I tried to smile as I gave all the fake, well-rehearsed answers Em had used flashcards to quiz me on, but saying them out loud to real people wasn't the same as saying them in my living room. After an entire week, my head swam with all the excuses and half-truths. Each one plunked into my stomach, heavy as a stone.

I'd spent months—years!—imagining what it would be like to finally go to human school, to finally make human friends. But how would I ever make real friends if every answer I gave, every word I spoke involved some kind of lie? No one would get to know the real me. *Duh. The real you is half fish. How could you think that wouldn't matter?* My thoughts berated me, called me a fool. How could I have been so naïve, so hopeful? As I sat in the cafeteria, looking around the table at all the classmates I'd never be able to get truly close to, a wave of disappointment washed over me with so much force I wanted to cry, wanted to run to the grottos and never come back to this place where I so clearly didn't belong.

I mumbled an excuse to the too-cheerful strangers around me and headed away from the crowded cafeteria as fast as my new legs would take me. Malibu Hills Prep boasted a sprawling, palm tree-lined campus up in the mountains. I didn't know where most of the paths led yet, so I let my instincts carry me along one that wound up to the top of a hill.

When I rounded a bend, my breath caught. Stretched out before me lay a stunning view of the ocean far below the mountains. A solitary turquoise bench stood at the overlook, and I sank onto it. The crashing of the waves posed a challenge to my leg control but also soothed me with its rhythmic familiarity. I'd always have the ocean. And my family, and Caspian … So what if I wouldn't be able to make real friends at the place I'd be spending seven hours every day? It didn't matter.

Except it did.

"You're in my spot."

My head spun around. I'd been so caught up listening to the clashing waves and getting lost in the whirlpool of my own thoughts that I hadn't heard anyone approaching. I swallowed as I drank in the sight of the guy standing in front of me, looking better in a t-shirt and jeans than anyone had a right to. My eyes darted from his dark hair to his jawline to the unmistakable outline of his biceps under the sleeves of an open leather jacket.

I was supposed to say something. *Talk, damn it!* "Oh, I … "

"Scooch over," the guy said. My thoughts were still flopping around like fish in a net, but I must have done as he'd asked because a second later, he slid next to me on the bench. "No one else ever comes up here."

"Really?" The waves rolled beneath us, majestic as they crested white and glinted in the sun before smashing against the rocks. "But it's so beautiful here," I said.

"Yep. It's a great view." He took a sidelong glance at me and the corner of his mouth quirked up. "Especially today."

My face heated, so I trained my eyes on my lap. "I … um … I just came up here 'cause … " I didn't know how to finish that sentence without seeming like an antisocial freak.

"You needed to get away for a while. To regroup."

I blinked. Turned to look at him again. "Yeah. It's just, I'm new, and everyone was asking me so many questions … " and I was telling so many lies …

"Hey, you don't have to explain anything to me."

After a week of being asked to do nothing but explain myself when I couldn't, those words—his words—sparked a rush of relief so palpable, my body sagged against the back of the bench. "Thanks."

"Oh, don't thank me. It's a strategy." He said it like he knew something I didn't. Like he knew everything. I wasn't sure whether the cockiness irked me or made me more curious.

Who was I kidding? Who wouldn't be curious? "A strategy?"

"Sometimes I think you get to know a person better when you don't question them." Did that mean this boy with his sculpted features and confident voice wanted to get to know me? "Sometimes," he continued, "you learn the most about a person from what they don't say."

He crossed his legs, resting one ankle on the opposite knee. The move shifted his weight until we were only inches apart. I let the silence fill that remaining space between us. After what he'd just said, it seemed appropriate.

When several seconds had passed and I hadn't said anything, he smirked as understanding dawned on his face. Silence was fine with both of us.

His eyes met mine then. I had to resist the urge to take his face in both my hands and study them up close. As the afternoon sun hit them, the hazel came alive with golds and greens and rich browns.

I was probably gaping at him like a codfish. With all the effort I could muster, I dragged my gaze back toward the view. So did he.

Without the need to make conversation, I didn't need to lie. I could finally relax.

And I did. Sitting there next to him in silence, I felt like myself at school for the first time. "I really love the ocean," I whispered.

We stayed there like that until a bell sounded from down the hill, signaling the end of lunch.

Then he finally spoke again. "You're Lia." It wasn't a question. "But you spell it cool." Also not a question.

"Yeah," I sputtered. He'd noticed me enough to find that out? "Lia Nautilus."

"I'm Clay." He swung on his backpack and faced me, pinning

me to the spot with his first full smile of the afternoon. It was dazzling. "See you around, Nautilus."

And he did. He seemed to be there on that bench whenever I needed to get away. He was the only one who didn't bombard me with questions I couldn't answer, who just let me talk when I was comfortable. Soon, I talked more and more.

Without knowing it, Clay totally saved me those first few weeks. He showed me someone could be my friend even if I couldn't say everything I wanted to. Instead of going home and pleading with my parents to re-enroll me in Mer school, I had the confidence to stick it out because of Clay.

Spending time with him proved even if I couldn't be completely open with humans, I could at least be genuine. So, I started making more of an effort with a few other people— including Kelsey, who told me (after I dodged yet another of her questions one day after school) that every girl deserved to have an air of mystery.

At first, I definitely included Clay on my growing list of new friends. I still met up with him on the outlook bench often and sometimes sat at his table in the library or spent time with him in the courtyard after school, exchanging jokes and banter.

But the day he casually took my hand to lead me up that same winding path, then leaned in close to tuck a stray lock of hair behind my ear, I knew the attraction was undeniable. If I'd been anyone else, I could have kissed him, right then. The problem was there was no way I could get involved with a human.

Letting myself be tempted would put my whole Community at risk. As hard as it was, I did what I had to and started putting distance between the two of us. I just couldn't be around him without wanting to do something I shouldn't, so I started spending more time with my other friends and made sure Clay and I weren't alone together. And I stopped going to that bench entirely.

Now, a year later, we still say hi to each other in the halls occasionally and talk in the classes we have together, but I've

made sure we're not close friends. Even though I sometimes want
to turn back the clock, pull him toward me on that path (as if
I'd ever have the nerve), and kiss him, I'm used to the way things
are. Or, I was, before I had to watch him and Mel lip lock on a
daily basis.

I sigh now as I stand in P.E. watching Genevieve and Jaclyn
whisper about me. Clay standing there next to me makes me feel
stronger. Just like it did back then.

Another muffled guitar riff from his hidden headphones
reaches my ears a second before the coach calls his name. He lifts
his hoodie up over his head without revealing even a hint of the
earbuds and tosses it to the floor.

As he deftly spars with Coach Crane, getting not only several
fast punches through her blocks but also some swift, clean kicks,
I'm struck again not only by the surety of his movements, but
also by the confident expression on his face. Like he's sure he
can take on any challenge and keep fighting. Does Melusine
appreciate that confidence? Does she even know him?

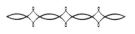

I'm not obsessing about Clay. I don't notice the way his dark hair
meets the creamy skin at the nape of his neck. I don't notice the
stubble dotting his jaw or the arresting, serious expression he gets
when he's listening to someone, the way he is now. I definitely
don't notice the way he subconsciously strokes Melusine's hand
as he holds it across the desk. I'm focusing on social studies class.
I'm dutifully taking notes. Is it my fault Clay and Melusine sit
between me and the board?

"Watch the drool," Kelsey whispers from the seat next to
mine. She's right. I thought I crushed this crush last year when I
made myself stay away from Clay. I give Kelsey a look of wide-
eyed innocence, like I don't have a clue what she's talking about,
and try to concentrate on what Mr. Reitzel is saying.

"After reading your last round of papers, I got the impression that many of you feel disconnected from the material we're studying."

"No offense, Mr. Reitzel," Kelsey says, "but we are kinda disconnected from it. By a couple hundred years." Everyone chuckles, including Mr. Reitzel.

"It does seem that way, doesn't it? So I guess my job is to help you realize that just because something happened a few centuries ago doesn't mean it can't affect you on a personal level today. That's kind of a hefty order."

I smell an assignment coming on.

"And your next assignment should accomplish just that." He picks up a stack of assignment sheets and passes them out. "These explain the project that will take us through the end of the quarter."

He hands me my assignment sheet. "Your Family History." Oh, no! My family history is more suitable for a marine biology class than it will ever be for social studies. How am I going to flounder my way through this one? I make a conscious effort to keep my breathing even and not let my face show anything more than the typical annoyance most students are exhibiting at the extra work load. "You're each going to go back as many generations as you can, using research tools that I'll teach you about. Then, you'll draw connections between every generation of your family and something you've learned in class about the historical events of the time. To keep things interesting," Mr. Reitzel continues, "you'll be working in teams of two."

The room fills with subtle but discernible noise as everyone shifts toward their desired partners. Kelsey and I have already leaned close together over our assignment sheets, and Melusine has pushed her seat so close to Clay's their thighs are touching.

"Not so fast," Mr. Reitzel says, holding up a hand. "Since the point of this project is to learn new things and make new connections, I'd like you all to get to know someone new."

Typical. Why do teachers wait until you've finally gotten

accustomed to their routines before yanking the sea grass out from under you? As if I weren't nervous enough about this assignment already. Kelsey and I exchange disappointed glances. Then again, maybe this is for the best. Maybe I'll get a stupid partner who won't get suspicious when I have to fabricate my entire half of the project.

Mr. Reitzel starts reading off a list of pairs, and soon Kelsey is moving across the room to sit with Matt Greene. Matt's nice and he gets good grades; the two of them will make a good team. Melusine looks none too pleased as Laurie Kennish sits down next to her. I smile. I wouldn't want to have to put up with Laurie's caffeine-fueled energy levels for an entire quarter.

Then Mr. Reitzel says my name. "Lia Nautilus and … Clay Ericson." Now I have a whole new reason to be nervous.

Breathe, I tell myself as Clay's eyes meet mine and he smiles at me. Time skips and he's lowering himself into the seat Kelsey vacated. The seat next to mine.

"So, I guess we're partners," I say. Way to state the obvious.

"Yep. Got any family secrets I should know about now, Nautilus?" he jokes.

"You'll just have to wait and find out." Except that can't happen. "How about you? Anything poster board worthy?"

"Oh yeah, tons."

"Like what?"

He leans in close and whispers, "I'm a prince in disguise."

"Really?" I ask, making my skepticism evident. "I didn't know princes liked to wear jeans with so many holes."

"I'm keeping a low profile." He winks at me, and I hope I'm not blushing. What would he say if he knew I was the distant cousin of the ocean's most infamous princess?

We read through the requirements of the project together: a poster board, oral report, and fifteen-page research paper.

"It's going to be an awful lot of work," I say. "We should probably get started sooner instead of later."

"For sure," he agrees. "I can't today. I'm gonna check out this cello rock band up in Santa Cruz, so I gotta cut out before bio, but why don't you come over tomorrow after school?"

"You're," I lower my voice, "ditching?"

"I read ahead. No harm, no foul. So, tomorrow?"

"Yeah, tomorrow."

I know this is just some random partnership for a school project. I know spending time with Clay can't possibly help me get over the way I feel about him. But I can't help looking forward to tomorrow.

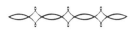

"Lia, get your butt downstairs. We're going to be late again," Lapis calls out before her platform shoes clack back down the stairs.

This is the third outfit I've tried on. I'm usually not picky, but today I keep changing my mind. I want to look fashionable, but not too trend-obsessed. Pretty, but also sexy—but not like I'm trying to look sexy, you know? Above all, I have to look like I don't care how I look. I don't want Clay thinking I dressed up to go over to his house because that would be super lame.

I settle on a pale blue, formfitting sweater and skinny jeans. I don't normally wear jeans (it feels strange to have layers of denim separating my legs), but I figure it's a good idea in case we sit on the floor while we work. As I slip into white ballet flats, I wish again that I could wear heels.

"Liii-aaa!"

I stick my clear but uber shiny lip gloss in the front pocket of my backpack and hurry down the stairs.

Once I'm at school, the day slogs by. Each class drags on and on until finally I'm dismissed. As soon as I see Clay waiting in the parking lot, it's like the time continuum decides to play catch up all at once and suddenly my heart is racing.

"Hey, Nautilus. You ready to get our study on?"

"Sure am."

He holds open the passenger door of his blue Mustang convertible and I slide in, thankful I stuck with the jeans. As he settles into the driver's seat, Clay pushes a button, and the top of the car folds back. Within minutes, we've turned onto the Pacific Coast Highway, and the ocean air whips through my hair. The waves sparkle through the window, and it's like we're in a movie scene or something. The Beach Boys should be crooning about California in the background. Then the wind lashes a strand of my hair into my freshly glossed, highly sticky lips. I smash back to reality and bat the hair out of my face. I must look so spazzy.

"And guys think we have problems," Clay says with a grin as he brakes at a stoplight. His hand moves toward the button that will put the top back up, but I place my hand on his, stopping him. This small touch of my skin against his shouldn't feel so electrifying. I inhale sharply, taking in a full breath of the salty sea air.

"Leave it open," I say. "I can handle it." Clay has a stack of napkins from a local coffee house sitting in his cup holder under a tin of mints. I grab one, swipe off the offending lip gloss, and throw my head back, welcoming the rush of wind that makes my hair fly out in all directions.

The light turns green, but we don't move. I look over at Clay in time to see him staring at me.

A honk from the car behind us jolts him into awareness, and he steps on the gas. The wind gets stronger as we pick up speed, and Clay's smile tells me he's enjoying the feel of it as much as I am.

Clay's house isn't as close to the water as mine or as ridiculously huge, but it's gorgeous all the same. His mom bought it after the book deal for her latest fantasy series about fairies earned her a cool six figures. My dad read about it in the *Malibu Surfside News*.

"Is your mom home? I should introduce myself."

"No. She usually writes at this café around the corner till it gets dark. You hungry? Want anything from the kitchen?"

A couple minutes later, armed with two bottles of water and a bag of sweet potato chips for Clay, we head up to his room.

I've never been to his house before, let alone in his room. I'm expecting it to be the way I've always pictured a guy's bedroom—messy with a smell like gym socks or sweaty sheets. When he opens the door, I'm pleasantly surprised.

The room is pretty neat, with the exception of a somewhat disorganized looking desk, and all that meets my nose are the faint scents of laundry soap and … something I can't quite place.

"Is that … cinnamon?"

"Hmm? Oh, I polished my guitar earlier. My grandfather's old polish kind of smells like cinnamon."

I don't see a guitar anywhere. He must have put it away. "I didn't know you played."

"Yeah, since I was a kid." He unpacks his backpack and spreads the books and materials we'll need across his cluttered desk.

"Is that your band?" I ask, indicating the t-shirt he's wearing, which features some sort of indie group.

One corner of his mouth twitches up. "I'm not in a band. This," he points to the shirt, "is a fellow musical prodigy." I shake my head at his arrogance but lean in and examine the shirt. The different band members are actually the same person over and over.

"Mozart?"

"The late and great. You seem to love staring at my chest, Nautilus." He's only poking fun at me, but I pull back.

"You wish," I say. "Let's get to work."

He brings in another chair, and we sit at his desk, creating a study schedule. Then, we start writing out family trees with names we'll research in computer lab.

A while later, I've made a list that's a good combination of fake names and names of real ancestors who never set foot on land and won't come up in any databases. I feel Clay's eyes on me, and I look up just as he looks down. It's probably nothing. Maybe he was staring off into space, or maybe I have lint on my sweater. I turn my attention back to my work.

We continue in silence, but I still feel like Clay's watching me.

"Lia?" he finally asks. "Can I ask you something?" His voice is quiet and uncharacteristically serious.

"Sure."

"Why … why did you stop hanging out with me last year?" He's looking down now, his eyes fixed on his paper.

Because you're human. Because I can't like you. "Because I got super busy. Y'know, first year at a new school." That sounds lame even to me. "Everything was a little overwhelming."

"I wasn't trying to overwhelm you."

"No, I didn't mean it like that. I just had a lot going on."

"So, you just stopped returning my calls?" He's trying to keep his tone casual, but hurt slips into his voice. I wish I could explain to Clay that I put distance between us for his own good.

"I'm sorry." It's the truth. He finally looks up, and his eyes bore into mine. For a second, they're filled with something raw and sad. Then, just as quickly, he breaks eye contact, and his trademark smirk slides back in place.

"Well, I just had to find out how anyone could blow off a guy as awesome as me. I've been wanting to ask you for a while, but we're somehow never alone."

"I didn't blow you off." Except I did.

"Hey, I just thought we were friends, Nautilus, that's all."

"We are friends." We shouldn't be—not when I feel this way. But I say it anyway.

"Promise?" His small smile is genuine now.

"Promise," I say. And I mean it.

Chapter Five

My house is too quiet. I don't hear music blasting from Lapis and Lazuli's room, or the telltale clanking of pots in the kitchen that means my dad is cooking dinner, or even Emeraldine's complaints that she's trying to study and everyone better keep it down. A strange stillness fills the house, putting my nerves on edge.

"I'm home!" I call out tentatively, dropping my backpack by the door. "Dad?" No response. "Em?"

No one's in the living room. I check the kitchen and the den. No one. The dining room. Empty. I run upstairs and search but don't find anyone. Could they all have gone somewhere without letting me know?

If they did, they must have told Amy. I head down to the grottos, shedding my jeans and shoes along the way. No matter how cute and lacey it can be, underwear is an unnecessary hindrance I gave up on a long time ago.

The moment I open the door to the antechamber, the chatter of voices makes me breathe a huge sigh of relief. I can even make out my mother's voice, which means she's home early from the Foundation. Curious, I step into the canal, lower my now-naked bottom half into the cool water, and relax. The rushing sensation of invisible tides flows up and down my legs as they meld together into one strong, golden tail that propels me into the main ballroom, then into the hallway as I follow the voices to Amy's room.

"What are we doing?" Everyone turns to look at me from around Amy's bed, huge smiles on their faces.

"Lia! Look!" Amy squeals. I look, but all I see is Amy, lying on her sponge bed with a soaking wet blanket covering the top half of her tail.

"What am I looking at?"

"Just give it a second, will you?" she answers back.

In a flash, Amy's shining purple tail disappears. In its place is a pair of pale, gangly legs! It only takes half a second for her tail to return, but those were definitely legs.

"Ah!" Now I'm the one squealing. I throw my arms around Amy and let go just in time to see her legs flicker into existence again. My whole family cheers.

"My baby cousin has legs!" Before I can stop myself, I'm squeezing her into another hug.

"Not a baby anymore," my mom says, giving Amy a smile.

"Sure isn't. Those are some damn sexy legs you got there, Aims."

"Lapis!" Emeraldine admonishes, beating my mom to the punch.

"All Lapis means is we better watch out. Amy'll be beating the boys off with a coral rod soon enough." Amy blushes at Lazuli's words.

"Of course she will. She's a Nautilus woman," my dad says with a wink.

"She certainly is," my mother adds.

"Can I go upstairs, Aunt Nerissa? I want to take a walk."

My mother smiles warmly at her but shakes her head. "Let's

wait until you can maintain all your limbs for a few minutes, shall we?"

Amy's legs are still morphing into a tail and back again every few seconds.

"How do I keep my legs?" Amy asks.

The twins share a knowing look. My father scratches the back of his head where his hair is still thick and glances at my mother, who gives a tiny nod.

"I'll go get dinner ready and leave you ladies to … talk," he says before swimming to the door. "Congratulations, Amy."

Once he's out of earshot, my mother sits on the bed and strokes a hand through Amy's long, strawberry blond hair. "Amethyst, maintaining your legs can be a challenge. Walking doesn't come naturally to us. Until the wars drove us to learn how to survive on land, trips above water were rare. Even the most accomplished Mer had never kept their legs for more than a few hours for such a visit. Most only ever used their legs at all for … the obvious purpose."

"Sex," Lapis clarifies. Even Below, Mer need legs to have sex. Our reproductive systems are built like humans', but our tails cover up … the necessary body parts. That's why getting legs is part of puberty.

"For mating, yes," my mother says. "Of course, we considered this when we first decided to live on land. That's how we discovered the key to maintaining legs, at least at first, is to contemplate their original purpose. This won't be necessary after some practice, but for right now, a certain level of maturity and self-awareness will go a long way."

Amy tries to follow this, but she looks confused.

"What you want to do," Em interjects, "is embrace your natural impulses. You don't need to act on those urges—thinking about them will be enough. You'll see."

"Does that make sense, sweetheart?" my mother asks.

"Um … yeah. Thanks." When my mother leans in to hug her, Amy shoots me a puzzled look, and I smile reassuringly.

When Mom gave me this same talk about self-awareness and natural urges, I had no clue what she meant. Until Lapis and Lazuli gave me a talk of their own afterwards. I remember lying on my bed, the way Amy is now, watching my new legs melt into familiar golden scales every few seconds. I willed with all my might for the legs to just ... stay. I closed my eyes and visualized it, thinking maybe that's what my mom had meant, but nothing happened. Then, the twins came into my grotto bedroom.

"Any luck, little sis?" Lazuli had asked.

"No," I pouted.

"Let me guess. Mom's little heart-to-heart left a lot to be desired."

"It ... helped. Kind of."

"Lucky for you," Lapis chimed in, "we're going to help a lot more. It's actually simple. What are your legs for?"

"Walking," I said like it was a no-brainer.

"Urrr!" Lapis made the sound of a game show buzzer. "Wrong. But thanks for playing."

Lazuli sat on my bed. "As usual, you're thinking like a human. You're a Mermaid, Lia."

"Gee, thanks for the update," I said sarcastically.

"As a Mermaid who's supposed to live in the ocean and would never need to step foot on land, what are your legs for?"

Oh! That. "Um ... s-sex."

"Give the Mergirl a prize!" Lapis announced in her game show voice.

"So what does that matter?" I was nervous about where the conversation was heading. I was only fourteen then, and talking about sex with my boy crazy older sisters wasn't something I was comfortable with. It still isn't.

"If we were all living Below," Lazuli explained, "the only time we'd even have legs is right before we—"

"Got it on with some buff young Merstud," Lapis concluded. "So, all you have to do is think slutty thoughts and your legs will stay firmly in place."

"Thoughts can't be slutty!" I argued, trying to poke holes in their theory. They'd played pranks on me before, and I wasn't going to let them pull the algae over my eyes this time.

"That's true," Lazuli conceded. "So, you should feel free to think whatever you want without getting all guilty about it."

"Personally, I like to think about what it would feel like to—"

"Okay, enough. I get it."

"Do you?" Lazuli asked, looking pointedly at my ever-disappearing legs. They hadn't held for more than ten seconds at a time.

"Lia, listen," Lapis said, her voice losing all trace of theatrics, "you don't need to be embarrassed. You're older now, and these kinds of thoughts are natural. At your age, they're practically required. Now, close your eyes."

I looked at her skeptically.

"Trust me," she said.

I closed my eyes.

"I want you to imagine … um … "

"Caspian," Lazuli suggested.

My eyes flew open. "He's my friend!"

"Your friend has gotten totally ripped. Don't tell me you haven't noticed."

Of course I'd noticed. That was the year Caspian went from being a wiry kid to looking like he'd stepped off the cover of one of Em's hidden romance novels. "I'm not picturing him that way."

"Relax," Lazuli insisted. "I'll keep it PG." I glared at her in warning before closing my eyes again. "Well, PG-13." She told me to picture his biceps, his abs, his new legs (which I'd only seen a handful of times, but already knew were muscular and strong). "Now open your eyes."

I looked down to see my legs holding steadily.

The twins smiled at me, looking almost proud. "Well, what do you know? Our little sister's all grown up."

In the months that followed, I kept what the twins said in

mind while I practiced. It didn't feel right to keep thinking about Caspian that way, so I focused on guys I'd seen in magazines or on TV and even imagined a few of the characters from my favorite books. I got the hang of it soon enough.

Now I look at Amy with her new legs still flickering in and out; she's growing up, too. It's my job to help her get the hang of it.

"Don't forget to shell call your mother after dinner," my mom tells Amy. "She'll be so excited. Your uncle and I might just have to plan a surprise, now that everyone in the family has legs." She gives Amy another hug before heading upstairs.

As soon as my mother leaves, Emeraldine pulls Amy into a hug of her own. "I'm so proud of you. Make sure you let me know if you need anything. When you're ready, I'll take you for a pedicure." Amy's face lights up. "Lapis, Lazuli," Emeraldine continues, "let's go help Dad with dinner." Clearly, Em doesn't want the twins corrupting our little cousin.

Em swims out of the room, expecting the twins to follow. "You got this?" Lapis asks me.

"I got it."

"You're a knockout, Aims," Lapis says as she leaves.

"You'll have to borrow some of my miniskirts to show those off," Lazuli says with a nod at Amy's legs as she follows Lapis out, leaving the two of us alone.

"Careful," I say. "Some of Lazuli's miniskirts are downright dangerous." Amy laughs, still beaming. "Didn't I tell you your legs would be beautiful?"

"They're nice aren't they?" Amy's grin reaches her ears. "Okay, so tell me how I really do this." She's looking at me expectantly. Here goes.

I launch into my own version of the talk. It's more watered down than the one I got from the twins, but I cover all the basics. Amy doesn't look as uncomfortable as I did afterward.

"That makes sense," she says, sounding a little overwhelmed.

"If you're having any trouble," I tell her, "just think about a boy you like."

"I've been thinking ... " Clay trails off.

"About?"

"Your legs."

I swivel my chair around to face Clay, but his eyes stay focused on the computer screen. Only the lift at the corner of his mouth tells me he's aware of my surprise.

"You've been thinking about my legs?"

"Yep. They're the problem."

"You have a problem with my legs?"

He turns to face me. "I have no problem with your legs." I look down, in case I'm blushing. "But they're what's causing all your trouble in self-defense. Last week, when we covered punches, you were fine. But now that we're covering blocking with the legs and kicking, you're spending all of class—"

"Tripping over myself. Yeah, I know." I want to joke about him looking at my legs, but we're already in dangerous territory. *He's a human*, I remind myself. *He's a human with a girlfriend.* I steer us onto safer seas. "Shouldn't we be researching our ancestors?"

We're in the computer lab that's attached to the library, and we're supposed to be looking up our relatives in a census database. Mr. Reitzel has left us to our own devices while he grades papers right outside.

"I've already found out my first ancestors to come over from Europe in the late 1800s opened a restaurant in New York. That's enough work for today. Now, since we're officially friends again, I want to help you conquer this P.E. problem."

"Well, since we're officially friends again," I say with a smile, "I'll be honest and tell you I don't think there's much hope in that department."

"There's always hope, even for something you think you've

crossed off your list. It just takes a little creativity."

"So, Mr. Creativity, where did you learn your mad fighting skills?"

He hesitates. "Can you keep a secret?"

"I'm just about a master at it," I answer honestly.

"I didn't have a choice. I was getting picked on bad in middle school."

"Really?" I find this kind of hard to believe. Clay's rough-and-tumble look makes him come off pretty tough. Plus, one glance at his arms makes it obvious he's a strong guy—not exactly the type you'd want to mess with.

"Really. I was scrawny back then, and I was always hanging out in the back of the science lab at lunch, writing songs." He pauses, like he's waiting for me to call him out on his behavior. Does he think it's embarrassing? When I stay quiet and keep listening, he continues.

"Anyway, this was when my dad still lived with us and, y'know, big navy man saw his son come home with too many bruises. He called up one of his squadron buddies and had me learn how to defend myself. No bowing or colored belts or anything. Just how to avoid a punch and how to dish one out when it's necessary."

"Were you able to stop them from bullying you?"

"In time I got 'em off my back, yeah. The growth spurt also helped a lot."

"If all else fails, maybe you can beat up Coach Crane for me," I joke.

He looks relieved, like he thought I might make fun of him. "I don't know if even I'm up to taking her on." We both laugh, our computers forgotten. "Hey, I wanted to tell y—"

Melusine chooses that moment to interrupt.

"Can I borrow my *boyfriend* for a teensy sec?" She puts just a hint too much emphasis on the word "boyfriend."

"Hey, Mel, what's up?" Clay asks her.

She grabs his wrist and moves toward the door of the computer lab. "We'll be right back," she tells me.

She picked her moment carefully; Mr. Reitzel is engaged in a conversation with the librarian. Through the tinted glass wall that separates the computer section from the rest of the library, I watch Melusine guide Clay into the book stacks, where they disappear from view. What's she doing with him back there? Is she angry we were talking? Friends are allowed to have conversations. Is she re-staking her claim to let me know she can? Maybe it has nothing to do with me. Maybe she just felt like a quick make out session in the middle of class.

A few minutes later, Melusine walks back in. Without so much as a glance at me, she takes her seat next to Laurie Kennish on the other end of the room. Clay follows a moment later and sinks back into the chair next to mine.

"You guys have fun?" I ask, keeping my voice nonchalant.

He doesn't answer. He looks pretty dazed. His eyes are all unfocused as he stares blankly at his computer screen. Oh, great. Melusine must be some kisser. It takes all my effort to withhold a sigh.

"So," I try, "any tips you learned from your dad's friend that might help save me from Coach Crane?"

Clay's voice is distracted when he says, "Let's just get back to work."

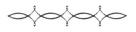

"Why are guys such much moody?" I wince. That came out wrong.

"You mean, why are guys so moody?" Caspian corrects. A powerful kick of his tailfin propels him even farther out into the ocean and sends resounding ripples toward my face. I kick my own tail to catch up.

On land, when I'm talking to older Mer, I speak a mean Mermenglish—grabbing English words I need and sticking them into Mermese sentences. But, when I'm underwater like now, that's nearly impossible. No other language travels as well through the muffling waves as Mermese, which switches between high-pitched sounds that pierce the water and melodic notes that dance across it.

Caspian has a thing for languages, so he fixes my grammar without thinking. Can you say annoying in Mermese? Ugh. Tonight, though, I need his advice. As soon as I catch up to where he's swimming in figure eights through a rich, green kelp forest, I ask, *"So why?"*

"Are you calling me moody? Should I be offended?"

"Not you."

"Of course not." The moonlight filtering from above glints off his silver tail as he twists his body through stalks of kelp as thick as tree trunks. I follow, accidentally disrupting a school of sassy *señorita* fish. I enjoy the tickle of their feather-light fins against my stomach as the tiny things rush back into formation.

"Are we talking about one guy in particular here?" Caspian asks. His voice sounds only mildly interested, but he's slowed down.

"No ... it's just a general question." I probably shouldn't be asking Caspian when I can't give him the full story, but I really need a guy's opinion. What's the point of having a guy for a best friend if I can't take advantage of his inborn expertise?

"Just general, huh? Well, speaking for my entire gender in general, sometimes it's hard to know what a girl's thinking." He stops swimming and his blue eyes fix on my face. *"And what she's thinking about you."*

Is that it? Does Clay think that I think he's flirting? 'Cause I so don't. I tear off a piece of kelp and munch on it as I roll this possibility around in my mind. I rip off a leaf for Caspian and offer it to him. We enjoy the salty, green apple-like taste for a minute in silence.

"Look, Lia, there's a difference between being moody and being a jerk. If a guy doesn't treat you right, he doesn't deserve you."

But that's just it—Clay treats me great ... when he's talking to me. We've met four times over the past two weeks, and he's usually super chatty. One minute he's joking around, and the next he's kind of cold and just wants to work on the project.

If Caspian's right and Clay's confused about what I might be thinking, then I'll have to make it clear to him that I understand he has a girlfriend and our friendship won't get in the way of that. *"That's a big help. Thanks, Casp."*

Caspian smiles. The blond hair floating around his head looks almost like a halo in the dark waters. I wish we were allowed to swim in the ocean during daylight, but there's too great a risk we'll be seen. Luckily, I can see much better in the dark, and obviously underwater, than a human can because of the shape of a part of my eye called the Crystalline lens. My dad explained to me once how my eyes are actually more like a seal's or a seabird's than a human's. When he first told me that little tidbit, I felt like more of an imposter than ever. My eyes may look human, but they're no more human than I am. I have to say, though, it sure is useful, and it makes swimming after dark much more fun. Still, it would be heaven to be able to sun myself on the rocks out in the open ocean, the way my ancestors did. The sweet freedom of it is almost unimaginable.

Yet another rule confronts me as the Border grows nearer with every flick of my tail. The row of bioluminescent bamboo coral that the Foundation planted five thousand feet out from the coast halts my progress. No land-dwelling Mer is allowed to swim past it without special permission, and its eerie blue light assures that no one can claim to have accidentally missed it.

We both stop to stare. *"You ever wonder what it would be like to swim over it? To just keep going?"* I ask.

"It would be dangerous. Especially for you." He's right of course. Going too deep into the ocean means entering the warzone. That could be fatal for any of us, but for me—a cousin of the hated Little Mermaid and the daughter of the two heads of the Foundation—well, it's no secret I'd be a high prize for very public execution by the many *udell* still dwelling under the waves. The *udell* hate everything the Foundation stands for. They think my parents and everyone who follows them are a bunch of human-

lovers who've turned our backs on our own ways. To them, I've betrayed my own kind by living on land, and they'd relish the chance to kill me if I ventured into their midst.

That's why on one level, I'm grateful for the Border.

On the other, I can't help feeling trapped. The hardest part of living on land is that no matter how many friends I make or how much time I spend trying to fit in, it's not natural for me. The call of the ocean is constant. It thrums through me like a current in my veins.

During the day, when I'm surrounded by humans and I'm busy with school, I can suppress the urge to swim out to sea. At night, lying in the saltwater grottos soothes it enough so I can sleep. But, when I'm out in the ocean like this, the temptation to ignore every warning I've been taught and embrace my innate urge—to answer that call by swimming farther and faster than I've ever dared—reaches its peak. The sea whispers to me, sings to me, tells me to explore my one true home. Sometimes it scares me.

Caspian hears it, too. Resisting can be almost painful. But not swimming up to the Border, not swimming in the ocean at all, that would be worse.

"The rules exist for a reason," Caspian reminds us both.

"I know."

I refuse to be melancholy. We still have the entire stretch of the coast, and that will have to be enough. So, I resort to the two words in Mermese that are always the right thing to say: *"Let's race!"*

Chapter Six

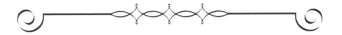

*A*s soon as I see Clay, I'll tell him we need to talk. As soon as I see Clay, I'll explain that I understand he has a girlfriend and our friendship does not equal a flirtation. As soon as I see Clay, my mouth goes dry.

He opens his front door wearing a sleeveless white shirt. His loose-fitting workout pants ride low on his hips. My immediate goal becomes keeping my attention on his face. His eyes are … eager.

"Are you coming in?" Excitement jolts through his words.

"What's going on?"

"C'mon." His hand wraps around my forearm, and he pulls me into the entrance hall. Then he steps behind me and covers my eyes with his hands.

"What—"

"No peeking."

His hands are cool on my cheeks and forehead. They feel good after the heat outside. And they smell faintly of cinnamon, a scent I'm starting to equate with Clay.

"Walk with me?" His breath tickles my ear. I hesitate, then nod, and he moves forward with me in front of him. At first, each step with my eyes closed is unsteady, the way it was when I first started using my legs, but soon we're moving in sync.

I sense that it's time right before he whispers, "Stop." He uncovers my eyes. "Surprise!"

We're standing in the doorway of his den. He's pushed all the furniture against one wall and covered the floor in exercise mats.

"You've finally found your calling in men's gymnastics?" I quip.

"I've finally decided to stop taking no for an answer. You're going to stop fighting me about helping you in self-defense and start fighting me for real."

"Clay, you didn't need to do all this." It was really thoughtful.

"Sure I did. I couldn't spend one more day watching you get clobbered."

Does that mean Clay cares about me or that he's embarrassed for me because of my lack of coordination? I've spent every P.E. period this week falling on my butt while Coach Crane scribbled viciously in her grade book. Whatever Clay's motive, I totally need his help.

"So, how do we do this?" I ask.

His smile widens.

Forty-five minutes later, Clay has run me through the basic maneuvers from class—blocks, punches, and even some kicks. Surprisingly, I'm still on my feet. It isn't that he's been explaining the process any differently, but unlike Coach Crane, who throws us at each other and expects improvement, Clay lets me take my time and repeat each move until I get it right. He isn't barking out orders or corrections; he isn't even teasing me for my lack of skill, the way I feared he might. He's quiet as he watches me, only talking to make subtle corrections to my form.

"Let's practice roundhouse kicks, Lia."

Anything but that. "What about weapons? Shouldn't you come at me with a rubber knife or something?"

"Weapons come way later. For now, just remember to keep as much distance between the weapon and the victim as possible. Okay, let's see that roundhouse."

I take a deep, steadying breath the way Clay suggested and assume the fighting stance he helped me perfect. Roundhouse kicks are the hardest because both my legs have to move in such different ways at the same time. I try to keep my front foot steady while I lift my back leg up and bend it in the air. Right when I'm about to bring it forward toward the couch cushion Clay is holding up as a target, my front leg attempts to bend at the same angle and I fall in a heap.

Clay drops the cushion and is at my side in a blink. "You okay?"

"My pride's hurt a little."

Strong hands help me to my feet, and I get back into position. "I've noticed something," Clay says as he steps behind me. "You seem to want to move both of your legs in the same way whenever you kick."

"That's … weird."

"The body wants what it wants." He kneels and wraps his cool fingers around my back ankle. I shiver. My legs have been sensitive ever since I got them. When I look over my shoulder, Clay's staring up at me.

"Pivot this foot so it faces forward," he says, applying light pressure to my ankle. "When you kick, you can think of the whole thing as one circular motion. Even though your legs are doing different things, they're moving in one direction to achieve one goal." He rises. "Try it."

His touch has made my legs feel stronger, like I don't have to focus to maintain them. I picture the kick as one fluid move like Clay suggested. I pivot my foot, lift my leg, and in one powerful swishing motion, I've executed my first successful roundhouse. It isn't perfect, but my shin hits the cushion with enough force to make Clay shout, "That's it!"

After a dozen more practice runs, I'm getting the hang of

it. I'm imagining how fun it will be to land all my kicks next class and see the shocked look on the coach's face. The fantasy is interrupted when Clay's phone rings. Some rock song I don't recognize.

It's probably Melusine. Every time Clay and I have worked on the project after school, she's called around now. It's like she can't stand to go without talking to him for more than a few hours. Can you say needy? "You can get that," I say.

"I can call back."

"Aren't we pretty much done?"

"Ready to be rid of me, Nautilus?"

"No! I just mean, those are all the moves we've covered in class." The phone stops ringing. Knowing he chose not to answer it makes me smile.

"I talked to Coach. We're learning ground fighting next week. You and I should get a head start."

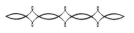

Clay's body presses against mine. I'm lying on my back on the mat with Clay on top of me, and I'm desperately trying to remember to keep my breathing steady. I've never been this close to him before.

"Now, wrap your legs around me and pull me in."

I didn't hear that right, did I? "What?"

"It's for the Switch Back Sweep—a jiu-jitsu move Coach said we'll be starting with." He gives me a half-smile, like he understands my hesitation. "Don't worry, Nautilus, I won't read anything into it."

I wrap both my legs around his waist and press against the small of his back to pull him toward me. He's even closer now, our bodies touching from hip to chest.

"Good." He takes a deep breath. Is this affecting him, too? "That will get your attacker off balance."

He shifts his torso upward and places his hands below my collarbone. His fingertips rest above the neckline of my tank top. Against my bare skin.

"So, next, you want to move my hands."

"Move your hands?"

"Right, because from here, I could attempt a choke."

"Right. Yeah. Okay." It's hard to sound cool when I'm so aware of his weight on top of me. It should feel claustrophobic or intimidating, considering he's posing as an attacker; instead it feels like he's protecting me, covering my body to keep me safe.

"Hold my right wrist and forearm with both hands, thumbs down, and pull my arm over your shoulder so I fall forward." I follow his instructions, feeling his muscles move under my palms.

"Now put your left leg down and turn your hips so that your, um, butt faces that corner." I do, and our bodies shift against one another to accommodate the change. Clay talks me through how to use his own arm to place him in a chokehold while I hook my other hand underneath his knee. That's supposed to put me in the power position, but I keep messing up and having to go back a few steps.

"I feel like a pretzel," I mutter. Clay's so much bigger than me that this feels impossible.

"Stop assuming you can't do it." Clay's tone is serious. "If using this move could help save your life, could protect someone you love from getting hurt, you would do it. And you'd get it right. You can do this, Lia." Hearing Clay talk about me with such confidence, like he believes in me, is motivating.

He's right—I can do this. I bring one hand around to create the chokehold at the same time that I angle my hips toward the corner, reach under his knee, and lift with all my strength. My body rolls over Clay's. I've flipped us over.

It's empowering. Like I can handle myself, protect myself.

I release Clay's arm and look down at him. That's when I realize the ending position of this move has me straddling him. His hazel eyes meet mine, and I stop moving. A part of my brain knows I should get up, move away. But it's as if my body is fused to his. My breath still comes in hard pants from the exertion, and the room is warm now despite the central air conditioning. All I seem to be able to do is stare at Clay. At Clay's lips.

A lock of my hair has fallen out of its makeshift bun and hangs between us. His thumb skims my forehead and the shell of my ear as he tucks it away. We're so close together that Clay fills my entire field of vision. Every detail of his face is exquisite. I want to stroke his cheek, see what the light stubble there feels like. His tongue peeks out to lick his lips, and I'm seized by the urge to press my mouth to his. His chest rises and falls beneath me; he's breathing hard, too.

The blaring rocker notes of his ringtone are the worst sound I've ever heard. We stay frozen until the jarring noise rings out again and shatters the heat between us. Clay's large hands grip my waist and lift me up. Coming back to my senses, I take over and move on my own. His girlfriend is calling. His *girlfriend!* What's wrong with me?

"I should get this," he says, his voice ragged. "I didn't answer it before."

"Yeah, you should." I take another step back, away from Clay, and busy myself with fixing my hair while he answers the phone.

"Hi, Mel. Yeah, sorry I didn't pick up before. Lia's here and we're ... working on school stuff." A pause. She must be speaking. Then, "It's good to hear your voice."

My heart aches and my throat constricts. Of course he wants to talk to her—they're together. I want to run out of the room, to be anywhere else. I could escape to the bathroom, but that would mean missing the rest of their conversation. I'm torturing myself, but I stay.

It doesn't do me any good. Melusine must be talking now because Clay's quiet, but I can't hear her end of the conversation. Minutes drag by like hours until Clay says, "Got it. Talk to you later, Mel."

I look up from where I've been pretending to futz with my

shoe. Clay's expression, so open and exposed earlier, has shuttered off. Is he angry at me for what almost happened? At himself?

"We've gotten enough done. You should probably go home." He doesn't sound angry exactly, just … cold.

I don't want to leave on such a strained note. "Thanks for helping me with self-defense. You're a real lifesaver. Or grade saver … " Great, now I'm rambling. Clay stares at me, silent. "I'll see you and Mel at school," I continue, walking out of the den and into the hallway. It seems like forever ago that Clay and I moved together down this same hallway with his hands covering my eyes. Clay follows me to the door.

"We're okay, right?" I ask.

"Sure," he says, but his tone is the opposite of comforting. "See you at school." His voice is robotic, like he's only saying what he has to to get me to leave. I want to say more, to make things better, but as soon as I step over the threshold, he shuts the door without a second glance.

Chapter Seven

I'm so tied up in knots that it's all I can do to slap a fake smile on my face when I walk in my front door and find my whole family in the living room.

"Look who walked up the stairs all by herself," my mother announces, gesturing to where Amy sits on the couch beside her.

"Stairs are complicated," Amy says, only half-joking.

"Now that we're all here," my mother says, "your father and I have a surprise. It's a congratulations gift for Amy, but I think you'll all enjoy it."

"I left it next door," my father says, rising to his feet.

We spend the next few minutes trying in vain to wrestle clues from my mom. Then it happens. My dad comes in holding a wiggly, furry, happy—puppy!

"PUPPY!" Amy and Em cry out together.

We rush forward as my dad places the tan, shaggy bundle on the ground. In her excitement, Amy loses focus and flops to the floor, her purple tail back in place and the cotton skirt she's wearing now rucked up around her waist.

My parents take in an audible breath. We've never had any pets in our home before. They believe restricting fish to bowls is cruel, and land animals make them nervous. How will this four-legged creature react to a Mermaid in her true form?

The puppy tilts its head in curiosity then runs right toward Amy. We all watch as it sniffs her tail. Then—taking advantage of her position on the floor—the puppy jumps right up to her chest and licks everywhere he can reach.

"He likes me!" Amy exclaims through her giggles. "Is it a he, Uncle Edmar?"

"It's a he," my father confirms, letting out a sigh of relief. "I finally have another male in this house."

"Do you like him?" my mother asks.

"What do you think?" Lapis asks sarcastically, kneeling to scratch his head.

"He's just about the handsomest puppy ever!" Lazuli adds, dropping to the floor to get in on the action.

"I always told you dogs would be Mer-friendly," Em says, holding out her hand for the puppy to sniff before petting him. "They love water." Emeraldine has been trying to convince our parents to get a dog for ages.

Except for one family that has a couple turtles, no one in the Community keeps a pet. Dogs, cats, hamsters—they're just too foreign for parents who grew up in the ocean to get used to. I'm friendly with a family of bottlenose dolphins and three different sea lions that I play with sometimes on my swims, but I certainly don't own them. Amy hands me the squirming puppy. Shaggy beige fur frames big, brown eyes.

"Hello," I say. He barks once. I think I'm in love.

"Stop hogging my new boyfriend, Lia," Lazuli jokes, reaching out for him.

"We're just getting to know each other." I put him down on the ground where he scurries between all of us, then tugs on a shoelace from Lapis's knee-high boot.

"Look! He has good taste," she squeals.

"Thank you, thank you, thank you!" Amy says to my parents. We all repeat the sentiment, and they smile, looking both pleased and relieved.

"I can't believe this," I say. "I thought you'd never let us have a land pet."

"We're constantly telling you girls to acclimate, so we figured we'd try to ourselves," my father says.

"But no one else in the Foundation—"

"There's a first time for everything," my father cuts me off with a warm smile.

"We'll be pioneers," my mother adds.

"Who knows, maybe we'll even start a trend," my dad says.

"Besides, this way Amy will have good motivation to learn to walk." My mother glances around to make sure we're listening. "And I expect all of you to help out by taking turns walking this little guy in the meantime." This has to be the first household chore in history we're all enthusiastic about.

"Hey, Em," Amy says as Em rubs the pup's belly, "you should call Leo. The two of you can take the puppy on his first walk together."

"Maybe. I think he has plans tonight." Emeraldine gets up and walks toward the kitchen. Her cheery tone sounds forced when she says, "I'll get our new little monster some salmon. I think we have some that's cooked."

"Nice try, Aims," I whisper. Em told me she talked to Leomaris at the party. They're still together, but they couldn't come to any decision. She believes in following tradition and he says that's not the type of marriage he wants. I guess they're at a standstill. A really strained standstill. I haven't seen this little of Leo since before they started dating. And I definitely haven't heard any more talk about an engagement.

"I hope they work it out soon," Amy says, voicing my own concerns.

"They will." I hope I'm right.

Amy closes her eyes, and a moment later, she's pulling her

skirt down over her new legs, which of course the puppy has to sniff.

"Great job!" I say, complimenting her improved leg control. Then, keeping my voice low so the others won't hear: "So, I guess you've found a guy to think about?"

"Yeah, there's someone." Amy ducks her head, and I know better than to push for details, no matter how much I want to.

"I can't believe you got my parents to get a dog," I say instead. "You are so their favorite."

"We should get him a studded collar," Lapis suggests.

"Gross," Lazuli says. "I refuse to let you turn him into a punk rock puppy. I say rhinestones all the way."

I take another look at the furry mutt. He doesn't exactly strike me as the rhinestones type. Then again, I can't picture him in studs either.

"Uncle Edmar, what's his name?" Amy asks.

"That's up to you."

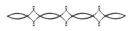

Even a brand new puppy isn't enough to distract me from dreading school tomorrow. I keep playing through possible scenarios in my head. In most, Clay decides we shouldn't spend any more time together; I picture him talking to me in that same cold voice, telling me I'm a threat to his relationship so we'll need to split up the work for the project and finish it alone. If he actually said this, I couldn't disagree with him. He'd be right.

Still, I much prefer the scenario that occurred to me right before I fell asleep—the one where Clay tells me he felt exactly what I felt, the same crackle of heat between us, and he's breaking up with Melusine. He grabs me to him and, before I can say anything, kisses me the way I wanted him to kiss me on that mat. But then what? My logical brain knows we can't be together. Sure, it's a nice fantasy—a wonderful, tail-curling, butterflies flying, spine tingling fantasy—but we have no future.

Besides, it'll never happen anyway. I can still hear Clay from his phone call with Melusine: "It's good to hear your voice." He likes *her*. Wants *her*. Kisses *her*. And he's probably about to tell me we can't even be friends.

By the time I get to school, I've done everything I can to brace myself. Then Clay drives into the parking lot in his Mustang, and I'm back to full-on nervous mode. He gets out and walks right toward me.

His words are the very last ones I expected.

"So, you coming over today?"

"Huh?" He can't mean what I think he means.

"You came over the last couple Fridays, so I figured you'd come today. We didn't really make any history headway last night, with the self-defense and all."

"You don't have plans with Mel tonight?" I hedge.

"I haven't talked to her yet today, but we don't have anything planned. She knows you and I have to get the project done. So, you're coming, right? Our report's not going to write itself."

"Sure."

"Cool, Nautilus."

If I could do a cartwheel, I totally would.

"It's weird that none of your ancestors have come up in any of the databases. You sure your family's not from outer space or something?"

Stay calm. "Hey, one of those sixty-three Margaret Smiths could have been related to me," I tell Clay, using one of the many generic-named, made up relatives on my list. "Anywho, I spoke to Mr. Reitzel and he said, since I'm not getting enough results online, I can use interviews with my parents as research sources in our bibliography. So we're covered."

I dig out the notebook where I wrote down the interviews—combinations of complete fabrications and tweaked truths—and place them on Clay's desk. We're in his room again and, in an attempt to show him I respect his relationship, I've scooted my chair as far from him as I can. His desk is on the small side though, so we're only a foot apart.

"We're lucky we've got that Denmark connection. That can be the focus of our poster board," Clay says.

It's actually true that I have ancestors from Denmark—well, from the waters surrounding Denmark, but why quibble? My mother's side of the family, including her distant royal relatives, lived in that area for thousands of years before the Little Mermaid refused to kill her prince and unleashed the curse by prizing a human life above her own immortal one.

Devastated and enraged at the loss of their immortality, the Mer dethroned her father, blaming him for her actions. He was executed. In the ensuing turmoil, ruler after ruler came to power, promising to find a cure for the curse.

As each one inevitably failed, a mutiny would break out to depose him. His supporters would cling to their hope and take up arms, arguing that all the current leader needed was more time to break the curse—that he almost had an answer—while others would rally behind a new leader who pedaled a new, useless method to save us all.

No sooner did the most recent leader take power, and begin strengthening his army, than those who saw the flaw in his plan turned to someone else who claimed access to better magic. What's worse, criminals have always taken advantage of each new war to loot and ravage cities, spreading the violence and destruction past the battlefields, so even those who don't seek to fight must arm themselves to protect their families.

Every new leader has brought more false hope, but no end to the anarchy. With each failure, the cycle continues, causing nearly constant chaos and peril. The sea has been in a state of continual war for two centuries. Hatred of many of the previous leaders is strong, but none is stronger than the hatred aimed at the memory of the Little Mermaid and her father. All their descendants, no matter how distant, became targets for annihilation.

It grew far too dangerous for my mother's family to stay anywhere near Northern Europe. At first, my ancestors took refuge in the waters near North America, but within a century, the wars spread and those were just as unsafe. The only choices for anyone with royal blood were to live in hiding or leave the ocean for good.

After a boatload of internal debate, I told Clay my mother's family lived near Copenhagen in Denmark until they came to America just before World War I. That way, I'll be able to discuss U.S. immigration and the First World War for my part of the paper. Thank the tides he bought it. I hate lying—especially to Clay—but I seem to be getting plenty of practice.

"Did you find anything else about that Danish opera singer?" I ask, steering the conversation toward Clay's family.

"Not really. I found plenty about her career, but there's nothing much about her personal life." He shuffles through a few printed articles on his desk, then reads, "'After giving birth to a son out of wedlock, Astrid Ostergard withdrew from public life, eventually becoming a veritable recluse.' Other than that, all I found was that her son moved his family to New York in the late 19th century. He's the one who opened up that restaurant I saw the picture of online."

"And that's on your mom's side?" I ask.

"Yep. A lot of his descendants died in World War I and even more in World War II, including my mom's only uncle, so I think she's the last one left. That's why every one of my annoying cousins comes from my dad's side of the family."

"And there's some info on your dad's side?"

"Enough for a paragraph or two. I think I'll focus mainly on Astrid, though. It's strangely cool to find out you're related to someone who was famous."

It isn't always cool. I don't know what's worse, that one of my distant, ancestral cousins is infamous for bringing death to millions, or that she's been immortalized as a cartoon character.

"Do you think Astrid's who you get your musical talent from?" I ask.

"Could be. My dad's the one who taught me to play, so maybe I get it from both sides."

"When can I hear some of your stuff?"

"Oh." He looks surprised at my request. "I don't know. I just sort of play for myself lately."

"You said you're a musical prodigy," I tease. "You must expect me to be curious."

"I don't know. I wouldn't want you turning all groupie on me."

I blush. "Why don't you play at any of the clubs around town?"

"I just don't," Clay says abruptly. Then, his voice softens, "You rocked it in P.E. today. Coach Crane looked like she was about to have a coronary from the shock."

I pretend not to notice the change of subject. "Well, you did it." I never could have survived today's kicks without his help last night.

Clay lifts my chin with his thumb and forefinger and looks directly into my eyes, "Hey, stop that. *You* did it. All I did was help bring it out of you."

His face is close enough that I can see the green and gold flecks in his eyes. The same heat I felt last night rises between us now. As if just realizing he's touching me, he drops his hand, but he doesn't move farther away. Something else flashes in his eyes. Decisiveness?

"My dad stopped coming."

"Hmm?" I ask, confused.

"To my performances. I stopped playing guitar in public because he was the one who taught me ... the one who always cheered me on. It was our thing." Clay picks at the sleeve of his leather jacket where it's draped off one end of his desk. "After the divorce, he came to a few shows. Then a few less."

Clay's voice is thick with hurt. "You don't have to talk about this," I tell him.

"No, I want to tell you." He looks right at me before glancing down again. "When he moved onto the naval base in Point Loma, he got a girlfriend in town and stopped driving up to see me altogether."

"Clay, I'm sorry." It's not enough, but it's all I can think to say.

"I still write songs—I can't really stop myself—but I haven't been able to play for anyone since. So, please don't take it personally."

"I understand."

He pastes his familiar smirk back on. "Well, Nautilus, I've told you my deepest, darkest. What's yours?"

Despite his well-practiced expression, his eyes are still vulnerable. He needs me to answer, if only to divert the conversation away from him. My secret? Telling him I have a tail would make him think I'm either a.) crazy or b.) a disgusting, fishy freak.

"I'm kind of lost," I blurt out instead.

"Your house is in walking distance."

I whack him on the shoulder. "That's my secret, genius. I sometimes feel like I'm … lost." Articulating it for the second time makes me realize it's true.

"What do you mean?" Clay asks. He's listening now, his gaze completely focused on me.

"My parents have this image of me. All these expectations. They've worked so hard to build … the family business."

"The Foundation for the something or other of sea animals?"

"The Foundation for the Preservation and Protection of Marine Life," I supply.

"Right! I see your dad on the news all the time."

"They expect me to devote my life to it, too."

"And you're not sure if it's for you?"

"It's a really important cause, and I totally admire everything they've done, but I don't know if I can live up to their example." I'm so human in the way I look at things sometimes that I'm afraid if I ever did try to take on a Mer leadership role, I'd be ousted as a fraud. "My older sister Em works at the Foundation part-time and she's perfect at it."

"I didn't realize you had a sister other than the twins."

"Yeah. Em's in college and she does everything right. She's smart, well-spoken, sophisticated—just like my mom. Then there's my little cousin Amy—she lives with us and she's definitely the sweet, adorable one. The twins are the witty, sexy ones. I'm just … me." I sigh. I've never put it into words like that before; it's like Clay's honesty opened up some kind of dam, and everything just came rushing out.

He turns his chair slightly so that we're facing each other, the front of his knees touching the front of mine. Then he takes my hand where it rests on my thigh.

"You know, no one expects you to have it all figured out." He says as he rubs a soothing circle over the back of my hand with his thumb. "You're not lost. You just don't know where you belong yet.

"Oh, and for the record," he continues, "Amy's not the only sweet one and, even without meeting her, I doubt Em is smarter than you." He's been looking at my hand resting in his, but now he looks up at me with a mischievous gleam in his eyes. "And if Mel asks, you didn't hear this from me, but the twins definitely don't have the market cornered on sexy."

Did Clay just say he thinks I'm sexy? Am I still breathing? "Yeah, right. They hook up with new guys at practically every party, and I've never had a real kiss." Why did I say that? What's wrong with me?

"You've never been kissed?" Clay's voice is all surprise. My face flames.

"I've had the opportunity." I backpedal. "Lots of opportunities!" That's kind of true. There have been at least three

81

Merboys who have leaned in for kisses after less than spectacular first dates. "It just never felt right, so I didn't go through with it." Clay is listening carefully, but he looks curious, not judgmental. What the heck, I can't possibly embarrass myself more than I already have, can I?

"I guess I'm just waiting for that heart-pounding, music-swelling, shooting star moment ... and I don't think I'll find it until it's the right person leaning in."

"That's—"

"Probably stupid, I know. I sound like I'm in middle school."

"I was gonna say, kinda cool," Clay finishes.

"This coming from the guy who makes out in the hallway every day."

Clay withdraws his hand from where it still rests on top of mine and runs it through his dark hair, looking away from me. "Yeah, sometimes I don't know what comes over me when I'm with Mel."

"You guys are just really, I don't know, passionate. I wish I had that with ... someone."

"That's just it. We're not. Well, I guess we are."

"That makes sense," I say, rolling my eyes.

"When I'm kissing Mel, all I can think about is kissing her more."

Yuck. How did I get in this conversation?

"But, we don't have that much in common. I mean, she's never heard of most of the stuff I like, and she's not interested when I tell her about it. She's never asked to hear my music." He looks up at me. "Somehow, we always manage to do whatever she suggests doing."

Now it's my turn to be surprised. "You don't really strike me as the pushover type."

"Well, whenever she suggests something, it sounds like the right idea. It's only later, when I'm home alone thinking about it, that I realize shoe shopping isn't my idea of fun. It's weird. When I'm with Mel or I'm talking to her, I'm so sure that everything's right. That we're right. But … "

I straighten up in my chair. "But what?"

"I don't know. When I'm by myself playing guitar or studying or just lying in bed at night and I think about her, I have so many doubts. She's not the type of girl I picture myself with."

I want to jump. I want to dance. I want to scream with joy.

"Then as soon as I see her the next day at school and we start talking, I feel like there could never be anyone else for me."

I want to hit my head against the desk.

"Do you love her?" I shouldn't be asking, but the question is out before I even think it.

"It sure feels like I do sometimes." He looks genuinely torn. Then, he shrugs and slouches in his chair. "Whatever. It's not like figuring it out will make a difference. My parents loved each other, and look how that ended."

"Clay, I don't think that's—"

"It feels good being with Mel. That's enough."

I should be happy that Clay's not sure he loves someone else, but the fact that he's okay to settle, like he thinks love isn't worth searching for, makes me sad.

It's not that I have to see Clay every day, it's just that we need to get started on our poster. At least that's what I tell myself on the way to Clay's house on Saturday morning. Technically, I didn't ask Clay if I could come over, but he mentioned his mom had plans and he'd just be hanging out at home.

I usually spend Saturdays swimming with my sisters in our pool during the day and in the ocean at night. We all look forward to spending an entire day not worrying about maintaining our legs. But ever since Clay's self-defense lesson, maintaining my legs has been easy. All I have to do is remember what it was like to have Clay pressed against me and my legs stay firmly in place.

Still, the water calls to me. It whispers deep in my head, but I don't care. For once, there's something I'd rather do than swim. Even if all we do is talk like we did last night, I'd rather be with Clay.

Soon, I'm reaching around the unwieldy poster board to ring his doorbell. He doesn't answer. After three more tries, I'm about to head back home when I remember Clay sometimes does homework outside. It's a gorgeous, sunny day; maybe he's in his backyard and didn't hear the bell. I try the side gate. It's unlocked, so I head through it and walk along the side of the house. Leaning the poster board against the wall, I peer around the corner into the backyard. Clay is by the gazebo. But he isn't alone.

Melusine stands with her arms draped around his neck and her face mere inches from his. She leans in even closer. Oh no, I'm going to have to watch them kiss. But, no. Right as I'm thinking I should turn away, her full, pink lips head toward his ear instead of his mouth. Music—so beautiful it's almost painful—escapes her lips and pierces the air.

She's singing.

The dark, alluring melody is captivating, and it takes my addled brain a moment to realize she's singing in Mermese. But I don't recognize half the ancient words. I nearly forget to breathe as I shift my focus from the song to the effect it's having on Clay. His eyes are glazed over, like he's lost in some dream world. The spark of intelligence, of awareness, is gone.

Although I've only ever heard it spoken of in scandalized whispers and harsh warnings, I know exactly what's happening: Melusine is sirening Clay.

Chapter Eight

I want to scream Clay's name. I want to run forward and push Melusine off him. I want to save him from the mental slavery she's trapped him in. But before I can do any of that, I do something far more dangerous.

In my shock, I lose my control. My brain registers the familiar tingle slip-sliding across my legs right before I fall. My tail hits the paved walkway with a resounding *Thwack!*

Melusine snaps her head around. I hold my breath. I'm hidden around the corner of the house, but if she investigates, she'll find me for sure. I scoot back as far as I can, dragging my tail against the rough concrete. If Melusine finds me, who knows what she'll do to keep me quiet? I'm a Mermaid, so she can't siren me, but she's definitely dangerous. Does she have access to other magic?

Melusine glances around the yard again, then turns her attention back to Clay. She slides a hand down his chest as he stares off into space. Bile rises in my throat.

With my fins exposed and with Clay in trouble, it's harder

than it's ever been to focus. I take deep breaths and force myself to picture Clay the way he usually looks, his knowing eyes full of laughter. I think of the comforting words he offered me in his bedroom, of his thumb stroking the back of my hand. With the feeling of invisible tides crashing against my lower body, my legs slide into place. I get up as fast as I can without making a sound, then slip back into my flip-flops and pull down my now-ripped skirt. Then I hesitate.

I hate leaving Clay with Melusine. If what I've heard about sireny is true, Clay has no free will; Melusine could make him do anything. I tell myself there's nothing I can do now. I force myself to grab the poster board and leave before I lose my legs again.

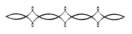

I have to tell my parents. They'll know what to do. They always know. Once I'm inside, I drop the poster board and run into the living room. Amy sits in her new favorite spot on the couch.

"Where's my mom?" I ask, trying to keep the desperation out of my voice.

"Lia! Guess what? I thought of the perfect name for him," she says, gesturing to the sleepy ball of puppy on her chest. "Barnacle! Get it? Because he lies on me all the time. Barney for short. Isn't it perfect?"

"Where's my mom?" I try never to be short with Amy, but Clay's in trouble, and no one else knows.

"Upstairs getting ready for that benefit," Amy answers. "You okay?"

"Fine!" I shout as I race upstairs.

My mom sits in front of her vanity. A sad look haunts her face, but it disappears when she catches sight of me in the mirror. She plasters on her usual smile.

"Hi, seashell."

"Mom, what's the matter?"

Her smile falters. "It's nothing. Just a few new wrinkles, that's all."

"Oh."

"I'm being silly. Human women deal with them. I just always hoped … well, never mind." She trails off, but I know what she's thinking. No matter how practical my mom is or how much she acknowledges that the curse is permanent, she was raised to believe it would be broken someday. She thought she'd get to live out the rest of eternity with everlasting youth and beauty. For her and my dad, the aging process must be a reminder of everything they've lost.

"Did you need something, Aurelia?"

I meet my mom's steady gaze. What will she do when I tell her Melusine's sirening Clay? "I … Mom, have there been any major crimes since we surfaced?"

Her brows furrow. "Just some petty theft and teenagers tagging a few buildings. Other than that, the only real crimes we've ever had were some incidents of violence against humans, but that was years ago when we first moved up here. Why?"

"What type of violence?"

"I'm ashamed to say there were a few bar fights—Mer who foolishly thought they were superior to humans and weren't used to the effects of liquor. Some Mer reacted badly when they saw seals being mistreated at a carnival, and things got violent. That's about the worst of it."

"What happened to them?"

"The Foundation ruled in favor of fines and Community service. We also made enrollment in our Mer-Human Relations classes mandatory for Community members who were having trouble adapting."

"That's it?"

"There were a handful who still insisted humans weren't equal to Mer. That Mer were somehow better. You know views like those aren't tolerated up here, so anyone who adhered to that outdated way of thinking was persuaded that life Above wasn't a good fit for them, and they returned to the ocean." She studies my face. "Why are you so interested in this all of a sudden?"

Because I saw Melusine commit a crime. I saw her sirening a human. The human I …

"What would you and Dad do if there was a big crime? Like something really bad?"

"Well … " She's looking at me questioningly now. "At that point it wouldn't be up to your father and me and the other board members. We'd open up the proceedings to the Community and vote on the best course of action. We'd do whatever it took to keep humans from getting suspicious."

Whatever it took? What does that mean? Sireny is one of the highest crimes there is. If I tell my parents what I saw, they won't be able to keep it quiet. Then what? Melusine would probably be sent Below, where she could easily be killed. If she dies, will Clay die too? I don't know how sireny works. With Melusine Below, would the spell wear off, or would he still be sirened? Would he spend the rest of his life wandering around up here like some mindless zombie with no one controlling him? Is there a way to break Melusine's hold over him?

I want to think the Community board or the elders could force her to let him go, but the truth is, even they might not know how to control magic this ancient, this secret. If they do know, and they get her to release him, will he remember anything afterward? Has he seen anything he shouldn't, like her tail? If he has, what will the Community do to him to keep him quiet?

"Aurelia, I'm glad to see you take an interest in Mer affairs, but what sparked all these questions on crime?" My mother looks concerned.

I can't tell her—not until I know more about what might happen to Clay. "Um … Amy asked me about it, and I didn't know what to tell her," I lie.

The tension in her face vanishes. She rises from the vanity and crosses to her walk-in closet. "Don't tell Amethyst anything that might worry her. Everyone who seeks refuge here has given up their natural home for a chance at a peaceful, safe life on land. You can tell her that we've all worked very hard to build a life here and we won't let anything jeopardize that."

I nod. My parents have spent years creating a sanctuary for everyone. I can't tell them something that will destroy that sense of security and call their leadership into question. Not until I have answers.

"Do you have plans while your father and I are out?" my mother asks as she rifles through her closet. "You've been spending an awful lot of time working on your project. I hope you're being careful around that human boy. No problems focusing?"

"Nope." Except for sitting on the side of his house in my tail where absolutely anyone could have seen me.

"Will the two of you be studying again tonight?" She frowns.

"No." Going over there tonight wouldn't do any good. I need to find a way to help Clay, but if I can't turn to my parents, who can I ask? I need to talk to someone who knows about sireny. "Enjoy your benefit, Mom. I'm going to Caspian's."

Caspian's house is just a short swim through the tunnels. I ring the bell at the underwater entrance, and he ushers me into the grottos. Unlike my family, Caspian's uses the upstairs mostly for show. Not only are they more traditionalist than my parents, but Caspian's grandmother can't go into the house above at all. She's one of the oldest Mer who's come on land, and by the time she did, it was too late for her to master her legs. The entire time I'm saying hello to her and his parents, all I can think about is getting Caspian alone so we can talk.

It's still too light out to go in the ocean, so I suggest we go to the swimming pool and get some sun. Really, I'm just looking for privacy, and Caspian's bedroom in the grottos—while cool with its stalactites and crystal-imbedded walls—is a cave without the luxury of a door.

"I'm glad you suggested this," Caspian says several minutes later in his saltwater pool. "I've hardly seen you this week."

"Yeah, I've been really busy with my history project."

"The one on your ancestors? You're still working on that?"

"It's worth twenty-five percent of my grade."

"So, you're spending a lot of time with that Clay guy, right?"

"I kind of have to," I answer, trying not to sound defensive. "The project's made me think about my ancestors and how much I don't know about them." I swim in a slow circle around him. "Do you ever think about yours?" I hope that sounded more subtle to him than it did to me.

He raises an eyebrow. "About my ancestors? Honestly, I try to avoid it, with Adrianna and all." He lowers his voice when he says her name.

"Still, you must get curious about her," I press. "Don't you ever ask your parents about her? Or your grandmother?"

"I did a few times when I was little. My grandmother's so ashamed of the scandal she won't even say the word 'siren' out loud. And I can tell it upsets my parents."

I hear the words he's not saying: that it upsets him, too. For years, I've avoided the topic of sireny around Caspian to spare his feelings, and I hate what I'm about to do.

"But you know some stuff about her, right? When she was imprisoned, what happened to the man she sirened?"

A grim look settles on Caspian's face. "He was executed."

It takes me a second to find my voice. "E-executed? By who?"

"It was after the Mer monarchy fell and the wars started, so I guess whatever faction was ruling at the time. None of them ever stay in power long."

"Why would they execute an innocent human? Imprisoning Adrianna I can understand—she knew the penalty when she sirened him. But the human was a victim." My volume rises.

"I guess they couldn't risk him telling other humans what had happened to him."

"But nothing like that would be sanctioned today, right? Not up here." I fight to tamp down my panic. Our community would never execute Clay, would they?

"I'd like to think it couldn't happen, but Adrianna's crime was only a century ago." Caspian's right; a hundred years is nothing for Mer. Change comes very slowly to a culture as ancient as ours. "Lia, why do you look so worked up? It's not like any sirens exist anymore. Adrianna's been the only one in six hundred years."

"Yeah, but hypothetically, why would they execute a human now? If he started talking about Mermaids, wouldn't people just think he was nuts?"

"It's hard to say what he'd remember. Sure, Mermaids would sound crazy, but accusations of brainwashing could be a real threat if the authorities suspected us of being a cult or something. Why do you look so nervous?"

I smooth my brow. "It's just such a scary thought."

Caspian raises a hand out of the water and squeezes my shoulder. "You don't need to worry, Goldfish." I smile at the pet name he's used since we were kids. "No one knows any siren songs anymore."

"What if someone does?" I ask, hearing Melusine's eerie song in my head.

"Teaching those songs has been illegal for centuries, and all the shell records have been smashed. Let's just drop it."

Then how did Melusine learn that song? Was it passed down through her family in secret all these years? Sung to her like a lullaby when she was a baby? I cringe inwardly at the sinister image.

"How do you stop a siren?" I ask, my voice urgent. "I mean, how would you?"

"For tides' sake, I don't know!" Caspian snaps. I back up at the force of his anger. He's never spoken to me like that before. "Why are we talking about this? Sireny is the reason my family went from being respectable Mer nobility to virtual pariahs."

"Casp, you're not pariahs. Now that you're on land, your family has a fresh start."

"In the eyes of your parents and a few others maybe, but plenty of the Mer here still won't let us into their homes." Caspian stops near the pool's edge. "Do you know what it's like to tell my six-year-old sister why her new friend's parents won't let her come over for a play date?" His blue eyes shine with sadness.

My own sting with unshed tears. How many times have I gone to a birthday party that Caspian wasn't at? How many times have I heard people whisper when he walked into a room? I hate that my questions have reminded him of his pain. I want to tell him what I saw. I want to explain why I've brought up a topic that hurts him. More than that, I'm in too far over my tail, and I need to confide in him.

But involving Caspian would be unforgivably selfish. He'd insist on helping me, even if it meant implicating himself and his family in another siren scandal. That's the last thing they need. So instead, all I say is, "I'm sorry, Casp. I'm really sorry."

After a few awkward laps around the pool, we bring the conversation around to lighter topics, like the recent dance at Caspian's school and all his lame excuses for deciding to go without a date.

The whole time, I'm thinking about the horrible, empty look in Clay's eyes. If Caspian doesn't know anything else about sirens and I can't ask my parents, there's only one place that might have the information I need.

Chapter Nine

"Dad," I ask Monday morning over breakfast, "can I start working after school at the Foundation?"

My dad coughs on a bite of his sturgeon scramble, but recovers quickly. "Of course you can."

My mother covers it up better, but the slight angling of her head tells me she, too, is surprised. "What brought this on?"

"I'm a junior now, so I figure it's time I take more of an interest in our Community." My parents look skeptical. "Plus, I've been spending kind of a lot on shoes lately." Understanding dawns on their faces.

"Aurelia, you know we're more than happy to help you girls assimilate in any way we can," my mother says, "and shopping is pretty much a requirement for assimilation in this neighborhood." As she sprinkles pink sea salt onto her plate, a new designer watch sparkles on her wrist.

"Yeah, and I'm super grateful, but I still feel like I should contribute," I say. Across the table, the twins gawk at me like I've grown tentacles, but Em smiles approvingly. Amy is too busy sneaking Barnacle pieces of sturgeon under the table to listen.

"That's very responsible of you," my dad says. "How about helping me in the P.R. department?"

That won't get me anywhere near where I need to be. "Actually, I was thinking I could help with the Information Input Initiative."

"You want to spend all your time listening to dusty old shells?" Lazuli says, shock evident in her voice.

Luckily, I prepared myself for a question like this. "Someone has to do it, and I'm good with computers." My parents and most other Mer raised Below are hopeless when it comes to technology. My offer will be too tempting for my parents to refuse.

"When would you like to start?" my mother asks.

"How's today?"

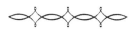

"Lia, you look a little green."

"Huh?" I haven't been listening to Kelsey. Melusine and Clay stand at the end of the hall. One of her hands rests on his t-shirt clad chest, the other grips his bicep possessively. That's what she's turned him into. Her possession.

"Are you sick?" Kelsey's voice buzzes from a million miles away.

Melusine leans up to kiss him. Hunger gleams in his eyes, and it reminds me what he said about something coming over him when they kissed. Whatever he's feeling right now, she's forced it on him. This stunning seventeen-year-old girl with her glossy black locks and striking figure is a monster.

"Kelsey, can you go get Mel to talk to you?"

Kelsey looks over her shoulder in realization. "Lia, you really shouldn't be watching their smooch fests. It just upsets you. Why don't we head out to the courtyard?"

"Go talk to Mel," I beg. "Please?" It's stupid, but I have to separate them, even if it's just for a few minutes.

Kelsey studies my face, then marches up to them. She taps

Melusine on the shoulder.

"Sorry to interrupt this entirely appropriate use of a public hallway," Kelsey says, "but I need to ask you a question about biology."

Melusine tears her mouth from Clay's only long enough to say, "We're not in the same biology class."

"I know, but I'm organizing the field trip, and I have questions for everyone. Urgent questions." With that, Kelsey pulls a surprised Melusine away from Clay by the arm and leads her farther down the hall. "Do you suffer from seasickness?"

Clay just stands there, staring blankly after Melusine, until she calls behind her in a sultry voice, "Go talk to your friends as long as you want, baby. I'll see you later."

He snaps into action, his eyes roaming the hallway, presumably looking for his friends. They land on me, and he walks over.

"Hey, how's it going?" His voice is the robotic one I've heard him use before, but now the lifelessness makes sense.

"You have lip gloss on your face," I say. His mouth is smeared with it.

When he just stands there, I pull some polka dot tissues from my bag. "Here," I offer. Clay doesn't move to take them. "May I?" I ask.

I brush a tissue gently across his mouth, wiping away the remnants of her lecherous kisses.

His hand covers mine, and he looks down at me, clearly trying to regain focus. He then takes the tissues from me and finishes the job himself. "Thanks," he says.

I take a step back. "I can't come over to work on the project today," I say. "I have some other research to do."

"Another project?" he asks in a voice still not his own.

"A big one."

I usually swim through the underwater entrance to the Foundation. Today, though, I'm coming straight from school, so I enter the towering office building through the doors of blue-green glass meant for human visitors. I walk past a gleaming, white alabaster sculpture of a dolphin on my way to the reception desk. A giant aquarium comprises the entire wall behind the desk, and my eyes linger on a basketball-sized, turquoise discus fish as it swims from the left side of the tank to the right before disappearing into a clump of java moss.

"Aurelia? Your father mentioned you were coming." I turn my attention to one of the two receptionists, who I recognize from a few of my parents' parties. I'm used to seeing her in a bright yellow tail and traditional *siluess*, so the sight of her in a well-tailored suit disconcerts me. In her current outfit, the only hint she's Mer is that she wears her copper hair long and flowing, as does the other receptionist.

"Follow me," she says with a smile. She steps out from behind the desk, and the heels of her black patent stilettos clack against the marble floor. I know in order to work on the upper floors and interact with humans, Foundation employees must pass leg-control tests, and only the best of the best would be allowed to work in the front lobby, but it still irks me that she can manage to walk so gracefully in stilettos. I've taken my golden pair out a few times to practice, and I always stumble across my upstairs bedroom like a zombie with a broken foot.

She leads me to a long row of elevators, then uses a small golden key to unlock the last one on the right. "This one leads *downstairs*," she tells me with a knowing look.

The brushed chrome doors slide open with a *bing*. "Press seven for the research department. I'll let your father know you're here," she says. I thank her. Then the doors close, and the elevator takes me underground.

I can sense the salt water before the doors even open. I step out onto an elevated slip-resistant walkway built over a deep canal. Mer in suits move quickly along the walkway while Mer in fins swim up and down the canal before disappearing behind any of the countless doors that line the walls. My father exits one of the doors and swims toward me.

"Hey, angelfish. Better keep your legs on—there's no water in the file room. Apparently it's very bad for the computers."

He shows me how to find the room where I'll be working and gives me my instructions. I'm supposed to listen to the beginning of a shell and enter its topic and orator into the database, then label it with a correlating number. This will eventually allow Foundation members to search for and locate information easily. My father's eyes gleam with excitement when he tells me the long-term goal is for Mer linguists to transcribe the contents of each shell, creating a digital file of each one. Shells are fragile, and it's not unheard of for a tsunami to wipe out entire libraries.

"Think how many problems technology can solve," my father says. "I'm telling you, it's proof we should always respect humans. There's so much we can learn from them. Just look how savvy they are." He shakes his head as if he can't believe something as miraculous as a computer exists. "Computerized information is a valuable tool we hope will benefit us as much as it's benefitted humans."

Since so much work goes into keeping an entire Community of Merfolk operating in secret, though, this project is still low-priority. Fortunately for me, that means I should be left more or less alone in the file room.

I'm glad I've been set such a boring task—hopefully, I won't be expected to get much accomplished on my first day. I picture the surprised excitement on my parents' faces when I volunteered to work here, and a pang of guilt rolls through me for feigning interest. But this is the only place with access to the information I need.

Once he's escorted me to the right room, my father heads off down another canal to get ready for a meeting with the Ocean Intelligence Commission.

As soon as the door to the file room shuts behind me and

I'm left alone with shelves upon shelves of shells brimming with information, hope surges within me. Centuries' worth of knowledge fills this room—the answers I need to help Clay must be here somewhere.

I head directly for the row of computers and login using the information my father gave me. If I'm lucky, some of the books that have already been entered will be on sireny, and I'll be able to find the information quickly.

Even though I'm alone, I look over my shoulder one last time before gathering up the nerve to type "S-I-R-E-N" into the search box. The look of the word in black and white letters makes my heart race. Doing what I'm about to do—looking up information on something highly illegal in Foundation files without permission—is the most criminal thing I've ever done.

"For Clay," I whisper. With a shaky hand, I click the search button and hold my breath.

Only three hits and none of them have text entered into the computer yet—not even summaries. Just three titles with orator names and file numbers. Well, it's a place to start. Besides, there must be a lot more information in the shells that haven't been recorded yet. It'll just take some extra digging.

I scribble down the numbers and make my way to the cases of labeled shells. The array astounds me. Tiny balier shells that I assume hold short children's stories to encyclopedia-like tomes in massive diadema shells, and everything in between. The first number corresponds to a yellowed, spiny murex shell, slightly larger than the palm of my hand.

I carry it over to a long, glass table and choose a seat at one end where I'm partially concealed by the shelves but still have a clear view of the door, just in case. I lift the shell to my ear and wait.

When humans place shells against their ears, they hear the ocean. My science teacher says it's the echo of your own body's blood flow and the amplified noises from nearby, but that's only because he doesn't have any other explanation. It's really a hint at the secrets within. You take the shell home, place it on your mantel or in your drawer, and have no idea that you've actually found a *konklili*—a Merbook.

Now, as I press it to my own ear, instead of the crashing waves a human would hear, I'm greeted by a dry, scholarly voice. At least the Mermese he's using is modern.

"*Dangers of the Seven Seas, first recorded by Cleodora Charybdis and voiced here by Seger Murrow.*

"*The first sighting of the highly poisonous blue-ringed octopus of the Pacific and Indian Oceans … *"

As the voice rattles off facts about the deadly blue-ring, I grab a thin whalebone stylus from a bowl in the center of the table and drag it along the natural spiraled indentation on the shell's surface until it hits a tiny groove. I pause and bring the shell to my ear again.

"*Many have feared the Croatian sea serpent of the Adriatic for centuries, but few know of its—*"

I slide the sharpened whalebone to the next groove and the next, holding the shell to my ear each time. Finally, the voice says:

"*Once present in all the world's oceans, but prevalent mainly in the Atlantic and Aegean, dwelled the most scheming and maniacal of all aquatic predators, the siren.*"

I sit up straighter in my chair.

"*While the threat of sireny has been all but eliminated since the 10,160s, no record of sea predators would be complete without the inclusion of this deadly monster.*" Hmm … the 10,160s … I do the math in my head, converting from the tidal Mer calendar to the BC/AD distinction humans use. So … that would be the early 1400s on a human timeline.

"*Of course, the danger of the siren arose from its Mer intelligence paired with its abominable cruelty to humans.*"

The speaker confirms my worst fears when he details the horrors committed by sirens throughout history. By the time he almost casually mentions a siren named Xana who ordered a man under her spell to gouge out his own eyes while she watched in amusement, I feel sick. Who could choose to do those things? Would Melusine ever hurt Clay that way? Would she enjoy it like the sirens in the recording did?

I don't understand why she's doing this to him. Why would anyone siren another person—steal that person's life from them? Does Melusine just want Clay to be her boyfriend? It doesn't make sense. How could she do something this horrible to him just so he would date her? Maybe she really is an *udell* like the rest of her family, and she thinks it's no big deal to keep a human as a slave. Maybe … I swallow, picturing the disturbing glee in her sapphire eyes … maybe she just thinks controlling him is *fun*. Feeling even sicker than before, I force myself to focus on the recording.

When the speaker moves on to tiger sharks, I take a few deep breaths before walking on shaking legs back to the shelves for the next *konklili* on my list. This one is a gleaming canarium shell. In my eagerness to erase the last shell's grisly images from my mind, I press this new one to my ear before I even return to the table.

Its title, Maritime Music, puts me on edge again. This *konklili* could tell me how Melusine found a siren song to use on Clay— and how I can reverse its effects. Moving the stylus as fast as I can, I skip the section on Mer-made instruments and the one on orca whale calls, before hearing the words I've been waiting for.

"The only music ever banned from the ocean is the Song of the Siren."

I listen in anticipation as the thin, wheezy voice of an older Merman explains the dangerous effects of siren songs, their illegal status, and the harsh punishments associated with using them. He talks about sireny as a stain on Mer history and sounds exactly like Mr. Reitzel did earlier this semester when we reviewed slavery in America.

After fifteen minutes of background information I already know, one fact reaches my ears that's completely new.

"Siren songs drew their magic from the call of the sea that all

Merfolk hear. The songs harnessed that call and focused it outward, onto a mortal. Thus, the siren song and the call of the ocean were intrinsically linked. The same force with which the ocean lures all of us was intensified a hundredfold to lure the mortal to the siren."

So that's why siren songs are so powerful. Most Mer magic consists of potions made from rare sea ingredients. These are hard to get even when you live in the ocean, which is why we don't use potions much on land. But spells rooted in the magic of the sea itself? It's no wonder siren songs have such a hold over their victims. How can I break that strong a hold on Clay?

The recording doesn't answer my question. Instead, it goes on to discuss specific changes to siren songs over time. The oldest siren songs were, unsurprisingly, in Mermese. Then, during the reign of King Nereus (what humans classify as the Middle Ages), a powerful siren named Loralei Rhiniss started a new trend. She enjoyed enchanting sailors and pirates, then commanding them to drop their beautiful jewels and other treasures into the sea. Loralei took twisted pleasure in translating the siren songs and using human's own languages against them.

After that, siren songs were often rewritten in French, Arabic, Greek, Chinese, and many other human languages. Apparently, one of the first English siren songs on record was sung by a Mermaid who heard a bard singing on a ship off the coast of Tudor England and used his own song to siren him. She brought him to a hidden cave and commanded him to sing and dance for her until he died of exhaustion. Later, she bragged her hold on him was so strong that he never once paused, not even to beg for water. Both these human-language songs and the ancient Mermese songs were passed down in families—especially among the nobility—until they were banned.

I process this information. Melusine's song was in Mermese. Does that mean it's one of the most ancient songs?

I don't get a concrete answer, but then comes something much more valuable.

"The length of time a siren song stays in effect varies depending

on the power with which it was applied. According to historical record, mortals have stayed under siren songs for anywhere from a few hours to half a day. Long enough for sirens to toy with them before murdering them in cold blood."

Wait! What? Half a day max? That means if I can just keep Clay away from her for half a day, it will wear off! There's gotta be a way for me to do that. Just when a smile of relief is spreading across my face, the next sentence freezes it in place.

"Of course, once a siren song takes hold, it can be reinstated at any time by the same siren with as little as a few notes hummed into the mortal's ear. In this way, some sirens kept the same fishermen and sailors in their service for years, even after extended absences."

In a moment of perfect clarity, it occurs to me why Melusine calls Clay every day a few hours after school gets out. Why she pulled him away that day in computer lab! She's re-staking her claim. Even if I can get Clay away from her long enough for her song to wear off, she'll just claim him again the moment she sees him—and I'll be powerless to stop her. In my frustration, I've missed the last few lines, so I move the whalebone backward, making sure I catch every word.

"Because teaching a siren song became as punishable a crime as using one against a mortal, knowledge of the songs petered out over the generations. When the Dreaded Curse killed off all elder Mer, the knowledge purportedly died with them. At least, that was the belief held until Adrianna Zayle became history's only modern siren."

I use the stylus to pause the recording. Listening to information Caspian may not want me to know about his great-great-aunt, feels like a betrayal. Still, I need to know everything I can about sireny if I want to help Clay. With a twist of the stylus, I let the words continue. I learn that before Adrianna was imprisoned, she was subjected to a month-long interrogation and admitted she'd found a shell recording of an ancient Mermese siren song. As a direct result of this admission, authorities searched all Mer homes and seized any recordings that so much as described a specific siren song in detail.

"Once these shells were publically smashed, the world was declared free from the threat of sireny and has been free of it ever since."

Until now. Somehow, Melusine has learned one of these long-forbidden songs. If all the shell recordings detailing exactly how the songs work have been smashed, I don't know how I'll learn what I need to do to stop her. But I'll find a way.

With the section on siren songs over, I return the shell to its shelf and seek out the next one on the list. It's up high and I have to stand on my tiptoes to reach it. My hand closes around a small, brown sea snail shell. It's dusty, but I don't have anything to wipe it with, so the dust coats my fingers in a thin, gray film. Gross.

This is the last *konklili* on my list. The last *konklili* that mentions sireny registered on the computer database. I've sat through everything the other two had to say, and I still have no idea how to reverse what Melusine's done to Clay. This tiny shell, no bigger than a jar of my mother's La Mer face cream, better hold the answers I need. I put it up to my ear and—

"Aurelia? Are you back there?"

My mother's voice causes me to jump, and the small shell slips from my grasp.

I dive forward as it hurtles toward the ground. That *konklili* might be the only record of the information I need. I can't risk it smashing.

My hand shoots out right as the fragile shell record is about to hit the hard ground. When it hits my upturned palm instead, I let out an audible sigh. Of course, my mother picks that moment to round the corner. She finds me lying on my stomach, clutching an old, rare *konklili*.

"Are you all right?" Her eyes scan the floor. "Did something break?"

"Everything's fine, Mom," I say, hurrying to my feet.

"You know," my mother says, "some of the shells in here are irreplaceable. Maybe it would be more fun for you to work with your father in the P.R. department after all."

"No! You just scared me, that's all. I'm being super careful."

"Clearly."

I can't let my mom reassign me. "These shells need to be categorized, and it's not like anyone else is swimming up for the job." I don't mention that I've gotten exactly zero sorting done today. Hopefully, she'll be too busy with her own work to check.

My mother must know I'm right because all she says is, "Finish up and get your things together. Emeraldine is done for today, so she'll drive you home."

I won't have time to listen to the last shell. I stare at it. Not only is it the property of the Foundation, it's classified information on a restricted topic. Taking it out of this room is illegal.

Once my mother turns her back, I slip it into my backpack.

Chapter Ten

The stolen brown shell rests in the palm of my hand. I sit huddled in my walk-in closet with my bedroom door closed and homework spread out on my bed in case someone checks on me. Taking a deep breath, I press the *konklili* to my ear.

"Origin of the Siren."

I gasp at the title. This entire *konklili* is about sirens? Sure, it's small, but it still must have more useful information than the other two recordings combined. The speaker offers some general info. While she explains that most sirens were women because the victims of sireny were usually sailors and dock workers (positions historically filled by males), I grab a notepad and pen from my desk, then return to the closet, ready to take notes. I'm soon listening to the story of a Mermaid who, according to legend, became the first siren.

"Himeropa enjoyed what by all accounts was a peaceful, idyllic childhood with her family in the waters near Paestum, found in the human region of south-western Italy. In those ancient days, when Mer were known to humans, our kind often enjoyed surfacing

remote islands to soak up the sunlight, sample delicacies like lizard or turtle, and study the vastness of the sky. Beginning in their teens, Himeropa and her sisters Peisinoe, Thelxiepeia, and Agalope frequented an island where they did just that. The island was also a mating and nesting site for seabirds. Fascinated by these winged creatures, the girls spent many hours feeding and training them. It is said that Peisinoe even made siluesses from their feathers for herself and her sisters to wear while on the island."

Siluesses out of bird feathers? That sounds unhygienic to me, not to mention uncomfortable. I listen with increasing boredom as the voice in my ear describes the various tricks the sisters taught the birds. I need to learn about their sireny, not their penchant for feathered headdresses.

"Because the girls spent so much time above water, as a precaution, their mother taught them songs they could use to distract humans in case they encountered any."

Songs! I'm back at attention.

"Like many parents before her, the mother instructed her girls to stun any humans they might meet with the captivating music, then escape back to the safety of the oceans. One fateful day, the sisters needed to use these songs. A group of sailors whose ship was anchored nearby swam to the island."

I bite my lip as the recording details how the sailors found Agalope, the youngest of the sisters, asleep in the sun and attacked her. Luckily, her sisters were nearby and heard her screams. They sang the songs their mother had taught them and Thelxiepeia and Peisinoe escaped with Agalope into the waves. But Himeropa, overcome with fear for her sister and rage at the sailors, kept singing. She poured all her emotion into her song, and it grew more powerful than ever before. Instead of stunning the sailors, the song brought them under Himeropa's command. In her anger, she screamed for their deaths, and each one of them jumped off the island's cliffs to a watery grave.

"This is the first recorded instance of the crime of sireny. Unfortunately, it failed to slake Himeropa's thirst for vengeance. She

blamed all humans for the attack on her sister and practiced her newfound power on any human who happened by. She learned to channel her emotions into her songs as she had done with her anger that first day, and she taught her sisters to do the same.

"Soon, the sisters took to luring sailors from passing ships with their songs. Enchanted by the music, sailors would sail their vessels straight into the rocks off the coast of the island. Most drowned, but those who swam to shore were tortured by the sirens. It is worthy of note that Himeropa, Peisinoe, Thelxiepeia, and Agalope continued to bedeck themselves in the feathers of the birds that nested on the island and allowed these trained birds to perch on their shoulders and heads while they sang. Thus, they were usually mistaken by sailors who passed at a distance as bird women, an erroneous image which permeates references to sirens in human literature. Those who got close enough to see the sirens' true form did not often survive to tell the tale."

When I read *The Odyssey* in school last year, I came home mega confused. Sirens as birds? I don't think so. My mother explained it away as an early mistake made by humans. She said Mer perpetuated it to keep ourselves from being associated with sirens whenever we could. Now I know the whole story.

"Several historical sources go so far as to suggest that Himeropa, who like all Mer at the time was immortal, continued to develop her powers and was in fact the very same Sea Sorceress the Little Mermaid sought out. If this is so, then she was responsible not only for the torment and death of countless mortals, but also for creating the magic the Little Mermaid misused to curse us all."

After finishing the legend of the sister sirens, the shell discusses the spread of sireny and repeats many of the same facts from the other two *konklilis*. The smooth female voice in the shell is at odds with the horrifying stories it intones. I force myself to hear every gruesome detail, listening for anything about stopping sirens, but nothing comes. That night, nightmares slither into my sleep, and I wake up with an image burning behind my eyes: Clay, his tongue ripped out by a sharp-beaked bird creature with a coral-colored tail.

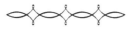

The picture doesn't look right. I straighten it before the glue sets. Perfect.

"So, I guess we're done," Clay says.

"We should run through the oral presentation one more time the night before, but yeah, I guess we are."

When I turn away from the poster board, Clay is frowning.

"What's wrong? Is something still crooked?"

"No, the board looks great. It's just now that the project's finished, you might ice me out again." He says it jokingly, but guilt nags at me.

"I never iced you out," I insist. I did, and we both know it, but since I can't explain my very good reason, my only course of action is denial.

"So then, you'll keep coming over to hang out now that the project's done?" His smile is devilish. I swam right into that one. It makes me smile, too.

All this week, I've been worrying about what excuses I could use to continue keeping an eye on Clay once we finished our report. After countless hours in the records room at the Foundation, I still haven't found anything that even hints at a way to stop Melusine, so there isn't anything I can do for Clay, but I can't just abandon him while I'm searching.

"You don't think your girlfriend will mind if I keep coming over twice a week?" My tone is light, my question serious.

"Well, the project's not due for a while … maybe we just don't mention we're finished."

"You can lie to her? I mean," I quickly cover, "you feel okay about that?" I didn't think someone under a siren's spell could lie to the siren.

Creases line his forehead. "It's not like you and I are doing anything wrong. I'm just not sure that Mel would understand that we're ... friends."

Under normal circumstances, I wouldn't feel right about coming between two people in a relationship. But when one of those people is using ancient ocean magic to control the other, I figure the typical rules of propriety don't apply.

He sighs. "It just took you and me so long to get to this place, and I don't want anything to mess things up again."

Seeing the honest, open expression on Clay's face makes me feel justified for putting his phone on silent while he was in the bathroom. I'm sure Melusine made her daily afterschool phone call, but since Clay didn't hear it, he's more himself than usual.

His mental clarity will be short-lived. Eventually, he'll see his missed calls and call her back. So, I intend to make the most of this time I have with him—with the real him.

I turn my gaze back to him, and I'm caught off guard. The sun streaming in from his bedroom window highlights the angles of his face, outlining his jaw and brightening the green in his hazel eyes. No, I can't get distracted. I need to use this time to make sure Mel isn't hurting him.

"So, why don't you think Mel would understand? Is she super controlling or something?" There, that was subtle.

"Not exactly. I just can't seem to say no to her." He shakes his head, confused. "I guess it's because I want to make her happy?"

No, it's because you don't have a choice.

"Anyway," he continues, "I'm afraid that if she told me not to spend time with you, not to be your friend, I might listen to her." As if realizing how that sounds, he holds up a hand. "Lia, please don't take that the wrong way. It's not like I'd want to. I just ... would." He runs his hand through his hair in frustration and lets out a pained sigh. "That doesn't make any sense!"

As Clay struggles with his muddled thoughts, I want to reach out to him. To take his hand and explain what's been done to him. But I can't. Not only would he think I'm crazy, but if he mentioned it to Melusine, it could put both of us in who knows how much more danger. Instead, I say, "Don't worry. I won't say anything about finishing the project. It can be our secret."

"But why does her opinion matter so much to me, Lia?" Anguish suffuses his voice and stabs into me. "I know she's my girlfriend, but it shouldn't be all about her all the time, right?"

"No, it shouldn't."

"It's like the other day. After I talked to you about how I haven't played the guitar in front of anyone since my dad stopped coming to watch me, I realized I should try to share that with someone again. And I thought, Mel's my girlfriend and this is important to me, so I should share it with her."

For Clay's sake, I stifle the immediate spike of envy threatening to overtake me, and make my words as encouraging as I can. "Wow, it's really great you wanted to open up like that." It's a big step for Clay.

"But that's just it!" He's risen from his chair and he's pacing the room. "She wasn't even interested. I'd barely played a few bars before she took the guitar out of my hands, started kissing me, and—" He must remember he's talking to me because he cuts off the description. I'm probably blushing, and I want to turn my head to the side to cover it, but I don't. Clay needs me right now, so I keep my gaze fixed on him. "She didn't even want to hear it. She sings to me all the time, but the first time I want to share my music with her ... " He sinks onto the bed, like he's emotionally exhausted by his own outburst. "She didn't even care."

When he looks at me, his eyes are pleading—desperate for me to understand.

"She should," I say. "This matters to you, so it should matter to the people who care about you." I swallow. "It matters to me. I think it's really cool that you're so passionate about writing music. I wish I had something I was that passionate about."

"When we talked the other day, I figured out I'd been shying away from sharing my music for too long. Composing music is what I've always wanted to do with my life, and I can't let go of that just because my dad's not around anymore. If I want to be able to lead an entire symphony one day or write the score to a movie that whole audiences will hear, then I can't be afraid to play my music now."

Hearing Clay talk about his goals stirs something inside me. I want him to have the chance to accomplish everything he's ever dreamed of. "It must've really hurt when Mel didn't want to listen," I say, "but you can't let that change your mind. I bet your music is phenomenal."

"You're about to find out," he says.

"What?"

"I—can I … play my song for you?" Uncertainty laces his words. He's afraid I'll reject his music the way Melusine did. Not a chance.

"I'd love that."

A genuine smile spreads across his face, and he's never looked so handsome. He pulls out his guitar from its shadowy hiding place under his bed.

"C'mere." He gestures me over, and I sit beside him on his bed as he places the guitar on his lap. The wood is worn and old, but it's polished to a high shine. There's something intimate about seeing Clay's most prized possession.

"This is a song I've been working on for a while. It's the only one I've finished and I think it really captures … well, just listen."

His long, callused fingers strum the first few melancholy chords, and the room—the world—shrinks to the two of us on that bed as his music encompasses us.

"Think that there's a forever?
Or is that just a dream?
Don't think that I'll find it.
Hearts are not what they seem."

Clay's voice is deep and rough. It makes me feel things I can't name. After not singing in front of anyone for so long, Clay could be self-conscious, but he's not. By the second verse, he's lost in the music.

"Wish mine was laid open,
All its secrets laid bare.
In a bond of forever.
But I just haven't dared."

His fingers strum faster against the chords and his voice picks up volume as he starts the chorus.

"Come, come, come to me
Let's explore eternity.
Come, come, come to me
I want you irrevocably.
Come, come, come to me
And promise that you'll stay."

Then Clay begins an instrumental section that I can only describe as a cross between rock and classical symphony. No wonder he dreams of being a composer. His talent seeps into my skin.

As he sings, the raw emotion in his voice tells me I'm watching something private. I'm the first person he's played this song for, and it's like he's let me into a part of himself that no one's ever seen. When he finishes the final verse, his eyes lock on mine, and they're shining with both sadness and hope.

I'll stay. I promise. *And I'll figure out how to save you.*

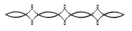

But my promise starts to seem impossible to fulfill. Every day after school that I don't spend with Clay, I spend researching at the Foundation. I sort and input just enough shells to keep anyone from getting suspicious and spend the rest of my time searching through any *konklilis* that might mention sireny, but I haven't come any closer to finding a way to stop Melusine.

In school, I'm tempted to run up to her and beg her to let him go, but I'm afraid of what she'll do if I confront her. No, my only advantage is she has no idea I saw her siren Clay. I might need the element of surprise later—if I ever find anything relevant in my research.

Then, one afternoon, after hours upon hours listening to the same facts over and over until my exhausted brain is spinning, I finally hear the words I've been waiting for.

"The siren Atargina held a sultan under her power for months until she was forced to let him go."

Forced to let him go? It is possible! My breath quickens.

"Another darker, far more powerful siren stole him away with her own deadly song. Like male sea lions fighting over a female, sirens living in groups have fought violently over mortals to prove rank and supremacy. In that far-off region of the Arabian Sea, few ships ventured and the competition for mortal slaves was fierce. The sultan was a prize to be won. Shell recordings from other sirens who bore witness to the event claim that no fewer than seven sirens sang to him at once in Mermese and he was bound to the one with the most powerful song, who was undoubtedly far more evil than her companions."

No. No, no, no! As high as my hopes were a moment ago, now they crash just as low. If I need another siren to stop Melusine, I'm lost. As far as I know, Melusine is the only siren since Caspian's great-great-aunt. And even if there were another—which I hope there's not—siccing her on Clay would only put him in more danger. I let my head sink onto my folded arms. Another dead end.

I make myself listen to the rest of the shell and three others like it, but I find no more references to stopping a siren. I've gone through every shell I can find on restricted magic, sorcery, music, crime, and Mer history—both the ones on the shelves and in the crates full of recent acquisitions—and I've found nothing. Heart heavy with disappointment after yet another fruitless research session, I decide to head home.

I came to the Foundation straight after school again today and I have my backpack with me, so I have to walk home instead of swim through the tunnels. If I wait for Em to drive me, I might blurt out everything and beg for my big sister's help. But she can't help. If searching through the best land-based collection of *konklilis* hasn't turned up an answer, she certainly won't be able to.

For the first time since I saw Melusine sirening Clay, I'm faced with the very real possibility that I may not be able to help him. This realization hits me like a steamship, and it's as if all the oxygen has left my body. This entire time, my anger at the injustice of what she's doing to him has propelled me forward, but now a deep, overwhelming fear overtakes it: What if I don't ever find a way to free Clay?

I keep my face impassive until I'm out of the lobby. As soon as I exit the green-glass doors, I break into a run. Passersby stare as I dash gracelessly by, but I don't care. For once, I'm grateful for my flat shoes as they slap against the concrete. Tears well up behind my eyes and burn to be let free. It's only through years of practice that I keep them from running down my cheeks and forming fat, sad pearls. Clay's song plays in my mind, as it has at least three times a day since he sang it, but even that doesn't comfort me.

I run until the blurred office buildings become boutiques and frozen yogurt shops, run until they become houses, then bigger houses. When I reach the white and glass of my own house, I don't stop.

I go in the side gate, rush through the backyard, and clatter down the wind-worn wooden steps to the beach below. When hot sand fills my shoes and impedes my progress, I slip out of them and leave them behind.

I don't know how to stop Melusine. I don't know how to save Clay. I don't know what else to try. All I know is that I need the ocean.

I need it to envelop me. I need its constant, steady call to drown out the endless questions in my head. It's not fully dark yet, and I'm not allowed in the open water, but the pool won't soothe my desolation. There's no one on our private strip of beach to see me and, for the first time, I'm past caring anyway. I run straight into the waves.

My favorite Capri pants, now sodden with salt water, rip beyond repair as my tail bursts forth, wrenched from my body at the same time as my tears. Pearls drop to the ocean floor as I swim farther and farther out to sea. The call is strong and so is the current. I relish the unforgiving push and pull of the water against my arms and tail. It gives me something to focus on. Something to fight against. I dive down deeper, swim faster. What else can I do?

I can't stop. I can't think. I can't—but then I have to. The blue phosphorescence of the Border comes into view. Desperate not to stop—not to feel—I swim along the Border, back and forth, my tail whipping from side to side, my heart pounding. But I can't outswim my fear or my helplessness.

I've gone as far as I can go, escaped as far as I can escape. On the cold ocean floor, right next to the blue coral Border built to keep me safe, I curl my tail around me and sob.

My dad wakes me from a fitful sleep at 4:30am. I have to get to school early for today's biology field trip.

"Are you sure you're up to going?" he asks.

"I'm sure."

It's a boating trip, and it's mandatory for the entire eleventh grade. My parents offered to get me out of it. They're worried about me venturing onto the open ocean with a boat full of humans, but we're not going far from the coast and certainly not out past the Border line. I assured them my leg control has been strong enough to handle it since last year; I also pointed out that

Melusine's father has enough confidence in his daughter to let her go.

That's my real reason for not bailing. If Melusine will be there with Clay, then I'll be there, too. I know I have no recourse to protect him—a thought which makes me feel just as helpless as it did yesterday—but I can't desert him.

We're out on the ocean in time to watch the sunrise. Partway through, I'm distracted by movement to my left when Melusine pulls Clay's arm around her shoulders. She's wearing his leather jacket, which leaves him in only his thin t-shirt. The pale pink light plays over his profile, and I hope he's not too cold in the morning chill.

The science teachers work with the crew to catch various specimens of fish and other small sea creatures. They put some that we're allowed to touch into sectioned off tubs filled with salt water. The sight of fish flopping their tails in the nets fills me with sympathy. Some of the other girls display disheartened looks that match my own, so one of the crew assures us the salt water will keep all the creatures alive until we're ready to throw them back in. I feel better until the nets pull up old shoes, a tire caked with filthy oil, and even a neon orange shopping cart. What humans do to the oceans disgusts me if I let myself think about it.

Still, as the day wears on, the field trip turns out to be pretty fun. I've seen all of these creatures on my swims, but the undiluted sunlight allows me to make some observations that I never could under the waves. It's also a boon to both my confidence and my grade when I can answer so many of my bio teacher's questions. With the waves rolling under the boat, it's challenging to keep my legs in place, but with Clay walking around in that t-shirt, his arms shining with sun lotion, I manage it.

I call him over whenever possible to come examine a starfish or a crab. He seems only too happy to leave Melusine's side, which must mean that she hasn't sirened him yet this morning.

"You know, your song's stuck in my head," I tell him with a smile.

His face lights up. "Of course it is, Nautilus." His voice has a cocky lilt, but his eyes tell me my words mean something to him.

"I keep singing it in the shower without even realizing it."

"That's a nice image."

I blush. "Thanks again for sharing it with me."

"Thanks for listening." This time, nothing masks his sincerity.

Melusine waltzes over and slips her hand into the back pocket of Clay's jeans possessively. A look of annoyance passes over his face, but he doesn't stop her. "Hi, Lia," she says in her melted-candy voice. "What are we talking about?"

A gray cloud moves in front of the sun, blocking its warm rays.

"I was just telling Clay how much I dislike people who insinuate themselves in conversations they're not part of."

"I hate that, too. But you know what's so much worse? Girls who throw themselves at guys who are already taken. It just doesn't get any more pathetic."

The air between us tightens with tension. I'm about to retort when Clay speaks up.

"Isn't this octopus cool, Mel?" He lifts a small brown and yellow octopus from the tub in front of us. Clay's still standing close to me, and the octopus wraps a tentacle around my arm. "Look! He likes Lia."

"Apparently he's not the only one," Melusine says with a pointed look at Clay.

"What's that supposed to mean?" he asks. The wind picks up, and it's chilly again. The waves roll more sharply beneath us.

"I think you and I haven't spent enough alone time together today. Come on, let's go to the other side of the boat." She makes her tone sultry and adds, "There's no one else over there."

These words are meant just as much to bother me as to tempt Clay. But knowing what I know, instead of making me jealous, they scare me. The second Melusine gets Clay alone, she'll siren him—I just know it.

Clay must not want to be alone with her, because he gestures to the creature that's now suction-cupping its way up my arm. "I want to get some pictures of the octopus."

Melusine glares first at me, then at the eight-tentacled creature. "Oh, please. It's a common California two-spot. Any idiot would know not to waste time on it. Now come on."

"Why do you think it's okay to talk to me like that?"

She must be used to keeping him under her spell, because she's taken aback by his question and disobedience. She recovers quickly and puts on a baby-faced pout as she sidles up to him.

"I'm sorry, handsome. I don't know what's gotten into me." Just then, the boat lurches to the left, and a few students around us gasp and grab onto the railings. "I've just been feeling so seasick," Melusine continues, taking advantage of the choppy water. "I think I'd feel better at the other end of the boat, but I don't want to be alone. Please come with me?" Seasick? Melusine? Yeah, right.

Clay hesitates.

I want to beg him not to go, but I can't give him any good reason. I shiver, and I'm not sure if it's from the now-biting cold or my own foreboding.

"I feel so awful," Melusine says, bringing a hand to her forehead.

"I'll come with you." Clay guides her toward the other end of the rocking boat, throwing me an apologetic look over his shoulder.

I'm about to follow them when one of the science teachers steps in front of me, blocking my path. "All marine life must remain in the designated area."

It takes me a moment to realize she means the octopus now wound around my upper arm and shoulder. I start pulling him off, but he's stuck fast to my skin and it's not an easy task. By the time the octopus rests safely back in his tub and the teacher has rushed off to stop another student from trying to bounce a blowfish like a basketball, Melusine and Clay are out of sight.

I head toward the stern, moving as fast as I can. I walk against the salty wind, and it pushes me back, but I fight it. As I move around the other side of the ship's cabin, Clay's voice reaches my ears, and I duck back so I won't be seen. Relief floods me; if he's using that harsh a tone, she must not have sirened him yet.

" … and you don't seem sick now. You just wanted to get me over here and you didn't care that I was doing something else. Why is it always about what you want?"

"Maybe letting you get this out of your system will do you some good," Melusine says, sounding bored. I can barely hear her indifferent words over the howling wind.

"I'm serious, Mel. When was the last time we had an actual conversation? Or did something we're both interested in?"

"You always seem interested."

"Yeah … " Clay sounds confused by this, but makes himself keep going. "I guess it's partly my fault for not saying anything earlier, but everything is so clear this morning. I'm sorry, but this … us … we're just not working out."

"Is that what you wanted to get off that chiseled chest of yours?" she asks in a condescending voice. "You won't feel that way in a minute. You may not love me now, but you will."

She takes a step closer to him and sings in Mermese.

Clay's eyes glaze over and his face, so resolute a moment before, goes slack. She's carving him out, leaving him empty, and I can't stand it. My insides are on fire. Fury at what she's doing to him rises up in me, wild and hot.

"Stop!" I cry, stepping out from behind the cabin.

But she doesn't hear me. She's lost in her own magic. The frigid air is thick with it. The waves crash against the side of the boat. I don't know what sound to focus on—her sickening song or my own blood rushing in my ears. I have to stop this. When I open my mouth again, it's not a scream that comes out.

"Come, come, come to me
Let's explore eternity."

The words rise almost unbidden from my throat. Melusine

snaps her head around to look at me, and in her moment of distraction, so does Clay.

"Lia?" His voice sounds far away.

Melusine realizes her mistake and sings again, louder. Clay sinks back into a trance, his expression dead. I do the only thing I can think of. I sing, too.

"Come, come, come to me
I want you irrevocably.
Come, come, come to me
And promise that you'll stay."

As my volume increases, so does Melusine's. Our words are whipped up by the sea wind that scrapes against both our faces. The magic of our two songs crackles and clashes, ricocheting off the surrounding waves.

Clay takes a step away from her and a step back. His body sways with the movement of the boat and the push and pull of the conflicting melodies.

I keep singing, hoping against hope something in Clay will recognize his own words and be drawn to them. But Melusine's voice is stronger.

She looks menacing now, her sapphire eyes cold and sharp, her hands balled into white fists. Her voice is confident and clear as she unleashes her ancient Mermese song, and Clay moves toward her once more. She places a hand right where Clay's shoulder meets his neck, and her long nails dig into his skin.

Not again. She can't do this to him again.

Her lips twist upward in a victorious smile so frightening it makes me falter. In that second of silence, I grow aware of the ever-constant call of the ocean. The sea whispers all around me, causing a memory of something I read to bubble to the surface of my consciousness:

"Siren songs drew their magic from the call of the sea that all Merfolk hear."

120

I focus on the ocean's call and the sensation of longing it creates within me.

"Come, come, come to me
Let's explore eternity.
Come, come, come to me
I want you irrevocably.
Come, come, come to me
And promise that you'll stay."

I stare into Clay's empty eyes, begging him to move toward me. His song pulses deep inside me as I sing, and I feed it the fear and need and love I have for him. With all my strength, I push my voice over the thrashing tempest.

Then he's walking. His feet move across the wooden deck, away from Melusine. She continues to sing, but it's as if he can no longer hear her. He takes his place beside me.

The waves and wind settle to an eerie calm. I have won.

I turn to Clay and he stares back at me, glassy-eyed.

"Clay?" I ask. But he's silent, awaiting my command.

I have sirened him.

Chapter Eleven

"This is a field trip, not karaoke night!" one of the science teachers shouts as she stomps her way toward us. Panic seizes me. This woman overheard us! I look at her—her hands on her hips, her beady eyes staring at us … why isn't she sirened? I guess because Melusine and I directed our songs at Clay. "What are you three doing over here?" she continues, voice sharp. The lecture's about to start. Now, march."

She doesn't feel like a part of my reality. So much has changed in the last few minutes, and this dowdy woman is oblivious to all of it.

The ebb and the flow of ocean magic still thrums through me. But I'm on a boat with an entire junior class of humans and I have to act normal. Clay's still staring at me dutifully. I have to keep him acting normal, too. So, I walk in the direction of the teacher's pointed finger, and Clay follows me step for step, all the way across the deck. Surrounded by witnesses, Melusine can do nothing but walk behind us. Her glower scorches my back.

When we stop in the throng of other students, Clay slips

his warm, strong hand into mine. A thrill of excitement shoots up my spine. But then I remember: Clay isn't holding my hand because he wants to, he's holding my hand because the siren song—my siren song—is forcing him to. Up front, one of the crew members holds up the octopus, and even his googly gaze looks accusatory. What have I done?

On the bus ride back, Clay slides into the same bench seat I do. He still isn't talking much unless I ask him direct questions. I must've asked some variation of, "Are you okay?" at least a hundred times. He just smiles and asks what he can do for me, but his eyes remain empty.

Then, I spot a sea lion on a nearby cliff. "Oh! Look out the window!" I say, trying to start up a normal conversation.

He does. And he doesn't stop. He stares out the window long after we've passed the sea lion and entered the boring city streets. He looks when there's nothing to see.

A few rows in front of us, Kelsey takes advantage of Clay's apparent distraction and turns around to face me over the back of her blue nylon seat. She stares pointedly at Clay, then at Melusine (who sits alone on the long bench at the back of the bus), then at me before mouthing, "OMG!" She shoots me a huge, congratulatory grin before flipping back around. To Kelsey, this must look like a dream come true. If she only knew …

The short bus ride back to school feels like it stretches on for hours. I let Clay stare blankly out the window so I don't have to see the vacant look in his eyes. When we finally pull into the school parking lot, I say, "Clay, we're here." He doesn't react. The truth of what I have to do settles on top of me like a heavy weight. "Clay," I try again, "you can stop looking now."

He turns his head back toward me, "Oh. Okay." His voice has more of a spark than it did earlier, but he still sounds out of it.

I swallow. Clay has rested his hand on my thigh. My heart speeds up, and warmth suffuses me at the feel of his solid, confident touch.

Considering that, traditionally, the only time Mer show their legs is right before they … Well, touching someone's legs is one of the most intimate, titillating gestures you can make. His hand looks so innocent, sitting there on my leg, but I've never felt like this before. I doubt I could summon my tail right now if I tried.

I don't want to move. I don't want to breathe. I just want to feel the exquisite pressure of Clay's hand. But when students file past our seat and out of the bus, the moment needs to end. Any second now, I'm going to move Clay's hand and get up.

A disgusted sigh reaches my ears. Melusine walks up next to us on her way to the exit. She stares at Clay's hand on my thigh, then pins me with a glare that says, "You'll pay for this. It isn't over," as clearly as if she'd spoken the words.

I can't waste any more time sitting here like a hormonal idiot. Clay is the victim of powerful magic. Magic I don't understand. I need to find a way to make this right.

"Clay, we should get up now." My voice comes out a whisper, but it may as well be the shout of a general. Clay gets up so fast, he almost bangs his head on the ceiling of the bus. With his hand gone, my leg feels cold.

"O-okay, go do whatever you want now," I say to him once we're off the bus. He doesn't move, just stares at me. What am I supposed to do? "Be yourself," I try. "Please." My voice breaks with the intensity of my wish, but Clay doesn't magically snap back to himself. He takes a small step closer to me and looks as lost as ever. If I … sirened him … and I want to free him, why isn't that enough?

If I can't end the spell myself, then I have to keep an eye on him until it wears off. It's gotta wear off sometime like Melusine's did, doesn't it? School is over, but Clay's mom might be home and I can't risk her seeing him like this, and my house is out of the question. I gaze out across the emptying asphalt desert of the school parking lot. Where am I supposed to take him?

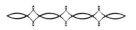

124

"What flavor do you want?" the pimpled teen behind the old-fashioned, gilded register asks Clay. The place is done up like a 1950s ice cream shoppe with two p's and an e. Of course, to cater to all the beach-ready dieters near here, it only serves frozen yogurt.

Clay turns to me. "What flavor do I want?"

I glance around at the other patrons, then back at Clay. "That's up to you. What flavor do you want?" I ask.

He scrunches up his face in thought. "I ... " He's searching his mind for the answer, but it's taking great effort. "I want ... "

"Spit it out, buddy," says a guy in line behind us. "Some of us want to get back to the surf."

I shoot him a death glare and he backs off, but several other people in line have begun to stare.

"Cold Apple Pie, two scoops!" Clay shouts. His face crumples in exhaustion.

Pimpled guy stands open-mouthed until I say, "You heard the man," then place my own order for Salted Caramel Swirl. By now, we've caught the attention of the whole place, so I forgo toppings and pay for our over-priced dessert before guiding Clay outside.

What was I thinking? I stole your free will, but here, have some fro-yo? Stupid.

By the time I lead Clay onto a more secluded residential street, his gaze has sharpened a little and he eats his yogurt without me telling him to. I wonder ...

"What's your favorite food?"

His face scrunches up again, but not for as long as before. "Sushi," he answers.

"Really?" I expected his favorite food to be burgers or pizza or something else stereotypical for a human boy.

"Yes."

I hadn't meant that as a question, but it's a good sign he answered quickly.

"What's your middle name?"

I pepper him with questions as we pass by the bougainvillea-covered gates of one home after another. Each question takes him less time and effort than the last. Thinking about himself and his own desires seems to lessen the sireny's grip, little by little.

By the time I've found out Clay's favorite color (bright blue, like his car), his favorite song (The Verve's "Bittersweet Symphony"), the type of dog he'd like to have (a Shiba Inu), and how old he was when he lost his first tooth (five and a half), our frozen yogurt is long finished and I'm running out of innocuous questions, but Clay's voice has more life than it's had since the boat trip.

For each answer Clay gives, I give my own. I don't know how aware he is or what he'll remember, but it feels more like a conversation this way. While we walk, he slips his hand into mine, warm and solid. I have to fight to keep my breathing even and focus on talking. As I rack my brain for more harmless facts to inquire about, other questions arise unbidden in my mind. What are you looking for in a girl? Do you have real feelings for Melusine? And of course, the one that's been burning inside me for over a year: How do you feel … about me?

But I can't let myself ask any of them. Clay would tell me anything right now—even things he wouldn't want me to know. I've already violated him enough, so I bite my lip to keep from asking the questions I yearn to have answered.

"Now you ask me a question. Anything you want to know." Maybe giving him some piece of myself will ease the guilt squeezing my chest.

"Why does my neck hurt?" Clay asks.

"Your neck hurts?" I ask, concerned.

"Yes."

The window! I let him stare out that window for at least twenty minutes. The guilt grips my chest even tighter.

A low stone wall runs along the gate of a nearby mansion. I sit Clay down and reach a tentative hand forward. With a deep, steadying breath, I inch my fingers closer until they graze the warm skin on the back of his neck.

I want to run my fingers over the skin, explore his rich

mahogany hairline. But that's not what this is about. My carelessness has brought him pain, and it's up to me to soothe it. I've never given a message before. Certainly never to a boy. *Please let me do it right.*

His neck feels so different from my own. Corded muscles run along his spine and down into his shoulders. They shift as I press against them with my thumbs and the pads of my fingers. Tension coils there in knots. Closing my eyes, I focus on the way it moves under his skin. I press harder, deeper—willing the pain away. My thumbs make small circles until his tension yields. The knots disappear, and Clay sighs in relief, turning his head from side to side.

I'm still touching him, my hand resting right where his neck meets his shoulder. I withdraw it and take a step back.

Lost in thought, I go too long without saying or doing anything. With nothing to distract him, Clay stands up and turns to face me. Suddenly, he's the one touching me. He's running his palms up my bare arms. My skin tingles under his touch, and I gasp. He strokes the back of his hand across my cheek where I can't help but lean into it. He's so close.

"Clay … "

He's going to kiss me. It's as certain as the tides.

This is what I've wanted. Every time we huddled over our display board or practiced a self-defense move, I've wanted to know what it would be like to feel him, to taste him. I've been waiting for what feels like forever for my first kiss. If I'm honest with myself, I've been waiting for Clay.

Now the wait is over. We've strolled into the lush, green hills overlooking the ocean, and the sun is shining down on us to create a perfect, romantic moment.

Only, it's not perfect.

As he leans in, his eyes remain open and filled with hunger. It's the same blind hunger I've seen a million times when he makes out in the hall with Melusine. My heart sinks. That hunger isn't for me. He can't even see me right now.

His breath skates across my lips before I turn my head away.

"Clay ... stop," It hurts me to say the words, but the fact that he instantly obeys me proves I'm right. It's the spell making Clay want to kiss me. It's not real at all.

Then his tone, his whole demeanor, suddenly changes.

"Lia?"

His voice is groggy, like he's finding his way back from a dream—or a nightmare. The spell must be wearing off. The universe sure does have a cruel sense of timing.

"Clay? How are you feeling?"

"Were we ... did I just try to ... what time is it?"

"About 6:00."

"I should get home. Do you need me to walk you first?"

"No, but I'll walk you to your house. It's on my way." It isn't strictly on the way, but I doubt Clay's in any condition to notice, and I don't want to leave him alone just yet.

We walk the rest of the way in silence.

"I-know-what-you're-looking-at," Kelsey sing-songs.

She's not wrong; I've been watching him all day. I've also been watching for signs of *her*.

"Did he kiss you? How perfect was it? Was it like hot new outfit perfect or like chocolate soufflé perfect?"

I pick at the poached salmon I brought for lunch. I have no appetite. "We didn't kiss."

"Oh." Her face falls but then immediately perks back up. "That's no reason to look like a melted Popsicle. The important thing is that he broke up with Mel—and he talked to you about it! That's big. It's huge! You should be doing a happy dance!"

I muster up a big smile for Kelsey's sake, but it's soon replaced by a yawn. I stayed up most of the night. I didn't have any *konklilis* on sireny at home, but I needed information more than ever. So, once everyone was asleep, I crept up to my room and made a list of everything I've learned about sireny so far. I had to make sense of what happened out on that boat ... how I did what I did, and what in the Seven Seas I'm supposed to do now.

I nearly fell off my spinny desk chair when I remembered the tale of the Tudor-era bard. The one who was under such a strong spell the siren bragged about her power over him. How could I have not seen it before? He was a bard—a musician! She used *his own song* to siren him. Maybe that's how she achieved such a strong hold. Did his own words strengthen the bond? I used Clay's song ... maybe that's why I overpowered Melusine. She knows far more about sireny and magic than I do, so it's the only reason that makes sense.

Now, in the light of day, all I can think about is where Melusine is. She didn't come to school today, and I'm a wreck trying to figure out what that means. Is she bowing out in defeat or spending the entire day casting a spell so ancient and heinous I've never heard of it? Maybe, while I'm trapped here going to A.P. Bio and pre-calculus, she's using these same hours to concoct some evil plan to get Clay back. And why does she want him anyway? The question plagues me again. Is he just a boy toy to her, or does she want him for something worse? Not having any clue what that something worse could be makes waves of fear rise up in me and swell higher than ever.

As for Clay, I've spent the entire day both avoiding him and keeping him in my sights—which is no easy feat. I want to be near him so I can check that he's okay, but I need to leave him alone to ensure the sireny has entirely worn off. My rational brain assures me that the spell wore off last night and that I'm being too cautious. But the memory of Clay's empty eyes and dead voice ... I can't bear to talk to him again until he's back to himself.

I've even ducked into the girls' bathroom a couple times today when I've seen him coming down the hall, telling myself it's because I want to give him the space he needs. I'm definitely not avoiding him because I'm terrified a part of him hates me for violating him. No, that's not it at all.

In history class, my luck runs out. Mr. Reitzel gives us time to work on our projects and all of a sudden, Clay is making his way over to me. He sits without a word. After a pause that makes my stomach leap up and lodge in my throat, he says, "We need to talk about yesterday."

His eyes are clear and he sounds fully back to himself, but his voice is more serious than I've ever heard it, and I'm afraid. Afraid that he remembers Melusine and me battling over him on the boat. Afraid that he's figured out I'm not a normal girl, that he thinks I'm a freak. Afraid that he knows I've wronged him. I dig my fingernails into my palms, the pain of each small crescent moon keeping me from panicking.

"I need to apologize," he says.

What? "Apologize?" I parrot.

"Yeah. Lia, I'm really sorry."

He's apologizing to me? It's like the universe is tilting, off-kilter.

"The way I treated you yesterday, it wasn't right."

"Clay, you didn't—"

"No," he holds up a hand, "let me say this. I almost kissed you."

"That's ... that's okay." *I almost let you.*

"No. No, it's not. Not right after I broke up with Mel. I can't imagine how that made me look ... or what you must think of me."

"It was a strange day." Talk about an understatement. "A lot happened." Like me weaseling my way into your mind.

"I-I'm still not exactly sure what I was thinking. I plead temporary insanity."

For breaking up with Melusine? For wanting to kiss me? For both? "For what?"

"For taking advantage of our friendship like that. I'd never want you to feel like some rebound."

Does that mean he doesn't want me now or he wouldn't want

me ever? "I totally understand." Even though I don't.

"I'm glad one of us does." He smiles, but it isn't his usual cocky smirk. It's almost … sheepish. "My friends say I've been zoned out lately. They think it's stress. I don't know what it is, but I'm sorry I acted weird. Everything yesterday was kind of a blur. I guess because so much changed so fast." Frustration fills his words when he says, "I was just so sick of Mel bossing me around. I couldn't take it anymore. But, that's no excuse for involving you." He looks up at me and raises one eyebrow. "Forgive me?"

"Of course," I say. If he knew what I'd done to him, he could never forgive me.

"You rock, Nautilus."

I don't. I don't deserve his praise. I need to change the subject—and I need information. "So, have you talked to Mel today?"

"No, she didn't come to school."

I don't know whether to be relieved he hasn't spoken to her or disappointed he doesn't know anything.

"But she texted me. She wants to talk later, so I'm heading to her place after school."

"No!"

I can't let him go over there. That's what she's planning! She didn't come to school today because she's waiting to get him alone—to get him away from me—so she can siren him back.

"Don't worry. I'm just going to drop off a few of her things so she knows it's really over."

"Clay, please don't go." I grab his hand and look him directly in the eyes, hoping he'll understand my urgency. "Trust me. She'll hurt you."

"She can't hurt me if I don't let her. I have to talk to her. I owe her that. But I won't let her mess with my feelings," he says, squeezing my hand before releasing it. A sinking feeling hits my stomach.

No, you won't. Because I'm going to mess with them first.

I shouldn't do what I'm about to do. It's wrong. It's so wrong.

But what other choice do I have? I fight to push my thoughts down, to smother the little voice inside that's screaming at me not to do this.

When the bell rings and we walk out of the classroom, I grab Clay's arm with a trembling hand and pull him away from the crowds of students making their daily exodus through the double doors. I set my jaw and tell myself I have to do it. If I don't, she will.

"Nautilus, what—"

I try to force myself to stop shaking. I lean up and, before I can talk myself out of it, I hum Clay's song in his ear.

I can only manage a few bars before I choke on a sob, disgusted with myself.

But it's enough. His worry lines smooth out, his face a blank canvas. I swallow. Now's not the time for me to give into my emotions. I place my hands on either side of Clay's face and look directly in his eyes.

"Clay, I need you to do something for me. I wouldn't ask, but it's important."

"Anything," he says, his voice a creepy monotone. It almost throws me, but I stand firm.

"I need you to … " To what? If I tell him not to go to Melusine's, she'll just try this same stunt again tomorrow. " … to go to Melusine's house, but no matter what she does, tell her it's over. Even if she sings to you."

Talking to him when he's like this is like talking to a zombie. I'm so scared he won't understand. "Clay, are you listening?"

"Yes. I'll go to Melusine's house and tell her it's over."

"Even if she sings to you."

"Even if she sings to me."

"As soon as you leave, you should come straight to my house and tell me how it went. Okay?"

"Okay."

I lower my hands and give Clay permission to go when he asks. I watch his retreating back and feel worse with every step he takes. Yesterday, when I sang to Clay, I hadn't planned it or even thought it through—I had just wanted to save him. Sirening him yesterday had been an impulse. This, this was a choice.

I'm still questioning that choice hours later.

"What whirlpool are you spinning in?" Lazuli asks as she moves her carved ivory dolphin forward three spaces and clips it to the board. She's beating me. Everyone is—even Em, who despite her skill in nearly every other area, fails miserably at *Spillu*.

I usually love to play. The board is beautiful, a family heirloom with spaces alternating between mother of pearl and the weathered wood of a sunken pirate ship. It's one of the only pieces in our home that's made from both Mer and human materials, not one or the other. The game requires focusing and thinking a step ahead of your opponent. But tonight, I have an opponent more real than my sisters. And all my thoughts are on Clay, who's with her right now.

"I win!" Amy declares as she clips her onyx sea lion to the winning square. She stands and does a victory dance around the patio. Her stance is wobbly, but she stays upright and everyone applauds.

"Go, Aims! You're gonna be hitting the mosh pit with me any day now," Lapis says.

"I highly doubt that," my mother calls from the pool.

"Dancing is so much more fun now that I have feet," Amy says. My father abandons the shrimp grilling on the barbecue and spins her around the sunken outdoor fireplace.

They laugh, but their merriment sounds muted to me. Distant. Clay still hasn't come. What if it didn't work? The *konklilis* said if a person had been sirened once, humming the song would reinstate the spell ... but what if it wasn't enough? What if Melusine was able to regain control? She could be making him do anything right now.

I have to suppress a shudder. I should have taken him into a classroom or something and sung the whole song, just to be safe. But it was all I could do to get through a few hummed lines. Even doing that to him made me feel dirty. Now, I wish I'd had the nerve to do it all the way. What if my squeamishness is the reason Clay's not safe tonight?

"How 'bout a dance, angelfish?" my father asks, offering his hand.

Before his words register, the security system buzzes. Someone's at the front gate.

I pop up like a flying silver carp. "I'll get it. It's for me. A book. I left a book at Clay's last week and I need it."

My mother hurries to lift herself from the pool. "Aurelia," she says sharply, "you should have mentioned that human boy was coming over. I'm in no state to—"

"He's not coming in. He's just dropping off a book. Promise!" I'm already heading toward the front door.

As soon as I'm outside, I run. The serenity of the warm evening with its light, jasmine-scented breeze is at odds with the anxiety roiling inside me. When I reach Clay, he could be back under Melusine's power. Maybe she sent him here to rub her victory in my face. Maybe she sent him here to hurt me.

I stop in my tracks. The truth sinks in as a stitch blooms painfully in my side. This could be a trap. Clay's stronger than me, much stronger. If Melusine commanded him to strangle me to death, I couldn't do anything to stop him. I picture myself gasping for breath as I die under his squeezing hands. Hands that just yesterday held mine as we strolled together.

The darkness of the long driveway stretches out before me. I'm the one who ordered him to come talk to me. If he is still under my power, he'll wait out here all night if I don't go to him. My legs reach a decision before my brain does, and I run toward the gate again. The gate! That's what I'll do. I'll keep the gate between us. Once I talk to Clay, I'll know if—

But Clay isn't there.

Chapter Twelve

I should have checked the security camera. I'd waited for Clay for hours, and I wanted so badly to know he was okay. So, when I heard the buzz at the gate, I just assumed ... But it's not Clay.

It's Melusine.

For one heart-stopping moment, I'm sure it's her.

Then I get closer. While this girl also has a thin figure and shiny dark hair, she's shorter and younger than Melusine.

"Staskia?" Amy talks about her antics incessantly, but it's been a while since I've actually seen her best friend. Defined cheekbones have replaced the baby fat, but the freckles and bright eyes are the same.

"Hey, Lia! Is Aims around?"

"Sure. C'mon in." I unlock the gate and usher her in, my heart rate returning to normal. I peer behind her into the darkness, hoping for a glimpse of Clay. No one's there.

"Why're you using this entrance?" I ask. Other Mer almost always swim to our house through the underwater tunnels.

"Practice," she answers, lifting one leg a few inches and shaking it. An ankle bracelet jingles there, and several toe-rings decorate her flip-flop clad feet. I went through a toe-ring phase, too. I'd been so excited to have toes that all I'd wanted to do was show them off. "I was hoping Amy and I could take Barnacle out and practice walking."

"She'll love that," I say. "Congrats on your legs, by the way. Amy told me the whole story."

"Thanks! It was only mildly mortifying. You coming?" she asks as she starts up the driveway.

Something rustles near one of the brugmansia trees that line our outside wall.

"You go ahead. I'll be there in a minute."

She walks up the winding path with slow, deliberate steps. Only once she's out of sight do I risk whispering into the darkness. "Clay? Are you there?"

He steps into the pool of light near the gate. The dark shadows under his eyes make him look haggard. "I didn't know if I was supposed to interrupt," he says.

His voice lacks the zombie quality it gets right after he's been sung to, but he sounds so confused that he must still be under the effects of sireny. At least that means he's probably too out of it to wonder about the conversation he may have just overheard. The question is, whose sireny is he under—mine or Melusine's?

I locked the gate after letting Staskia in, and I keep it locked now. I don't want to think that Clay might be here to hurt me, but I have to.

"Clay," I keep my voice calm, "did you go to Mel's?"

"Yes. I just left."

He looks so worn out. All I want to do is reach forward and comfort him. But I can't. Not yet. It might not be safe.

"How do you feel?" Maybe asking him questions about himself will bring him back, like it did yesterday.

"Like my thoughts are … " he concentrates, "muddled." Then he locks eyes with me. "Like I want to touch you." He moves his hand through the bars of the gate and takes mine. I should pull away. What if it's a trap? But I don't. It may just be a spell making him want to touch me, but what if he really needs the physical comfort? He's been through enough—I can't deny him. And I don't want to.

I let him bring my hand to his chest, the bars of the gate pressing against my own. I can feel his heart beating under my palm. Steady. Rhythmic.

"What happened at Mel's?"

"I told her we were over. Then I came here. Wait ... " He looks away, trying to piece together his thoughts. "Why did I come here? You asked me to, right?"

"Yeah. I thought you might need moral support," I say, in case he remembers this conversation later. But he's lost in thought again, trying to make his way through the fog.

"She kept me there for hours. She kept apologizing over and over. She even tried singing me her favorite song. It's strange, I used to love that song. Every time she sang it, I'd think about how perfect she was for me, and how much I loved her. But I don't love her. I don't." His tone is vehement. "This time when she sang, all I could think about ... was you."

It worked. My humming worked. Melusine tried to siren Clay back, and she failed. He came back to *me*.

He takes my hand, still clasped in his, and rests his cheek against it. He looks so tired. I thought that if I could just get Clay through this night, I'd be overjoyed. But I don't feel joyful. I don't feel victorious or powerful or even relieved. All I feel is guilty.

And I'm about to feel worse.

I lean forward, the metal bars cold against my face. If I don't do this, he'll be defenseless soon. "I'm sorry," I whisper. Then, I sing.

She breezes through the halls like nothing's changed. It makes my insides churn.

She can't hurt Clay, she can't hurt Clay, she can't hurt Clay, I repeat to myself like a mantra. In the parking lot first thing this morning, I hummed into Clay's ear the second I saw him to make sure he'd be safe from her.

But I have no idea if *I'm* safe. Violent spells died out long ago, but then again, so did siren songs. As I walk from class to class, a constant sense of foreboding plagues me. I expect her to corner me any second.

By lunch, she still hasn't spoken a word to me—or to Clay. In fact, she seems to be ignoring both of us. I want to find this comforting, like she's acknowledging defeat and giving up. I want to, and I almost do. Then, right after the bell rings, something sends me reeling.

Melusine stands out in the courtyard, the sun shining off her ebony tresses. She lets out a girlish giggle as she strokes the arm of the person next to her. Jake. He's a member of the water polo team, and he's ridiculously attractive. From the way Melusine squeezes his arm muscle over the sleeve of his team jacket, it's clear she thinks so, too.

I nearly collapse under the weight of my own stupidity. How could I be this dumb? I've been so busy worrying about Melusine re-sirening Clay that the obvious possibility never occurred to me. Instead of trying to get Clay back, she can just siren another unsuspecting victim to replace him. And it looks like that victim will be Jake. She takes a step closer to him, molding her body against the side of his, and he smiles, completely oblivious to the danger he's in. Then, she glances over her shoulder, meets my eyes, and winks.

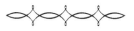

Usually, I look forward to the end of the school day and the freedom it brings. But today, I dread it. Each passing second drags me closer to … How can I do it again? How can I keep defiling Clay's mind this way? This will be the fifth time. The *fifth time* I commit an act so despicable it's been considered a high crime for centuries. I can't go through with this.

But if I don't … It seems like maybe Melusine's moved on to Jake, but what if she's just messing with me so I'll let my guard down and stop singing to Clay? Is she planning to swoop in and siren Clay again the second he's free from my influence? After all, he's the one she chose to keep as her fake, hypnotized boyfriend for weeks on end, not Jake. An image rises in my mind of Melusine sticking her tongue down Clay's throat in front of the lockers. Of the haunted look in his eyes when he tried to explain to me why he was with her and couldn't. Of his determination when he tried to break up with her on the boat. What else was she doing with him? I can't let him go back to that.

That's when I make an oath. I promise myself that I'll siren him again to protect him, but I won't do anything else to take advantage of him. It will just be temporary—until I can find another way to make sure he's safe from Melusine.

"Clay," I whisper, when the time comes and we're half-hidden behind an ivy-covered column in front of the school tennis court, "I won't make you do anything you don't want to do. I promise."

After I sing to him, I tell him to do whatever he'd normally do at home, hoping it will ease my guilt. I'm almost glad that today I'm expected to intern at the Foundation—I can't stand to be near him, knowing I'm the one who's sucked the life from his eyes.

When I arrive at work, my mind still swims with thoughts of Clay and what I've done to him. Some secretary or other is researching in the file room today, so I type information on one *konklili* after another for over an hour until she leaves. The mindless data entry only gives me time to dwell on how much worse everything's become. This morning I thought sirening Clay was my only problem. Now … what can I possibly do to protect

Jake if Melusine does decide to siren him? I might not know him as well as I know Clay, and I might not … feel the same way about him as I do about Clay, but I can't just let him or anyone else be the victim of Melusine's brainwashing. I can't sit by while that happens—it isn't right. But what can I do to stop it? While the shells I've listened to say it's possible for one siren to enchant many humans at the same time, I don't know if I have that kind of power—and I won't risk weakening my protection of Clay. A vein throbs in my temple. Even if I could siren Jake, Mel might just pick someone else. I can't brainwash every boy she shows interest in. She'll turn me into a monster no better than she is.

Clay's expressionless face when I left him this afternoon rises to my mind's eye. If I'm not a monster already …

I jump when the secretary slams the door behind her. Alone at last, I go through title after title, looking for anything that might help me. I can't keep this up. Sirening Clay is wrong. It's sick. I have to find another way to put an end to Melusine's magic, and I have to do it now.

By the time I trudge through the front door, the only thing I have to show for my research is an angry red indentation biting into my ear from listening to so many *konklilis*. I try to do homework, but I can't focus on my English paper … or my lab prep questions … or my problem set for pre-cal. The twins are out at their music lesson, and Amy's over at Staskia's. Em is embroiled in a heated conversation on her cellphone with what must be Leo. It doesn't sound pretty. With none of my sisters here to distract me and my tension tight enough to snap, taking a dip in our hot springs grotto sounds too enticing to pass up. Maybe it will give me some clarity.

I sigh as my body sinks into the satiny pool deep under the house. The heat of the water sends pleasant chills all the way from the top of my head to the tips of my unfurling fins. When I've spent an entire day maintaining my legs, letting my control slip and my tail stretch out is a longed-for release. Allowing water to glide over my tail and between each golden scale is bliss. The pure pleasure of it almost silences the constant stream of fearful thoughts that assaults my brain. Almost.

My eyes fluttered shut at the first touch of the hot water on my thirsty skin. Now, I open them again. Amy insisted we hang twinkle lights down here, and they make the abalone surface of the cave walls sparkle an iridescent silver-blue. It's calming.

The serenity of my surroundings, the rejuvenating water, and the freedom of spreading my fins all combine to soothe my frazzled nerves, and I take deep, relaxing breaths. I won't be able to help Clay or anyone else if I can't think straight. I haven't slept properly in days, so, as the heat claims me and my eyes drift closed again, I let myself doze.

"Hello, sunshine." The voice is syrupy sweet.

My eyes snap back open. Standing above me, one hand on her popped hip, is Melusine. I sit up straighter along the stone edge of the pool, scrambling to regain my awareness. Am I dreaming?

"Your mom let me in. She's so eager for us to be friends."

"She doesn't know you." Doesn't know you're a monster.

"No. You haven't told her much at all, have you?" She affects a pout. "Keeping secrets, Lia? What a bad girl you are."

"W-what are you doing here?" I surreptitiously reach behind me under the water, trying to find a sharp rock I can wiggle loose. She wouldn't try anything with my parents right upstairs, would she?

"Aren't you going to invite me in for a dip? I've had such a trying day." She pauses, but I remain silent. What kind of game is she playing? "I'll invite myself then," she says, and removes her high-heeled Mary Janes. Part of me wonders if she's been using some kind of magic to balance in them on the slippery floor of the grotto.

She removes her skirt without a modicum of modesty and before I can even turn my gaze away, her slender coral tail's in place and she's sliding into the water.

"Ohh," she groans, the sound almost guttural. "This is divine."

"What are you doing here?" I repeat, this time with more force.

She leans her head back and swishes her tail lazily through the water. Back and forth, back and forth ...

Right when I'm about to ask again, she looks at me, and the intensity in her eyes belies her relaxed posture. "I wanted to let you know I'm not mad at you, Lia. For taking Clay. For," she glances around as if double checking that we're alone and whispers, "sirening him away from me." She smiles like we're both in on a secret.

Part of me wants to wipe the smile off her annoyingly symmetrical face and scream that "sirening" isn't the password to some secret clubhouse. But I'm so shocked by her words that all I say is, "You're not?"

"No." She makes the word lilting, soothing. Then she glides toward me through the water, her movements serpentine. She stops with less than a foot between us. "In fact, I have a little proposition for you."

The steam rises from the water and clings in small droplets to her hair and skin. "You watched me talk to Jake earlier. Isn't he delectable? All that water polo sure does a body good. Have you seen his arms?" she asks, and she runs a hand up one of mine before stroking it back down.

I shudder and shrink back, but she doesn't move her hand away. Her manicured nails lightly graze my skin. "Jake's tall and buff and even passably intelligent. And from what I've heard in the girls' locker room, he'd make a very *talented* boyfriend."

This time I knock her hand away. "You can't have Jake. I won't let you."

She lets out a throaty laugh, and the sound echoes off the domed walls of the grotto. "Oh, I don't want Jake."

"You don't?" The heat, so calming when I was alone, is now oppressive, addling my brain.

"Nope." She leans in close again and whispers in my ear: "He'd be the perfect present. For you."

"What?" She can't mean what I think she means.

"I know you sirened Clay practically by accident. That song you sang? He tried to sing it to me a few times. As if I have the patience to sit through his scribblings."

I glare at her. That bitch.

"So," she continues as if she hasn't noticed my reaction, "you only managed to get him under your power because he'd written a song. Not every guy in school spends his time sitting around mooning to music—thank the current—so it's not like you could siren anyone else. But I can." Her lips curl into a devious smile. "I'm offering you a trade. You let Clay go, and I'll siren Jake for you. I'll even put a ribbon around his neck."

"NO!" I don't think I've ever been so disgusted. My head pounds with it. "You're sick."

"Come on, Lia." She keeps her voice nonchalant, but her eyes flame. "Jake's more popular than Clay. He's much more—"

"That's enough! You stay away from both of them, do you hear me? If you try to siren either one of them, I'll go straight to the Foundation and you'll be sent back to the ocean. They'll drop you in a warzone. I don't think you'd like being torn tail from limb by crazed rebels."

"Aww ... what a brave little bluff. Got any more?"

"I'm not bluffing. I'll tell."

"Right," she says, her tone dripping sarcasm. "Even if we pretend that you'd be able to tell on me without revealing your own recent musical proclivities, you'd still have to reveal Clay's identity. And who knows what they'd do to him?" She puts on a mock-fearful expression, her eyes going wide. "Don't think I don't know about your little crush. You'd never put Clay's life at risk by telling on me. It's cute really."

She wraps her tail around mine under the water, a gesture far too intimate, and says in her low, melodic voice, "No one likes a tattletail."

I can't take it anymore. I push her back by the shoulders, her heated skin nearly burning my palms. "Don't touch me."

But she just keeps talking. "You want Jake for that? Bet he feels good. You could be like a normal girl, Lia, with a normal human boyfriend. All you have to do is release Clay back to me and I'll fix everything for you." She tries to keep her voice composed, but a wild, desperate edge sneaks into it.

Wait …

"Why do you want Clay so much? You don't even seem to like him."

"You're such a child." In a blink, Melusine has summoned her legs and is rising out of the steaming water. "Don't worry your pretty little head about it." She shimmies back into her skirt, the fabric hugging her damp legs. Picking up her enviable Mary Janes, she turns back to face me. "Consider my offer, Lia. I'm trying to … I'm not your enemy." For a moment, the sibilance of Mermese creeps into her voice, and she sounds like she's hissing. She must work so hard to conceal her accent. "And trust me— you don't want me to be." With that final threat, she's gone.

Chapter Thirteen

The biggest change is the touching.

The way he takes my hand in his when we walk to class.

The way he drapes his arm across my shoulders—strong and safe—when we sit at our desks or in the library.

The way he pulls my hips a few inches closer to his body when we practice self-defense.

Or now. The way he reaches across the small table and curls a strand of my hair around his finger before tucking it behind my ear.

We're at my favorite sushi place near Paradise Cove. I swore to Clay I wouldn't make him do anything he didn't want to do, and I remember he said sushi is his favorite food. So, I figure if he had the choice, he'd like to come here. *Yeah, but would he come here with you?* a little voice inside me questions. I ignore it.

On the days I go to the Foundation (where my research still hasn't turned up anything), I have to siren Clay at the end of the school day, then call him later in the evening and sing to him again. That way, if Melusine tries anything, he's out of her reach.

But I want Clay to be able to be himself. So, any day I'm not expected at the Foundation, I spend the entire afternoon with him. As long as we're together, it's safe to let the enchantment wear off. Some days, we hang with his friends, so they can see him acting normal. But today, it's just the two of us. As we sip iced green tea and wait for our order—the siren song waning with every passing minute—Clay's almost back to himself.

"So they did this experiment where they tested different frequencies of sound. They made them visible with some type of powder and showed that sound creates these beautiful geometric patterns. It's gotten like, three million views. Pretty awesome."

"Sound has shape?" I ask.

"Yeah, we just can't see it. Imagine all the other incredible stuff in the world we must not know about. Maybe we'd be able to see it if we just knew where to look." He lets his gaze drift out over the ocean view from our table on the restaurant's balcony. "Did you know humans have explored less than five percent of the ocean? Crazy, right?"

"Actually less than one percent if you include the deep ocean instead of just the ocean floor," I correct automatically. Then I look up at him. Is it weird I know that?

His smile widens. "Maybe one day I'll take some scuba lessons. Get out there and explore some of it myself."

"You'd want to do that?" I'm surprised. "I thought you wanted to write songs and symphonies."

"I do. Think about all the songs I'd be inspired to write after deep-sea diving."

It's comforting to hear Clay talking like himself again.

"Of course, the ocean's not as beautiful as you are." Well, almost like himself. Even once the sireny wears off enough that Clay's personality comes back, that part sticks. I guess being enamored with your siren is too essential to the spell to just fizzle.

My face must fall at his words because he says, "What? I thought girls liked guys to tell them how beautiful they are." The waitress hears Clay's words as she sets down our plates and shoots me a dirty, jealous look before disappearing.

"As a general rule we do, but ... "

"But, what? Guys tell you so often that you're sick of hearing it?" His smile is cheeky.

"Trust me, that's not it." The twins—with their bouncing blond curls and their bouncing bikini tops—always have guys fawning all over them, but my love life makes watching a sea slug sound exciting.

"Well, you are. I've always thought so."

Really? Has he really always thought I'm... or is that just the spell talking?

"So, gorgeous, what'll it be? Beach Breeze?" he asks, gesturing to the California roll topped with sweet shrimp that I always order. "Or Too Hot to Handle?" He opens his chopsticks and points them at the spicy tuna concoction he insisted we try. I love tuna as much as the next Mermaid, but the slices of jalapeno stacked high on top of this one have always scared me off.

"Too Hot," I say decisively.

Clay raises an eyebrow in challenge as he loads wasabi on top of it. But I'm not backing down. I cross my arms over my chest and try to look like I couldn't be bothered. What am I getting myself into?

Clay lifts a piece between his chopsticks, dips one corner in soy sauce, then brings it to my lips. I lean over the table, and take a bite.

"What you'll need to remember to ace your lab," my A.P. Bio teacher lectures, "is to carefully consider all your observations."

As we review the carbon cycle for the umpteenth time, I take his advice.

Observation 1: Melusine has left Jake alone.

I've seen him approach her in the hall a few times, but she's ignored him. I'm not sure whether to be grateful she hasn't sirened him or confused as hell about why she hasn't. All those hallway make out sessions made me think maybe Melusine wanted Clay as some kind of boy toy arm candy. But if that were true, she'd just siren Jake. What is she hiding? If I can figure that out, maybe I can find a way to help Clay. One that doesn't involve stripping him of his free will multiple times a day.

Observation 2: Melusine hasn't so much as talked to Clay since her failed attempt to get him back.

This would make sense if she'd moved on to Jake, but she hasn't. As far as I can tell (and I've been watching closely), she hasn't moved on to anyone.

Observation 3: She hasn't talked to me either, but she keeps … watching me.

She's doing it now. Clay's not in bio this period, but Melusine is, and I can feel her gaze on me right this minute, heating up the back of my neck. I look over my shoulder, and our eyes meet across the rows of long, black-topped tables. She smiles at me. She's biding her time. But until when? And for what?

Observation 4: Melusine knows I'm watching her, too.

So, she's not going to do anything in front of me that might reveal a clue to her plan.

Conclusion: I need reinforcements.

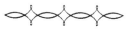

"So, you want me to spy on a seventeen-year-old girl, but you can't tell me why?"

I hesitate. Then nod.

"And you don't know what I'm looking for?"

"Something fishy?" I joke, trying to lighten the mood.

"Ha ha," Caspian says sarcastically. He swims around me in a slow circle, assessing how serious I am.

We've swum out to a cave we discovered as children. When

we were little, we dubbed it Star Cave, because starfish of every color—yellow, purple, pink, orange, red—cover the rocky walls like wallpaper. It's only accessible from underneath, so humans never come here, and it's well within the Border line so it isn't off-limits. Under the waves, the limestone is thick with soft lichen.

Once you break the surface, moonlight streams in through a small crevice in the mountainside. It plays off the walls and water, scattering in a million directions, making magic. The ceiling stretches high enough that both of us can sit comfortably on the rocky platform along one side. I can still stand up if I bend a bit, but Caspian, now a towering 6'3", couldn't if he wanted to. Luckily, with his tail in place, that isn't a problem. We could never outgrow this cave—we've shared too many memories here. One wall still bears the drawings we scrawled as children, clumsy stick figures of humans on their mysterious legs. We'd wanted so much to be older, more grown up.

The day Caspian showed me his legs for the first time, he took me out here to our cave and brought a towel with him. Of course, by the time we got here it was soaked, and I kept asking him about it, but he wouldn't say a word. He hoisted himself up onto the ledge, tied the towel around his waist, and squeezed his eyes shut. His silver scales—so much like my gold ones—transformed into two well-formed legs.

I'd looked on in awe, but even though his legs were so fascinating to me (so much thicker and more masculine with their light dusting of hair than my older sisters' legs), I'd known I mustn't touch them. I still haven't.

My mind flashes to when Clay and I were sitting on the school bus, his hand on my thigh. I can still feel it resting there. But I can't let either memory distract me now. The stakes are too high.

"Look, Caspian. I know I'm being vague. I can't tell you much because I don't want to put you in any danger." That's partly true. I want to protect Caspian. If any of this ever gets out, I won't have Caspian's family's reputation more tarnished by sireny than it already is. But there's another reason I can't tell him that Melusine's a siren. If I did, I'd have to tell him I'm one, too.

And he'd never speak to me again.

Maybe that sounds melodramatic, but it's true. To Caspian, I'd seem no better than Adrianna, who condemned his whole family line to ridicule. And maybe I'm not. If what I'm doing got out, wouldn't my family fall just as far? Maybe even farther, since we're supposed to be the upright, moral figureheads of the Foundation. Of the whole land-dwelling Mer Community. I picture my parents and my sisters disgraced because of my actions. Little Amy, her face stained with the tears of rejection—shunned because of me.

But I can't undo what I've done and I can't stop doing it. Not until I find another way out. That means it's even more important that I figure out what Melusine is plotting as soon as possible. Then I can stop her, release Clay, and put all of this behind me. Hopefully, Caspian will never have to know the whole story. And he'll never have to hate me.

"All I can tell you," I continue, "is that Melusine has access to ancient Mer magic and she'll use it to hurt someone if we don't stop her."

"Do you know who?"

"A human named Clay. Maybe others, too."

"Isn't he her boyfriend?"

"Not anymore."

"Look, Goldfish, I'm always here to help you, but I barely know these people. I know you go to school with them and all, but what does this even have to do with you?"

"I'm responsible for Clay. He's … " What? My friend? My soul mate? My victim? "My boyfriend." Well, what else am I supposed to say?

He opens his mouth then closes it again. Then he opens it and says, "Oh." He leans back against the wall, crossing his arms over his chest. "I didn't realize you were dating anyone."

"It's sort of a new development."

"Lia, I'm not judging, but ... a human? I know the twins mess around with them, but actually dating one? If your parents found out they'd—"

"Murder me? Yeah, I'm aware. That's why they can't know." I level my gaze at him. His eyes, shockingly blue even in the dim light, narrow for a fraction of a second. Then he nods once. He won't tell them.

"Are you being safe?" he asks.

"Caspian! Clay and I are so not there yet." He raises one eyebrow at me. "Oh! You mean with my tail ... Yeah, my control's good, and I'm being really careful. He has no idea I'm a Mermaid."

I thought this would appease Caspian, but he still looks like he sucked on something sour and is trying to hide it.

"He won't find out about Merfolk from me," I say. "But if you don't help me, he very well may find out from Melusine. I've been thinking, it's common knowledge that her family has been *udell* for generations. Maybe she and her father aren't as pro-Emergence as they claim. Maybe they're secretly *udell*, too. Maybe they came up here because they're plotting something."

"I don't judge people by their family's reputations."

I rest my hand on his tan forearm. "I'm not, believe me. But she's done something ... awful. Worse than awful."

"But you won't tell me what?"

"I can't. Only that if we don't stop her, she might do something worse. Something that would put all of us at risk."

"It's that serious?" he asks, his voice back to its usual measured tones.

"I think so, yes."

"And you can't tell the Foundation?"

I shake my head.

"If I started investigating her, I'd have to meet up with you a couple times a week to fill you in." He pushes his wet, dirty blond hair back from his forehead. "Your new boyfriend wouldn't mind that?"

"No boyfriend could ever stop me from spending time with you, Casp." I look up at him, my eyes imploring. "Please? I really need you on this one."

Caspian's quiet for a long time. To a stranger, he might look like he's stopped listening, like he's tuning out the world. But I know better than to disturb him. Caspian always gets like this before he makes a decision—quiet, reflective. That's why when he makes a choice, I can trust it's the right one. Finally, he says, "Got a plan?"

Chapter Fourteen

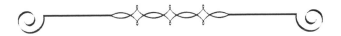

"Dinner's delicious, Mr. Nautilus," Caspian says, adding another swordfish steak to his plate.

"Well, Em helped tonight," my father says smiling.

"Leo's one lucky Mer," Caspian says.

"Don't I know it," Leomaris agrees, giving Emeraldine's hand an affectionate squeeze.

My parents insisted it had been too long since my sister's boyfriend had come over for dinner. So now, Leo sits across from me, his Burberry blazer the same latte brown as his hair. The twins took Amy on her first trip to the mall, so it's just my parents, Em and Leo, and me and Caspian at the dining room table. Leo looks at Em like he's just as crazy about her as ever. It gives me hope that they can work it out.

Emeraldine thanks Caspian for the compliment and squeezes Leo's hand right back.

"It's impressive you're already so good in the *qokkiis*, Em," Caspian says, using the Mermese word for kitchen. "Neither one of my parents learned until after they got married."

At the mention of marriage, both Em and Leo's expressions turn dark, and they cast their eyes down at their plates. I guess they still haven't figured everything out.

Caspian looks at me apologetically and whispers, "I thought everything was back to normal."

"I can't believe it's not," I whisper back.

"I'm so glad you could join us," my mother says to Caspian, rescuing the conversation.

"Me, too. Actually," Caspian's eyes meet mine for an instant before shifting back, "there's something I wanted to speak to you both about. I know Lia's been interning at the Foundation, and I was wondering if you would help me get an internship of my own."

A warm smile spreads across my dad's face, and my mom's eyes soften. "Of course, Caspian," my dad says.

"It would be our pleasure," my mom adds. "The linguistics department, right? I'll just make a call on Monday and set up a meeting for you. With your language skills, it shouldn't be—"

"Well, no." Caspian clears his throat. "Thank you, but no. I was thinking I'd like to help with some field work in … ingredients collection."

Both my parents lose their smiles. Leo and Em share an apprehensive look. Ingredients collection is a lowly job. The only one the Community members would agree to give Mr. Havelock because of his family's politics. I heard my parents talking about how it was a shame no one trusted him to be a medic, like he was Below.

If ingredients collection didn't require potions expertise, it would be considered menial labor. But that isn't my parents' main objection to Caspian's newfound interest.

"It's too dangerous," my father says. "Covert dives into rebel-occupied zones of the ocean … " He shakes his head. "It's one of the reasons we don't use many potions on land."

"We could never let a minor go out into the open ocean," my mother says. "Not only would your parents never forgive us, but it's against our laws for you to cross the Border. You know that."

We do know that. Both Caspian and I are counting on this rule to keep him out of as much danger as possible—and get him as much alone time in Melusine's house as we can. Still, Caspian pretends to be disappointed. "Couldn't I still help with researching ingredients or something? I got to know Melusine at your party." That's stretching the truth if I've ever heard it. "And I know Melusine and Lia are good friends." Never mind, that is. "I was hoping that Mr. Havelock would agree to mentor me."

"But, Caspian," I say, just like we practiced, "you've always wanted to go into linguistics. You're so good with languages— your Mermese is perfect. And you're such a good speaker." He can be shy, but he's tactful, thoughtful, diplomatic. "I thought you dreamt of negotiating peace treaties Below one day."

"Yes, Caspian," my mother agrees. "You'd be such an asset."

"That is what I always thought I'd do, but recently, I've become much more interested in potions ingredients," he says, justifying his request so my parents won't be suspicious. "I want to learn more about where they grow, how to harvest them. You know, my grandmother did a lot of growing when she lived Below, and she knows so much about so many potions and their components. She won't live forever, like she should, and—" His voice catches, as if he can't contain his sadness. I'm impressed by how convincing it sounds. "I don't want all the expertise in our family to die with her."

The corners of my father's mouth turn down in sympathy, and my mother reaches across the table to pat Caspian's hand. Who would have thought honest, noble Caspian would be so good at manipulating people? I have to stifle the urge to applaud. This is going to work, it's really going to work.

"Caspian, that's an admirable goal." Uh-oh. Too much resolve colors my mother's voice. "But, your grandmother would be just as proud of you if you followed your own current. Why don't you let me organize an internship for you in the linguistics department at the Foundation? I can arrange for you to work under the tutelage of Ervin Zung."

I have to stop myself from gaping. That's such a good opportunity; my mom's practically bribing Caspian to forget about ingredients collection. If she weren't about to ruin everything, I'd be touched that she cares about him so much. I study Caspian's face. What if he decides to take it? An internship that high up in linguistics would be Caspian's dream job. I bet that's a lot more promising than putting himself at risk to help me.

It's selfish of me to want Caspian to refuse the opportunity. Maybe I'm a bad friend. In the long pause that follows, an almost imperceptible tick pulses in Caspian's jaw. If he takes the linguistics job, how will I ever figure out what Melusine is up to? She'd be too wary of one of my sisters, and there's no one else who'd do it for me. No one else I'd trust enough to ask.

"I don't know what to say," he murmurs. "*Tallimymee*." That's the most respectful phrase for thank you in Mermese.

No, no. Please don't take it. Please don't take it.

"That's a more generous offer than I ever expected," he continues. My parents look hopeful. I try not to look panicked. "But I'm afraid I'm set on potions collection."

I let out a breath and try to look concerned instead of relieved. Inside, I'm rejoicing.

Once several more attempts at convincing him fail, my parents realize they won't change Caspian's mind. After that, it doesn't take them long to agree to arrange an internship with Mr. Havelock. They stipulate that Caspian won't be going into the water or even working with real ingredients. He'll be limited to research. That's exactly what we were hoping for.

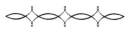

"It's never going to work."

"Why not?" I ask, concern evident in my voice.

"Because your hand is too high." Clay wraps his fingers around my wrist and moves my hand down so it rests on his hip bone. "That's better," he says. It's been over an hour since I last sang to him, so the playfulness is back in his tone.

Shifting my weight, I try the throw again and push Clay off me like I'm supposed to.

"Nice improvement," Coach Crane says, marking something in her grade book. Was she talking to me? "Now try hold number four," she instructs as she heads to where Kelsey struggles to throw Matt off her.

Clay moves into position and wraps his arms around me from behind. My back presses against his chest. "So this is what it takes to get you close to me. Good to know," he whispers in my ear, his voice low, husky.

I bite my lip. I tell myself it's just the spell making him say it, but it feels so good to have his body pressed against mine, his arms holding me. To know, at least on some level, he wants me close to him.

"What are you doing to that boy, Lia?"

"What?" I'm so startled, I nearly bang my head on the door of my gym locker.

"Clay is totally under your spell," Jaclyn says from over by her own locker.

"No, he's not!" I say instinctively. Then I tell myself to breathe. It's a figure of speech. They couldn't know.

"Oh, he so is," Genevieve insists, snapping her gum. Well, she's changed her tune since our last conversation.

"We've seen the way he looks at you," Jaclyn says.

"So, you and Clay … are you officially official now or what?" Genevieve asks.

"You bet they are," Kelsey says as she emerges from one of the showers wrapped in a polka dot towel. "He's so into her."

"Already?" Jaclyn jokes. She and Genevieve erupt into giggles.

"I'm glad he's with you now," Genevieve says as her laughter subsides. "That new girl Mel's a total biatch. So undeserving of his hotness."

She slips her P.E. t-shirt over her head and reaches into her locker for a Ralph Lauren polo. Her bra is the prettiest one I've ever seen. Cream silk with a lace overlay and a delicate bow right between the pillows of her breasts. She notices me noticing. "You like?" she asks, adjusting its cups slightly. "Ryan came in the dressing room with me while I was trying it on." Ryan has been Genevieve's boyfriend for the last few months. They're kind of the school's power couple. Jaclyn and her boyfriend Nick, who's a senior and vice president of the student body, are a close second.

"We had to sneak him past the salesgirl," Genevieve continues. "Of course, he paid for this one," she indicates the bra, "aaand a bunch of other goodies."

"He's the one who'll be enjoying them. Am I right?" Jaclyn says. We all laugh. It feels good to let myself laugh with them.

Then Jaclyn says, "My boyfriend isn't big on bras. He likes me best in nothing but bikini cut panties." I blush. Isn't this kind of TMI?

"My boyfriend likes thongs. He says anything bigger's a grandma panty." Genevieve turns to me. "What about you, Lia? What does your boyfriend like?"

"My boyfriend?" The word still feels strange in my mouth. Boyfriend. Strange and wonderful. "My boyfriend likes me in boyshorts. Low-rise boyshorts." I have no idea if that's true, but it's so fun to say. Besides, Clay seems like a boyshorts kind of guy.

"When am *I* gonna have a boyfriend?" Kelsey asks, sinking onto the bench that runs between the gym lockers.

"When you man-up and kiss Matt," I say. I've never given her dating advice before.

"You really think I should?" She's looking at me like I'm an authority on the topic. I nod.

Genevieve shuts her locker. "Ryan says even when Clay's not talking about you, it's *très* obvious he's thinking about you. Whatever you're doing to the guy, it's working. See you around, Lia. Text me if you wanna hang."

I don't even have her number. But all I say is, "O-okay."

"Perf!" Jaclyn says. It's like I've been accepted into the girlfriends club. They both give me girly single-finger waves as they exit the locker room. I wave my finger right back.

Later, I replay the conversation as I float on an inflatable lounger in our pool. The tips of my fins dip over the edge and into the water, my tail soaking up the last rays of sun.

When Genevieve and Jaclyn see the way Clay looks at me, they assume his feelings for me are real. What would it be like if they were? What would it be like if he really were my boyfriend? I allow myself to relish the sweet fantasy of it as I skim my fingertips across the glimmering water. *Where is he right now? I wonder. What's he doing right this minute?*

Suddenly, I feel … a tug. The sensation isn't in my stomach exactly, but deeper—in my center. It's a light tug, but it's startling in its unexpectedness.

When I was just a guppy and I'd go out into the ocean with my sisters, Em was entrusted with my safety. Still just a child herself, she'd been terrified I'd swim off on my own. More than once, I tried to follow the call of the ocean straight into the intrepid waters past the Border. Always the problem-solver, Em took a seaweed rope and tied one end around her waist and the other around mine. No matter where she'd swim or where I'd swim, we were connected and were always tugged back toward each other.

Now, the tug at my center feels like the tug of that long-ago seaweed rope. But I know that waiting on the other side for me isn't Em. I know, without knowing how I know, that if I tugged back on that rope, I could pull Clay to me. Compel him to stop whatever he's doing and come to me.

I close my eyes and focus on the sensation. The roar of waves assaults my ears.

I open my eyes and look at the ocean stretched out below the hillside, but the water is as calm as it was before, rippling softly in the twilight breeze. The roaring in my ears has stopped just as quickly as it started. Suspicion seeping into my bones, I close my eyes again and focus on the tug. The roaring assaults me full force. There's a voice behind it—a mesmerizing, compelling call. My eyes fly open again.

Last year, when I first started at Malibu Hills, I caught a human strain of the flu. It was essential that I stay warm and dry, so my parents bundled me up in my upstairs bedroom. I wasn't allowed in the ocean for a week. By the fifth day, the call of the ocean was so strong that my every thought was consumed with swimming out as far as my fins could take me. By the seventh day, my family members had to take turns supervising me so I didn't escape into the waves. By the time I was well enough to resume my daily swims, the call had been deafening.

Now, it's louder. I have no doubt the roaring sound I heard when I closed my eyes was the call of the ocean, but it was stronger, deeper than ever before. Only one explanation makes sense: This is the call used by the siren spell. My siren spell. Bracing myself, I close my eyes a third time. The roaring waves, interlaced with their tempting whispers, return. I force myself to focus, to reach into them and latch onto that tugging rope. Following the rope with my mind, I sense safety and warmth before an image of Clay blossoms behind my eyes. He's sitting in front of the fireplace in his living room, reading a book. I innately know he's not in any danger, just as I know he's alone, he's comfortable, and his book is about music theory. He shifts his feet underneath him as he turns a page.

Shocked by how real the image is, I lose focus and the roaring fills my ears again as my consciousness crashes back into my own body, my own skull. I wrench my eyes open, panting. At some point, without even noticing, I splashed from my lounger into the salt water of the pool. But it isn't enough. With the call of the ocean ringing in my ears, my skin itches for the sea.

It takes all my control to wait out the rest of the sunset. I need to get in the ocean. Now.

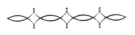

"Relax, Lia," Caspian says, from where he wades near the opening of our cave. *"Just because I haven't found anything yet, doesn't mean I won't."*

"But you've been inside her house. Three times!"

"In Mermese, please," Caspian reminds me. He doesn't sound condescending, just insistent. I grumble. I'm sitting on the cave's rocky platform and both our heads are above water, so we don't need to use Mermese. But since I don't go to Mer school like he does and my parents don't make my sisters and I use Mermese around the house, Caspian insists I practice sometimes when we're together to keep my language skills sharp. I can't fault him for it; it's for my benefit. He certainly doesn't need the practice. Still, English is so much easier.

At the determined glint in his azure eyes, I relent. *"But you've been inside her house. Thrice!"* He nods approvingly at my formal, academic wording.

"And you what? Expected that I'd instantly find evidence that Melusine and her father are udell?"

When he puts it like that, I sound stupidly optimistic. Maybe I let my hope run away with me, but I thought that as soon as Caspian got into the Havelocks' home and had some alone time to poke around, he'd at least find a few dark artifacts or contraband *konklilis*. Something …

"Where have you looked thus far?"

"I've been all throughout the public rooms of their grottos, and I've been spending most of my time doing research and filing in Mr. Havelock's office."

"And there's nothing in his office?" There must be. I don't trust that oil spill of a man.

"Just way more than I ever wanted to know about some of the ocean's most disgusting potion ingredients. If I told you what was in the tonic for children's scale spots ... " He shudders.

"What? I took that a few times as a kid." I hold up my hand. *"On second thought, don't tell me."* I slide off the platform and into the water, hoping it will soothe my anxiety. Not only am I worried about the Havelocks, but—despite the three hours I spent in the ocean last night—I'm still worked up from tapping into the siren bond. My need for the ocean feels deeper than ever. Submerging myself in the waves helps dampen the call so I can focus on our conversation.

"Where else is there to look?" I ask.

"Mr. Havelock hasn't left me unsupervised yet, so I haven't been able to wander around. I haven't been to the aboveground levels at all, but I doubt anything's up there. The two of them seem to go up into the human part of their house even less than my family does."

That's not suspicious by itself. Sure, it fits with *udell* behavior, but it could also describe any Mer family that just got to our Community and is still adjusting to life Above.

"My bet," Caspian continues, *"is that if they are hiding something, it's in the sleeping chamber caves. Those are at the very back of the grottos where the private rooms are. I haven't had a chance to go back there."* He swims closer to me, levels me with a serious gaze. "Hey, Lia?" He switches back to English. It's a gesture of goodwill; he doesn't want his next words to offend me. "Before I invade this family's privacy, just tell me you're sure about this."

"I'm sure."

"Then your wish is my command," he jokes.

"Don't say that."

I try not to think of them as commands. When I tell Clay to avoid Melusine, to go straight home after school, to say whatever he'd normally say in his classes and around his friends. I try to think of these as ways to protect him, to keep his life as safe and normal as possible. He follows these instructions happily and never thinks to question me. Well, almost never.

"Why don't you want me to kiss you?" Clay's face is so open, so vulnerable. I'm not sure if he'll remember this conversation, but I don't want to hurt him either way.

"I do want you to," I answer, and it's the truth, "but—"

"Then why do you always pull away or turn your head? Do you want me to leave you alone?"

"No. I just ... I want to kiss *you*."

"Huh?" His thoughts are already all mixed up, and I'm just making things worse.

"Never mind. Let's go to the pier."

At the Santa Monica pier, I can distract him with funnel cake and shooting games and oversized stuffed animals. When we ride the Ferris wheel, my head resting on his shoulder, I can distract myself into almost believing it's real.

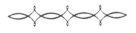

"Once she'd achieved fame throughout Denmark for her voice, Astrid Ostergard was invited to court to sing for the royal family," Clay says, pointing to the opera singer on our display board. "Once she moved into the palace, she was reported to have numerous affairs, which must have been true because by the time she left court, she'd given birth to a son and I couldn't find any record of his father. So," Clay says, crossing his arms across his chest and raising one cocky eyebrow, "we can conclude I'm destined for musical greatness and sexual debauchery."

The class chuckles.

"Okay, Mr. Ericson," Mr. Reitzel admonishes lightly. "Let's not digress." Even he sounds amused.

I jump in and discuss the (largely edited) details about my

ancestry, careful to make them sound more like a family tree and less like a family coral reef.

"And so, Clay and I discovered that we both have some family from Denmark who immigrated to the United States before World War I," I finish.

"Yep," Clay says. "Who knew we'd have so much in common?" He winks at me, and I hope I'm not blushing in front of the entire class.

"I did!" Kelsey shouts from her seat. Everyone laughs but Melusine. Her glare is downright dangerous.

"All right, you two, excellent work," Mr. Reitzel says. "Next up, Laurie and Mel."

I'm quick to return to my seat. I've been looking forward to Melusine's report for the last few weeks. Maybe, just maybe, it will reveal something useful.

Laurie begins the report and, in her usual exuberance, talks so fast that Mr. Reitzel has to remind her to slow down twice. She tells us the entire story of her family's immigration from Ireland in five minutes flat. At least I don't have to wait long to hear from Melusine.

"My family immigrated here, too," she says. Is it only by comparison that she seems to be speaking so slowly? Her voice seeps out like thick honey. "From … an area near the coast of France. I come from a long line of … seamen."

A few of the boys snicker, and one of the water polo players shouts, "I bet you do."

She pins him with a look so icy, it silences him faster than any threat of detention ever could.

"As I was saying," she continues as if she'd merely paused to pinch a bothersome flea between her fingernails, "you could say my ancestors hardly ever stepped foot on land." She laughs, the sound tinkling around the room. "Sadly, war drove my family from their home, first toward America and eventually right here. Until this year, I'd never been among any … Californians."

"When you say war, you mean World War II? That's what

drove your family out of France?" Mr. Reitzel asks.

"Sure," she replies with an indulgent smile. I guess people hear what they expect to hear.

Laurie chirps up again, and the two of them spend the rest of their report discussing Ellis Island. Melusine doesn't actually say her family was there, but no one else notices. It never occurred to me to be that honest in my presentation. It's so ingrained in me to hide all the Mer parts of myself; I never considered another alternative.

Still, Melusine's transparency hasn't helped me get any closer to useful information. I should have known she'd be too smart to let anything slip. Evil? Yes. *Udell?* Probably. Stupid? No. My stress creeps into the muscles of my neck and shoulders, tightening them with tension.

The thought has barely swum to the surface of my mind when Clay's hand reaches up behind the back of my chair and messages my neck in slow, deliberate circles. My tension dissipates under his talented fingers. Is it the siren bond informing him of my desires, or is it just him? Either way, his touch sends electricity tingling down my spine. My whole body hums with it.

I can still feel it hours later when I'm out with the twins. I've bailed on hanging with them after school a lot lately, and I really miss talking to them. Sure, their antics can sometimes be eye-roll worthy, but if anyone knows about guys, it's them. Plus, spending time with the twins means giving myself some much-needed space from Clay's hands. His warm, strong, wandering hands …

"Have you ever … " I pick up a bar of soap from a nearby shelf and smell it, an excuse to collect my thoughts. It smells like peppermint and cake batter. Lazuli's taken us to a specialty shop that sells bath products handmade to look and smell like desserts. "I mean I know you've … "

"You know we've what?" Lazuli asks, opening a tester of shampoo and holding it under my nose. Caramel apple. Not exactly what I want my hair to smell like.

"This place is like a brothel dipped in bubble gum," Lapis says, cringing as she sniffs a bottle of strawberry frosting face wash.

"Hey, I endured that vintage record store you dragged me to last week. Besides, where else could I buy this many chocolates without adding to my waistline?" Lazuli asks, brandishing a pink and black box of two dozen small soaps, each carved to look like a decadent chocolate truffle. "Nothing's worse than a Mermaid with a muffin top. Now, stop complaining. Lia was trying to ask us something."

"Never mind. What do you think of this one?" I ask, holding up the peppermint soap.

Lapis tilts her head, staring at me. "Oh no you don't. Don't go changing the subject. You have boy face."

"She does!" Lazuli squeals. "She has boy face." She turns to me. "You have boy face."

"No I don't," I insist.

I'm met with two identical looks of skepticism. Despite their drastically different interests, the twins are sometimes scarily alike.

"I was just wondering ... I mean, I know you've hooked up with a bunch of guys from school ... "

"Very true," Lazuli says. "But we haven't tapped anyone younger than us, so the junior class is all yours."

"In case you're worried about sloppy seconds," Lapis finishes.

"Ew. No. What I mean is, have you ever thought about," I look around, checking that no one can hear me in the nearly empty store and lower my voice, just in case, "actually dating a human? Like getting serious?"

The teasing looks vanish. The twins glance at each other, communicating silently like they have since they were toddlers. Then Lapis puts a hand on my shoulder and steers me to an overly-stuffed chintz couch in a secluded back corner of the shop. As she and Lazuli sit down with me, I wish I'd kept my mouth shut.

"It's that guy you're doing your project with, isn't it?" Lapis asks.

"Clay." Lazuli says. "Clay Ericson, right?" The look she gives me is understanding, but grim. "We've heard rumors about the two of you around school, but we figured you were just messing around—finally."

"We didn't think you'd ever consider anything serious," Lapis says. I can hear the part she doesn't say: *We didn't think you'd ever be that stupid.*

I can't bring myself to admit they're right. This conversation is painful enough without having to talk about Clay. Besides, what would I say?

"No, it's not about Clay. It's … hypothetical," The lie sounds lame even to my own ears. Great. Now they'll really rub it in.

But the twins don't call me on it. Don't taunt me. In fact, when Lazuli speaks, her voice is comforting. "I've never *hypothetically*," she emphasizes the word, "thought about getting serious with a human guy."

"Me either," Lapis says. "No matter how tempting a mortal guy might be, he's just not worth it."

"But what if he's—"

She cuts me off, "He's not worth it."

"Lia," Lazuli says, putting her hand on mine, "you know you'd never be able to tell the truth, never be able to be yourself."

It's the advice I would have given myself before all this happened. But now, after everything I've been through with Clay, after feeling what it might be like to be with him … I want to know—no, I need to know—that if I get us to the other side of this, if I stop Melusine and find a way to free him, and if by some miracle he can forgive what I've done and feel something real for me, then I need to know that there's hope for us. Some hope that we can be together.

"And not to sound momish or anything," Lapis adds, "but there's a reason we don't choose mortals for mates." Her voice is forbidding when she says, "You don't want a seal, do you?"

These words hit me like a splash of icy, Arctic water. "No," I whisper. Seal is a slang word. It means a baby born from a Mer-human union. A seal looks just like a human baby and can't survive living underwater, but it has an innate affinity for the sea. It hears a muted version of the call of the ocean and can never be satisfied with life on land. As far as anyone knows, none have existed for hundreds of years, but stories from before the curse tell about Mer who lived for eternity with broken hearts after being forced to abandon their children to the human world. Seals are a major reason Mer-human romances are so deeply frowned upon, are taboo; they are creatures who belong to neither world and can never be happy.

I can never have a life with Clay. I have to find a way to free him—then I have to let him go.

Lapis and Lazuli must see their words have sunk in. They don't belabor the point the way Em would. I'm grateful for this because I don't think I can bear to hear the words again.

All Lazuli says is, "You okay?" I nod. I don't trust myself to speak.

Lapis squeezes my shoulder. We all get up and head back to the main area of the store.

"You know, Lia," Lazuli says, the smile back in her voice, "you're way too young and hot to be worrying about choosing mates. If you like … someone hypothetical," (I'm glad she didn't say his name. I don't think I could stand hearing it right now), "then you should just have fun with him."

"Definitely," Lapis says. "That hypothetical guy of yours sure has one grabbable ass." She and Lazuli laugh. "Enjoy that boy while you can, that's my advice."

On the way to the register to pay for Lazuli's box of chocolate soaps, we pass the baked goods inspired items. From among the cookie-dough lip gloss and devil's food bubble bath, I pick up a simple bar of cream-colored soap with little brown flecks. I lift it to my nose and inhale the sweet, familiar scent of cinnamon. This one I don't put back.

That night, I use it in the shower. Later, when I lie in my sponge bed under my blanket of salt water, I zero in on that rope connecting Clay and me. Tapping into that part of myself will make the call of the ocean almost unbearable, but I can stand it if it means knowing Clay is safe in his bed. Knowing he's warm and content. I rest my head on my arm, and my skin smells like cinnamon. I fall asleep with the scent and the feel of Clay swirling around me.

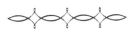

"If you won't let me kiss you, can I at least hold you?"

"Um ... I don't think that's a good idea." No matter what the twins say, I can't let myself enjoy my time with Clay. They don't know the whole story. They don't know that Clay isn't my boyfriend by choice.

"I can't stop thinking about how much I want to touch you," he says, sounding so sincere.

My cheeks burn. My pulse skyrockets.

We're lying in the grass in Clay's backyard. He's tried to kiss me three times today. That's up from yesterday. My hold on him must be getting stronger.

Every day, I tell him no. Every day, it gets harder to refuse him.

Today, at this moment, with Clay spread out on the grass, his shirt off so he can fully relish the sunshine, it's nearly impossible.

I came over on the pretext of doing homework, so now I sit up and try to refocus my attention on my history textbook. But my gaze keeps sliding to Clay's bare chest, to the line where the dark denim of his jeans meets the skin of his cut abdomen.

"You know you want to." His voice is teasing. "I don't get why you keep saying no."

I tear my eyes away from the tantalizing expanse of skin and meet his eyes. "One day you will."

"Fine," he says and stands up. "We'll study." I breathe a sigh of … relief? Disappointment? But then, instead of getting his textbook, he sits right behind me, one leg on either side of my body, and reads over my shoulder.

He rests his chin at the base of my neck, and his stubble tickles the soft skin there. It's an entirely new sensation. New, but not at all unpleasant.

My tank top is low-cut in back, and I can feel the sun-warmed skin of his chest against my nearly bare shoulder blades. My breath hitches.

When I don't move away, he tentatively wraps his arms around me. I don't shrug them off. They feel too much like they belong there. Like they've been missing for years. There can't be any harm in relaxing back into his strong embrace, in letting all my worries fall away for a few minutes, can there?

We sit like that, bodies fitted together, in a sun-drenched moment of bliss. The scent of fresh-mowed grass and of azaleas and of Clay's skin creates a heady combination that has me closing my eyes so I can take it all in. So I can capture this living daydream in my memory. After—when all this ends—I want this moment crystallized for keeps.

Clay raises his chin and replaces it with his lips. A slow kiss covers my shoulder, his lips firm and cool against my heated skin.

"Mmm … sun-kissed," he says.

"Clay-kissed," I murmur.

He plants a trail of kisses across my shoulder, toward my throat. As soon as his lips make contact with my neck, a shudder runs through me and I want to grab him to me and hold him there forever. Somewhere in the back of my mind, I know I should stop this. I know this isn't real. But it feels so real.

"This is what I wanted," Clay says against my skin. "To touch you. To taste you."

His words melt into the air and caress me alongside his lips.

"Lia, you're all I've … " He falls silent. Then pulls his head back, his arms loosening, "What … what was I saying?"

I keep my eyes closed—squeeze them shut—willing time to freeze. Clinging to a feeling that's already slipping away.

"Lia, what were we talking about?"

I work hard to keep the quaver out of my voice when I say, "I guess we both zoned out for a minute there. Don't worry about it."

I stay still as a stonefish. Clay's body remains molded to mine, and I wait to find out what he'll do. Some days, once the claws of the siren spell retract their grip, Clay continues to hold my hand or stroke my cheek. The persistence of these small touches after the spell wears off makes me hopeful that his feelings are real. I hold my breath. Are they real now?

The moment stretches into eternity, and Clay keeps holding me. My heart swells with relief as his arms stay wrapped around me. He wants to hold me. Wants to touch me. I'm enough. Even without the spell he wants—

When he peels his skin away from mine a mere millisecond later, something shatters inside me.

He scoots backward in the grass and twists his body away from mine. I feel the loss of him in every part of myself.

"What were we doing?" he asks, bringing a hand to his forehead in confusion.

I gesture toward the textbook. "Studying." My voice sounds dead.

"Oh." He looks down at his own shirtlessness but doesn't ask. He just picks his t-shirt up from where—only half an hour ago—he threw it eagerly onto the floor of the nearby gazebo.

As he slips the soft cotton over his head and tugs it down over his stomach, I can't force my eyes away, even though I should. Two minutes ago, he was mine to look at, mine to touch. Now … now I'm an intruder.

When he glances up, I lock eyes with him and beg him without words to remember how he felt before. To feel that way now. He looks down at the crushed grass.

I stand and take a step toward him, but he backs away. I stop walking, stop breathing.

"Lia, I'd really," he runs a hand through his mussed dark hair, "like some time alone."

"Oh." There's more to say. There must be. But I don't know what it is.

"I feel like you're always here, even when you're not. Like you're inside my head." He still sounds disoriented, but his voice gains clarity with every stinging word. "I just need some space."

"Of course." Of course he doesn't really want to hold me. He doesn't even want to spend time with me. It was ludicrous to think he might. "I'll leave right now."

"Sorry," he says. "I don't want to be rude. I just feel like I really need time to myself. Does that make sense?"

"Yeah," I say, stuffing my book into my backpack, "it makes perfect sense."

Now that I'm ready to go, I stand there in silence. I've forced myself into his life. I've stolen his freedom, and I need to give it back.

But I can't. It isn't safe. Not with her out there, waiting. I open my mouth and hate myself:

"Come, come, come to me
Let's explore eternity.
Come, come, come to me
I want you irrevocably.
Come, come, come to me
And promise that you'll stay."

My voice comes out strangled with unshed tears, but it doesn't make my magic any less potent. Any less dangerous. The worry vanishes from his eyes, iced over by rapture that isn't real. He moves toward me, the tide pulled to the moon.

Clay wraps his warm, toned arms around me for the second time in the past hour, holds me tight against him, and kisses my hair.

I let myself breathe in the grass-stained, sun-soaked, cinnamon scent of him before I extricate myself from his embrace and pull away. I can't give Clay his freedom, but at least I can give him freedom from me. Freedom from my unwanted presence.

I put a few feet of space between us. Space Clay asked me for.

He starts to step forward, but I put up a hand to stop him.

"Can I hold you?" he asks.

"No. Spend some time tonight on yourself." I want to protect Clay, not consume him. "Try not to think about me or about what I want. Try to think about what *you* want."

He tilts his head as if my words are unfathomable. "But all I want is you."

I leave him standing there, alone in the middle of his backyard. Once I'm out of sight, a tear slides down my cheek, a single pearl of sadness.

Chapter Fifteen

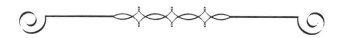

"*H*ow's *it going, Goldfish?*" Caspian calls out. He's waiting outside the underwater entrance to his school, where he asked me to meet him since it's on my way home from the Foundation through the grottos.

Seeing Caspian at the end of a long day is usually all it takes to make me happy. But I can't bring myself to feel that way today. I haven't been happy since I left Clay's yesterday afternoon, and I feel like I may never be happy again. Like I have no right to be. Still, I shouldn't inflict my mood on Caspian.

I make myself smile. "*Well, genius, didn't you say you had an exam in Mer history today? How'd it go? Another perfect score for Mr. Zayle?*"

His face lights up. "*Well, there were one or two tough questions,*" he says. I roll my eyes at his modesty and poke him in the ribs. His laughter makes my plastered-on smile feel even more fake.

"*So, did you just ask me to meet you here on my way home so you could brag?*" I swat playfully at his side with my tail as I swim away from the entrance.

He puts a hand on the small of my back and guides me down a deserted side waterway. *"I asked you to meet me here so I could tell you that Mr. Havelock left me alone while he was on a dive yesterday. Melusine was out, too, and I spent four hours searching their entire house—the upstairs and the private grottos."*

"And?" In Mermese, the word comes out a harsh, insistent hiss.

"And ... Lia, I think you're wrong." My face must fall the same way my stomach does because Caspian rushes to reassure me, *"At least about Mr. Havelock. Maybe Melusine is planning something. I don't want to argue with you about it."* Of course he doesn't. When we'd race as kids, he'd let me win just so I wouldn't get upset.

"All I'll say is," he continues, *"I didn't find anything strange in either of her rooms or anywhere else. But if she is up to some scheme, I'd bet my last sand dollar her father's not in on it."*

"Casp, just because you're trustworthy doesn't mean other people are."

"Lia, I'm telling you, Mr. Havelock is ... cool." Cool is one of those words that doesn't really translate into Mermese, so Mer our age use Mermese sounds to approximate it. It comes out sounding similar to the English word but more melodic. I'm surprised to hear Caspian use it, though. He's such a purist when it comes to languages.

"He's gone out of his way to be nice to me," Caspian says. *"He even sat me down and explained all the reasons he thinks ingredients collecting wouldn't be a good use of my potential."*

"I'm sure my parents put him up to that," I counter.

"It's thoughtful of him regardless. It can't be easy to confess to someone you barely know that your own job isn't good enough for them. He knows so much about potions and medicinal sea plants. He must have been a top medic Below. The man's brilliant."

All this talk about Mr. Havelock being nice and thoughtful doesn't gel with the condescending elitist I met at my parents' party. What could have caused Caspian to come down with such a case of hero-worship?

"He even knows how to write in Mermese!" Caspian announces,

grabbing my arm and shaking me in his excitement.

Well, that explains his newfound mancrush. Written Mermese hasn't been used in thousands of years. Before we discovered how to seal our voices in *konklilis*, Mer kept written records on red algae leaves, the way humans did on papyrus. But preserving these records underwater was difficult. It required covert trading with human merchants for wax that we could infuse with magic and use to coat the leaves. Once *konklilis* and shell calls were common, written Mermese became extinct. It's now a dead language studied only by the highest-level scholars.

And, of course, by Caspian. He started teaching it to himself when we first learned to read and write in English. We were taking turns writing our names on wide-lined paper in childish scrawl at our all-Mer elementary school when Caspian raised his hand and asked our teacher how to write his name in Mermese. She explained that she didn't know and that very few Mer did. When he kept asking, she spoke to his parents about getting him a *konklili* on the history of the language. He sped through that and asked for more. Eventually, his parents enlisted mine to find resources for him. As there was no teacher in our Community school qualified to teach him, Caspian taught himself.

For a while, he tried to teach me, too. I was interested at first because I thought we could use it to write secret messages to each other, but the artful characters were so numerous and so difficult for my small, uncoordinated fingers that I decided I much preferred English. Since then, in typical Caspian fashion, he's mainly kept his studies of the written language to himself.

But it's one of his passions. If Mr. Havelock knows written Mermese, it's little wonder Caspian admires him so much.

"I was shocked when I found a letter written to his family Below and coated in wax—a whole letter in Mermese! He must know konklilis can be intercepted by one of the underwater factions. Anyway, I read it—for you, because you were suspicious."

"What did it say?" I ask before the words are even out of his mouth.

"It was about how wonderful life is Above. How much more peaceful and safe it is. He begged his family to give up their udell thinking and move up here."

"But I thought … "

"You thought wrong. He's changed his entire life to be here, just like our parents did, and I don't think he'd jeopardize that for some dangerous scheme. After reading his letter, I can't believe he's still an udell. He's a smart man. He even knows some ancient Mermese characters." Caspian goes off excitedly on a tangent about sketches of Mermese letters so old not even he had ever seen them before. As he takes out a pen and scribbles a few on his hand to show me, I question how I could have so completely misjudged Mr. Havelock.

Is it possible he has no idea that his daughter committed the high crime of sireny? That she bent a human to her will for weeks without his notice? How could a parent not know such a thing about his own child?

Later, when I reach the underwater entrance to my house and my own father asks me how my day was, it hits me. My parents are as oblivious to my sins as Mr. Havelock is to Melusine's. I've tricked them. Lied to them. After all they've done for me, I've failed them. I look at my father's kind smile. If he knew what I'd done—what I'm doing—he wouldn't even recognize his own daughter.

I'm still worrying about it a few days later. And it's not my only worry. I'm spending some time alone in my upstairs bedroom this afternoon, and all the thoughts I wish would disappear are bubbling to the surface. When school got out, Clay practically begged me to come to his house or go on a hike or go kayaking—anything, as long as we could spend time together. But that was only after I'd hummed in his ear. Only after I'd brainwashed him into liking me.

I can't let myself listen to those pleas. Instead, I have to remember that he requested more space. Space away from me.

Thinking about it makes me cold inside. Maybe soaking up

some sun will help lift my mood as it warms my body. I change into a bright yellow bikini, hoping some of its cheeriness will rub off on me.

"Stas and I are taking Barney for a walk," Amy calls from downstairs.

"'Kay!" I call down. Good. Everyone else is out, so I'll have the whole house to myself—a rare occurrence. I head outside, looking forward to the quiet. Soon I'll have to call Clay; the siren song will be wearing off. Doing it will make me hate myself a little. Maybe not enough. It can wait another few minutes.

I pull one of the beach chairs close to the pool's edge so I can watch the sunlight shine golden white off the water without blinding myself. Then I stretch out against the canvas fabric of the chair, wiggle out of my bikini bottoms, and let them drop to the ground as my eyes slip shut. I'm just starting to feel the sensation of tides rushing against my legs in transformation when the memory of Clay holding me against his warm chest rises unbidden to my mind. The way he put his arms around me, the way his smooth skin electrified mine. When I open my eyes, my legs haven't budged.

Usually, letting my tail free is the most natural act in the world. It provides a relief I crave all day. But when my thoughts drift to Clay ... to *being* with Clay, it's the only time my legs have ever felt like they belong, like they don't want to go away until they've wrapped around him.

I close my eyes again and exhale in one long, slow breath. *Don't think about Clay*, I tell myself. *Think about school.* School ... history class ... Clay sitting close to me at his desk while we worked on our report, leg to leg. *No! Okay, I'll try P.E.* Coach Crane ... bad hair gel ... self-defense ... Clay underneath me as I flip us out of a submission hold. *Bad brain, bad! Pre-calculus. Clay isn't in my pre-cal class.* I run through mathematical formulas in my head.

Tides push and pull along my legs. My bones and muscles shift and fold, and my scales slip free, like blossoms after too long

a winter. This time, when I open my eyes, my tail flows out from my waist, decadent and sparkling in the sun.

The distant noise of the front door opening and closing startles me. Amy must be back.

The view of the ocean stretches out below me, and the palms sway in the breeze. The sea air's salty tang refreshes my senses, and the warm California sunlight kisses my face, chest, arms, and tail.

"Wow."

Clay!

Panic like I've never felt seizes me, strangling my insides. I must have imagined his voice. He can't be here, can he?

My beach chair—thank the current—is facing toward the ocean, away from the back door. Staying as still as I can so that my tail remains hidden from his view, I crane my neck around the back of the chair.

He's there. Clay is standing right there. And I'm lying here, IN MY TAIL. This can't be happening.

"Your pool is ginormous!" he exclaims.

He's not looking at me. He, like most of our visitors (human and Mer alike), is taken aback by our pool. My parents have done their best to make up for the no-swimming-in-the-ocean-during-the-day rule by building a swimming pool that wraps around nearly two sides of our house's exterior and has a disappearing edge like a waterfall. Once you get in, it looks as if the pool flows seamlessly into the Pacific Ocean below. All I can do is hope Clay's distraction lasts long enough for me to transform back into my legs.

I squeeze my eyes shut, preparing to do exactly that. But my heart pounds in fear and my breath comes in shallow gasps. I can't concentrate to save my life. Literally. In my terror, my body has decided swimming away from danger is my best option, and I can't calm down enough to call my legs to the surface. Clay could walk over here any second. What am I supposed do?

"Is that my dad?" I ask too loudly, pointing inside the house.

"Where?" Clay turns his head around to look, and I catapult my body into the pool, knocking over the beach chair in the process.

It clatters against the concrete, diverting Clay's attention.

"Guess not," I say as I peek my head out of the water. "I thought I saw him. What are you doing here?" As I talk, I move as quickly as I dare toward the edge closest to Clay. As soon as I reach it, I press my tail up against the wall of the pool. If he stays right where he is, he shouldn't be able to see it. But if he comes any closer …

"I ran into Amy and her friend outside. You have history's cutest dog. Why haven't you ever invited me over to play with him? I know you say your sisters are too distracting for us to get any work done here, but I'll put up with any level of distraction for that amount of tail-wagging." He brings his hand up to his forehead, cupping it over his eyes as he looks down at me. I hope like I've never hoped before that the glare from the sun hitting the water blinds him enough to conceal the truth. "Amy let me in and said you were upstairs doing homework."

"Clearly, she was mistaken." And her mistake might cost me absolutely everything.

He takes one dangerous step forward. My hand starts to shake. To make it stop, I clutch the lip of the pool so hard my knuckles turn white. A tiny, far down, secret part of me has always wished something exactly like this would happen. That Clay would somehow find out what I am without me telling him, and I'd be able to be honest with him for the first time ever. Now that I'm faced with the reality of that fantasy, I realize how idiotic it was. This isn't going to end in lovey-dovey smiles and truthful confessions. This is going to end in screams of disgust and me on the front page of some sleazy supermarket tabloid alongside an alien mummy and vampire Elvis.

Clay's eyes widen as he spots something.

My tail. He's spotted my tail under the water. This is it. It's all over.

Chapter Sixteen

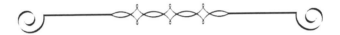

His mouth opens into a small "o" of shock.

But, no ... he's looking just to the right of me. He's staring at something, but it's too far over to be my tail.

Clay walks to the edge of the pool near where my beach chair lies on its side. I press even more firmly against the wall. He's close enough now that all it'll take is a single look into the water. I can barely breathe. In fact, there's a definite risk I'll stop breathing altogether, faint, and wake up just in time to be photographed for that tabloid. I try again to transform into my legs, but now that I'm in the water, it's even harder than before. The fact that Clay could discover me with the slightest turn of his head makes it impossible to focus.

Instead, I keep my wary eyes on him, but he's still looking at something else. He bends over and reaches for something on the ground that I can't see.

"Well, well, well. Now I know why you launched yourself into the pool so fast."

He does?

"And why you're glued to that wall. Do you want to tell me what you were doing out here?" One corner of his mouth turns up in a devilish smirk. "All alone?" he asks, holding up something yellow. Bright yellow.

My bikini bottoms!

Considering I'm trapped only a few feet from a human boy who could easily look into the pool and see my tail, it's ridiculous to be embarrassed that he has my bikini bottoms in his hand. But I can't help it. Clay thinks I'm naked.

Suddenly, I feel naked.

"Clay, give those back!"

"I don't know, Nautilus," he says, still smiling. "You didn't want them before. Maybe I should just keep 'em." I guess that answers my unspoken question. If Clay can be this snarky and disobedient after I gave him a direct command, then the siren spell has completely worn off since I cast it after school.

"That's not funny!"

"I think it's pretty funny," Clay says, still smirking. He puts a finger through one of the leg holes and spins the bottoms around it, a bright yellow blur against the blue sky. "Maybe you should just come out here and get them."

I wish I could. If Clay would just leave me alone for two seconds, maybe I could concentrate enough to change back.

"Clay, I'm really thirsty. Would you go get me a bottle of water from the kitchen?" I put on my sweetest, most feminine smile. "Pleeease?"

He chuckles. "Nautilus, there is no way I'm letting you off the hook that easily."

I squirm, feeling as if I really am trapped on a hook. He moves closer, squats down by the edge of the pool. "Maybe I should just peek down there," he whispers, "and see what you're hiding."

"No! Don't!" I shout.

A growl pierces the air, and a ball of scruffy tan fur tackles Clay. "What the ... hey!" Clay loses his balance and falls from his squatting position onto, as Lapis called it, his grabbable ass. Barnacle jumps up and down on his chest. If I weren't in such a precarious position, this would be hilarious. Barney is so tiny, and his threatening barks come out in high-pitched little yelps of ferocity. "Looky who's defending your honor," Clay says, his voice brimming with amusement. "Stand down, good sir. I was just teasing her. I'm a gentleman."

Barney cocks his small head to the side, his ears lifting as if he's considering Clay's words. Then, with another growl that sounds more like a whine, the puppy sinks his tiny teeth into the bikini bottoms and decides to play tug-of-war.

"Oh no you don't," Clay says, tugging back.

This is exactly what I need. Clay's attention is focused on Barnacle. I release my grip from the edge, my fingers stiff from my tight hold, and relax my arms by my sides. I force myself to steady my breathing. Then, I concentrate on the sounds of Clay's laughter, low and rumbling and unintentionally sexy.

My muscles shrink and separate, interlacing with the bones of two separate legs. Almost afraid to believe it, I slit my eyes open and peer down into the blue. Two long, familiar legs tread water beneath me.

That's not all I see.

Now I really am naked from the waist down. After almost being discovered with a tail, a little case of nudity shouldn't bother me, but ... Clay ... right there in front of me ... I slam myself right back against the wall of the pool.

He and Barnacle roll on the nearby grass, continuing to fight over the bottoms I now desperately need. "Little monster!" Clay mumbles between laughs.

"Barney!" I call. "C'mere, Barney. C'mere!"

More used to my voice than Clay's, Barnacle runs to me so fast on his teeny puppy legs that he looks more like he's jumping across the lawn, my yellow bottoms clenched securely in his mouth. He's so excited by this game that he runs right past the lip of the pool and into the water.

He yelps, his fur dripping, as I lift him up under his belly with one hand. With the other, I wrestle the yellow fabric from him. The teething pup's baby teeth weren't sharp enough to do any real damage, so, moments later, Barnacle shakes himself off on solid ground as I shimmy back into yellow safety.

Out of the corner of my eye, I see Clay watching me from where he still sits on the grass. Now, it's my turn to tease him.

In a well-practiced move I often use when I have a tail, I dive down deep. This time, instead of letting my fins splash out of the water behind me, my legs—with toes gracefully pointed and muscles toned from swimming—shoot out of the water and give Clay quite a view.

As I swim back up, I angle my face just right. When I hit the surface, I flick my head back so my hair flips in a perfect cascade, sparkling with thousands of water droplets that catch the sunlight at every angle. Maybe it's unfair to use a classic Mermaid move against Clay. But after what he pulled with my bikini? Revenge is sweet.

In a much more human-teen-movie move, I adjust my bikini top, needlessly straightening the straps. Clay's eyes follow my fingers just as I'd intended, and I angle my body toward him, ensuring he gets an eyeful.

When I raise my head, our eyes meet. And his are hungry. Not in the disturbing way they get when he's been sirened—that wore off when he first got here. No, this is a natural, human boy hunger, and it's directed at me. It sparks a glow inside me from the tips of my recently recovered toes to the ends of my recently flipped hair. I've never felt this ... sexy.

The look on Clay's face—of slack-jawed wonder—is empowering. It's only there for a second; then he gives me a knowing smile.

"Well played, Nautilus." He gets to his feet and ... unzips his jeans? I gulp. Maybe I went too far with my little game.

"Clay, what are you doing?"

"What does it look like?" he asks as he pushes the denim

from his hips and lets it pool at his feet. He kicks his jeans to the side. Now he stands in front of me in only a tight white V-neck t-shirt and blue cotton boxers, his legs tan and muscular. "I'm going for a swim."

He walks closer. "You can't show me a pool like this and expect me to resist the temptation," he says. His muscles dance under his skin as he raises his arms above his head and dives into the water.

When he comes up for air, I gasp. He's much closer than I expected. He's inches from my face, so close I can see the water clinging to his eyelashes in iridescent beads.

"Salt water," he says in surprise. His tongue peeks out to lick his full bottom lip before disappearing again inside the cavern of his mouth. I track its progress with my eyes and think how much I'd like to taste the salt on his lips. How much I'd like to taste him.

"Yeah. It's more buoyant." I murmur the well-rehearsed excuse without thinking. I can't think about anything right now, not with Clay so close to me.

And he's moving even closer. He's leaning toward me, his breath cool against my wet skin.

My world spins upside down as Clay dives forward. He wraps his arms above my knees, lifting me into the air as he stands, and throwing me up over his shoulder so my upper half hangs down his back.

My screams and laughter blend together. "Clay! Put me down!" I giggle, pounding my hands lightly against his back.

"Now, why would I do that?" His laugh vibrates against my thighs as it rolls through his chest. Barnacle barks from the edge of the pool, eager to join in the excitement.

Clay walks around the shallow end of the pool with me still hanging over his shoulder, and I let out an undignified squeal as I whap him on the back, just above where his sodden white t-shirt meets the waistband of his equally wet boxers.

"Aurelia!"

My laughter dies half-formed on my lips.

Just like that, my world spins upside down again.

My mother has never looked so scandalized. My father has never looked so uncomfortable. And I, dangling in a bikini over the shoulder of a human boy whose hands are all over my bare legs, have never been in so much trouble.

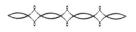

Clay is gone. With as much politeness as my mother could muster, and that wasn't much, she asked him to leave. I didn't even manage a goodbye. I just stood there by the pool and watched as he walked through the glass door, through the living room, and out of my house.

I should be planning what to say, how to explain my behavior. But how can I possibly explain? Instead, I stay motionless, listening to the drip, drip, drip of the water onto the concrete until my father throws me a towel.

"Cover your legs before your mother has a heart attack." My parents know legs aren't considered as blatantly sexual to humans as they are to Mer, but walking in on me with so much of my legs exposed—worse, with a boy actually *touching* my legs—must shock them. Still, it can't shock them more than the risk I took by getting in that water in front of Clay.

I expect them to yell right away. Instead, they're quiet. The silence scares me more. My mother, the consummate politician, has been rendered speechless by my behavior.

She paces back and forth in front of me, but doesn't say a word. My father stares at nothing, wringing his hands.

Then, after several long, tense minutes in which my stomach tangles itself up like strings of seaweed on the beach, the storm starts.

"How, Aurelia? How could you? You went in the water with a human! Have we taught you nothing? You could have lost your control at any moment. Imagine if he'd seen your tail! What were you thinking?" Her shouts continue in an endless stream.

I don't interrupt. I don't try to argue. How can I, when she's right? If my parents had come home ten minutes earlier, I would have been in my tail in front of a human.

My father usually soothes my mother's anger. He's the jokester to her disciplinarian. But he doesn't try to quiet her now. All he says is, "You endangered all of us."

I nod, my eyes downcast.

My mother curses in Mermese. She never curses. "Have you slept with him?"

"No! I haven't even kissed him." Even though I could have. I've tried to do the right thing, really, I've tried.

Her shoulders lose some of their tension, but her pinched expression remains. "Maybe human school was a mistake. I have the utmost respect for humans and we want you to fit into this world, but—"

"But you can't forget you're not one of them." My father's voice is so quiet it's almost like I'm hearing it inside my head. "You're not human, Lia. You never will be. You're Mer."

My mother looks at me for the first time since she saw me in the pool with Clay. She steps right up to me and puts one of her hands on each of my shoulders, demanding my full attention, as if she didn't have it already.

"Friends are one thing, Lia. Friendships with humans are necessary to survive here and can teach you a great deal. But romance, romance is off-limits." She keeps holding me—even jostles me once by the shoulders—until I nod again. "You know this. Don't set yourself up for misery."

She lets go of me and releases a labored sigh, as if I've sapped away all her energy. Now, my father moves closer, looking grimmer than I've ever seen him. "You're better than this, Aurelia."

I snap. I can't listen anymore. "How do you know?" *You don't know that I've wanted him since last year, that I've buried my feelings so I could be who you wanted me to be, that I've saved him, that I've cursed him—that I've fallen face over fins for him.* "You don't know me."

"We know that you're too smart a Mermaid to chase after a fantasy." Now my mother's voice is calm, collected, steely.

My father's sounds like it might break when he adds, "We brought you here—gave up everything—so you could have a better life. Not so you could throw away your entire future. You're not to spend any more time with that boy. Understand?"

I nod one last time. But this time, it's a lie.

Amy waits for me in my grotto bedroom. "Lia, I'm so, so sorry! When I let him in, I thought you'd still be upstairs. How mad at me are you? How mad at me are they?"

"I've never seen them madder, but not at you. They just assumed I let him in."

"I'll tell them! I'll go upstairs right now and—"

"No, you won't. There's no reason for them to be mad at both of us. I don't think they could take worrying about your judgment and mine."

"I screwed up," she says, looking about ready to cry.

"Yeah, you did, but it happens. I've been screwing up way worse. And I don't know how to stop."

"Is there anything I can do?" she asks.

"Will you go distract them? I need to go back upstairs and make a phone call."

While I've been getting yelled at, Clay's been out there unprotected. Letting my sireny wear off while we're together is one thing, but letting him leave like that means Melusine could reclaim him any time.

Once I'm in my upstairs bedroom with the door locked, I call him up with shaking fingers.

He picks up right away. "Lia, are you okay? Your parents seemed really upset. How can we fix this?"

I don't know what to say, so I don't say anything. I just sing.

When I get home from the Foundation the next day, the way Amy greets me—a mixture of eagerness and temerity—tells me she wants to talk. She must still feel bad about yesterday.

I've started researching Community bylaws at the Foundation in hopes I'll find something to pin on Melusine besides sireny (nothing so far). I'm exhausted from pushing my brain to understand all the legal Mermese. So, it's tempting to ignore Amy, but I've been doing that too much lately. Between spending time with Clay, worrying about Melusine, researching at the Foundation, and meeting in Star Cave with Caspian, I've spent almost zero time with her.

"Hey, Aims, have you walked Barney yet?"

Her face lights up, and she shakes her head.

"Get him leashed up and show me what those new legs of yours can do."

For the first few blocks, she's uncharacteristically silent. I pretend not to notice as I chatter on about school and compliment her leg control.

This must make her feel more at ease because she says, "So, that boy you got caught with … " She trails off, as if now that she's broached the subject, she doesn't know what to say next.

"You going to lecture me, too?" I ask. I widen my eyes in mock-fright, and she giggles.

Last night, my parents gave me what I thought was the lecture to end all lectures. I was wrong. When Emeraldine got home from campus, she gave me a lecture of her own. Everything from why it's dangerous to get involved with a human to how wonderful love can be once you've found the Merman of your dreams. Apparently, she and Leo have had some serious convos the last two weeks. I don't know what kind of conclusion they've come to, but when she talked about love last night, her smile finally met her eyes again. She practically glowed when she told me that, one day, she wants me to find a love like hers so I can be as happy as she is. I let her talk. I wish she could understand that not everyone falls for the Merboy next door. Love isn't always as predictable as a fairytale.

Once Em felt she'd given me enough sisterly advice, the twins came in and gave me their own earful about how dumb I was to get caught. They told me that no matter what they got up to, they never let Mom and Dad know enough to get this worried.

Considering the echo in the grottos, I'm sure Amy heard every word. But she won't RSVP to the criticize Lia party. Instead, she asks, "Clay, right? That's his name?"

"Yeah. He goes to my school."

"Clay," she repeats, as if testing the feel of it. She stops walking, letting Barnacle sniff a nearby tree. "He likes you, doesn't he?"

"I don't know," I answer honestly. "I thought he didn't, but then yesterday it seemed like maybe he does." By the time I got my legs back yesterday, the spell had totally worn off, but Clay went right on flirting with me. It might mean nothing, but maybe, just maybe it means …

"*You* like *him*, though." It's a statement, not a question. I don't know whether it's my behavior from yesterday or my current blush that gives me away. Either way, I don't deny it. At thirteen, Amy looks up to me, and I don't want to set a bad example by feeling this way for a human, but I don't want to lie to her either.

"Yeah, I really do."

"Do you love him?"

The question catches me off guard. I know the answer, but I don't know if I can bring myself to admit it out loud. I say the closest thing I can to yes. "I think so."

"So, you love him even though you're not supposed to?"

"Yeah, I've tried hard not to, really I have, but I can't help how I feel."

She looks at me for a long moment, studying me. Then she tugs on the leash. We walk for another few minutes in silence.

Amy's conflicted expression means she has more to say. I wait.

By the time Barnacle stops again to investigate a garden gnome, a determined expression has settled on Amy's face. But her voice comes out shaky. "You remember when I first got my legs … "

I wait for her to continue. When she doesn't, I say, "Yep, I remember."

"You know how you told me that if I had trouble keeping them, I should think about a boy I like?"

"Yep," I say again.

"Well, it didn't work."

"What do you mean? You're doing great with your legs. I never could've walked this long on a public street so soon."

She shakes her head. "You don't understand. When I was practicing, thinking about boys in my class—even thinking about guys on TV—it didn't work. It still doesn't work." Her voice is barely above a whisper when she says, "But, when I think about Stas, well ... " She gestures at her legs.

Wait. What? "Staskia? You ... think about Staskia?"

"I think about Staskia." She says the words like she's wanted to say them for a long time, like she's needed to say them. How long has she wanted to tell me this? How long has it been since I really talked to her? Should I have already known? Maybe if I wasn't so wrapped up in Clay, this wouldn't come as such a shock.

"Does Staskia know? Have you two ... ?" I gesture wildly. *Oh yeah, real mature, Lia.*

"No! I mean, not yet. I haven't said anything exactly but, well, sometimes we hold hands while we walk and I thinkmaybeshefeelsthesame." She says the last part very fast and now she's blushing as red as a flame angelfish. "Do you think your parents are gonna be mad? Do you think they'll tell my parents?"

I stop to think about it. I've heard that, before the curse, homosexuality (what translates to *glei elskee* or same-love in Mermese) was accepted in Mer culture. Most Mermaids mated with Mermen, but Mermaids mating with Mermaids wasn't uncommon, and neither was Mermen with Mermen. Mer also sometimes took advantage of their immortal lifespans to explore the company of both genders.

But once the curse stole our immortality, we started

dying off in droves. All Mer who'd lived longer than a normal human lifespan, nearly eighty percent of the population, died immediately. The wars decimated our remaining numbers. With such a strong need for repopulation, being gay became frowned upon as the worst form of selfishness.

Now, Mer are expected to mate young and produce children. My parents adhered to this idea themselves and have certainly encouraged it within the Community. We've hardly ever discussed same-love. My parents support gay rights for humans, but humans aren't dangerously under-populated. Now that I think about it, I have no idea what their reaction will be. But I know what mine needs to be.

"Thanks for telling me, Amy. If it ever seems like I'm too busy to talk, just pull my hair or something until I listen." That's what she did as a toddler, and the memory elicits a smile from her now. "I'm never too busy to talk to you, got it?" She nods. "You don't have to tell anyone else in the family until you're ready. And don't worry about what they say. You're growing up, and you have to do what feels right to you."

"You ... you don't think I'm weird?"

"Not at all. Do you think I'm weird? Falling for a human and all?"

"Not any weirder than you were before."

"Gee, thanks," I say with an eye roll. I'm happy she's smiling.

"So, now what?" she asks.

"Now? I guess we love who we love. What choice do we have?"

I can't worry about what my parents think or what my sisters say, or even what I would have thought of myself two months ago. I need to be with Clay.

Chapter Seventeen

My parents may not know what "grounded" means, but they sure know "you're only allowed at school and home, no exceptions." Then I ask if I can go to Caspian's for dinner. I want to spend time with a boy who's Mer? They say yes right away. Instead, I walk straight to Clay's house.

I have to be honest with myself. I'm in love with Clay. I'm in love with Clay and I can't keep trying to stop it, to force it back into some deep dark corner of myself. It wasn't supposed to happen. If I'd been born and raised in the ocean like I should have been, we'd never have met. But I wasn't and we did and now I love him. I don't know if his feelings for me are real—I can't know as long as he's under my spell. Not knowing feels like an orca whale lying on my chest, making it impossible to move or even breathe. But it doesn't change the fact I love him.

I know I can't have him. I know we have no future. And, since he's sirened, it would be beyond wrong to kiss him, to touch him, so we have no present, either. But it doesn't change the way I feel. I don't care what we do; I just want to be with him.

When he opens the door, he seems so happy to see me, and it lifts my spirits as it breaks my heart.

"My mom's at a writers' conference in NorCal for the week. Wanna come up to my room?"

We lie together on his bed, and it takes everything in me to resist his advances. To tell him no and refocus his attention on our conversation. We talk for over an hour, spread out on the softness of his flannel bedspread. I ask questions and answer questions and laugh and feel him close to me. It's the sweetest torture I've ever known.

When it gets late, I gaze at Clay. At the trust in his eyes. Maybe, just this once, I should go a night without sirening him. He's supposed to tell me every time Melusine talks to him, and she hasn't in three weeks. Maybe, if I give him a night of freedom, by morning he'll know how he really feels. It's a dizzying thought. But it's a selfish one. Leaving him unprotected would be a mistake.

With a sigh, I lean in, and it scares me how easy it's gotten to siren him, how routine it's starting to feel. I hum and watch the mist close in over his eyes. Then I leave.

I'm turning onto my own street when I stop dead. Heavy, booted footsteps run toward me. By the sound, they're at least a block away, but they're speeding up and they won't be far off for long. I reach in my bag, clutching around desperately for my pepper spray. My dad gave one to each of us when we got our legs and started walking by ourselves.

"It's a human weapon," he'd explained when he showed me how to use it. "Now that you'll be doing human things like walking home alone, you should have it."

At the time, I'd teased him for being too cautious. Now, I silently thank him as my hand closes around it. I pull it out just as a dark shadow rounds the corner.

I drop it, and it clatters to the sidewalk.

"Clay!"

"Lia!" His voice is a strangled cry as he collapses three feet away from me. I run to him, crouch down.

"What is it? What's wrong?" He's shaking all over and deathly pale.

"Mel came by … " Each word is a struggle. He swallows, fighting to draw ragged, rattling breaths. "Brought tea. Feel strange. Had to—" His eyes fall shut.

"Clay?" I shake his shoulder lightly, not daring to jostle him more. "Clay!" He doesn't respond. I feel his forehead and it's burning. I take his pulse and it's racing.

Wait! I can fix this. He's under my siren spell. "Clay," I say, making my voice stern, "wake up. Open your eyes."

It's not the instant cure I expected. He convulses, his limbs smacking against the unforgiving pavement. Sweat pours down his face.

What's happening to him? I need to make sense of the words he fought so hard to tell me. He saw Melusine? It's only been fifteen minutes since I left him, twenty tops. Maybe she watched the house, waiting for me to go. The hacking and sweating and struggling for air, that isn't sireny. I didn't think there was anything worse, but this, this looks worse. He said something about tea. Damn it! She must have slipped him something. Some kind of potion. But if she did, where is she now? And what was she trying to do? Kill him?

It sure looks that way. He's breathing, but he's wracked by violent tremors.

"Clay!" This time, it comes out a sob. What am I supposed to do? A human doctor will have no idea how to help him, and a Mer medic won't keep this quiet. I need to save Clay from dying, not risk the Foundation executing him for knowing too much. Besides, whatever Melusine's given him, it reeks of ancient dark magic. Modern medics might not know any more about counteracting it than human doctors would. The seconds pass, and my panic rises. I can't just sit here in the street while Clay's life's in danger. *Think!*

I need someone who knows about ancient potions. There's Melusine's father, but he may have brewed this one. Who else is there?

Then I have an idea, and all I can do is hope it works. Clay is too heavy for me to lift, but I can't leave him here. What if he's picked up by an ambulance? If we were in the ocean, I could carry him easily. Here on land, I feel so helpless. I drag him as gently as I can behind a hydrangea bush.

He lies there in shadow. Eyes closed, face pained. I stroke his cheek. "I'll be right back," I promise. Then I run.

By the time I reach Caspian's door, I'm panting and holding a stitch in my side. I've never run that fast. Tides, I wish his parents trusted human technology enough to buy him a cellphone.

It takes a long time—what feels like a thousand loud knocks and urgent doorbell rings—for Caspian to answer the door. He's wet and wears only a pair of shorts, their drawstring hanging loose. He must have been in the grottos in his tail. His family rarely receives visitors up here.

"Lia? Are you all right?"

"Grab your car keys. Hurry!"

He asks a constant stream of questions while we drive, but I only tell him to go faster.

"This is residential. The speed limit's twenty-five." Caspian is as careful with driving regulations as he is with everything else.

I push down on his thigh, so his foot hits the gas and we speed up.

"Turn here!" I say, grabbing the wheel and spinning us around the corner. "Stop!"

He hits the brake hard. We both pitch forward, then smash back against the leather seats. Caspian looks up and down the seemingly empty street. "What is it?"

"C'mon." I get out and lead him to the bush, breathing a sigh of relief when Clay's still there. But my relief doesn't last long; he's even paler than before, and his breath is shallower. Caspian stands there, frozen in shock. "Casp, help me!"

He shakes himself out of it, and together we carry Clay to the car, laying him across the backseat. I get in with him, his head resting on my lap. "Melusine gave him some kind of potion. We

She stares at me for another long minute, her eyes hard. *"I will not speak of it."*

"What? Why not?" Caspian asks.

Then I understand. She's not staying silent for my sake. She hates me now. It's written on her face, and it hits me in my stomach. No, she's not helping me. She's protecting herself. This woman's entire life has been so scarred by the stain of sireny that she doesn't dare speak the word aloud. She would never tell Caspian anything about Adrianna, and she won't say anything about this sireny now. But will she involve herself enough to help Clay?

"Please!" I beg. *"Please help him. He's a victim."*

She turns her head away from me.

"Of course she'll help him, if she can," Caspian says. *"Can you, Olee?"*

Will you? I wonder.

She raises a hand to Caspian's cheek, his eyes wide with worry. He may not know Clay, but no one is more caring than Caspian. She must know he would never forgive her for letting an innocent die. She pats his cheek.

"What I can do is remove the susceptibility spell. Like most of our potions on land, this one was weak. I can mix an antidote."

"Weak?" I ask. But she doesn't respond. She won't be talking to me again.

"On land, potions ingredients from the sea can't stay as fresh," Caspian says. *"Mr. Havelock explained it to me. They dry out on their own or they're preserved, so all potions Above are weaker than they should be."*

"Clever boy," his grandmother whispers. She swims back to her chest, and the rattling of glass again fills the room. She mixes ingredients that smell salty and acrid. *"This will take time."*

"Does he have time?"

She doesn't answer me.

"Olee, Lia asked if—"

"Hey, Casp," the last thing I need is for him to realize she's

need to get him back to your grandmother—now."

This time, Caspian breaks every speed limit in the California handbook.

His parents are at his sister's turtle shell harp recital, so we head straight down to his grandmother's grotto. I transform into my tail so fast, my skirt rips. Caspian's shorts meet a similar fate as he carries Clay at top speed toward his grandma. I expect her to look surprised, maybe even scandalized, when we burst into her private room late at night with a convulsing human.

Instead, she stays quiet, collected. She raises a hand, fingers gnarled with age, and beckons us farther into the room. She's wrinkled and hunched with thin wisps of white hair. The garnet scales of her tail curl up slightly at the edges and have lost their sheen. But her pale blue eyes are sharp.

"MerMatron Zayle, this is a-a friend of mine. He's been poisoned and I didn't know who else to bring him to. I think he's dying. Can you help him? Please?" My words come out in a rush of Mermese.

She shifts her gaze to Caspian. He repeats the request, grandson to grandmother: *"Olee, please?"*

She uses the same gnarled hand to gesture at a slab of rock protruding from one wall of her cavern-like room. It's the only surface that's elevated enough to stay dry. She must use it as a table because she clears away a few empty dishes right before Caspian lays Clay down. Clay's still sallow, still sweating.

I hold my breath as she examines him. Caspian puts a hand on my shoulder in comfort but I barely feel it. Like I did, MerMatron Zayle takes Clay's pulse and feels his heated skin. Unlike me, she uses two fingers and her thumb to open his slack jaw. She scrapes a fingertip across his tongue and sniffs at it. Is there potion left? Does she know what it is?

"Save a sample," Caspian says.

She nods. She hasn't uttered a word, and she still says nothing as she abandons Clay and swims out of the cave. She's not giving up, is she? I rush to swim after her, but Caspian stops me and she returns hefting a large copper chest that's covered in verdigris and rattles when she sets it on the table. She opens the heavy lock with a long fishbone key and lifts the lid. Glass vials line the entire chest, each one filled with a murky liquid or dark powder.

They clang together when she pulls one out and pours indigo dust onto the finger she touched to Clay's tongue. Her fingertip turns a sickly orange and she nods, as if this is what she suspected.

I can't stay quiet any longer. Not while Clay lies a foot away, fighting for his life. *"What is it?"*

"Susceptibility tonic," she answers. *"Partly."*

I look at her blankly. *"What's susceptibility tonic?"*

"I'm not surprised you haven't heard of it. It's old. Older than I am, in fact." Her voice is quiet. Even in the echoey cave, I need to strain my ears to make sure I don't miss a word. This becomes harder when she lifts various clinking vials from the chest and mixes their contents into an empty one. *"A susceptibility tonic is the closest Mer ever came to creating a love potion."*

"Melusine gave him a love potion?" Caspian's words drip with disgust. *"She tried to force him to love her? Sick."*

"Yeah, sick," I whisper.

"It doesn't look like it worked so well," he comments, watching Clay's prone form.

"It was well-mixed. It would have performed its office successfully," she finds my eyes with hers, *"if the boy weren't already under another form of Mer magic."*

Oh, no. She knows.

Chapter Eighteen

"Another form of Mer magic?" Caspian asks, the corner mouth turned down. "He's human. *What other Me could he have been exposed to?"*

I brace myself. This is it. She's going to tell him, and h to hate me. She'll probably tell my parents and the Fou too. I can't begin to fathom their disappointment. Wil Clay live? Will he even survive long enough for them that decision? Maybe Caspian's grandmother will refu him now. I look at him lying there. I can't let him d they lock me up or throw me into a warzone tomorr let him die tonight. When she accuses me, when C at me, I'll just have to convince them what I've done fault.

She studies my face. Her lips purse. This wom known me all my life, who has taken me in her ar her grandson and told me stories of her life Below looks at me like she doesn't know me. Like I'm suppose I am.

"What other Mer magic?" Caspian repeats.

need to get him back to your grandmother—now."

This time, Caspian breaks every speed limit in the California handbook.

His parents are at his sister's turtle shell harp recital, so we head straight down to his grandmother's grotto. I transform into my tail so fast, my skirt rips. Caspian's shorts meet a similar fate as he carries Clay at top speed toward his grandma. I expect her to look surprised, maybe even scandalized, when we burst into her private room late at night with a convulsing human.

Instead, she stays quiet, collected. She raises a hand, fingers gnarled with age, and beckons us farther into the room. She's wrinkled and hunched with thin wisps of white hair. The garnet scales of her tail curl up slightly at the edges and have lost their sheen. But her pale blue eyes are sharp.

"MerMatron Zayle, this is a-a friend of mine. He's been poisoned and I didn't know who else to bring him to. I think he's dying. Can you help him? Please?" My words come out in a rush of Mermese.

She shifts her gaze to Caspian. He repeats the request, grandson to grandmother: *"Olee, please?"*

She uses the same gnarled hand to gesture at a slab of rock protruding from one wall of her cavern-like room. It's the only surface that's elevated enough to stay dry. She must use it as a table because she clears away a few empty dishes right before Caspian lays Clay down. Clay's still sallow, still sweating.

I hold my breath as she examines him. Caspian puts a hand on my shoulder in comfort but I barely feel it. Like I did, MerMatron Zayle takes Clay's pulse and feels his heated skin. Unlike me, she uses two fingers and her thumb to open his slack jaw. She scrapes a fingertip across his tongue and sniffs at it. Is there potion left? Does she know what it is?

"Save a sample," Caspian says.

She nods. She hasn't uttered a word, and she still says nothing as she abandons Clay and swims out of the cave. She's not giving up, is she? I rush to swim after her, but Caspian stops me and she returns hefting a large copper chest that's covered in verdigris and rattles when she sets it on the table. She opens the heavy lock with a long fishbone key and lifts the lid. Glass vials line the entire chest, each one filled with a murky liquid or dark powder.

They clang together when she pulls one out and pours indigo dust onto the finger she touched to Clay's tongue. Her fingertip turns a sickly orange and she nods, as if this is what she suspected.

I can't stay quiet any longer. Not while Clay lies a foot away, fighting for his life. *"What is it?"*

"Susceptibility tonic," she answers. *"Partly."*

I look at her blankly. *"What's susceptibility tonic?"*

"I'm not surprised you haven't heard of it. It's old. Older than I am, in fact." Her voice is quiet. Even in the echoey cave, I need to strain my ears to make sure I don't miss a word. This becomes harder when she lifts various clinking vials from the chest and mixes their contents into an empty one. *"A susceptibility tonic is the closest Mer ever came to creating a love potion."*

"Melusine gave him a love potion?" Caspian's words drip with disgust. *"She tried to force him to love her? Sick."*

"Yeah, sick," I whisper.

"It doesn't look like it worked so well," he comments, watching Clay's prone form.

"It was well-mixed. It would have performed its office successfully," she finds my eyes with hers, *"if the boy weren't already under another form of Mer magic."*

Oh, no. She knows.

Chapter Eighteen

"*Another form of Mer magic?*" Caspian asks, the corners of his mouth turned down. "He's human. *What other Mer magic could he have been exposed to?*"

I brace myself. This is it. She's going to tell him, and he's going to hate me. She'll probably tell my parents and the Foundation, too. I can't begin to fathom their disappointment. Will they let Clay live? Will he even survive long enough for them to make that decision? Maybe Caspian's grandmother will refuse to treat him now. I look at him lying there. I can't let him die. Even if they lock me up or throw me into a warzone tomorrow, I can't let him die tonight. When she accuses me, when Caspian yells at me, I'll just have to convince them what I've done isn't Clay's fault.

She studies my face. Her lips purse. This woman who has known me all my life, who has taken me in her arms alongside her grandson and told me stories of her life Below, this woman looks at me like she doesn't know me. Like I'm a criminal. I suppose I am.

"*What other Mer magic?*" Caspian repeats.

She stares at me for another long minute, her eyes hard. *"I will not speak of it."*

"What? Why not?" Caspian asks.

Then I understand. She's not staying silent for my sake. She hates me now. It's written on her face, and it hits me in my stomach. No, she's not helping me. She's protecting herself. This woman's entire life has been so scarred by the stain of sireny that she doesn't dare speak the word aloud. She would never tell Caspian anything about Adrianna, and she won't say anything about this sireny now. But will she involve herself enough to help Clay?

"Please!" I beg. *"Please help him. He's a victim."*

She turns her head away from me.

"Of course she'll help him, if she can," Caspian says. *"Can you, Olee?"*

Will you? I wonder.

She raises a hand to Caspian's cheek, his eyes wide with worry. He may not know Clay, but no one is more caring than Caspian. She must know he would never forgive her for letting an innocent die. She pats his cheek.

"What I can do is remove the susceptibility spell. Like most of our potions on land, this one was weak. I can mix an antidote."

"Weak?" I ask. But she doesn't respond. She won't be talking to me again.

"On land, potions ingredients from the sea can't stay as fresh," Caspian says. *"Mr. Havelock explained it to me. They dry out on their own or they're preserved, so all potions Above are weaker than they should be."*

"Clever boy," his grandmother whispers. She swims back to her chest, and the rattling of glass again fills the room. She mixes ingredients that smell salty and acrid. *"This will take time."*

"Does he have time?"

She doesn't answer me.

"Olee, Lia asked if—"

"Hey, Casp," the last thing I need is for him to realize she's

spurning me and wonder why, *"I can't leave Clay, but it's getting late. I left my cell in the car. Can you call my parents and tell them we want to go on a swim now that it's dark? Ask for their permission to bring me home after curfew."*

He nods and squeezes my shoulder before swimming out the mouth of the grotto. Caspian can be persuasive when he needs to be. Between his skills and my parents' newfound eagerness for me to spend time with Mermen instead of a certain human boy, I don't doubt they'll say yes.

"It's not what you think," I say to MerMatron Zayle now that we're alone. Then again, maybe it's exactly what she thinks. Whatever my reasons, I have sirened him. Either way, she doesn't acknowledge me. But she's making Clay's anecdote, so I don't care.

I close the distance between Clay and me, then take his clammy hand in mine. Caspian's grandmother narrows her eyes but doesn't say a word. Then it dawns on me: She's afraid of me. When she looks at me, she sees a dangerous, cruel siren. I want to explain but she wouldn't believe me. So instead, I focus on Clay. I stroke his hair, damp with perspiration, from his forehead. He's groaning and his tremors haven't abated. I understand why now. Melusine's love potion is working inside him to bind him to her, but my siren spell is binding him to me. The two magics are warring within him, yanking him in different directions.

"Shh. It'll be okay. You'll be okay." His groans continue. I doubt he can hear me, but I keep whispering comforting words to him anyway.

I'm still holding his hands and stroking him when Caspian returns. An expression flits over his face, something twisted, sad—but then he sets his jaw and it's gone. *"Your parents hope we have fun. They said the moon is beautiful tonight."*

"Casp, I'm—"

Clay's groans grow louder, more guttural. He writhes violently, his head snapping from one side to the other. I cup the back of it in my palm to keep him from knocking himself unconscious on the stone slab.

"What's happening?" Caspian asks in horror.

"His body is trying to expel the magics, but without an antidote this is impossible. He will die trying."

Don't die. Please don't die.

I don't risk saying the words out loud. Another command from me may just kill him right now, so I bite my lips to keep from pleading with him to live.

More rattling and pouring, scraping and mixing as MerMatron Zayle hurries her motions.

"Can I help?" Caspian offers. *"Speed things up somehow?"*

But she pushes past him. Pushes me aside on her way to Clay.

She uses a mother of pearl spoon to spread a thick, putrid smelling paste across his tongue. Is it coincidence or some component of the magic that the paste is the same coral color as Melusine's tail?

For a moment, nothing happens.

Then, Clay's eyes roll back in his head and he sputters, attempting to spit out the paste. Old, crooked fingers clamp his mouth shut, forcing his head back until he swallows.

His body spasms, and it's worse than the convulsions of a moment ago. The spasms propel his body off the slab and slam him back down so hard I worry he'll break a bone. I want to hold him, help him, but I'm afraid of making it worse.

He breaks out into a sweat again and loses all his remaining color.

Then he falls still.

Chapter Nineteen

"Clay?" I ask. "Clay?" It feels like I've been calling his name all night. But there's no answer.

He lies there comatose. All the color drained from his face.

"Olee, what now?" Worry laces Caspian's voice.

"We wait," she says. She clears up her supplies, and I know what that means: if this antidote doesn't work, she's got nothing else to try.

I clutch his hand, stroke his face, and hope. If I'd just let Melusine keep him, if I hadn't intervened, she'd never have given him a love potion. If he dies tonight, it's my fault.

Ten minutes pass.

Then another ten.

We're all wading in stagnant water.

"Is there—"

A whimper. A whimper! I've never been so happy to hear a whimper.

"Clay?" I ask again, voice urgent.

"L-Lia?"

"I'm here. I'm here. You're okay. You'll be okay."

"Where … where … ?" His eyelids are heavy, weighed down after his body's battle, but he's trying to open them.

Caspian looks at me, mouth open, eyes panicked. Clay can't see the grotto, can't see our tails.

"Is the susceptibility spell out of his system?" I ask Clay's grandmother. *"Answer me."* I put as much power, as much threat behind the words as I can.

She gives me a curt nod and swims out of the room.

"Sleep, now," I tell Clay before he can open his eyes. "Just sleep."

Obeying my command and exhausted from his ordeal, he does.

On the car ride back, I sit in the backseat again with Clay's head resting on my lap. He's sleeping deeply now. No more shaking or sweating. His fever is gone, and his color is back. His breaths against my knee are steady and even.

I turn my attention to the driver's seat. To Caspian's profile, illuminated in yellows and whites by passing headlights. So far, the only words we've spoken to each other were my directions to Clay's house. He's silent now. Contemplative. He saw me tell Clay to sleep. Did it sound like the order of a siren or the comforting words of a girlfriend? Does he suspect?

No, I'm being paranoid. How could he? His grandmother was both too scared and too scarred to breathe a word. And Clay's energy was so sapped from fighting Melusine's potion that it's expected he'd fall asleep. I hope.

When we're only a few blocks from Clay's house, Caspian says, "You were right about Melusine. I didn't want to believe it." Of course he didn't; Caspian wants to see the good in everyone. I just want him to keep seeing the good in me.

"Do you think her father knows?" he asks.

I doubt Caspian's ever met anyone else who shares his passion for scholarship the way Mr. Havelock does, anyone else who he admires so much. I don't want to hurt Caspian—but I don't want anyone else to either.

"That was an ancient potion. Illegal and complicated. I think he brewed it."

"I thought so," is all Caspian says. Hurt settles in the set of his mouth.

"That letter you found about how much he loved the human world and wanted his family to move up here? He probably wrote it for your sake. Planted it to throw us off. You need to stop interning for him. That family is dangerous."

He nods, and I drop the subject. "I can't leave Clay tonight. I'm going to call my parents and say we swam so late that I want to stay the night at your place. I'll tell them your parents are home and I'm sleeping in the guest grotto. Cover for me if they call?"

Another nod. We pull up to Clay's house. Since his mom is at her conference, all the windows are dark.

"Hey, Lia?" Caspian asks as I'm using Clay's key to unlock the door. "My grandmother said the potion didn't work because of a second type of magic. What do you think it could be?"

I shrug, but I don't say anything. I'm so sick of lying.

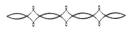

My mother pretended to be stern on the phone, but she could barely conceal her glee that I'm finally expressing interest in a Merman. Caspian, with his family's reputation, is far from an ideal choice, but at least he has a tail.

With that taken care of, I grab Clay's phone off the nightstand and send a quick text to his mom, scrolling through his earlier messages to make sure I word it the way he would. It's late and if he doesn't check in to say goodnight, she'll probably make the eight-hour drive back down here. Then I sit on the bed next to him. He looks so peaceful. All of his muscles are relaxed in sleep, and I've never seen his rugged features look more angelic than they do now. I make my voice as gentle as I can when I erase my earlier command, "Clay, you can wake up now if you want to."

He blinks and shining hazel gazes up at me. "Lia?" He glances around, sees that we're in his bedroom and it's late. "What are you doing here?" He tries to smirk at the implication, but he's too sleepy to pull it off.

I tell him as much of the truth as I can. "Mel stopped by—"

"Oh, yeah, I remember," he says.

"She gave you some tea that didn't agree with you. You've been pretty sick, but you're okay now. You're gonna be fine." He nods. My explanation must gel well enough with whatever he remembers.

Now there's only one thing left to do. He needs to get out of his sweat-drenched, salt water-splashed clothes. I didn't feel right changing him myself while he was sleeping. "Here, put these on."

I hand him a fresh t-shirt, boxers, and a pair of pajama pants from his drawer. Then, I turn my back.

"What? You don't want to watch the show?" he asks. This time, I can hear the smirk. I can also hear him pulling down his zipper.

"Are you wearing my workout pants?" he asks over the rustle of fabric.

"My skirt ripped," I say. I've had to roll the pants up about a zillion times, but I like knowing the smooth fabric against my legs belongs to Clay. That it's touched his skin the way it's touching mine.

I can feel his body behind me. "I won't need these." He rumbles the words right into my ear and presses soft cotton into the hand hanging at my side. I look down to see I'm holding the pair of clean boxers I gave him. "I don't wear them to bed," he says, his voice still gravelly from sleep. I'm positive I'm blushing, and I'm glad my back is turned.

Despite his swagger, as soon as I usher a pajamaed Clay back into bed, his eyelids drift closed. He's been through so much tonight. More than he should ever have had to endure.

"Need a pillow," he mumbles, already half-asleep.

"You have one right here," I whisper, guiding it under his head.

"Need a better one." He pulls me by the waist until I'm pressed up next to him on the bed. Then he rests his head in the crook of my arm, a contented sigh escaping his lips. "Perfect," he says. And just as he's falling asleep, "You smell like the ocean."

I can imagine the bliss of surrendering to sleep in Clay's arms. If only I could control my tail. Over the next few hours, every time Clay shifts or mumbles in his sleep, I sit bolt upright, terrified that either the potion or the antidote is having some deathly side effect. I have another dose of the cure waiting on the nightstand in case he needs it. I watch him sleep and whisper that he'll be all right, that I'll make everything okay for him.

When the first rays of pink sunlight peek through his curtains, I extricate my arm from under his head. Then I allow myself a second to admire him. I've never seen him like this before—after a night's sleep. His hair is mussed, his lips parted. I don't want to leave him; I want to stay here enveloped in his warmth, in this refuge of sheets that smell faintly of cinnamon. But he's fine now. I nudge his shoulder until he's awake just enough for me to siren him. To be safe, I sing the entire song. Now's not the time to leave him alone unprotected, and I have to go. I owe someone a visit.

The sun hasn't even fully risen when I reach her door. I ring the bell. Repeatedly. I'm sure it's set up to echo in the grottos below, like the doorbell is in my house. I'm also sure that at this early hour, she's still asleep. But I didn't sleep last night so I don't think she deserves to either. I press the doorbell again, and I don't remove my finger.

The ring drones on and on until the door opens. I must have woken her, but she doesn't look disheveled in the least. Sure, she has bed head, but in a sexy movie star kind of way. She's still tying the sash of a red silk kimono around her slender waist when she pulls open the door. It reveals a deep V of skin along her chest, all the way down to her abdomen.

"I thought you might come calling," she says, her lips curling into a sea serpent's smile. "Since you're not strangling me, I assume lover boy's all right?"

Oh, I want to strangle her—more than anything else right now. But this situation needs to be handled delicately. So, I reign in the violent urges, the hatred, and use them to infuse my voice with authority.

"We'll talk about Clay. In private. Where's your father?" I ask. I must have woken him too.

"On a dive," she says, still smiling. "Leviathan's breath has to be picked right before sunrise."

"Who will you be poisoning with that?" I'm determined to wipe that damn smile off her face.

"It helps prevent hair loss. Didn't you hear about Mr. Piskaret? Poor man."

I did hear about him, of course. Mr. Piskaret was a Merman just a few houses down from me who started going bald. He was over fifty, and it really wasn't that surprising. But he killed himself anyway. He couldn't take the constant reminder that he was aging. That he wasn't immortal. I don't understand this way of thinking, but it's common enough among Mer who grew up Below. It isn't vanity; it's a deep, irrevocable sense of loss.

"Such a tragedy," Melusine says, the pity in her voice almost believable. "My father and I are doing our part to help our Community and keep something like this from happening again." She sounds like a politician. She lies like one, too.

Enough of this. My parents raised me to be courteous, to be polite. I pride myself on both qualities. But she doesn't deserve either. I push past her and step inside.

She doesn't have the decency to look affronted. She just keeps up that infernal smile. "Come in," she says when I'm already standing by the table in the entrance hall. Nothing's on it but a towering silk orchid in a waterless vase. Like everything above ground in this McMansion, it's fake. Just for show. "Welcome to my house."

"This house is owned by the Foundation. You lease it at their discretion." That shuts her up. Good. She needs to be reminded of her place here. And I'm the one to do it.

"I won't stay long," I continue. I don't want to be near her any longer than I have to. "You know what you did to Clay last night and so do I. More importantly, so do two other Mer. And we have proof."

I expect her to bristle, to argue. Instead, all she says is, "You're looking a little worn around the eyes, Lia. Did you stay up all night playing medic to a human?" She studies me, and her tone loses all trace of mocking when she says, "You really love him, don't you?"

Telling her it's none of her business would be an answer in itself—and I don't answer to her. So I ignore her question and say what I left Clay's bed this morning to say. "I have a sample of the potion that Clay remembers you giving him. I have the thermos full of poisoned tea that you brought to his house—with your fingerprints all over it. And I have two witnesses aside from me who saw the effects. One is a potions expert who can testify to its contents and implicate your father in its complex brewing." I pause to watch this sink in. Em said all those human courtroom dramas were a waste of time. Good thing I didn't listen.

Melusine's smile FINALLY disappears. "Daddy didn't brew it. I did. I found his notes on susceptibility potions … " She blinks, and then her wide eyes meet mine. "I didn't know the potion would conflict with the sireny. I'm … I need him to love me. You don't understand—"

"I understand plenty." I pin her with my stare. She's not worming her way out. "Now you understand this: I don't care who mixed the potion. I have enough to get both you and your father thrown into a warzone for illegal brewing and violence against a human. I won't have to mention sireny at all."

She crosses her arms over her ample chest. "And what if I do?" she asks, her voice a dangerous whisper. "What if I tell them exactly what you've been doing to Clay?"

She doesn't scare me. Not anymore. "Who would believe the word of an *udell* poisoner?"

A part of me feels dirty for dismissing my own crimes this way, but my words have the desired effect. Her face falls, defeat dowsing her defiance. If I go to the Foundation, there's nothing she'll be able to do to save herself.

"And the priccce of your sssilence?" she hisses, her Mermese accent slipping through the cracks of her façade.

"I don't want to ever have to think about you again. You will not so much as blink in Clay's direction—or any other human's. You place one scale over the line and you and your father are history. You can kiss your safety in this Community goodbye. Got it?"

She nods once.

"Tell me you understand," I insist.

"I undersssstand. There's nothing else I could try anyway. Clay's all yours. Enjoy him." Spite infuses her words, but I don't care.

She'll stay away from him now. She doesn't have a choice. I turn on my meager half-inch heel and walk toward the front door.

"Do you think he loves you?" she calls out behind me. "Do you think he ever will once he knows what you are? What you've done?"

My body tenses, but I don't turn back to face her. With her question still ringing in my ears, I leave the house and don't look back.

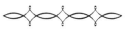

I've never ditched school before. In fact, I've had near perfect attendance all year. But wasting the rest of this monumental day cooped up in a classroom would be a travesty. Today deserves to be celebrated. Today is the first day that Clay is free from Melusine.

Today deserves to be savored. Today is the last day that Clay and I will ever be together.

Chapter Twenty

I go home, rush through a family breakfast, and grab my backpack for appearances. So many fake smiles. So many half-truths. Yes, I sure was out late with Caspian. No, we're not together ... yet. Yes, I admit he's handsome. No, I didn't sneak out of the guest grotto in the middle of the night. Yes, I'm sure. Every question wastes precious seconds.

Finally, I'm standing among the potted geraniums, my hand poised to knock on Clay's door. One more day. I'll allow myself one more day.

He opens the door dressed for school. I miss the intimate, bed-mussed appearance from earlier this morning, so I tousle his hair.

"Hey!" he exclaims in mock offense. His eyes are still glazed from my siren song earlier, but I won't let it bother me. Not today.

"Did Mrs. Halliburton come over yet?" I ask. Clay's neighbor checks in on him every morning before school while his mom's out of town.

"Yeah, she already left for work."

I grab his hand. "C'mon then! We're late for our adventure!"

"What adventure? We're just going to school."

"Not today, we're not."

Clay raises an eyebrow, "*You* wanna ditch?" Even with a mind still fuzzy from sireny, he's surprised. "You sure?"

I nod, my smile pushing up into my cheeks.

"Where are we going?" he asks.

"Anywhere you want."

He thinks. His own desires come to mind slowly, the way they always do when he's sirened. About a minute later, he tells me where he wants to go.

"You got it."

Clay's convertible is our own private world. It lets in the sea breeze and keeps out my worries. Clay serenades me with the cheesy songs he sings along to on the radio. I dance badly in my seat. By the time we've turned off the Pacific Coast Highway and away from the ocean, my hair is a tangled mess of wind and my tension has been laughed away.

The further inland we drive, the more daring I feel. For my sisters and I, trips into Los Angeles are few, far between, and short-lived. Since I got my legs three years ago, I've come into the city to go to a few museums and to see the ballet with my mother ("See, Aurelia, if ballerinas can do that with their legs, surely you don't need to worry about walking around school."). But those trips to L.A. lasted only a few hours. Being this far from the sea feels unnatural. It heightens the call of the ocean to a level that, just a few months ago, would have been uncomfortable. Now, though, after routinely harnessing the call to check on Clay through our bond, I'm more accustomed to the tug, and I can push it to the back of my mind. Which is a good thing because Clay and I plan to be here all day.

We drive through the wide residential streets, and I marvel at how all these people live a whole fifteen minutes from the ocean. Then we head to Sunset Boulevard and go into a store that must have been built for Clay. Three entire floors of guitars and music memorabilia. His eyes are so wide he reminds me of a blowfish. If blowfish looked windswept and sexy and wore low-rise jeans … okay, time to rein in my brain.

The clerk tells us some of Clay's favorite up-and-coming bands have performed gigs in the back room. Since it's empty during the day, I ask if we can see it. The awe on Clay's face as he stands on the black box stage and runs his hands reverently along the vintage posters lining the walls is enough to make the entire trip worth it.

But the day's still far from over. When Clay finishes drooling on at least half the guitars, he buys some new picks and a soft suede guitar strap, and we drive to our next stop.

We preview about a hundred food trucks and laugh at menu items like Squeeze My Meatballs and Berry Potter Pie. The Fishalicious Tacos tempt me, but Clay points out that L.A. is known for its gourmet burgers. Fish may be my fave, but since getting my legs, I've explored beyond the realm of Mer-cooked meals. I've learned to appreciate other human food, as long as it's not overly processed or chocked full of additives. The truck we settle on is painted bright green and boasts organic ingredients. Perfect! I follow Clay's lead, and soon I'm at the window, retrieving the juiciest burger ever. Afterwards, I steal Clay's napkins, and he chases me down the row of trucks, grabbing at me with ketchup hands. On foot, he's much faster than I am, so he catches me in no time. Living on land sure has its advantages.

Our next stop promises even more fun. The central plaza of the quaint outdoor shopping center buzzes with people. Clay drapes his arm around my waist as we walk, and several passersby shoot me jealous glances. I've always wondered what it would be like to try on clothes for my boyfriend like girls do in the movies. I find out when Clay pulls me into the first of several clothing stores, all featuring art-deco façades and high price tags. He compliments me on so many outfits that by the time we're done inside, I'm several shopping bags heavier.

Then we just stroll. We browse trendy odds and ends at kiosks and duck into intimate courtyards hidden among the shops. The European-style cobblestone walkways are newly built but romantic all the same. I've never had this much fun just walking around in public before. Back in the plaza, Clay stops me on a picturesque little bridge to admire the pond-like fountain below. I don't know if it's the look in his eyes, the fact that we're so far from the ocean, or the other human couples doing exactly what we are, but I feel … normal. More normal than I've ever felt. I bask in that feeling the entire drive home from Los Angeles.

When we get back to Malibu, I'm not ready for the day to end. My siren song has been wearing off all day. Soon it will be gone. My time is running out.

Clay and I head to El Matador Beach, which is within walking distance of both my house and his. The tightness in my chest lessens with the ocean in sight, but I don't welcome the relief. The closer we are to home, the closer we are to the end of our day. Our last day. No, I won't do this. I won't give into melancholy yet. It'll just make it that much harder to do what I must do.

There are couples here, too, walking hand in hand along the beach. They make this feel like a real date. I cling to the feeling, knowing today will be the last time I feel it.

It would normally worry me to be this close to the ocean around humans. That's why my family has invested in the stretch of private beach behind our house. But Clay's hand resting on my hip anchors my legs in place. I can even take off my shoes, bury my toes in the wet sand, and let the waves lap at my feet without fear of transforming. It's exhilarating.

Everything today has been exhilarating.

"Clay?" I turn to him, taking both his hands in mine. "I just want to say, thank you."

"Today was all your idea."

"Not just for today. These last few weeks, being with you has been … " I trail off, at a complete loss for what to say. How can you narrow down to a few paltry words something that means everything?

"A fairytale?" he asks, a teasing lilt to his voice.

"No!" I insist. "No. Being with you has been … real. This … us … has been real to me."

Tears sting the back of my eyes. I can't let him see so I squeeze them shut, will them away.

"Hey," he says in a comforting voice, "hey, what is it? What's wrong?" He cups my cheek in his palm, and I lean into his touch. "Do you think this isn't real for me? It is. Lia, I l—"

"Don't!" I say, my voice full of the tears I can't shed. "Please, don't say it. If you say it, I won't be able to—"

"To what? Lia, I don't understand."

Then his hand drops from my cheek. He staggers back and blinks several long, slow blinks.

No, no, it's too soon. It's not enough time. I want to turn my face to the heavens and plead for more time. Instead, I step close to Clay, wrap my arms around him and hold him close. I bury my face in his chest and inhale the scent of him—for the last time.

I can't do it. I can't let go.

Today was so wonderful. We could have a day just like it tomorrow. Just one more day and then I could let him go. That couldn't do any harm, could it? All I'd have to do is tilt my head up and hum. It would be so easy.

A hummed melody through my lips and we could have more time together. Clay could tell me he loved me. We could have everything. Everything I've ever wanted.

"Lia? What was I saying?" Confusion laces his voice again. I hate it. I hate myself for causing it. I hate myself for even thinking about violating him one more time when I don't have to. He's free from Melusine and now he'll be free from me.

It takes every ounce of strength to lift my head from his chest, to pull away from his body. This is it. The song has worn off, and I will never sing it again. I will give him his life back and let him live it without me.

All I have to do is turn around. Turn my back on him and

walk away. It's the right thing to do. It's the only thing to do.

But I don't do it.

My eyes meet his open, questioning ones, and I stop thinking. Grabbing two fistfuls of his shirt, I yank him up close to me. I raise myself on tiptoe and finally—finally—crash my lips against his.

He doesn't move. For an instant, he's completely still.

Then his lips part and I'm tasting him. He astounds my senses. My world becomes a whirlwind of supple lips and exploring tongue, of light stubble and sweet, gasping breath. I press the entire length of my body against his, twine my fingers in his hair, and lose myself in the heady, overwhelming taste of him. His lips and body are firm against mine, a buoy in the storm.

This. This is what I've longed for. For weeks. For a year. For my whole life.

Wrenching my lips from his is the hardest thing I've ever had to do.

I step back. He brings a hand to his lips, his expression stunned. I have no clue what he's thinking. There's no spell now to cloud his vision of me. Nothing to make him spend time with me, to make him love me. He's free to dismiss me now, free to reject me. Whatever he feels now is real.

I can't bear to find out.

With my heart still pounding and the taste of him still lingering on my lips, I turn and run down the beach.

Chapter Twenty-One

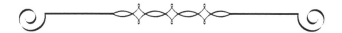

"Tell me it isn't true."

"Huh?" My head is reeling. All I want to do is be alone so I can crumple without witnesses. Why is Caspian standing outside my front gate? "Look, Casp, can we talk later? I've had just about the worst—"

"Tell me it isn't true," he demands again, his arms crossed over his broad chest. He's wearing a shirt. And shoes. I don't remember the last time I saw him in anything other than a bathing suit or a thrown-on pair of shorts. If I wasn't a hairsbreadth away from breaking down, I'd ask him about it. Right now though, I don't care. I just want him to go away and leave me to my grief.

"What are you talking about?" I ask. If I figure out what he wants, maybe I can get him to leave me alone.

"Tell me you didn't siren him."

The words are too crisp, too clear. The sun too bright.

This can't be happening. I'm imagining this. I must be. It's some morbid hallucination. Maybe I snapped when I left Clay, and now I've gone crazy and I'm seeing things—hearing things—

that aren't real.

I can barely keep my legs underneath me, let alone answer him. He takes my silence for the admission of guilt it is.

"You did." He tilts his head and stares at me like he's never seen me before. "I didn't really believe it. Didn't want to think … but it was the only thing that made sense."

"How did you find—"

"*That's* your response?" he shouts. "I say you're a siren, and all you want to know is how I found out?" He lets out a few choice curse words in Mermese. Caspian almost never curses. "You must think I'm an idiot."

"No, I don't," I insist.

"Oh, really? How else could I miss it? What other type of ancient, dangerous magic would my grandmother refuse to mention? What else would make someone fall asleep the second you told them to? You asked me all those questions about sireny," He shakes his head. It's a relief when his hair falls into his eyes and covers the betrayal there. But then he sweeps it back with one hand and I can't hide from his accusatory stare.

"Casp, please, it's not what you think."

"You didn't siren him?" Beneath the hate-filled sarcasm lives a weed of hope.

"I did, but—"

"How? How could you? I thought there must have been something I was missing. Some other possibility. If I just came here and asked you, if I were just honest with you … " He practically spits the word honest. He's shaking.

"I'll be honest. I'll be honest now, okay?" I say, my voice pleading. And I am honest. I tell him about Clay acting weird and moody, about seeing Melusine siren him, about endless hours of research that led to nothing, and about needing to find a way to help.

"And then, we were on this field trip, and she was so mean to him. Casp, she was controlling him. He tried to break up with her, and she was about to sing to him again so he couldn't. I couldn't let it happen. I sang this song he'd written. I just wanted to protect him."

"That worked? Using his own song?" For a second, the academic in Caspian wins out. *Maybe if I can hold on to his curiosity ...*

"Yeah, actually there's a precedent for it that I read about in—"

"How long ago?" He cuts me off.

"How long ago did I read about—"

"How long ago did you siren him?" His words escape through gritted teeth. *He needs answers.*

"Four weeks"

"Four weeks? The spell lasts that long?"

My face heats with shame. "It lasts half a day or so. Sometimes more. Sometimes less." I mumble the words. *He's going to know what they mean.*

"You've sirened him every day for four weeks?" A mixture of shock and utter disgust darken his face. *Seeing Caspian look at me that way breaks me.*

I can't keep up the strength in my legs, so I let my weight clunk down to my knees in the gravel driveway.

"I had to. I had to. She would've just taken him back. Please understand! She would've ... I couldn't let her. I just couldn't."

"So, you did this for him? To help him?"

"Yes!" I exclaim, so relieved he seems to get it.

"That was really your only reason? You're telling me you didn't like it at all?"

"What? No!"

"Oh, please. I heard the way you called him your boyfriend." He spits that word, too. "Are you telling me you don't like having him cling all over you? Admit it, Lia. It's been fun for you."

I shake my head in adamant denial. But I might throw up, because it has been fun. A part of me has had more fun these past four weeks with Clay than I've ever had before. That's why I had to leave him on that beach. Because I couldn't bear to hear him say he doesn't feel the same, doesn't love me—and how could he when every moment we shared was a lie? Spending any more time with him … I'd be too tempted to do it again. To siren him just to keep feeling the way I feel when he's near me. I've promised myself I'll never do that again. Not ever.

"What did you make him do, huh Lia? Did he kiss you? Touch you? How far did the two of you go?"

"That's enough!"

"Is it? He's not your toy, you know. He has feelings."

"I know that."

"Do you? Do you know I have feelings?" His voice breaks, but he continues. "Did you even think about what you were doing to me? You sent me into Melusine's house, and I went because I trusted you. I have always trusted you. Done anything I could to help you. And you didn't even think about me." He looks down at my face from where he towers above me. Disappointment shines in his eyes. And hurt. So much hurt.

"I did think about you."

"Don't. Don't lie. Not again. You know how much my family suffers from just the ghost of sireny, and you've dragged me into it again. Dragged my grandmother into it. Into this sick game of yours."

"Caspian, I didn't have a choice."

"Yes, you did. You had a bad choice, but you had a choice. Do you understand what you chose to risk? Your choice could affect your family for generations." His shouts grow louder, meaner. "Your parents. Em and the twins. Amy. Amy's grandchildren. Her great grandchildren. All of them would be despised if anyone found out what you did."

It's true. It's all true. Tears finally pour down my cheeks as I picture my family shunned by the very Community they've worked so hard to build. Pearls mix among the gravel that digs into my knees.

He doesn't acknowledge my pain. He just keeps talking. Each word twists the hook in deeper. "And don't forget the human. You think you did this to protect him? You enslaved him. Just like

Adrianna did to her human. Just like all those other sirens did. How could you cause that kind of pain? How did you become like those monsters? You don't care about anyone, do you?"

"Yes!" Now I'm the one shouting. "Yes, I do! I care about Clay more than I have ever cared anyone. Maybe I made a bad choice, but I did it for a good reason." I get to my feet, my own conviction giving me strength. "I stopped. Do you hear me? I stopped today. Now that we have enough on Melusine to keep her in line, I let Clay go. Do you think I don't know his love for me wasn't real? That every touch … Of course I know! That's why I stopped sirening him today and why we can't be together. I'll never let myself get close enough to him to be tempted to sing again. No matter what I feel for Clay, I'm not going to push myself on him." I'm shaking now, too. Badly. "Leaving him was the hardest thing I'll ever do, and I did it because I *do* care."

Caspian stills. His voice is low, roughened from his earlier shouts, when he asks, "You stopped sirening him? You swear?"

"I swear." My oath is solemn, my eyes wet. "And I'm the one who'll have to live with that choice for the rest of my life."

Silence.

Then Caspian clears his throat. "It's good you've stopped. It means I won't have to turn you in." The stark relief on his face tells me that's a choice he dreaded making. "But I can't forgive you for this. Not ever. You're a siren."

I'm everything he's always hated.

"Caspian, don't!" I beg.

He holds my gaze for a long, life-altering moment. Then, just as I left Clay, Caspian leaves me. He turns his back and walks away down the street.

As his tall frame gets smaller and smaller, my heart breaks for the second time today.

"Your face looks as tragic as a beached baby seal," Lapis says from the living room.

I don't respond. I barely hear her. I'm halfway up the stairs before she rests a hand on my shoulder.

"Hey, what's wrong?"

I have no words. I have no tears, either. Maybe I shed them all with Caspian. Maybe I've dried myself out. That's how I feel inside: dried up, withered, dead.

I shrug off her hand and shake my head. "Alone," I say. "I just need to be alone." That's a lie. What I need is to be with Clay. For Caspian to forgive me. But neither of those is going to happen. Alone is all I have to work with.

Lazuli has come up behind her now, and both of them look back and forth between me and each other, unsure what to do. They're concerned, but I can't bring myself to care. So, I take advantage of their indecision and retreat to my upstairs room.

Over the next few hours, they take turns trying to get me to unlock the door. When nothing works, they tell me Mom and Dad will be back from the Foundation soon and Leomaris is coming to dinner, so my parents will expect me to come down.

I sit on my bed, clutching a pillow to my chest. I must look like the perfect stereotype of some angst-ridden teenage girl. Only I'm not. If I were a stereotypical teenage girl, I could text my bf a few emoticon hearts, and we'd get back together. But I can't. I can't get Clay back because I never had him. And I never will. He deserves someone so much better than me. Someone who would never do what I've done. Someone who he loves for real. These last few weeks have been nothing more than a dream. A beautiful, tragic dream.

Well, I'm awake now. I'm awake, and it hurts more than anything has ever hurt. I'll never have the dream back.

Dry, giant sobs wrack my body. I gasp for air as the sheer force of them cleaves me in two. They go on and on and on until I'm curled up on my bedspread, exhausted. My chest aches, my head aches, and I focus on that because it's easier than thinking about what I've lost.

The sun has set by the time I drag myself from that bed. My parents are calling me downstairs and, while I don't want to go, I really don't want to answer their questions about my absence. Without comprehending how I got there, I'm sitting at the dining room table with a plate of food in front of me that I don't eat. Lapis and Lazuli keep shooting me sideways glances, but everyone else focuses on Emeraldine and Leomaris.

I don't understand why until they say they have an announcement. Their happy faces seem surreal when I'm struggling with such gnawing sadness.

"We're getting married!" Emeraldine practically squeals. That's right, Emeraldine, my proper, self-possessed sister is squealing.

Her words cut through my fog like a jet ski through still waters. While everyone else cheers, I look at Em and Leo. Really look. Their grasped hands lie on the tabletop, and their radiant smiles fill the room. Em has never looked this happy. Leo, too, looks almost delirious with it.

"So, did you two decide to go traditional, or are you sentencing yourselves to seventy-odd years of monogamy?" Lazuli asks. At the looks on my parents' faces, she adds, "What? We were all thinking it."

Leomaris comes to the rescue. "We still haven't decided. We know it'll be … a challenge to navigate such uncharted waters." He stops to laugh at his own lame joke, and my father joins him.

"But," Emeraldine picks up, "we don't want to waste precious time that we could be spending together worrying about what problems we might swim into."

"That's right," Leo says. "We can't solve everything. Some things we'll just have to figure out as we go along."

He turns and shares a smile with my sister. She melts in her chair and snuggles her head against his shoulder, bringing his hand up to her lips for a kiss. "Some things are worth the risk."

You know that moment when you've been swimming down

deep in dark waters and you break the surface and your hair flips back slick out of your eyes and the sun hits your face for what feels like the very first time? That's how I feel right now. I look at my sister, and I look at Leo. Ever since they were fourteen, I've thought they were this perfect couple, with absolutely nothing working against them. But they're not. They have to work at it. They have to make tough calls and be honest and communicate even when it means risking pain. They fight for each other. And they do it because they love each other.

If I ever want to be that happy, I have to take a risk, too. If I don't want to spend the rest of my life curled up in my room, I have to stop mourning something I haven't even lost yet. And I have to stop telling myself I'm not strong enough to face the possibility of Clay rejecting me without resorting to sireny. Because I'll never be strong enough if I don't give myself the chance. I have to fight for Clay—even if it means fighting my own fear.

Maybe he doesn't feel what I feel. Maybe he never did. But how will I know unless I go to him? I have to go to him.

I make a decision right then and promise myself to stick to it no matter what: I will leave him alone tonight so there's no doubt the spell has completely worn off. Then, tomorrow morning, I will tell Clay I love him.

Chapter Twenty-Two

I don't remember what time I finally fell asleep. It was all I could do not to summon my legs, jump from my sea sponge bed, and run to Clay. Now that I've decided to tell him how I feel, I can't think of anything else. Does he feel the same? Will he tell me he loves me, and mean it? Will he flat-out reject me?

I spent hours last night reliving each of our conversations and trying to decipher what his real feelings might be. All I managed to do was stoke my own anticipation.

But I stayed put. I forced myself not to go to him. If I want to know his real feelings, it's crucial that I give the spell time to totally leave his system.

Now, pre-set music drifts down into the grottos to wake us up in lieu of sunshine. Usually, I'm one of the last ones up, especially on a Saturday. But today, as the lights embedded high in the cave walls brighten on their timed dimmer, I'm already swimming out of bed. Is Clay awake yet? What's he thinking? Is he thinking about me? Does he hate me for running away?

A somber mood plagues our house this morning. In my

anxiety over seeing Clay, it takes me a moment to remember why. It's the anniversary of the curse. It's harder for my parents than for my sisters and me, but no one brings it up. It's not something you talk about. Community policy is to resist spending the day in mourning; instead, we're supposed to carry on with the lives we have. That's what I intend to do.

When my entire family is awake and upstairs, I tell my parents all my homework is done and Caspian invited me to spend the day in his pool. Fresh pain stabs into me at the thought of Caspian. At the disgust on his face, at the hurt in his eyes, at the determined set of his shoulders as he walked away from me last night. As he left me. Saying his name out loud hurts. But it's the only way my parents will let me leave the house after catching me with Clay just three days ago. So, I smile big and hope they buy it. They do—hook, line, and sinker.

I put on one of my favorite outfits: A t-shirt that's just the right combo of clingy and casual, and a short but not too short white canvas miniskirt. I need to look better than I've ever looked. This day may be the day Clay tells me he loves me. If he does, I want to look beautiful for him. Tides, just thinking about it makes a whole school of butterfly fish circle in my stomach.

If he does the other thing ... if he rejects me ... says he doesn't love me and never did ... well, I'm hoping the outfit will help me feel beautiful for *me*. Maybe it'll keep me confident enough to stay on this side of a breakdown. Either way, by the time I leave my house, I feel powerful.

By the time I reach Clay's house, I'm back to terrified. But I push myself forward. Step by step, I make my legs carry me up his walkway to his front door. His doorbell has never sounded so loud, so resonant.

But he doesn't answer. His car's in the driveway, so I know he's home. I ring again. And wait.

And ring. And wait. He must still be sleeping. I fidget with my t-shirt. Should I risk waking him up? I pull my cellphone out of its waterproof case and call his number. The blaring rocker beat of Clay's ringtone blasts into the street from his open window. His phone plays note after note, but he doesn't answer. When I call two more times, he still doesn't answer.

Disquiet replaces my giddiness. Clay never goes anywhere without that phone. He's probably just in the shower. Yeah. Or he hates me and isn't taking my calls. Maybe it's a sign I should save myself the heartbreak and just go home.

But something feels wrong. I'm like a fish that just smelled danger.

I go around to the side gate. It's unlocked, as usual. The backdoor is also unlocked—that's unusual.

"Clay?" I call as I enter, trying not to sound nervous.

When there's no answer, I head to the bottom of the stairs. "Clay?" I say again, louder.

I go up the stairs, my anxiety escalating with every step.

Then I'm standing at his bedroom door. I listen for running water from the bathroom beyond. Nothing. "Clay? It's Lia. I just want to talk for a minute."

The door isn't fully closed. I push against it, and it opens with a creak. And reveals a scene from a nightmare.

My heart plummets to my stomach. Ritualistic symbols line the walls in a translucent, sickly blue ink. They're the ones Caspian found in Mr. Havelock's office. The ones he scribbled on his hand to show me. The ones that were so old, even Casp couldn't translate them. Melusine and her father have been here—in Clay's room.

The biggest symbol glares down at me from the wall above Clay's bed. Then my eyes shift to the bed itself.

"NO!"

I'm barely aware of my own scream. All my attention fixates on the sight before me. The bed sheets hang off the bed, as if someone dragged a body across them. As if someone dragged Clay's body across them. Whatever happened here, it was violent.

Staining the sheets are several drops of blood. I fight to swallow down my terror.

They've taken him. They've taken Clay.

Chapter Twenty-Three

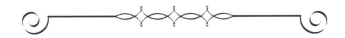

I bang on the Havelocks' front door. I pound my fists against it to no avail. I can't get around to the back, and their underwater entrance is sure to be even more heavily fortified. I glance up and down the quiet, tree-lined street. No dog walkers. No children playing hopscotch. Not a person in sight. Good.

I pick up a rock that lies among the California poppies and hurl it through the window. I wrap my sweater around my arm and reach in through the shards of glass to unlock the door. Moments later, I'm standing in the Havelocks' dark entryway.

I venture deeper into the house than I have before. An eerie stillness permeates the place. I check all the most likely hiding spots for an entrance to the grottos and find it in a back closet off the kitchen.

Down, down, down, I go, winding ever closer to the underwater caverns below. Are Melusine and her father down here? Did they not hear me up above? I keep my footsteps as light as I can. If they have Clay down here, maybe I can still catch them off guard.

The grottos in my house are welcoming. We keep them lit all the time except when we're sleeping, and our twinkle lights reflect off the iridescent walls to give the place a warm glow. These grottos couldn't be more different. The farther down I go from the sunlit kitchen above, the darker it gets. By the time I reach the antechamber, it's as pitch dark as you'd expect an underground cave to be. I can still see just fine, but in the darkness, the moisture clinging to the walls makes the whole place feel dank and cold.

When I reach the antechamber, the water shines inky black. I leave my shoes at the edge and hike my skirt up over one shoulder like a beauty queen's sash across my chest. I transform so quickly, I barely feel it. The black ripples swallow up my golden tail.

I move as fast as I dare through the large grottos meant for public rooms. Unease eats away at my insides as condensation drips off the walls and echoes through the cavernous darkness, dwarfing me. I don't hear anyone. They must have Clay in the private grottos in back. I shiver at the thought of him down here. He won't be able to see a thing, and for him, it will be much, much colder. I swim faster.

A hallway leads me even deeper under the house. The entrance to the next cave is much smaller—a bedroom probably or an office. I plaster myself against the wall outside so if someone's inside, they won't easily spot me. Then I peek my head around. No one. I do the same thing at the next room. And the next.

I've checked every grotto; Melusine and her father aren't here. But they may have hidden Clay somewhere.

The blood I saw on Clay's bed sheets scares me. Maybe they left him somewhere, and he's hurt and needs a doctor. Maybe he's d—no, I won't think it.

Forget stealthy.

"Clay?" I call. "Clay?"

I check every inch of the grotto, every possible hiding place. He's nowhere.

Back upstairs, my wet lower half drips onto the polished

wood floors. I search every room here, too. Every closet, every bureau, under every bed. I even venture into the crawl space attic, but it's empty. Clay isn't in this house.

Where, then? Where would they take him? *Think.* What do I know? They took him from his room sometime last night or this morning. They painted creepy ancient symbols on his walls. Why? The only reason to use ancient Mermese aside from scholarship is dark magic.

They're using Clay for some kind of spell. But what spell and why Clay? Are they afraid I'll charge them with poisoning him? Are they planning to kill him to get rid of the evidence? That makes no sense—Melusine knows I still have other witnesses and a sample of the poison.

They've had him for what must be hours. Whatever they're doing to him, they've probably already started. I have to find him fast.

What would they need for a spell? I'm not trained in magics—especially dangerous, illegal magics. But I've read about them in my sireny research. For some magic, you need ingredients, usually some kind of dried sea plants or body parts of sea creatures (yuck), but it's different for every spell. What you always need is power. For small things like making medicines, the power comes from the ingredients and from the Mer doing the mixing. But for big spells, you'd need a bigger power source. For an ancient spell so powerful it requires long-forgotten Mermese symbols, you'd probably need the biggest power source.

You'd need the ocean.

My body erupts in goose bumps. They've taken Clay out to sea.

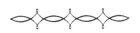

Like all Community-owned houses, the Havelocks' is beachfront. Yanking my skirt back down from where I hiked it up across my chest earlier, I run out their backdoor. After the dark interior, the sunlight blinds me. How can the sun be this bright when Clay is hurt and in danger? I don't wait for my eyes to adjust before running toward the waves.

Blue vastness. Water stretching as far as my eyes can see. It's always seemed so beautiful, so infinite. Now, it's terrifying. Clay is out in that blue somewhere, and I have no idea where. If I'd gone to him earlier, this may have never happened. If I'd kept him sirened, I could use the bond now to find him. Without it, what chance do I have?

I used the bond so many nights when I didn't even need to— to watch him read or sleep. To feel the cozy, reassuring warmth of his contentment. Now I need it, and it's gone.

Or is it? In all that research I did, there was never an account of what happened to a mortal *after* he was released from sireny. I guess all victims were murdered or forgotten by their sirens. No siren has ever loved her mortal. Until now. Until me. I love Clay. And I'll try anything. Standing by the ocean, my toes nestled in the damp sand, I close my eyes and reach out with my mind to find Clay, as I have so many times before. I expect to feel the call of the ocean assaulting my senses. I expect to have to push past it like I always do. But it doesn't come. All that raw power is gone. It must have left me when my last siren song wore off.

Now I don't know how to find him. The salty, sea air fills my lungs, the wind whips through my hair, and the cool waves lap at my toes. I'm about to open my eyes, when I feel … something. Something so quiet I almost miss it. It's not a strong tug like it was when Clay was under my spell. That felt frantic and mighty, like the call of the ocean itself. This is faint. A very faint drawing feeling. Before, the siren bond felt like if I took control and pulled it, I'd call Clay to me. But this is something different. This feels like I'm the one being pulled, being drawn away. Will it draw me toward Clay? Only one way to find out.

I open my eyes and look up and down the beach. It's private, like the one behind my house, but Melusine's neighbors are closer than mine. I don't see anyone. Still, it's broad daylight. It's against Community law for me to transform in the ocean now, for me to risk exposing myself and everyone else.

But Melusine and her father have Clay. Without another thought, I dive into the frothy waves and swim out as far as my human legs can take me. Then, in a flash of golden tail, I dive deeper.

Whoa! My eyes flick everywhere at once. I've never been in the ocean during daylight. It's even more startling in its beauty than our blaringly bright, flower-lined street was when I first got my legs and ventured up from the dim seclusion of the grottos.

The sunlight filters through the water, creating the richest, most brilliant colors I've ever seen—turquoises and aquas, chartreuses and viridians, all punctuated by magenta and electric orange. I wish I had the time to enjoy it, to play with the fish that match my set of neon highlighters. But stopping isn't an option.

I close my eyes to the wonders surrounding me and search again for that faint drawing feeling. It's stronger now that I'm in the water, but still nowhere near as powerful as it was just yesterday when I was still a siren. The sensation guides me forward by the thinnest of threads, and I follow it. I picture Clay at the other end of this bond, and I swim faster. Rock formations, stalks of seaweed, and brightly colored fish all blur past me as I pick up more speed. My tail beats up and down and I slice through the water. Nothing can stop me.

Until something does. I come to a complete halt at the sight before me. Its blue bioluminescence is fainter in the daylight, but there's still no mistaking the neatly planted row of bamboo coral. The Border.

How could I have reached it so quickly? I close my eyes, and the bond urges me onward. I gulp in fear, swallowing water that flows back out through my gills. How could she?

Melusine needs to be in the ocean for whatever spell she's casting, but it never occurred to me that she'd go *past* the Border. I know she grew up in the open ocean, but returning after she'd deserted the land Below to live Above? Going back into the warzone? It could be suicidal. What spell is worth putting herself and her father in that much danger?

I don't know. But I know what's worth it to me. Clay. He has to be alive, doesn't he? I wouldn't feel the bond otherwise. But how is he still breathing? Will he be alive by the time I reach him? I look again at the Border. Will I be able to stay alive once I swim past the very barrier built to keep me safe?

I peer into the water over my shoulder. I should go back. Surely, I should go to my parents. Bring a search team from the Foundation. I pull my body vertically, wading in indecision. Would they even believe me? I'd have to tell them about the bond, and once I did, they'd see me as a siren—a criminal and a monster—and they wouldn't trust me. Even if they thought I was telling the truth, they might think Clay was a liability and let him die. I can't let that happen. I have to go myself.

Caspian's angry words from the night before replay in my head. I wish we hadn't fought. If I don't come back ... No. I won't think about that now. I can't.

Just as it always does when I'm at the Border, the call of the ocean whispers to me to go deeper. Compels me to explore my true home. I stare out in front of me, beyond the Border, into what seems an endless watery mystery. Into a warzone. Into everything I've ever been taught to fear.

"Where you go, I go," I whisper.

With one more hard flick of my tail, I swim over the Border.

Chapter Twenty-Four

I'm on the other side of the Border. The *other side*. I never thought I'd be here. The water, the fish, the kelp canopy—it all looks the same, but it feels different. It feels forbidden.

For the first few miles, I tell myself that nothing has really changed, that I'm still safe. But deep down I know with every sweep of my arms and swish of my tail, I'm foisting myself farther from that safety. It's like I can suddenly feel every inch stretching behind me, separating me from home. I grow hyper-aware of the speed I'm traveling, of the sound my fin makes as it pounds through the water, of the brush of fabric against my stomach ... I gasp, and my sharp inhale forces a flood of water through my gills. Fabric against my stomach! My shirt! How could I be so stupid? Tides, I'm wearing a human t-shirt. Why didn't I think to change into a *siluess*? If anyone sees me ... Out here, I'm not the sheltered little darling of the Community founders. Out here, I'm in enemy territory with a price on my head because I'm a relative of the old royal family—of the Little Mermaid herself. It doesn't matter how distant a relative I am, it's still grounds for public execution if I'm captured.

I fight to even out my breathing. Panic won't do any good. I pause only long enough to untangle a sharp shard of cockle shell from the kelp. While I swim, I use it to cut off the cap sleeves and the fabric that covers my abdomen. At least the fabric is metallic. Most Mer clothing sparkles or shines with precious gems or pieces of shell, so from far away my ripped shirt will now pass for a *siluess*. But up close, it'll look like polyester.

I'll just have to make sure I don't get close to anyone. With the population so decimated from the curse and the wars, I should be fine as long as I stay away from Mer settlements. Of course, the bond could be leading me straight into the ocean's most populated village. All I can do is hope that's not the case.

I'll have to stay as close to the surface as I can for as long as I can. That's the best I can do. Avoiding the occasional boat will be a small price to pay for the comfort of sunlight and the diminished risk of encountering other Mer. Having a plan soothes my nerves.

Until another pull from the bond destroys that plan. My insides lurch as the bond urges me downward. I stare at the endlessness of the water stretching below me, and I dive deeper.

And deeper.

And deeper.

I've never been this deep. The expanse of ocean on my side of the Border doesn't go down this far. The water here is murkier, rich with minerals, and it takes my eyes time to adjust.

My vision sharpens just in time for me to dart out of the way. A pack of four sea horses glides in my direction, and my mouth gapes open as I gaze at the colorful, stately creatures. These aren't the itty-bitty things I've held in my hands. Each of these is as big as a, well, as a horse.

They're all so dazzlingly beautiful, it almost hurts to look at them. These are the creatures my ancestors rode across the ocean for generations. Ever since I was a little girl, I've dreamt of seeing one, but they only live down deep. Undiscovered by humans.

The stuff of legend.

One changes from light pink to deep purple as he swims in front of a towering purple rock. His companion dips its bright yellow head in my direction, inviting me to follow. Oh, how I wish I could. How I wish I could pet them and ride them into safer waters. Instead, I let the majestic animals continue past me, and I push myself forward with my fin. I glance back over my shoulder and watch them grow small with distance. Once they're out of sight, loneliness settles over me, seeps into me.

Eventually, all traces of sunlight disappear. The water grows colder. Colder than I've ever felt. My skin is smoother than a human's for added water resistance, but it's also much thicker. So, while I'm aware of the cold, it doesn't bother me. But if Clay's down here and somehow still alive, he must be freezing.

The deeper I go, the more the water pushes against my arms and tail. I cycle through different strokes to keep my muscles from tiring, but at the speed I'm compelling myself to travel, it's a losing battle.

Then I'm forced to slow down as the waters in front of me darken further, and a shiver spiders its way up my spine. For miles on either side of me, and rising so high over my head I can't see where it stops, a forest of dense black coral blocks my path, swaying menacingly in the current. I gulp, my head snapping from side to side, searching for any way around, any way over, any way but through. The scared little girl part of me—the part I've been fighting since I crossed the Border, no, since I saw Clay's empty room—that part wants to cry as another fateful yank at my center from the bond pulls me forward, dragging me straight into the thick, sharp blackness.

I grit my teeth and swim ahead, letting that blackness swallow me. Once I'm inside, I can see next to nothing. Even with my enhanced eyesight, I only make out vague shapes of what's right in front of me. Skeletal stalks of spiny coral wind upward from the ocean floor, pressing in on me from all sides, grabbing at me like crooked, bony fingers. I have to make my way forward—

there's no other option—so I stretch my arms in front of me, feeling my way blindly as I twist my body this way and that, weaving through the stony, treacherous spikes.

Ah! Pain sears my skin as a jagged spine of coral scrapes along my forearm. *Don't be bleeding. Please, don't be bleeding.* One open wound, one drop of blood, and I'll attract every shark from miles around. Since Mer blood smells like whale or seal blood to sharks, it whets their appetites even more than human blood does. If I'm bleeding and I ever make it out of this forest, I won't survive long enough to stop Melusine. I jerk my arm close to my body, squinting at the red welt there. I suck on it but don't taste the telltale copper of blood. *Just a scratch.* My whole body sags in relief, sending my tail colliding into more of the knife-like coral spokes. I shrink in on myself before any can pierce my scales, not daring to twitch another muscle.

What am I going to do? The outlines of the coral skeletons that trap me appear more sinister than ever. Monstrous.

Any move I make will risk injury, blood I can't dare spill. But I can't just stay here paralyzed forever.

Do it for Clay. Get to Clay.

I repeat the words to myself as I reach my arms back out, give my tail the smallest of flutters, and inch my way onward. In the silence, a quiet but constant crunching meets my ears, alerting me to the hundreds of sea creatures that lurk in this forest, feeding on whatever they've managed to sink their teeth into today. I'm surrounded.

Now that I've focused on it, the sound magnifies, making me that much more desperate to escape. With strokes even slower and more calculated than before, I weave my way over and under, beneath and between. When blessed blue peeks through the black up ahead, I want to weep with joy. It's the first sign I might actually make it out of this hellish darkness. I arch my back and extend my tail all the way as I writhe through a tight gap in the coral toward that promise of blue openness. I'm going to make it, I'm—

I suck water through my teeth as I'm yanked backward. A glance down at my fin makes me want to curse; it's caught between two of the spiny, black branches. Wincing, I twist around to examine it, and my hip jostles another large stalk.

A pair of glowing, yellow eyes pierce the darkness.

They blink open right behind me and send my heartbeat skittering. Images of a medieval sea serpent or a giant squid that could squeeze the life from me plague my imagination. I twitch my tail back and forth, frantic to get free. Those yellow eyes inch closer to me, and all of a sudden, I'm panting, nearly hyperventilating as my gills flap faster and faster. It takes all my willpower not to just rip my fin free. I tell myself those glowing, terrifying eyes belong to something harmless, a manta ray maybe or a large crab, and force myself with all my might to believe it. Without making any sudden movements, and being careful to only touch the coral where it isn't sharp, I pull back one of the branches at the same time that I curl the now-bruised left point of my tail inward.

It works! With my tail free, I glance back at those eyes, growing ever closer. Belonging to I-don't-want-to-know-what. A resounding *snap!* makes me jump, heart clanking against my ribs now. Teeth? Could it be massive, snapping teeth?

I'm halfway through the gap; if I can just make it out … My body undulates through the barbed branches that jut out at every angle. With one last powerful thrust of my tail, I propel myself forward.

A loud thrashing and grinding behind me tell me whatever was following me is stuck in the sharp coral barbs.

Free at last from the forest's clutches, I surge forward without looking back, emerging into the freedom of open ocean. I'm about to let the relief wash over me when I look down at the most devastating sight I've ever seen.

A battlefield stretches out below me, the ocean floor strewn with spears, swords, and bodies. So much gore. So much blood. It stains the sand. Body parts litter the ground. Tails of every color lie sliced open—a macabre jewel box spattered with red and crusted brown. Turned up faces stare at me with vacant eyes.

It's scenes like this that I've been sheltered from my entire life. I'm frozen in place, eyes fixed on the massacre below me. What caused these senseless deaths? Were they fighting to depose another self-proclaimed leader? Were they throwing away their lives to install someone new? Someone who tempted them with promises of breaking the curse, of restoring immortality? Or had they lost hope altogether and turned to violence and anarchy out of desperation?

Permanent agony contorts each lifeless face. So much suffering. Bodies battered and bloody, limbs twisted at odd angles, fins hacked off.

My stomach seizes. I can't let myself be sick here; I can't defile these dead any further. I kick my fin and launch myself behind a thicket of fan coral just before I lose my meager breakfast. Wiping my face with the back of my hand, I move to straighten up. Voices. I duck back down.

"*This sword'll be all right. Once we clean it off,*" one rough voice says in Mermese as it gets closer.

"*These will fetch something, too,*" another, even gruffer voice replies. Through the coral, I can see a hairy hand rip a strand of polished limpets off a fallen fighter's chest. "*You won't miss it, will ya, fella?*" He nudges the body with his tail, and the head lolls toward the side, the glassy eyes staring into mine where I duck down low. Stuffing the limpets into a sack, the thief laughs.

I curl my tail toward my chest, making myself as small as possible. If these men plan to sell the stolen possessions of the dead, just what would they do with me if they found me? From my hiding place, I can see both of them are large and burly, with corded muscle winding like sailing rope beneath their skin. A layer of thick hair covers their chests and arms. One bears a squid ink tattoo of a tiger shark on his bicep. If they see me, I won't stand a chance of fighting them off. As they pick their way through the gore, moving closer to me with every body they disturb, I will myself to be invisible.

"*Let's do a sweep of the coral. A stingray spear could've rolled in there.*"

Every one of my muscles tenses.

"*Nah, brother. I got more than I can carry as it is. We oughta get outa here before the sharks come and feast on all this.*"

"*Guess you're right. I'm hungry anyway. Starril must be getting lunch ready by now.*"

"*Bet that's not all she's getting ready.*"

Only once their crude jokes and barking laughter fade out of earshot do I relax. I peek over the coral, but there's no one else. With one last, mournful glance at the destruction, I swim away from the scores of dead fighters.

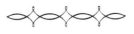

The bond pulls me farther and farther out to sea. I'm deep enough now that the ocean floor stays in my sights. I'm too deep to see any trace of the sun, but I've been swimming for so many hours that it's undoubtedly set already. What did my parents think when I missed dinner? When they called Caspian and realized I didn't spend the day with him? They must be worried. Are they looking for me? It would never occur to them that I'd swim out past the Border, so if they are searching, that means my dad is driving around Malibu, stopping at every sushi restaurant and yogurt shop, while my mom and sisters call all my school friends. If I weren't so worried about Clay, I'd feel terrible about it. But right now, my focus needs to be on getting to him.

What looks like a settlement comes into view below me. My instincts scream at me to hide before someone sees me. But as I inch closer, the town's utter disrepair tells me it's been long abandoned.

Homes and buildings made of what once must have been pristine white coral and polished stone are covered with algae.

Amber windows are cracked and spires towering upward from rooftops have entire chunks missing. An eel slithers between broken ceiling beams. A tentacle peeks out at me from the opened doorway of a dark dwelling some creature now calls home. Weeds shoot up through the seashell-tiled streets.

Anything valuable has been stripped by looters, but remnants of life still linger here and there. A kelp doll lies half-buried in the sand. Urchins and anemones overrun carefully laid seaflower beds. As I pass each abandoned house and storefront, I can almost feel the hustle and bustle, hear the echo of store clerks and shoppers, of families with children. Where did they all go? Are they hiding in far off caves from the constant battles? Are they dead?

The bond pulls me through the eerily beautiful streets until I reach what's left of the deserted town square. There, looming above me and the rest of the settlement, is a castle of crystalized ice and the same white coral. I try to picture it as the gleaming structure it must have been, but it's hard to see past the dinginess from decades of grime. The many towers that twist into the blue water above are gray with barnacles. The oyster shells lining its roof and pathways—once regal and shining—are splintered and filthy, the pearls ripped from their bellies long ago. But even in its ruin, the palace is impressive. I swim a few feet closer and suddenly, the bond stops short.

No more pull. Just a gentle, pulsing sensation telling me I've arrived. Whatever Melusine is doing to Clay, she's doing it in that castle. Kicking my tail, I move through the arching entranceway into the darkness within.

Chapter Twenty-Five

I swim alone into the elegant, decaying entrance hall. I'm hoping Melusine and her father will be distracted by the intricacies of whatever magic they're performing. With any luck, I can get Clay before they notice me, and we can make a break for it. Since we're in the water, I should be able to pull his extra weight without much trouble. It's not much of a plan, but it's all I have.

I expect to see Melusine fin-deep in an ancient ritual. I expect to see her father brewing some sickly-colored potion. I expect to see more creepy symbols defacing the walls. But I don't. I don't see anything. Because before my eyes can properly adjust to the darkness, someone grabs me from behind.

I struggle to pull my arms free. When I fail, I kick my tail, sending up swirls of sand and current. Then, whoever's behind me presses wadded up kelp against my mouth and nose. A second pair of hands closes over the gills on either side of my neck. I thrash my head back and forth, trying to dislodge them, but it's no use. I'm breathing in whatever noxious potion is on the kelp, and I'm growing dizzier by the second. Soon, all I see is black.

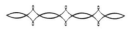

Pushing up the dead weight of my eyelids is a struggle. Once I manage it, I wish they were shut again because the sight that greets me is worse than any I could have imagined. Clay, bound from his shoulders to his ankles in seaweed with his face bruised and bloody, floats several feet in front of me, his eyes glued shut by the layer of ice clinging to his eyelashes. His skin a frosty, death-like blue.

My screams pierce the water.

"Relax." The saccharine voice is too calm, too cool. *"He's alive. For now."*

I drag my eyes away from Clay and focus them on her. We must be in one of the other rooms of the palace. My intuition tells me we're deep inside. Huge chunks of the columns that hold up the arched ceiling lie like ruins across the floor. An intricate mosaic of abalone, mother of pearl, and troca shell pieces peeks through layers of sand and dirt. I only catch sight of it because it shimmers in the light from above. About a hundred transparent, glowing jellyfish are strung around the large chamber like Chinese lanterns, casting the room in a greenish sheen.

Melusine wades in the center of it all, casually flicking her tail with the current. I want to lunge at her, want to rush to Clay, but I can't do either. I, too, am bound in seaweed. It winds too tightly around my arms, pinning them behind my back. Then it loops downward around my tail, yanking my fin up toward my tied hands. It's almost too painful to bear and renders me helpless. I pull at my bonds, hard, but it's no use.

"What have you done to him?" I demand instead.

"It's a rather ingenious potion, if I do say so myself." Mr. Havelock sounds far too pleased with himself. He isn't looking at me; he's swimming at a steep angle, facing downward so he can draw more symbols on the dirty ground. *"It brings the human*

body temperature down nearly to freezing point, suspending function and making it possible for him to stand the temperature and the pressure this far down. It also keeps him breathing."

"*But it doesn't last long,*" Melusine adds. She swims between me and Clay. "*I'd give it till sunrise, tops. After that, his breath will stop.*"

Sunrise? How long until sunrise? How long was I unconscious?

Melusine leans close, her sapphire eyes cutting into mine. "*It's in about two hours,*" she says, answering my unspoken question. "*But don't worry, you'll be saying goodbye to lover boy long before that. We're almost ready.*"

"*Ready for what? What are you going to do to him?*" I tug at my bonds again. Ow.

She gives me an indulgent smile, as if I were a small child. "*Why, kill him, of course. How else did you think this would end?*"

I stop moving. "*Why? Why Clay?*" I don't understand. "*Is this all because he tried to break up with you?*" Even as I say it, I know how stupid it sounds, but why else would she have it in for him?

She laughs so hard, bubbles erupt near her mouth. "*Tides, Lia, just how high school can you be?*" Her lips curl into a superior smile. "*You still have no idea who he is, do you?*"

My bewilderment must be written on my face.

She turns her back to me and closes the distance between herself and Clay. "*You see, Clay here, he's not just any measly human. He's special.*" She runs the back of her hand down his frozen cheek and neck. I want to rip her arm off and feed it to a shark.

"*I thought maybe you'd figured it out, and that's why you wanted him so badly. Why you took him from me. But, no. You just looove him.*" She makes the word a taunt. "*Disgusting.*"

"*But useful,*" her father pipes up, still focusing his efforts on the growing number of symbols emblazoned across the floor.

"*Very useful.*" She looks back at me. "*It's all about love, you see. She loved him so much, she sacrificed everything for him.*"

"*Who did?*" What is she talking about?

"*The bitch who caused all our problems. The Little Mermaid.*"

"What in the Seven Seas does she have to do with Clay?" I'm losing my patience. Clay's floating there, icy and trapped and running out of time.

"Everything. He's where the story ends." She whacks Clay on the arm, and he drifts through the water. She moves to his other side and whacks him on the other arm. She keeps this up, treating his body like a bouncing ball, abusing him like it's a game.

"Stop! What story?"

"Come now," her father says, putting down his brush and swimming toward us. His puce-colored tail swipes through the water in sharp, deliberate passes. He looks down his nose at me. *"You know what story. Even humans know it. A beautiful young sea maiden makes an unimaginable sacrifice for the sake of love."* His voice sounds even more oily in his native Mermese.

"But in the real version, no one sang their way into the sunset to a happily ever after, that's for sure," Melusine says, finally ceasing her assault on Clay. *"Like a little idiot, the Little Mermaid believed that love would conquer all. So, she struck a deal with the Sea Sorceress when she begged her to permanently banish her tail. If the prince married anyone but the Mermaid, the Mermaid would perish on the first sunrise after the wedding."*

Of course, I know all this. When I don't say anything, Mr. Havelock picks up the thread.

"The Mermaid—your distant cousin, I believe?—managed to hold the prince's interest for a time, but then he married another girl. A human princess, as well he should have. You should always stick with your own kind." He glares at me and then at Clay, as if to make his point. *"But the Mermaid had sisters, like you do."*

"Except they were much smarter than yours are."

"Her sisters cared about her very much," Mr. Havelock continues, as if his daughter hadn't interrupted, *"and didn't want to see her throw away her immortality for a lower life form. They went to the Sea Sorceress and pleaded with her to spare their sister. They traded their lovely hair for an enchanted obsidian dagger. The Little Mermaid had a choice: kill her one true love with the dagger*

and turn back into an immortal Mermaid, or die herself at sunrise. Unable to take the life of the man she loved, the Little Mermaid chose her own death. And so, say the humans, ends the tragic tale."

"Not!" Melusine interjects.

"Most decidedly not," her father agrees.

"I know!" I make my impatience evident. Every Mer knows. *"She refused and dropped the dagger into the ocean. The dagger unleashed a terrible curse the moment it hit the water. Because she had valued a human's life above her own immortality, all Mer were stripped of our eternal youth and forced to live human lifespans."* I rattle off. *"But what does that have to do with Clay?"*

"All that research on his family and you never figured it out?" Melusine shakes her head in mock disappointment. She swims up close to me—too close—and clamps my chin in an iron grip. *"Clay is the only direct descendant of that very same prince."*

What?

Everything fades away. The bruising pressure on my chin, the smug look on Melusine's face, the seaweed holding me prisoner. All I'm aware of are her words and Clay's unconscious, frozen face.

How is that possible? Clay's an American. We don't have royals. If he's a prince, why isn't he sitting pretty in Denmark with a crown on his head? Denmark … His family is from Denmark … where the Little Mermaid's prince was from …

When we were going over our family histories, Clay said he was the last one left on his mother's side. The side descended from the opera singer, Astrid. The one who was banned from the royal court after a scandalous affair. Could that mean … ?

"Long after the Little Mermaid's prince had become king, an ancestor of Clay's fell in love with the prince's grandson. She had the grandson's baby in secret, then disappeared."

Astrid. It was Astrid. She moved to America to escape her shame and start a new life.

My thoughts whirl, and I have to concentrate on Mr. Havelock's words. *"My family has tried to track down the descendants of that baby for over a century. We nearly lost hope. And then help came from the most unlikely source. The humans."*

He moves toward Clay's immobile body. *"I despise humans, and I loathed every minute I spent among them each time I snuck up to land over the years to continue the search, the way my father and grandfather taught me. Humans multiply and pollute. Their sonar kills our whale and dolphin hunting companions, their thirst for oil and nuclear energy poisons our seas, their exploratory missions force us into hiding. Yes, human technology has devastated our home in many ways. But it has also made information easier to access than ever before. And this information led me to finding the one person I thought was lost forever."* He pats Clay's head like he's a prized racehorse. *"Ancestry websites, immigration documents from over a century ago, birth records—all right there at my fingertips once I taught myself to use human machinery. Yes, I have known this boy's identity for over a year now. Just enough time to finish preparing Melusine—to have her perfect her English and leg control—so I could bring her on land to perform her part."*

"The Little Mermaid should have killed her prince two hundred years ago. If she had, we never would have been cursed," Melusine says, releasing my chin at last. *"Killing Clay tonight will solve our problems. Killing Clay will free us all."*

Chapter Twenty-Six

I can't let her do it. I test my bonds again, pressing against them as subtly as I can. Pain shoots up my bent tail. The restraints don't budge. I have to keep her talking, keep them talking, until I can figure out what to do.

"*Why tonight?*" I ask. "*You've had plenty of time alone with Clay. If you wanted to kill him, why didn't you do it while you were still dating, or as soon as you knew I was on to you?*"

"*What day is it?*" Melusine spaces out each word like I'm an idiot.

Oh! I am an idiot. "*The two hundredth anniversary.*"

The water muffles Melusine's applause.

"*The curse can only be changed every one hundred years, at sunrise.*" Mr. Havelock explains. "*My family would have changed it on the one hundredth anniversary, but they had found no descendant. That's why tonight's so important, Miss Nautilus. Why the approaching sunrise is so crucial.*" In the green glow of the jellyfish, his face looks even more angular, even more intimidating. "*I'm glad you're here to celebrate with us.*"

"*Yeah, Lia, wanna party? Maybe when we wake Clay up, he can sing for us. If he's still breathing.*" Melusine laughs again, sending bubbles skittering around our heads.

I need to distract her. To get her out of my face and give myself time to think. "*If you didn't need Clay until tonight, why did you bother sirening him? Did you just want to mess with him?*"

"*I'll leave you girls to your gossip,*" Mr. Havelock interrupts. "*I need to retrieve the artifact.*" With no further explanation, he swims across the large room and disappears through an archway into the darkness beyond.

"*Alone at last,*" Melusine says, swimming around me in a slow circle before stopping in front of my face again. "*To answer your question, I might hate humans, but playing with them sure can be fun.*" She winks lasciviously at me. If we weren't in the water, I'd spit in her face. Instead, all I can do is clench and unclench my hands behind my back, causing painful, needling tingles. My hands have long-since gone numb. So much for taking her down while we're alone.

"*But no,*" she continues, "*I sirened Clay for a reason. Like I told you before, this story's all about love.*"

"*You love Clay?*" I ask in disbelief.

"*Don't be gross,*" she shoots back. "*I could never love a lower life form.*" She waves a hand, dismissing the idea. I bristle. My parents would never have allowed me or my sisters to refer to humans as lower life forms. They're not. And they're certainly not any lower than the despicable Mermaid in front of me who keeps talking as if she hasn't just insulted an entire species. "*The crux of the curse is love. The Little Mermaid loved the prince, and he broke her heart. She didn't just die for him. She died heartbroken. Understand? We don't just need Clay to die. We need him to die heartbroken. We need someone he loves to break his heart.*"

She lets her words sink in, then continues, "*That's why Daddy needed my help. He explained everything to me before we surfaced. Before we came to live in your stifling little Community. He told me that I needed to make Clay love me and keep him in love with me until the anniversary, so I could break his heart.*

"I thought it would be easy. Laughing at the right jokes, a few well-timed hair flips. How hard could it be to get a human boy to fall for someone like me? I mean, look at me."

I do, despite myself. I can't deny she's beautiful. Stunning even. I don't know which are more arresting, her dazzling, piercing eyes or her impossibly high cheekbones. Her diamond-studded *siluess* draws attention to her full, feminine chest. The water makes her ebony hair fan out in long, curling tendrils around her head. In the dim light, her coral-colored tail blends into her creamy skin, making her appear almost naked and decidedly sexual.

"But he didn't fall in love with me. He dated me, held me. But no matter what I did, he didn't love me."

I remember what Clay said. That love didn't matter. That it hadn't kept his parents together. It was almost like he didn't want to fall in love. Maybe he went out with Melusine at first because he didn't love her. Because he thought she was safe.

Boy was he wrong.

"Then Daddy and I remembered that in some other ancient spells, the siren bond had worked as a substitute for real love. It was a risk, but time was running out. So I sirened Clay.

"He obeyed me. Lusted after me." She smiles, knowing the words bother me. I'm jealous, even now. I've only ever kissed him once. A stolen kiss.

"He clung to my every command," she continues. *"It wasn't real love, but I hoped it was enough to satisfy the ritual. Then you came along and took him from me. At first, I panicked. I knew I had to go to any lengths I could to get him back before the anniversary."*

"So you poisoned him." Rage boils in my veins at the memory of Clay's painful seizures.

"When you came to me afterwards, when I saw how shaken you were, I realized you really loved him. And since you felt so strongly for Clay, there was a higher chance that under your siren spell, he'd experience real love. And after all, as long as a Mermaid breaks his heart on the anniversary of the curse, it doesn't matter

which Mermaid. So, I let you have him, and then I brought him here." She crosses her arms over her chest, a look of victory on her deceptively delicate face. *"I knew you'd take the bait."*

Her meaning seeps into my every pore. I'm going to be sick again. *"So, if I hadn't come ... "*

"Then we couldn't perform the ritual. Killing Clay would be useless if you weren't here to break his heart first."

"I won't do it. I WON'T DO IT!" No matter what they do to me, if it's in my power to keep Clay safe, I will. Or I'll die trying.

It's that last part that terrifies me.

"Oh yes you will, my dear." Mr. Havelock's voice is hard as he swims regally back into the room carrying a silver box the length of my forearm. *"If you refuse to see reason, we have ways of making you do our bidding."*

"They won't work," I say with more conviction than I feel. *"Even the ritual won't work. Killing Clay won't break the curse. It can't be broken. All the experts have agreed on that for two centuries."*

"And that's why we don't intend to break it," Mr. Havelock says. *"Just ... twist it. We don't know how to break the curse, but we can mollify the magic—lessen its effects—by giving it Clay's life."* His words are informed, but cold. Detached. *"Clay's life will replace the life of the prince, which should have been taken long ago. Clay's death will appease the curse for one hundred years."*

I don't want this to be true, but I don't know what to say against it. So, I poke at the glaring hole in their logic. *"And what happens then? Clay's an only child. If you kill him tonight, he won't have any descendants in a hundred years. We'll be right back where we are now."*

"That's the beauty of this ritual, Miss Nautilus." He strokes the silver box as he speaks. *"Once we kill Clay, any human life will do. We kill one human every hundred years in this same ritual and all Mer enjoy immortality."*

"That's why you don't want to mess with us," Melusine adds. *"As long as our family has the secret to the ritual, all Mer will recognize our power."*

"*You mean they'll have no alternative if they want to live. That's tyranny,*" I say. The residue from whatever they used to drug me has left a sour taste in my mouth.

"*That's how to ensure a dynasty.*" Mr. Havelock's voice loses its objectivity. A mad spark lights his eyes. "*Our family will rule for all time. Stretching through the generations. That's been the plan for nearly two hundred years. When the curse first took effect, no Mer were spared. Even the Sea Sorceress herself, who was quite old, began to wither. When she was on her deathbed, she told her nursemaid—my ancestor—all about the curse. And she told her where to find this.*"

With careful fingers, he undoes the latch on the box and opens the lid. I have to pitch myself forward in my bonds to see inside, yanking painfully on both my arms and tail. There, resting on a cushion of the finest seasilk, lies a dagger with a black blade.

It can't be.

"*The very same obsidian dagger that cursed us all those years ago. Beautiful, isn't it?*" He lifts it out of the box by its ruby-encrusted, iron hilt. The sharpened point of the long, spiny blade glints in the green light. Beautiful? I'd go with horrifying. Even from a foot away, I can feel its power. Dark and metallic, like spilled blood.

"*Just as our family has passed down the knowledge of the siren song for generations, we have also passed down this dagger in secret, as we bided our time. As we searched for the descendant we needed. Tonight, we will unify all Mer under our reign.*"

"*And you'll help us,*" Melusine says.

"*Like hell I will.*"

Mr. Havelock moves behind me. I try to crane my neck around to keep him in my sights, but it's impossible. Then Melusine places her hands on my shoulders. "*Allow me.*"

She spins my body around in its seaweed bindings. Mr. Havelock has seated himself on a gigantic chair fashioned from igneous rock. It's imposing and studded with hundreds of aquamarine gemstones, the symbol of royalty. This once-stately hall with its archways and mosaic was the throne room.

And Mr. Havelock looks too comfortable on the throne.

When Melusine approaches him, he hands her the dagger, and she accepts it with a bow of her head.

"Reason with her," he tells his daughter.

She swims back to me, and I keep my eyes glued to the dagger's obsidian blade the whole way.

Now she's right in front of me. Will she cut me? Stab me?

Holding the hilt, she rests the blade innocently against the palm of her other hand.

"Lia, remember when I told you we didn't have to be enemies? It's still true. I'm not the bad guy here."

"You sirened Clay," I spat.

"So did you. You had a good reason; you wanted to save him." She looks straight into my eyes with what looks like sincerity. *"I had a good reason; I wanted to save everyone."*

"You want to kill humans. And not just Clay. You want to kill a human—take an innocent life—every century. Forever." How could anyone do that? All those lives ... all the people she plans to murder, each with a family ...

"Grow up, Lia. There are always sacrifices." Then the tension in her expression smoothes out. *"You know, I think we've gone about this the wrong way."*

She turns me so I'm no longer facing her father, but I'm not facing Clay either. It's just her and me.

"We can be on the same side." The palm of her hand presses against the bare skin of my upper arm. She still grips the dagger in the other. *"You've grown up in the human world, and it's skewed your priorities. But this is your heritage. You're Mer, Lia. You have a responsibility to your own kind. Tonight, we can save our entire species from death. We can give them back the immortality they deserve for just one human life every hundred years. It's a small price to pay. The humans are lower than us. They die anyway."*

I don't want to hear this. I angle my torso back, away from

her, but it pulls on my bonds and I writhe in pain. She leans even closer, her face inches from mine. *"Their lives flicker out like the fire they rely on for survival. But ours shouldn't. Ours are meant to be so much more.*

"Don't you want that for yourself, Lia? For your family?" she asks. *"They'll die. If you don't help me tonight, your whole family will die. Your sisters, your parents."* Her cherry lips form vile words I don't want to acknowledge. I shake my head.

"Yes, they will. Your parents have only forty or fifty years left—and that's if they're lucky. You care about protecting people. Don't you want to protect them?"

Of course I do. How could I not? My parents have devoted their lives to protecting me.

"Even the little one—the one with that beautiful strawberry blond hair—Amy?" She runs a lock of my own hair through her fingers. It's one of the most intimate gestures among female Mer. I think of all the times I've done it to Amy.

"She'll die, too. You can save her. You can save all of them. All of us." She's still running her fingers through my hair. In this decaying, dangerous place, after such a terrifying day, the caress feels comforting. It shouldn't. But having someone stroke my hair is so familiar, so soothing.

"Join us, Lia. I'll make you a part of our dynasty. We can rule side by side. Everyone will know you saved them. They'll see how special you are."

I picture my family, the entire Community, and even all the Mer Below living forever because of me.

"Think how grateful they'll be to you for giving them their eternal lives back, their safety back. The wars will be over and you and your family can come back home. Here—to the ocean. Imagine what you could do with an eternity to explore, to discover everything the ocean has to offer you."

Immortal life in the ocean … it's the stuff of dreams.

"I know how strong the call is. I know the unquenchable need you have inside you to be out here in the deep. Trapped on land with

only a few miles of shallow ocean is no life for a Mermaid. I know you feel it."

It's like her eyes can see into me. Like she knows how out of place I feel.

"This is where you belong, Lia. All you have to do is choose it. Make the choice."

I know what I have to do.

I lean into Melusine's hand against my hair.

"I want that. All of it. I want my family to live. I want the ocean and the freedom. I want to stop hiding. I want eternity."

Chapter Twenty-Seven

A triumphant smile curls Melusine's lips. *"I knew you were smart, Lia."*

She touches the tip of the dagger to my temple. I force myself not to shudder. To stay perfectly still with the sharpened blade pressed against the vulnerable veins there.

Our eyes meet, and Melusine must see the resolve she's looking for. *"There's no reason for you to be our prisoner, when you can be our guest."* She drags the tip of the dagger down my cheek and neck with enough pressure that it must leave a line of raised, red skin in its wake. But she doesn't break the skin, doesn't cut me. This is a warning.

Obey.

As she circles behind me, bringing the tip to rest between my shoulder blades, I'm careful not to flinch. The cold, sharp point skims down my spine.

"Let's do this together." With those words, she brings the blade down between my hands, slicing through the seaweed ropes that bind me.

I only have one chance.

The instant my tail is free, I stretch it to its full length and kick out as hard as I can, walloping Melusine in the side.

The powerful muscles of my tail smack against her ribs. She grunts in pain, but I don't look back. I'm already swimming at full speed toward Clay. The seaweed bonds still hanging from my wrists and fins fly out behind me in the water like streamers.

If I'm anything, I'm a fast swimmer, and I reach him in seconds. Clay. His body bound, his skin blue, his face frozen. I have nothing that can cut through his bonds, so I duck below him, where the rope is tethered to a ring in the mosaicked floor.

My fingers are nimble, but the knot's a complicated one. There's movement behind me. I need to leave with Clay, and I need to do it now.

I work one strand of seaweed under another, then another. I almost have it.

Hang in there, Clay, I'm—

A large, cold hand closes around my neck from behind, yanking me away from Clay.

"You stupid girl," Mr. Havelock rasps in my ear. With his other hand, he grabs the top of my fin and folds my tail back up into that painful bent position. I lash out with my arms, twist my torso around so I can hit him with my fists, and try to free my tail, but he stands firm against my attack.

"Stop!" Melusine shouts. She presses the dagger to Clay's throat.

That stops me faster than ropes ever could.

"Don't hurt him," I say, raising my hands in surrender. *"Just don't hurt him."*

"I thought you wanted to fix the curse. To save your family." Did her voice break? A bruise is blooming across the pale flesh of her right side and abdomen.

"I do." I picture my family, picture the smiles that would light my parents' faces if I told them they could have the immortality they've always dreamed of. But they're not the only ones I picture. An image of Kelsey with her mischievous grin rises to my mind.

How many times has she been there for me when I needed her? We have so many of the same interests, the same worries about school, about family … we're the same age. How is Kelsey's life worth less than mine? It isn't. And neither is Kelsey's friend Matt's, or chatterbox Laurie Kennish's, or eager, well-intentioned Mr. Reitzel's. Their lives matter. I picture my parents again, who have spent years living alongside humans and trying to learn from them. They've always taught me to respect humankind, to be grateful to humans for creating a world that could provide Mer safe haven from the ocean in our time of need. My parents wouldn't be proud of me if I agreed to the ritual slaughter of human beings, no matter what the benefits. *"I do want to save my family,"* I repeat. *"But causing more death isn't the way to do it."*

"I thought you wanted eternity."

"I do." I answer honestly. *"But I want Clay more. You told me to make a choice? I choose him."*

"You fool."

"At least now we can get on with it," Mr. Havelock says, still clutching my neck in his cold fingers. *"I've waited long enough."*

"All right, Lia," Melusine says, *"it's time to break your precious human's heart so we can start the ritual."*

The ritual. They can't kill him now, or it will ruin the ritual! *"I'm not helping you. I'm calling your bluff. You can do what you want to me, but you won't kill Clay. Not now. You need him."* Only the fact that the blade tip rests against the soft indent of Clay's clavicle keeps me from fighting again.

"Oh, I won't kill him. Not yet. His death is too important. But I have no problem hurting him." She uses the blade to trace random patterns against the skin of his throat. *"You know the dagger's cursed. As soon as it breaks the skin, it burns like liquid fire. Even small cuts will cause poor Clay unbearable agony."*

The unsuppressed glee in her eyes is the only proof I need that she's telling the truth.

"We've still got an hour before sunrise," she says. *"So you do exactly what I tell you, or I'll spend all that time torturing him.*

Making him writhe and suffer before I slit his throat in the ritual."

The fight goes out of me. I can't let Clay's last moments be filled with pain. *"Don't. Please."*

"Do we have a deal? No more pointless escape attempts? Full cooperation?" She's still skating the blade against his exposed skin, tracing where the seaweed pulls taut against his chest.

"Deal," I whisper.

"Oh goody. This'll be fun."

Her father releases my neck and tail. There's nothing holding me now, but the instant I try anything—try to wrestle the dagger from her grip, try to free Clay and get him out of here—Mr. Havelock will overpower me again, and Melusine will take my actions out on Clay. There may be nothing holding me, but I'm trapped just the same.

"Unbind the land-dweller," Mr. Havelock instructs his daughter. *"He must be free and willing for the spell to work."* She nods, and the dagger glides across the thick seaweed ropes. They fall from Clay's body, leaving him floating there unconscious in a pair of cotton boxers nearly the same blue as his icy skin.

Melusine takes him by the arm while her father yanks at my own. Soon, all four of us swim right above the symbols that deface the floor. Mr. Havelock moves a few feet back and begins chanting in Mermese.

His creepy half-music fills the chamber.

"Stay," Melusine orders, like I'm a misbehaving puppy. Keeping a firm grip on Clay, she swims to where rows of supplies lie on the ground, just outside the circle of symbols. When she returns, she holds a small bottle containing a deep purple potion. Then she brings it to Clay's lips.

"What is that?" Urgency suffuses my voice.

"Don't worry—this won't affect the potion keeping him alive down here. I need him alive so I can kill him." She laughs at her own sick joke. *"All this does is make things a lot more interesting."*

Clay's hand jerks, and I gasp. He's waking up.

Melusine returns the sharpened dagger to his throat.

"Now, tell him exactly what you are and what you've done to him. Or I play slice and dice."

The ice clinging to Clay's eyelids chips off with a soft crackle. He opens his eyes.

Chapter Twenty-Eight

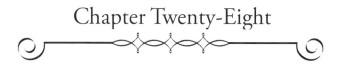

"*Don't move!*" I tell Clay, worried that even a small nick from the dagger at his throat will cause him searing pain. My words come out in the sibilant, melodic tones of Mermese. I don't realize my mistake until Clay starts thrashing, wild-eyed. How much can he see in the semi-darkness?

Melusine moves the blade an inch or two from his skin but angles it threateningly at him. "*Better tame your stallion, Lia. I wouldn't want to cut him by mistake.*"

I rush to Clay's side. He's choking and sputtering.

"Clay, stop moving. It's okay. You can breathe the water. Just let it in." It's strange speaking English underwater. The words are muffled, so I say them into Clay's ear. But my eyes never leave the dagger.

"Breathe. Shh. Just breathe and stay still."

It must take courage for Clay to take the salt water into his mouth and nose, but he does. Now that I'm close to him, I can see the potion has given him gills like mine—tiny openings along the sides of his neck below his ears.

He gasps again and again, no doubt getting used to the

strange sensation. I use the time to keep talking to him.

"Clay, listen to me. I need you to stay very still. We're both in danger, and there's a knife at your throat."

"Lia, are you okay?" His gaze searches my face. Melusine presses the dagger's tip up under his chin, and he must feel it because he doesn't dare move his head.

At least as long as he doesn't look down, he can't see my tail.

"I'm okay."

His eyes move as far to the side as they can, trying to see who's holding the knife. But Melusine floats behind him, out of his field of vision. Giving up, he says to me, "We're underwater."

"Yeah, we are."

"How are we breathing? How are we talking?"

"You're breathing because you drank a potion. A magic potion." There's no other way to say it. He blinks twice but doesn't question this. I guess waking up deep in the ocean with an unseen attacker threatening your life does wonders to suspend your disbelief. Or maybe he's in shock.

"I'm breathing … " I hesitate. Melusine raises an eyebrow at me from behind Clay and adjusts her grip on the dagger's hilt. "… because I can."

"You can breathe underwater?"

Melusine lets out an exaggerated yawn. "I'm getting bored, Lia. Start talking."

"Mel? Is that you? What are you doing here?" Clay asks, trying to see over his shoulder without moving his head. It's a useless endeavor, but he must be able to guess from the proximity of her voice that she's the one holding the dagger, because he says, "Why are you doing this?"

"I'm doing this because Lia's been lying to you. It's very naughty of her." She smirks at me as she ruins my life. "I'm just making sure she finally tells you the truth."

"Lia?" His hazel eyes, greener than ever in the chamber's emerald glow, are wide and questioning.

"She's right," I admit, shifting my gaze away from his. "I have lied to you."

"About what?"

I wring my hands, twisting my fingers together.

"I can breathe underwater because … because I'm a Mermaid." I move backward so he can see all of me—all of my long fish's tail.

His jaw drops.

The only sounds are my own heartbeat pulsing in my ears and Mr. Havelock's ghostly chant growing louder. The seconds stretch.

"This whole time?" Clay finally asks. "This whole time you've been a … a … "

Tides, he can't even say it. "A Mermaid? Yeah."

"But how … how did I not know my girlfriend was a … "

"Oh, she was never your girlfriend," Melusine interrupts. "Not really. Tell him, Lia. And you'd better hurry—that potion'll be wearing off mighty soon."

She says it so casually, but her words tighten my chest. How long before he stops breathing? Twenty minutes? Ten? Two?

I close the distance between us again so he'll be able to hear me. If it weren't for the dagger, would he recoil from me now? If he doesn't want to yet, he will.

At Melusine's dangerous look, I start talking fast. "She's right. I … I was never really your girlfriend." I look away.

"Yes you were. Lia, you were my girlfriend up until yesterday when you just ran off."

"No. That's why I ran off. I couldn't lie to you anymore."

"Because you're a mermaid?" His voice is all shock, confusion.

"No, because being with someone means choosing them, but you never chose me. You never had a choice."

I take a deep breath, the water flowing in and out of me. "Melusine—Mel—she's a Mermaid too, and she sirened you. She, um, she used a spell … a song … to brainwash you. To make you love her. I wanted to protect you." I stroke his cheek, feel his stubble graze my fingertips.

"Tell him what you did, Lia." Melusine's voice is menacing now, as she presses the blade harder against the flesh of his throat. He swallows.

I speed up, the words spilling out of my mouth. "I wanted to make sure she couldn't hurt you, so I sang to you." My voice cracks. "I brainwashed you."

"My song … " He trails off, putting the pieces together.

"Yes. I sang your song. Oh, Clay, every time I did it, I felt so awful. But I didn't know what else to do. And then you started acting like you liked me, like you wanted me, like you loved me."

"You liked it," Melusine accuses in a hiss.

I nod in shame. "I didn't want to like it, but I did. I used magic to control you, to control your feelings." My eyes well up with tears. "I'm sorry, Clay. I'm so, so sorry."

"So, I never loved you? It wasn't real?"

"No," I shake my head, the tears flowing freely now, dotting the surrounding water with the shimmering pearls of my regret, my grief. "I wanted it to be. I wanted it to be real so badly."

Clay's jaw sets. "Get away from me."

"Clay, please, I—"

"You used me." He clenches his teeth. "All those times you sang to me. I thought we were connecting. God, Lia, I thought … but no. You were making me think those things, you were making me feel that way. I can't even look at you."

Melusine may as well have cut me with that dagger. The pain couldn't be worse than this.

Her laugh pierces the water, and she releases Clay with a flourish, letting the dagger hang at her side. It doesn't matter now. The damage is done. He swims away from me.

"Brava," Melusine says. "I certainly couldn't have hurt him any worse than that."

Neither Clay nor I say anything. There's nothing left to say.

Clay's eyes are red. If we weren't surrounded by water, would there be tears in them?

Suddenly, the whole room vibrates. The symbols etched

below us glow. Mr. Havelock stops chanting.

"*That confirms it,*" he says. "*The human is heartbroken. He's ready to be sacrificed.*"

"*Thanks, Lia,*" Melusine says. "*I couldn't have done it without you. Ready to watch him die?*" A deranged look shines in her eyes as she rushes toward Clay, the obsidian blade aimed straight at him.

He sees her coming and tries to swim away, but with her natural speed in the water, he's no match for her. This deep down, the current is strong, and without a tail to combat it, Clay looks like he's swimming in slow motion. She'll reach him in seconds.

It can't end like this. Without planning, without thinking, I shoot toward her. My hand closes around her wrist.

Clay's voice echoes in my memory from a long-ago lesson: "Keep as much distance between the weapon and the victim as possible."

I wrench her arm upward so the dagger points away from Clay.

"Swim to the surface! Now!" I scream to him. He has to save himself before sunrise—before the potion wears off, and he stops breathing.

I squeeze Melusine's wrist as hard as I can and smash my tail into the spot on her abdomen I bruised earlier. The shock and pain of the impact make her loosen her grip on the dagger for the briefest of moments. That's all I need. I shake her arm violently, and the dagger flies out of her hand, plummeting toward the sea floor.

I let go of her and speed after it. Without the dagger, she can't kill Clay in the ritual. If I can hold onto it until sunrise, she'll miss her chance. Out of the corner of my eye, I see Clay hasn't listened to me; he's swimming toward us instead of toward the surface. But he's making almost no progress, his human legs still hindered by the current.

I dive toward the ancient weapon, my arm outstretched, my fingers inches from the hilt.

Thick arms wrap around my waist and yank me away from my prize. Mr. Havelock holds me back, and all I can do is watch in horror as Melusine's long-fingered hand closes around the rubied hilt.

She spins around, brandishing the dagger in my direction. Her other hand clutches her wounded side. *"You know, I didn't want to hurt you, Lia. But you're becoming a distraction. And we won't let anything distract us from bringing this curse under our command. Besides, you've pissed me off."*

She's coming closer. I fight to free myself from Mr. Havelock's hold, but he's too strong and he's bending my tail again.

"Father, will it disrupt the ritual if I kill this meddling bitch before I take care of the human?" Melusine asks, a crazed edge to her voice.

"No, my dear." His words cause water to ripple against the back of my neck. *"As long as we kill the human descendant before sunrise, spilling her blood first won't matter in the slightest."*

That's all she needs to hear. She gives her tail a mighty kick and comes at me, dagger raised.

I close my eyes. I don't want to see her as I die.

I'm sorry, Clay. I love you.

I hope with everything I am that somehow, as I'm dying, he'll get away.

Water rushes toward me. I try to prepare myself for the pain of the blade.

Guttural screams fill the throne room.

But they aren't mine.

My eyes fly open in time to see Melusine twist the dagger deeper into Clay's stomach. He's right in front of me, his arms spread wide to shield me.

"That works, too," Melusine says.

Shocking realization hits. He saved me. Clay swam in front of the blade and saved my life.

And now he's screaming. Covering the wound with his hands. Just as Melusine promised, the magic from the dagger inflicts burning agony.

I must be bucking like a bull shark to free myself, because Mr. Havelock wrestles me to the floor, forcing himself on top of me. He uses his body as a barrier to keep me from Clay. He holds me down by the throat, and uses his powerful puce tail to crush my own against the sharp shards of shell decorating the floor.

His eyes are wild, power-hungry. *"You can't stop this."*

His cold hands tighten around my throat, pressing both my windpipe and my gills shut. I can't breathe. My struggles do nothing but pound my head hard against the floor. I miss a raised chunk of quartz to my temple by mere millimeters. *He's right,* I think, as my vision goes black around the edges. *I can't stop this.*

"Stop assuming you can't do it." Clay's voice rings out in my mind. I'm back in our first self-defense lesson. "If using this move could help save your life, could protect someone you love from getting hurt, you would do it. And you'd get it right. You can do this, Lia."

I know what to do.

I stop struggling. I close my eyes and force all my focus, all my adrenaline into the most important transformation of my life.

My tail splits into legs, and I wrap them around my attacker to pull him closer, throw him off balance. Mr. Havelock never expected me to use my legs—it's too human an option for him to consider—so he's doubly thrown off.

I grab his left wrist and forearm the way Clay taught me, and pull until he falls forward. With his hands no longer strangling me, I breathe in the oxygen-infused salt water and the blackness in my vision clears.

I put one leg down and angle my hips just like I practiced, then reach around and use Mr. Havelock's own arm to place him in a chokehold.

My other hand hooks under the middle of his tail, and I flip us over—just like I did on the mats in Clay's den.

This time, I save my life.

Before Mr. Havelock can regain an advantage, I ram my knee

into his side. He groans, and while he's distracted by the pain, I grip either side of his head and smash it with all my strength against that chunk of protruding quartz.

The rage in his eyes glazes over, and they close.

When I let go of his head, it falls to the side like a stone. Is he dead? Just unconscious? I don't have time to find out.

I get off him and transform back into my tail so I can swim to Clay.

Clay's skin—still blue-tinged from the potion—is pasty now as he fights against the pain of the dagger. My heart pounds. He looks like death.

Even through what must be unbearable agony, he's smart: he's kept the blade buried in his stomach, pressing down around it to stem the bleeding. But his blood still seeps out in crimson curls that slither through the surrounding water.

Melusine wades just above him, her back to me. *I'm getting tired of this. We're wasting time.*

With no other warning, she draws back her tail and swings it forward, whapping it hard against Clay's back.

"No!" I shout. I make it to Clay, but I'm too late.

His body bows forward with the impact. The blade pops loose from his stomach, arching through the water and unleashing a rush of his blood that gushes forth in a cloud of deadly red.

I reach out to catch his falling body, but then the ground shakes and I go blind.

Chapter Twenty-Nine

Colorless, shining light bursts out from the cloud of Clay's blood and radiates in all directions. It happens so fast, I don't have time to shield my eyes from the brilliant brightness. A violent underwater earthquake rattles the entire palace. In my sightlessness, I reach forward and clutch Clay's body tight to mine.

As suddenly as the shaking started, it's over. I blink my eyes open, my vision returning to find the chamber engulfed in the same green glow it was earlier, as if nothing happened. To my left, Melusine's body lies crumpled against the bottom of one of the large columns. She must have been thrown against it in the blast.

"Clay?" I turn to look at the body in my arms. He took that blade for me.

His hazel eyes, always so full of mirth and mischief, are lifeless.

"No," I sob, dropping my head to his chest. "Why did you do it? Why did you die for me?" I convulse with sorrow.

Several long minutes later, I gather my resolve, move my hand to his face, and brush his eyes closed.

Chapter Thirty

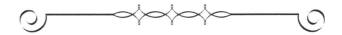

I can't let him go. I hold his cold body against mine. Even in death, he's so handsome. Like he's sleeping.

A groan. It's the softest, the weakest of sounds—and the most beautiful I've ever heard. I'm afraid to hope.

"Clay?"

I put my ear right against his mouth. Another small groan. He's alive!

Barely.

Barely will have to be enough.

Blood still seeps from the gaping wound on his stomach, but it's slow. He should have bled out long before now. As I run my fingertips over his blue cheek, understanding dawns. The potion! It's slowed all his body's functions so he could survive underwater—that must include his blood flow. But Melusine said it wouldn't last long, and that was nearly two hours ago.

She and her father are still unconscious. Now's my chance. I turn around and pull Clay's arms over my shoulders, anchoring them against my chest with my left hand. His injured stomach presses against my lower back. Without so much as a glance back at our captors, I flick my tail through the water and let the current pull me toward the arched doorway.

The palace is a maze. I swim through it as fast as I can, avoiding sharp turns or sudden movements so I don't jostle Clay.

"I'll get you out," I promise, hoping some part of him can hear me.

Room after room, until we're in the entrance hall, then back out into open ocean. I don't bother swimming through the streets of the settlement this time. I head straight up.

I don't have a bond to follow now, so I'm miles out into the ocean with no way of knowing how to find my way back to Malibu, back to our home. Fear shoots through me, and I push it down; I can't give in to panic.

I take comfort in the weight of Clay's body against my back, in the warmth of his arms against my chest. Wait, warmth?

Without stopping my ascent into ever-higher waters, I glance down at the arms I'm clutching. The blue tinge has receded a little. The potion's wearing off. Now, I can't do anything to quell the fear. If the potion wears off before I get Clay to the surface, he'll drown.

I redouble my efforts. I kick my fins as hard as I can, propelling myself upward with every stroke. I use one arm to slice through the water and push it back, while the other holds on to Clay.

"Hang in there. Please hang in there."

But then I have no more energy for talking. It takes all my strength to keep up my speed.

After what feels like ages, the darkness slips away. The light from the sky above brightens the water around us. It means we're getting closer to the surface—but it also means sunrise is nearly here, and the potion is nearly gone. We still have so far to go. Have I saved Clay from the ritual only to watch him die?

I fight the aching muscles in my tail and arms. They rebel against my speed, against Clay's weight pulling them down as I force them up.

The surface sparkles above us. Almost there. I want to tell Clay, but I don't have the energy.

Strangled gurgles meet my ears. Then choking sounds. Clay is fighting to breathe. And he's losing.

The potion has worn off.

He thrashes against me, his body seeking air that doesn't exist here. As he flails, he lets go of my shoulders, and his body sinks down, away from me.

I zoom downward, my muscles screaming, and grab him under his arms, his back against my chest. I pull him up. Up toward the surface, up toward the sky, up toward the air that I hope will come soon enough to save him.

A cramp bites into my side. I keep kicking.

The surface lies just above us.

Three feet.

A foot.

Inches.

With one final kick, I launch our heads out of the water.

Cold air hits my face. We break the surface the same moment the sun bursts into the morning sky. With the last bit of strength left in my arms, I hold Clay up.

"Breathe," I say, my voice ragged. "Please breathe."

As the sun blooms in the sky like a giant orange anemone, Clay gasps for air. Then he coughs, horrid and wet and hacking. Then he gasps again.

I keep his head above water as the pattern continues. Finally, he stops coughing, starts breathing regularly. And passes out.

It's only then that I notice the red staining the waves around us. With the potion gone, his blood is flowing fast, and he's losing too much of it. We're stranded in the ocean with nothing but endless crystal water stretching as far as the eye can see. How will I keep Clay from bleeding to death?

Hopeless tears sting my eyes. How have I gotten us this far just to lose him?

Vrrrm. Vrrrm. The blaring of a motor erupts into the isolated silence. I hear the boat coming before I see it—a tiny dot growing larger as it speeds toward us. What's a boat doing all the way out here so early? Is it fishermen? Drug lords? Whoever's on board, Clay will be safer on that boat than in the ocean.

I swim out of its direct path and wave one arm in the air, calling for help. The boat slows when they spot us. I close my eyes and concentrate with all my might until my legs kick below me. Now I'm as ready as I'll ever be to meet whatever breed of human is on that boat.

But, when I open my eyes, the boat is near enough for me to see its markings, and I know there won't be a human on board. I recognize that sleek aqua logo. A Foundation boat! The small kind we use for scouting missions and ingredients collecting.

"Goldfish!" a familiar voice cries out as the boat pulls up close and drops anchor.

Caspian reaches over the side to help me. I push Clay's unconscious, bleeding body into his strong arms, and he hauls him into the boat. He lays Clay across the deck, then grips me by my forearms and pulls me aboard, too.

He throws me a towel and averts his eyes, waiting for me to secure it around my waist.

Instead, I kneel and press it to Clay's stomach.

"The bleeding! We have to stop the bleeding!" My voice comes out high-pitched, foreign.

"Shh, it's okay. I'll do it," he says. His large hand replaces my shaking one. But instead of pushing down on the blood-soaked towel to staunch the bleeding, he pulls it away.

"What are you doing?"

Caspian doesn't answer. He just takes a small glass bottle from his pocket, uncorks it, and pours its contents on Clay's wound.

The bleeding stops.

I gasp. Caspian hands me a clean towel, and he ducks his head so that his eyes meet mine. "Lia, you've done enough," his voice is steady, soothing. "I'll take it from here."

His clear cobalt gaze begs me to trust him. And I do.

I step back and wrap the towel around my waist, then sit as Caspian uncorks another bottle and sprinkles a rust-colored powder across the gash.

All the blood smeared on Clay's body slides across his skin and back into the wound! Even the red staining his boxers seeps upward along the fabric, back onto his torso, and into his body. Caspian takes the towel soaked in Clay's blood and presses it against the wound once more. It comes back clean.

"Handy, huh?" he says, smiling at my slack-jawed expression. "I raided my grandma's potion stores. She made some of this stuff years ago, in case one of us had an emergency. Today definitely qualifies."

"How … are you here?" I stammer.

"The symbols," he says, pushing his dark blond hair out of his eyes. "I came to your house to say I was sorry for last night," he offers me an apologetic smile. "When I got there, your parents said they thought you were spending the day with me. I knew the only reason you'd lie to them was so you could see him. I told them I'd forgotten we were supposed to meet at the Lumber Yard mall. Then I headed to his house. I had to see you." He meets my eyes. "I had to make things right." Then he gestures me forward, "C'mere."

He lifts his hand as if to touch my top, but it's in shreds, so instead he says, "Lean forward." I lean awkwardly over Clay's prone body. "More," Caspian says, pressing on my bare lower back, until I'm almost lying on top of Clay, chest to chest.

Before my eyes, the blood leeches out of my shirt and off my skin the same way it did from the towel. Clay doesn't wake up, but he moans, and for the first time, it doesn't sound pained. I lift myself up, my makeshift *siluess* still dirty, wet, and ripped, but free of blood.

"When I got to his house," Caspian continues, "the front door was open. Then I saw his bedroom, and I worked out what must have happened."

"But how did you find us?"

"I told you: the symbols. The ones all over Clay's room. They were the same ancient ones I found in Mr. Havelock's office. Ever since I mentioned them to you, I've been researching. Cross-referencing them with different texts."

I shake my head. Of course he has. Caspian would never let a scholarly opportunity like that drop.

"And, Lia, I figured them out." His whole face lights up. "So when I saw the symbols all over the bedroom walls, I could read them. They said the place where the human sleeps needed to be marked with the place he would sleep forever. Then they gave a location."

That makes a warped kind of sense. According to legend, the Little Mermaid was supposed to kill the prince with that dagger while he was asleep in his marital bed—in his bedroom. Since the Havelocks took Clay from his bedroom, I guess they had to mark the place for the ritual to work.

"I knew Mr. Havelock had one of the Foundation's boats for his ingredients dives, and I'd seen where he kept the key. Maybe I should have told someone. I guess I wasn't thinking straight. I just kept picturing you in danger."

Caspian bends over a case covered in verdigris—his grandmother's copper potions chest—and pulls out yet another bottle, this one larger than the others. He sits down and props Clay's head on his leg, then pours a liquid the same rust color as the powder down Clay's throat. Although he stays asleep, Clay lifts his head toward the bottle and drinks greedily before falling back into stillness, his face content.

"That one'll help replenish the blood he lost Below." Caspian lays Clay's head back on the deck, then pulls a small tub out of the copper case and lathers a white cream over the gash on Clay's stomach. "That's the last one," he says, wiping his hands on yet another towel.

He eyes me up and down, searching for wounds, taking in the bruises around my throat.

"I'm fine," I assure him. "I'll be fine."

He stares at me in silent consideration, then turns his gaze back to Clay. To the deep stab wound now so neatly tended. "Tides, what did they do to him down there?"

I open my mouth to tell him, and my throat closes up. I'm not ready to talk about it. But the least I owe Caspian is an explanation. "I got in the way of their ritual. Melusine came at me with a dagger. Clay rushed in front of it to save me," I force out.

Caspian must want to know more, but he doesn't push. "Then he has my respect." He looks at me, and his solid stoicism breaks down. "I'm so glad you're all right."

He enfolds me in a huge hug. He was scared for me.

By the time he lets me go, I have just one more question. "I know you followed the symbols, but how were you right at this spot moments after we surfaced?"

"It wasn't quite as miraculous as all that," he says. "I only had your approximate location, so I've been circling this whole area for over an hour. If I didn't catch sight of you soon, I was going to dive down and search for you."

"Thank you. Thank you so much for coming." Now it's my turn to hug him. Without Caspian, I would be lost. Clay would be dead.

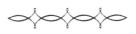

As Caspian steers us back home, I sit at Clay's side, gripping his hand in mine. I whisper to him that he's safe, he's finally safe, and everything will be okay. The sun has risen in the sky and it shines down, warming us.

Chapter Thirty-One

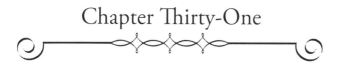

Clay's grip on my hand tightens as he opens his eyes.

"Lia, I had this dream you were … "

His gaze shifts from side to side, taking in his unfamiliar surroundings. He sits up and doesn't seem to be in any pain. Through the cream on his chest, I can see the wound is closed. He looks out at the shimmering water on all sides of the boat.

"Was … was it real?"

I nod, and manage a quiet, "Yes."

He stares at my legs then back at my face. "And you had me under a spell all this time?"

He keeps his tone steady, but betrayal lurks just under the surface.

"I didn't know how else to protect you," I say, my voice even quieter.

He drops my hand and scoots away from me. He makes the gesture casual, like he wants to rest his back against the side of the boat, but his message comes across loud and clear. I bite my lip to keep myself from crying.

"How am I still alive?" Clay asks, rubbing some of the cream on his chest between his fingertips and staring at it.

I'm afraid that if I talk anymore, Clay will hear the tears in my voice. When I don't answer, Caspian chimes in from behind the wheel, "You have me to thank for that. I brought some ... medicines with me. I'm Caspian." Caspian turns and nods in greeting.

"Have we met before?" Clay asks, tilting his head.

"I tend to turn up when you're unconscious."

"So, Caspian, are you a ... mermaid, too?"

I can't help it; I burst out laughing. All the panic, the fear, the rejection of the day escapes in wild laughter that shudders through my body. Soon, Caspian and Clay are laughing, too. A much needed release.

We dock at my house. We need to tell my parents where Melusine and her father are. Clay's mom is still out of town, so he agrees to come give a witness statement for official Foundation records.

"Better now than later," Clay says. "I want to put all this behind me. Move on."

My face falls. "All this" includes me. Clay wants to move on from me, and I can't blame him. He keeps a sizable distance between us as we walk up the dock.

The private beach behind my house—meant only for the families (some human and some Mer) who own houses on our street—is almost always empty except for the occasional neighbor. Now, it's crowded with people. Everyone speaks animatedly to one another. I don't recognize all of them, but the fact that so many cover their legs with long skirts or pants despite the heat tells me they're Mer. That's odd. I thought I knew everyone in the Community. Did we get more refugees? What's going on? Caspian must wonder the same thing because he raises an eyebrow at me. I shrug.

They're all so wrapped up in conversation that no one stops us as we go up the stairs to my house. When we walk through the back door, silence greets us. Everyone must be in the grottos.

We stop at the concealed entrance. It feels monumental to bring a human into the hidden depths of my home after a lifetime of secrecy. Caspian understands my hesitancy. He stops walking and gives me time.

All I can think to say to Clay is, "Careful, it's slippery."

As we head down the winding stairs to the antechamber, he's wide-eyed with wonder at the shimmering walls and the velvet water lapping along the slanted floor.

I can hear my sisters' voices now. And Leomaris's. And Staskia's. And my parents'. And … Caspian's parents'?

Even though Clay's stomach looks healed, I don't want to chance getting it wet. Besides, the grottos get deep, and he doesn't have a tail. So, instead of moving farther in, I call out, "Hello! I'm home, and I really need to talk to you."

I expect my family to be shocked beyond belief at the sight of a human in the grottos. Instead, I'm the one who's shocked.

When my parents enter the antechamber, I gasp. They've changed. These are not the parents I left this morning.

The wrinkles around my mother's eyes and mouth have vanished; the skin on her whole body is tight and glowing. Her hair, always beautiful, is now as lush, shining, and free of gray as any of my sisters' hair.

My father has hair! My father, who's been balding for over a decade, now has a head of thick, dark hair. Even more striking, the soft, cushy potbelly that usually sticks out above his tail has been replaced by a perfect six pack. My dad has abs … so weird.

Caspian stares at his parents with equal fascination. They look like they did when we were toddlers.

And no one—not his parents, my parents, my sisters, Stas, or Leo—seems surprised to see Clay. They shift to make room as a woman I don't recognize enters the antechamber from the inner grottos. She's breathtaking, with flowing auburn hair, almond eyes, and nearly translucent white skin. She swims to the edge of the water, where Clay and I stand with Caspian.

"So, Aurelia," she says the words to me, but her gaze fixes on Clay, "this must be the human you broke the curse with."

Chapter Thirty-Two

Broke the curse? There's no way to break the curse. Melusine and her father wanted to twist the curse, manipulate it to gain power. I want to tell my parents this—to tell them everything—but that'll have to wait. Instead, Clay gives his formal statement that the Havelocks kidnapped and attempted to kill him, and Caspian and I describe their location. My parents know where the palace is, and my father heads upstairs to call in a Foundation team.

"We need to retrieve them," my mother says. "Before they can take credit Below for what's happened."

"What *has* happened?" Caspian asks.

"As far as we can tell, all adult Mer in the Community, and possibly Below as well, have reverted back to their stasis ages," Caspian's father answers in a baritone so much like his son's.

Before the curse, Merfolk stopped aging at around thirty—what we call reaching stasis. That's why there was such a commotion outside ... and why I didn't recognize some of the Mer! They must've looked decades younger than they did the last time I saw them. My eyes flit to the beautiful Mermaid with the auburn hair. Her almond-shaped eyes are the same blue as Caspian's and her radiant garnet tail shimmers beneath her in the water.

"MerMatron Zayle?" I ask.

"Olee?" Caspian whispers.

Caspian's grandmother smiles. *"Didn't I tell you I was a looker in my day?"* Then she turns to Clay and switches to English. "How are you feeling, young man? It seems my potions worked wonders, if I do say so myself."

"Fine, thank you," Clay answers. He tries to maintain eye contact with her, but his focus keeps shifting to her tail. To all their tails. "Kind of like I jumped … er, dived into one of my mom's fairytale books but, yeah, fine."

"Glad to hear it," she says just as my father comes back downstairs, transforms, and returns to my mother's side in the water. "Now, I have a theory about all this," Caspian's grandmother continues, "but I need to know exactly what's happened to see if I'm correct."

Since Caspian was never Below with us, and Clay was unconscious for most of it, the explanation falls on me.

I try to recount every detail, every word Melusine and her father said about the curse, every step they performed in the ritual. Once I reach the end, Caspian's grandmother has me start all over again, and when I get to the part where Clay got stabbed, she interrupts me.

"So you chose a human's life over Melusine's promise of immortality for all of us?" she asks, her voice serious.

I nod, feeling kinda guilty.

"Thanks so much, Lia," Lapis says sarcastically. Amy shushes her from where she swims next to Staskia.

"You must really love him." A mix of awe and incredulity colors Emeraldine's voice.

Both of them fall silent when Caspian's grandmother poses her next question. "Then you attacked Melusine, risking your own life to save this human's?"

I remember grabbing Melusine's arm, hitting her with my tail. Then Mr. Havelock holding me back as Melusine came at me with the dagger. I nod again.

"You were willing to die for him?" she asks.

"It's not like I was looking forward to it. I was scared," I confess. "But I thought maybe while they were killing me, Clay might escape."

My parents stare at me in silence. They look … proud?

"But you didn't make your escape," MerMatron Zayle says to Clay. "You swam in front of the dagger to save Aurelia's life. Isn't that right?"

"Yes," Clay says. Our eyes lock. Then he looks away.

"And when your blood poured out into the ocean, that's when there was an explosion of light and a seaquake?"

This time, we both nod.

"Right before sunrise, when we all regained our youth," she murmurs to herself. Then, to the room at large, she says, "It's as I suspected." She points to Clay and me. "Their sacrifice broke the curse."

"But the curse can't be broken," I say. "Clay isn't dead."

"He was willing to die for you and you for him. That's what matters. Ancient spells are about balance. The Havelocks wanted to control the curse by killing Clay in place of the prince who they thought should have died, and by taking another human life every century to balance the immortal life of the Little Mermaid, who let herself die. They saw the curse as a spell about death."

"Isn't it?" Caspian's mother asks, her kind face a picture of bemusement.

"If it were, Clay here would need to be dead for a ninety-four-year-old like me to have my cleavage back."

"Niiice," Lazuli says, appreciating the humor. My father stifles a laugh behind his hand. Clay just mouths the words "ninety-four?"

"The Havelocks would have succeeded in taming the spell with all that death," MerMatron Zayle says, her tone serious again, "but they could never have broken it."

"Why not?" Leomaris asks, his attention focused on her words even as his hand strokes Emeraldine's hair. Em's gleaming green tail twines with his topaz one under the water.

"Because the curse isn't about death. It's about love." Now she looks at me. And at Clay. "The Little Mermaid accepted death so the one she loved might live. Both of you did the same. Your true love balanced the curse and broke it."

"True love?" I whisper.

"Yes. Only true love—free of uncertainty or hesitation," she pins Clay and me with a knowing gaze, "free of any type of magic—could have broken that spell and given us our immortality back."

But that means ... I look at Clay. That means he loves me.

Clay loves me.

Even after finding out what I did to him—that I lied, that I'm a Mermaid, that I sirened him—he still must love me like I love him, or we wouldn't have broken the curse.

I stand there, stunned into silence, as my fellow Mer rejoice.

"So we really have our immortality back?" my father asks. "This isn't temporary?"

I'm barely listening as MerMatron Zayle gives her confirmation, and everyone cheers and hugs. I need to talk to Clay, but he won't look at me. He's giving everyone else his rapt attention.

"Oh, Edmar," my mother says to my father, "once things settle down, we can travel home. Back to the ocean." She buries herself in his embrace. They must be thinking of the family they haven't seen in decades.

"I can see my parents!" Amy shouts, pulling me into a fierce hug. No sooner has she pulled back than Staskia pulls me into another—and squeezes tight. I've never hugged Staskia before, and I wonder if she's just caught up in the excitement, until she whispers in my ear, "Thank you ... now we can ... just thank you," and squeezes again. When she lets me go, Amy grabs her hand. The two of them share a look that puts a shy smile on Amy's face and makes her blush. Oh! Now that immortality's back and procreation isn't the only way to ensure our population survives, same-love will be viewed like it was before the curse—it'll be accepted instead of shunned. That means Amy and Stas will be accepted … whenever they're ready to be. They're both practically bouncing in the water, their shining faces trained on mine, expecting a reaction. I give them a giant smile, but it doesn't quite reach my eyes. I'm happy for them. So truly happy. I'm happy for all of us. But right now, I need to know how Clay's feeling.

He's talking to Caspian's family, thanking Caspian's grandmother for the potions that saved him.

"Thank *you*," Caspian's father says to him. "Because of what you did, my wife and I, Caspian, even our little daughter Coralline—all of our kind—are immortal, as we were always meant to be."

My parents swim up to him next. My mom gives him a lecture about how vital it is he doesn't tell anyone about us. After he's sworn up and down he'll keep our secret, they thank him, too. Thank him for saving me.

"I'm glad I could help. I'm glad we survived," Clay says. "Now that you have my statement against Mel and Mr. Havelock, I think it's time for me to go home. Return to the human world." He says it like a joke, and my parents laugh, but I hear what he's really saying. This isn't his world. Even if he loved me, really loved me in that moment when he saved my life, he doesn't want to be with me now. He's human, not Mer. He doesn't belong here, and he can't wait to leave.

Without saying a word to me, Clay turns and walks out of my life.

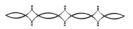

"There's still one thing I don't understand," my mother says to me after Clay has gone, after I've let him go. "How did you track that human boy all the way out to the palace?"

I gulp. It's time to tell them. So far, I haven't mentioned anything about sireny or the bond. I said I broke Clay's heart by confessing I'd lied to him. Everyone assumed I meant about being a Mermaid. Well, everyone except Caspian and his grandmother. I told myself I was waiting until I was alone with my parents to tell them; really, I was just putting it off so I wouldn't have to see their anger, their disappointment. But I'm ready to face them and accept my punishment. I guess now's as good a time as any.

"I found Clay because—"

"Because I'd taught Lia what the symbols meant," Caspian interrupts. "When I first deciphered them. She found Clay the same way I found her. By following the symbols in his room." His voice stays steady through the lie.

I open my mouth to argue, but Clay's grandmother drapes an arm around my shoulders and whisks me away.

"I need to tell them," I say.

"They'd be obligated to report you to the board, Aurelia. Even if by some miracle you weren't imprisoned, your whole family would be mired in scandal, the way mine has been for generations. They don't deserve that. They've been through enough. And so have you." She speaks slowly, as if urging me to see reason. "The Community needs to look up to them right now. All Mer need to. Do you realize now that the curse is broken, your family is next in line for the throne?"

I hadn't realized. My mother is such a distant cousin of the old ruling family that I've never thought of us as real royalty. "You think the Mer Below would want my parents to rule?"

"I don't know," she answers, "but it is your parents' right, and we'll all need strong leaders after what we've endured. We need leaders who can piece our civilization back together. Seeing how your parents have led the Community, I have faith they could do it."

I do, too. I know they could.

"But they'll never get the chance if sireny stains the Nautilus name the way it's stained the Zayles'," she tells me, her voice quiet but intense.

I look over at my parents, at my sisters. At their happy smiles. "So, they'd just never know?"

"You know. That's enough. It's over. Let it go." With that, Caspian's grandmother turns to swim back to the group.

"MerMatron Zayle?" I say, stopping her. "How did I track Clay to the palace? Shouldn't the bond have dissolved with the siren spell?"

"A siren spell uses powerful magic to join a Mermaid and a human. I've never heard of any other case where a victim outlived a siren spell, so I can't be certain, but my guess is that even though the spell is over—even though your hold over Clay is gone—the two of you will always be able to sense each other. You'll always be connected."

The weight of her words pains me. "Even if that's true," I say, "Clay wants nothing to do with me."

Chapter Thirty-Three

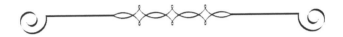

Everything's changing. My parents (who I still can't stop staring at) have sent emissaries Below to explain what's happened. They made an announcement themselves to the Community, and I've received more bouquets of flowers and baskets of seashells than I know what to do with.

As soon as it's safe, my mom and dad will take us on a trip Below. We'll see where they grew up and visit family we've never met. They haven't mentioned the whole reclaiming the throne thing, but they're thinking about it. They've appointed Emeraldine as an executive on the Community board, and I think it's so she can run things up here in case they need to spend time Below.

In the meantime, the entire Community has exploded in celebration. Parties, bonfires, parades. My parents have had to tell the human neighbors it's a Danish holiday and hoped they wouldn't Google it. I guess there's no better reason to celebrate than finding out you're going to live forever.

Forever. I keep trying to wrap my brain around that, but it's so unreal. I don't even know what I want to do when I graduate. What am I going to do with forever? Talk about possibilities. Do I work at the Foundation someday, like my parents have always expected? Will there even need to be a Foundation? Will everyone eventually move back Below? That scares me; the human world is the only one I've ever known. Should I go to college and pursue a career here on land? Should I go Below and spend all my days letting the call of the ocean guide me through the waves? The thought both exhilarates and terrifies me.

There's only one person I want to talk to about it. I want to sit on the flannel bedspread in Clay's room and stay up half the night telling him how I feel and listening to what he has to say. I want to fall asleep in his arms, surrounded by the cinnamon scent of him.

But I can't. He hasn't talked to me since he walked out of the grottos six days ago. With the changes in the Community, the normalcy of school should comfort me, but it doesn't. All I can think about while I'm there is Clay. Will this be the day he talks to me? For the last six days in a row, the answer's been no. Jaclyn and Genevieve throw me pitying glances in the hallway. Kelsey keeps grilling me about our apparent breakup, and all I can say is I don't want to talk about it.

Now it's Saturday, and I won't even get to see him. I want to rush to his house and make him talk to me. But I don't—for the same reason I haven't approached him in school. It can't be about what I want. Not anymore. I'm through pushing myself into his life if he doesn't want me. I have to let it be his decision. I have to let him come to me this time. Without any song compelling him.

But I'm losing hope that he will. I need to distract myself today. I could go to Caspian's, but he's probably busy. Since our story got out, he's gone from being a social pariah to a Community hero. Helping restore everyone's immortality must trump the hundred-year-old stigma of sireny. His sister has as many play dates as she could ever want, and Caspian, well, he's not doing too shabby in the dating department himself. Now that girls have stopped interpreting his natural reserve as proof he'll turn out evil, they're getting to know the real him. And the real him is awesome.

He'd still spend the whole day with me if I asked him to, so I don't. That leaves me with a big, empty Saturday. Em and Leo are meeting with Mer wedding planners, and Staskia's parents have taken Stas and Amy shoe shopping as a fitting reward for their leg control. I smile at the thought. They haven't told anyone else about their relationship yet—I think they're just finally enjoying spending time together without feeling guilty, without feeling like they're doing something wrong. Even with my mind so preoccupied with thoughts of Clay, it makes me feel good to know I played some part in their happiness. Since they're not here now to help distract me, I'm just about to head downstairs and see what the twins are up to when I get a text.

It's from Clay!

He wants to talk. He's coming over.

I rush to my closet. What I wear won't change whatever he plans to say, but I obsess anyway. It gives me something to focus on, something to keep my mind from spinning into a whirlpool. Four outfits later and nothing feels special enough. Then I have an idea. I pull down a box, lift the lid, and brush back the tissue paper. The gold heels glimmer up at me.

I'm waiting downstairs when the doorbell rings.

But it's just another human neighbor dropping by to get the number of my parents' plastic surgeon. I foist her off on my dad. She's asking him an uncomfortable series of questions about liposuction and facelifts when I get another text.

"Dad," I say, too excited to worry that I'm interrupting, "I'll be outside. Clay's here. He went around back, and he's waiting for me on the beach."

"Have fun," my dad says, looking like he desperately wishes he could leave with me. Instead he offers a polite smile to our neighbor as she launches into a gross description of her unsuccessful experience with chemical peels.

After giving my dad a bracing pat on the arm, I go out the back door and down the stairs. I stop at the edge of the cement walkway, stop myself from running to him.

He stands in the sand at the water's edge, his back to me as he stares out at the waves. The calm, sun-kissed surface of the water hides so much power in its depths. He heard me come down the stairs, so I don't call out to him. I just wait.

He turns to face me, but he doesn't step closer. "I didn't want to come in in case it's not okay with your parents. They weren't too happy to see us together that time by the pool."

"They know you're here," I say. "Since you saved my life and all, they've kinda stopped objecting."

"I talked to Mr. Reitzel after school yesterday. He said we got an A on our project. I guess we make a good team."

I try not to get too excited at his words. Instead, I say, "Melusine and her father have both been imprisoned here on land, where my parents can keep an eye on them until they're sentenced." The image of Melusine in one of the Foundation's jail cells makes me smile.

Clay nods.

"I'm sorry I haven't talked to you much the last few days," he says. "I needed time to think. It's been a while since there was no one in my head but me."

"I'm so, so sorry." No matter how many times I apologize, it's not enough.

"I know. I know why you did what you did."

"And I would never, ever do it again." My words are almost frantic in their intensity. He has to believe me. He has to know that no matter how badly I want him back, I'd never siren him again.

"I trust you," he says. He takes a step forward, then stops.

"I just wasn't sure I trusted my feelings. That's why I needed to take some time. I had to figure out what I felt. When we were underwater, you told me my feelings for you weren't real." He shakes his head. "But they felt so real. On the boat ride back, I thought I was lying to myself. I told myself I didn't love you, and I tried to force myself to believe it."

I'm desperate to interrupt, to ask how he feels now. But I let him speak.

"Then, in the … the cave below your house, Caspian's really hot grandmother said my feelings were real, that they had to be or we couldn't have broken that curse. I wanted to talk to you then."

"Why didn't you?" I'd wanted to talk to him so badly.

"You were all so happy. I felt like I was intruding. You're immortal, Lia. You're this beautiful, immortal creature … "

"Beautiful?"

" … and I don't fit into your world. I don't know how I can be a part of it."

I take a bold, deliberate step toward him, my gold stilettos sinking into the white sand. The distance that stretches between us is too wide to bear. "Do you *want* to be a part of it?"

A pause that stops my heart.

"Yes."

And then I'm rushing to him. My shoes fill with sand, and I kick them off. I'm barefoot when I reach him and just the right height to bury my face in his chest.

"Then we'll find a way."

He wraps his arms around me, holding me to him as he asks, "Aren't you going to live in the ocean?"

"I don't know. Maybe someday." I raise my chin so I can look right into his eyes. "But next year's senior year. I'm not gonna miss that."

He smiles. "A year, huh?"

I nod. "For starters."

"Lia? Remember that stage in the guitar store in L.A.? Well,

I went there yesterday and booked a gig. The last few days, I've been staying up and finishing these songs I started last year. I'd been stuck on them for a while, but now they're just flowing. I think it's time I sing them."

"So do I," I say. I know what this means to him.

"I'll be performing next Friday. Would you ... be my date?"

Our first real date! I want to dance with the glee of it.

"Yes!" I squeal.

"Good. Because I wouldn't want to share the night with anyone else." His eyes bore into mine, touching something deep inside me. "Not now that I know I love you."

I've stopped him from saying those words so many times when he didn't mean them. Now that he does, all I want is to hear them over and over.

"Will you say that again?"

"I love you," he repeats.

His hands come up to the back of my head, and he strokes my hair, touching me as if to ensure I'm real.

"I love you," he says again.

I look up into those hazel eyes as he brings his face closer to mine.

"I love you," he whispers.

Even though the beach is silent except for our breathing, even though it's drenched in afternoon sun, this is a music-swelling, shooting star moment. My heart pounds as Clay leans in.

He conquers me with a kiss.

His lips press against mine and what starts as a gentle exploration becomes so much more. I put every word I've wanted to tell him, every touch I've denied us both over the last three months into the kiss.

Clay crushes my body against his, and the kiss deepens even more as we discover each other. It's sweet and lush and fierce and full of promises. And so, so real.

When our lips part, my head is spinning. Clay rests his forehead against mine, and I luxuriate in his closeness.

"Lia?" Clay says, his voice husky.

"Yes?"

"You've had a few months to realize you love me. To understand what that means. For me, this, with you, it's all so new. I've never felt this way about anyone. I never thought I wanted to … I'm going to need to take it slow."

I reach up and touch his cheek, "I can do slow." After all, I have the time now. And for Clay, I can do anything.

THE END

Caspian's *Etallee Leedis*

(Pronunciation Guide)

Hello. Caspian here. Lia defined the Mermese words that came up in this story, but some of the more astute among you might be interested to learn their pronunciation. This page is for you. Remember, proper Mermese should have a lilting, musical quality, so be sure to elongate any double vowels and let your s's linger.

Best of luck in your linguistic pursuits,

Caspian Zayle

Allytrill: ALLEY(as in "Don't swim down that dark alley!") -TRILL(rhymes with "thrill"), noun
   - A graceful Mer dance performed in pairs on formal occasions

Glei Elskee: GLY(rhymes with "my") ELLE(as in the name "Elle" or the letter "L") -SKI(as in the human winter sport), noun
   - Literally translated: same-love; refers to homosexuality and same-sex relationships

Konklili: KAWN(rhymes with "dawn") -KLEE-LEE, noun
   - A shell imbued with recorded voices that Mer can listen to by holding the shell up to the ear; a Merbook

Olee: OH(rhymes with "foe") -LEE(rhymes "sugar kelp tea"), noun
- An endearing word for grandmother, similar to grandma, granny, or nana

Qokkiis: QUO(as in "status quo") -KISS(as in what lips do at sunset), noun
- Kitchen

Siluess: SILL-YOU-ESS(rhymes with "guess"), noun
- A traditional chest covering worn by Mer women

Spillu: SPILL-EW(rhymes with "fish stew"), noun
- A Mer game of skill and strategy played on a board of alternating light and dark panels that are equipped with clips to keep the game pieces from floating away

Tallimymee: TALLY(rhymes with "valley") -MY(as in "Those are my swim trunks.") -MAY, noun
- The most respectful form of thank you; usually directed at elders

Udell: U(rhymes with "woo") -DELL, noun or adjective
- A Mermaid or Merman who has a hateful, prejudiced view of humans
    - Describing such a Mermaid or Merman
    - Describing such anti-human prejudice or behavior

ACKNOWLEDGEMENTS

First and foremost, I'd like to thank *you,* for reading this book and joining Lia on her journey. I wish I could talk to you about all the details over sushi!

You never could have read Lia's story if it weren't for the hard work of all the people who made it into a real, shiny book you could hold in your hands or read on your screen. To my truly extraordinary agent Jennifer Unter who, when *Emerge* landed in her inbox, loved it enough to sign a brand new author and champion these mermaids. Jennifer, thank you from the bottom of my heart for being my partner and my guide throughout the entire process of bringing this book to life. I admire you so much, both as a businesswoman and as a person.

Georgia McBride. The mighty and magnificent Georgia McBride who is unstoppable. Georgia, you make dreams come true. Thank you for working your magic on mine.

To the other members of the invaluable team at Month9Books, who joined forces to make *Emerge* shine. To Jaime Arnold for her undying enthusiasm, savvy, and kindness. To Shara Zaval for truly *getting* this story and for pushing me to think even more deeply about it—when I first read your edit letter, I knew my book couldn't have been in better hands. To Cameron Yeager for her keen, careful eye. To Jennifer Million for all her hard work and for answering my questions. To Stefanie at Beetiful Book Covers for creating the gorgeous, ethereal cover that so perfectly captures this story. A special thank you to the members of the terrific team at IPG who have done so much to bring *Emerge* to readers.

The first-ever reader of *Emerge* is someone who has offered more encouragement and excitement for this story and for the Mer world than I could ever adequately thank her for. Denali, you are the best critique partner and friend anyone could wish for. Thank you for all the late night phone calls and for being Caspian's first fan.

I'm so grateful to all those dear friends who offered feedback along the way—who asked both the fun questions and the hard ones. To Kate for always knowing so much and caring about what's important. To Savannah for being the first person to insist I was a writer when I wasn't yet ready to call myself one. To Audrey, Hannah, Annabeth, Ethan, and Joel for all the thought-provoking notes—and all the snacks!

To my fantastic team of teen readers for keeping *Emerge* authentic, for pushing me to write faster so that I would finish, and for indulging my curiosity by picking out your tail colors. A heartfelt thank you to Anna L., Jamie, Judy, Anna R., Jasmine, Alexa, Jenny, Rachel, Andy, Michelle, Heeju, and Leah.

To everyone at C2 Education for your encouragement and for stoking my love of sharing books with teens. To Puneet for answering my marine bio questions. Most especially, to Jaehee—thank you for your support throughout the years and your excitement for this book!

The YA writing community has been more welcoming and wonderful than I ever could have imagined. To Skylar Dorset, the first stranger who read *Emerge*, and who subsequently became a friend. Thank you for convincing me my manuscript was ready to send out into the world. To Lori Goldstein for being a cheerleader for this book from the beginning and for all the excellent writing and publishing advice. To the incredible Wendy Higgins and the talented Jennifer Gooch Hummer for rallying behind this story and sharing your excitement. To all my fellow GMMG authors and all the members of the Sweet Sixteen debut group and of WO2016 for the endless and sincere encouragement. I love experiencing this whirlwind alongside you.

To the teachers I have had over the years who have incited and fostered my passions (and endured my unrelenting enthusiasm), especially those at Immaculate Heart and the University of Southern California.

I also owe a special expression of gratitude to my family. Thank you to my aunts, uncles, and cousins for your love and for being so happy for me throughout this process. To both my grandmothers, Roslyn and Georganna, who were great readers and storytellers. To another great reader and a great writer, Ingrid, who has been so loving in her support. To Günter for always taking a keen interest and for always being there to listen and advise. To Timon for his inquisitiveness, passion, and heart.

And, of course, to the two people without whom I would not be a writer. My parents, Andrea and Daniel, who are unparalleled. Mom and Dad, thank you for always treating me as someone capable, and for teaching me to value my intellect and follow my dreams. Thank you for your unwavering confidence in me—it gave me the confidence in myself I needed to get here, and I know it will continue to serve me well. Thank you for giving me all those books that sparked my imagination, and thank you for my education. Mommie, thank you for everything, especially for your love of words and for teaching me to both adore and question fairytales. Daddy, thank you for always being there with a kind word right when I need to hear one, for sharing my love of *Harry Potter*, for appreciating beauty, and for giving the *best* hugs. To both of you—I am so lucky to be your daughter, and I know it.

Most of all, thank you to Simon, for living a love story with me. You are all the good parts of every leading man I write and all the best parts of every day of my life. Thank you for the heart-pounding, music-swelling, shooting star kisses, and for the hours upon hours of conversations that took this book to new depths. Thank you for teaching me what having a great love really means. For you, I can do anything.

TOBIE EASTON

Tobie Easton was born and raised in Los Angeles, California, where she's grown from a little girl who dreamed about magic to a twenty-something who writes about it. A summa cum laude graduate of the University of Southern California, Tobie hosts book clubs for tweens and teens. She and her very kissable husband enjoy traveling the globe and fostering packs of rescue puppies. Learn more about Tobie and her upcoming books at www.TobieEaston.com.

OTHER MONTH9BOOKS TITLES YOU MIGHT LIKE

GENESIS GIRL
FACSIMILE
PRAEFATIO
THE REQUIEM RED

Find more awesome Teen books at http://www.Month9Books.com

Connect with Month9Books online:
Facebook: www.Facebook.com/Month9Books
Twitter: https://twitter.com/Month9Books
You Tube: www.youtube.com/user/Month9Books
Blog: www.month9booksblog.com
Request review copies via publicity@month9books.com

Their new beginning
may be her end.

BLANK SLATE: BOOK 1

GENESIS GIRL

JENNIFER BARDSLEY

BOOK 1 IN THE PRAEFATIO SERIES

PRAEFATIO
A NOVEL

"This is teen fantasy at its most entertaining,
most heartbreaking, most compelling. Highly recommended." -Jonathan Maberry,
New York Times bestselling author of ROT & RUIN and FIRE & ASH

GEORGIA McBRIDE

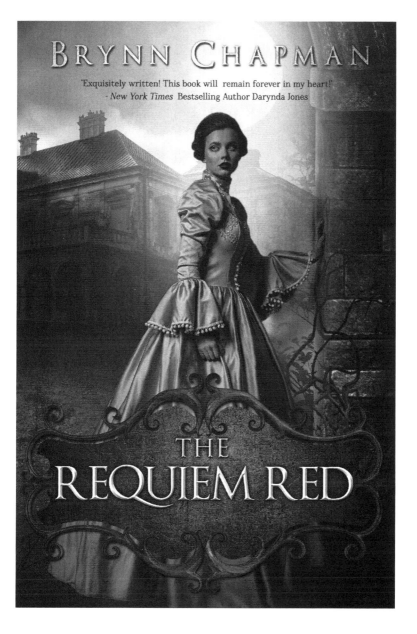

BRYNN CHAPMAN

'Exquisitely written! This book will remain forever in my heart!'
- *New York Times* Bestselling Author Darynda Jones

THE
REQUIEM RED